PRAISE FOR

"With her wonderful characters and resonating emotions, Melissa Foster is a must-read author!"

—*New York Times* bestseller Julie Kenner

"Melissa Foster is synonymous with sexy, swoony, heartfelt romance!"

—*New York Times* bestseller Lauren Blakely

"You can always rely on Melissa Foster to deliver a story that's fresh, emotional, and entertaining."

—*New York Times* bestseller Brenda Novak

"Melissa Foster writes worlds that draw you in, with strong heroes and brave heroines surrounded by a community that makes you want to crawl right on through the page and live there."

—*New York Times* bestseller Julia Kent

"When it comes to contemporary romances with realistic characters, an emotional love story, and smokin'-hot sex, author Melissa Foster always delivers!"

—*The Romance Reviews*

"Foster writes characters that are complex and loyal, and each new story brings further depth and development to a redefined concept of family."

—*RT Book Reviews*

"Melissa Foster definitely knows how to spin a tale and keep you flipping the pages."

—*Book Loving Fairy*

"You can never go wrong with the heroes that Melissa Foster creates. She hasn't made one yet that I haven't fallen in love with."

—Natalie the Biblioholic

"Melissa is a very talented author that tells fabulous stories that captivate you and keep your attention from the first page to the last page. Definitely an author that you will want to keep on your go-to list."

—Between the Coverz

"Melissa Foster writes the best contemporary romance I have ever read. She does it in bundles, tops it with great plots, hot guys, strong heroines, and sprinkles it with family dynamics—you got yourself an amazing read."

—Reviews of a Book Maniac

"She has a way with words that endears a family in our hearts, and watching each sibling and friend go on to meet their true love is such a joy!"

—Thoughts of a Blonde

SHE
LOVES
ME

MORE BOOKS BY MELISSA FOSTER

LOVE IN BLOOM ROMANCE SERIES

SNOW SISTERS

Sisters in Love
Sisters in Bloom
Sisters in White

THE BRADENS

Lovers at Heart, Reimagined
Destined for Love
Friendship on Fire
Sea of Love
Bursting with Love
Hearts at Play
Taken by Love
Fated for Love
Romancing My Love
Flirting with Love
Dreaming of Love
Crashing into Love
Healed by Love
Surrender My Love
River of Love
Crushing on Love
Whisper of Love
Thrill of Love

THE BRADENS & MONTGOMERYS

Embracing Her Heart

Anything for Love
Trails of Love
Wild, Crazy Hearts
Making You Mine
Searching for Love

BRADEN NOVELLAS

Promise My Love
Our New Love
Daring Her Love
Story of Love
Love at Last
A Very Braden Christmas

THE REMINGTONS

Game of Love
Stroke of Love
Flames of Love
Slope of Love
Read, Write, Love
Touched by Love

SEASIDE SUMMERS

Seaside Dreams
Seaside Hearts
Seaside Sunsets
Seaside Secrets
Seaside Nights

Seaside Embrace
Seaside Lovers
Seaside Whispers
Seaside Serenade

BAYSIDE SUMMERS

Bayside Desires
Bayside Passions
Bayside Heat
Bayside Escape
Bayside Romance
Bayside Fantasies
Bayside Dreams

THE RYDERS

Seized by Love
Claimed by Love
Chased by Love
Rescued by Love
Swept into Love

SUGAR LAKE

The Real Thing
Only for You
Love Like Ours
Finding My Girl

HARMONY POINTE

Call Her Mine
This Is Love
She Loves Me

TRU BLUE & THE WHISKEYS

Tru Blue
Truly, Madly, Whiskey
Driving Whiskey Wild
Wicked Whiskey Love
Mad About Moon
Taming My Whiskey
The Gritty Truth

THE WICKEDS

A Little Bit Wicked

BILLIONAIRES AFTER DARK SERIES

Wild Boys After Dark

Logan
Heath
Jackson
Cooper

Bad Boys After Dark

Mick
Dylan
Carson
Brett

HARBORSIDE NIGHTS SERIES

Catching Cassidy
Discovering Delilah
Tempting Tristan

STAND-ALONE NOVELS

Chasing Amanda (mystery/suspense)
Come Back to Me (mystery/suspense)
Have No Shame (historical fiction/romance)
Love, Lies & Mystery (three-book bundle)
Megan's Way (literary fiction)
Traces of Kara (psychological thriller)
Where Petals Fall (suspense)

SHE LOVES ME

Harmony Pointe, Book Three

MELISSA FOSTER

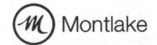 Montlake

Published by Montlake, Seattle

www.apub.com

Amazon, the Amazon logo, and Montlake are trademarks of Amazon.com, Inc., or its affiliates.

ISBN-13: 9781542018418
ISBN-10: 1542018412

Cover design by Letitia Hasser

Cover photography by Rafa G. Catala

Printed in the United States of America

For strong women who know exactly what they want in life and love

CHAPTER ONE

"AND SHE DOES this thing with her tongue" was not what Piper Dalton expected to hear when she walked out of Windsor Hall to join her construction crew. Piper and her father had owned Dalton Contracting for several years. She was used to hearing guys talk about all sorts of things, and she didn't think it was much different from the way women talked. She found three of the guys standing around a table where the plans for the old farmhouse they were renovating were spread out. Piper glanced at her project manager, Kase Force, a large man with granitelike features and an ever-present baseball cap, and lifted her brows. Kase and the two men he was with, Mike Renway and Darren Wilcox, had worked for Piper for the last few years. They were trusted and valued employees.

"Don't look at me, boss," Kase said, holding his hands up.

Darren, a baby-faced blond who looked closer to eighteen than twenty-five, said, "Mike was just trying to convince me not to get married in August."

Mike shrugged, flashing a cocky grin.

The guys knew Piper didn't have a problem with them shooting the shit as long as the work got done. But she did have a problem with three-times-divorced and far-too-cynical Mike trying to convince a man who was madly in love with his fiancée to think twice about tying the knot. Mike was in his midforties and didn't have a faithful bone in his body, but at work he was as dependable and hardworking as the rest of Piper's crew. She might be the boss, but it wasn't her place to judge her employees' personal lives.

"Is that so?" Piper crossed her arms, meeting Mike's steady gaze and cocky grin. She might be only a size two, but there wasn't a man on earth she wouldn't stand up to. "So, this thing she does with her tongue—does she do it to all the guys she blows, or just you?"

Kase and Darren chuckled.

Mike's brows knitted. "Um . . ."

"Yeah, that's what I thought," Piper said. "How about you let Darren be happy? I don't think he's the kind of guy who's into sloppy seconds . . . or thirds."

"Aw, come on, Piper," Mike said. "I don't see you running to the altar."

"Can you imagine Piper trading in her jeans and work boots for an apron and heels?" Kase shook his head. "You're too cool for that, boss."

"Thank you," Piper said.

"And too tough," Darren added. "You've got bigger balls than most of the guys I know. I mean, my girl is always hanging on my every word and giving me foot rubs. I just can't see you doing those things."

"Rubbing your *feet*? Really?" That kind of grossed Piper out.

"Not to mention you're about as unfiltered as a muddy creek, which is *awesome*, but some guys are too insecure for truths." Mike patted her on the back and said, "If you were ten years older, I'd beg you to marry me. You're everything I want in a woman. You're smokin' hot, you won't give me shit for swearing, you've got a good brain and a kick-ass job, and you don't mind having beer and wings at Dutch's for dinner."

Piper laughed right along with them. She had dinner at Dutch's Pub most days of the week, oftentimes with a few of her crew. She loved her job, and she didn't like watching her language. But she'd witnessed each of her four siblings falling in love, and it had definitely opened her eyes to what she was missing. She hoped one day to find a man who would love her the way her siblings were loved, but she wasn't looking to get married, nor holding her breath for that man to suddenly appear. She knew she wasn't most men's long-term cup of tea.

"So, what do you say, Piper?" Mike waggled his thick blond brows. "Want to hook up with an older man who knows all the tricks?"

Piper's phone rang, and DEBRA DUTCH appeared on her screen. "Saved by the bell." She walked away to answer the call. Debra's family owned Dutch's Pub, which was run by one of Debra's sons—Piper's close friend Harley.

"Hi, Deb. Is Delaney okay?"

Delaney was Harley's older sister, and a single mother to two wonderful girls. She had recently been diagnosed with breast cancer and had undergone a double mastectomy two weeks ago. Debra was taking care of her while she recovered. Delaney's diagnosis had rocked her family and friends to their core. Luckily, the cancer hadn't spread, and all the cancerous cells had been eradicated during surgery.

"Yes. She's getting stronger every day," Debra said. "Honey, it's Harley. He's had an accident at work and he needs a ride home from Harmony Pointe Hospital. I didn't know who else to call."

"Oh no. Of course I'll get him. Is he okay? What happened?" Many moons ago, the youngest Dutch sibling, Marshall, had been Piper's first love. He'd been as risky and rowdy as Delaney and Harley were responsible. Marshall had left town to attend college, but he'd quit after his third year and returned home so rarely since, even his family had no idea where he was living. Harley had always picked up the slack. Piper was sure that times like these, though rare, made it even more difficult for Debra.

"I don't know exactly. I just know he had an accident."

"Don't worry, Deb. I'll leave now." She ended the call and hurried over to the guys with her heart in her throat, hoping Harley wasn't hurt too badly. "That was Debra Dutch. Harley's in the hospital. I have to go get him."

"Is he okay?" Kase asked.

"I don't know."

"The cockblocker strikes again," Mike said teasingly. "Tell him I said thanks a lot."

Piper glowered at him, although Harley *did* have a habit of scaring off her dates. "Kase, I'll text you when I know something," she said as she headed for her truck.

"Give him my best," Darren called after her.

"Tell him his timing sucks!" Mike added.

Piper flicked Mike the bird as she climbed into her truck. She knew he was kidding, but she was worried about Harley.

Harmony Pointe was a small town, and her job site wasn't far from the hospital. A few minutes later, she rushed through the emergency-room doors, heading for the registration desk. The waiting room was crowded, and the woman behind the desk was on the phone. Piper's anxiety rose as she waited. She hated hospitals. The lights were too bright, the atmosphere too sterile, and the underlying thrum of pain was inescapable. *Oh God, is Harley in pain?*

She tried to keep from drumming her fingers on the desk as she waited for the woman behind it to get off the phone. She thought about all the times Harley had broken up barroom brawls, taking punches like they were given by children instead of grown men. He'd gotten a few deep gashes over the years from broken bottles and out-of-control patrons, and he'd *always* refused medical treatment, which left him with tough-looking scars from cuts that should have been stitched. Piper couldn't imagine a fight breaking out at the bar on a Wednesday afternoon, much less what had to have happened to land him in the hospital.

As soon as the woman behind the desk hung up, Piper said, "Hi. I'm here to pick up Harley Dutch. He came into the emergency room earlier."

The woman typed something into her computer, then pointed to a set of double doors. "You can go through those doors and they'll direct you."

"Thank you." Piper rushed through the double doors, scanning the curtained-off patient areas, and spotted Harley lying on a bed. His head was tipped back, his eyes closed. His jeans were rolled up on his right leg to his calf, and his right ankle was wrapped. That explained why he needed a ride home. She went to him, wondering how he'd gotten to the hospital. Her gaze moved over his face. He was truly a handsome man, with dark hair and a short beard. Though his eyes were closed, she knew how powerful his deep-set slate-blue eyes were. She'd seen women hanging on his every glance and men cowering when those eyes turned fierce. She couldn't help allowing her gaze to crawl down his beefy arms and broad chest to his waist. Harley wasn't lean or *cut*, and he didn't have six-pack abs. He was thick-bodied, brawny, and rugged. She never allowed herself to look him over—they were just friends after all. But now she couldn't help herself. Her eyes drifted to the impressive bulge behind his zipper—she knew he wasn't lean *there*, either. Harley was a few years older than Piper, and he had gotten quite a reputation in high school for the monstrous heat he was packing. Her pulse quickened, and she forced her eyes back to his face. He might be built like a grizzly and hung like a horse, but Piper had a feeling that despite his tough reputation and bravado, when it came right down to it, Harley Dutch was all cuddly cub inside.

Harley's eyes opened, and the smile that melted panties everywhere lifted his lips. Piper wasn't immune to his charms, but he dated the type of women who would dote on him, who wore pretty dresses and said all the right things. And as Piper's crew had so kindly pointed out, as much as she loved children and would adore a family of her own, she was never going to be a doting wife. For that reason, she was glad she was into *untamable grizzlies* and not cuddly cubs, because she didn't need to ruin their friendship over what could never be more than a few nights of incredibly hot sex.

"Hi," he said groggily.

"*Hey*," she said softly. "What happened? Your mom said you got hurt at the bar."

His brow furrowed. "I'm sorry, but do I know you?"

"What kind of pain meds do they have you on? It's me, *Piper*."

"Piper," he said softly, his face still a map of confusion. "Are you doing construction here?"

She glanced down at her T-shirt, jeans, and work boots, all of which were speckled with drywall dust. "Don't mess with me, Harley. You know I'm working at Windsor Hall, getting the house ready to go on the market. What happened? Are you okay?"

He looked down at his leg and said, "I sprained my ankle. Someone should be here soon to pick me up."

She crossed her arms and said, "That's *me*, doofus. Your mom called. She's taking care of Delaney, remember? Geez, did you hit your head?"

He nodded, smiling sheepishly, which took her by surprise. He didn't do anything *sheepishly*. Harley was more of a barrel-in-and-blurt-it-out kind of guy.

"Sorry if I should recognize you, but I can't remember anything."

"What . . . ?" Her stomach sank.

Harley was everyone's *rock*, including hers. He'd made it big on Wall Street after college, returning home about four years ago, when his father had taken ill, to help his family run their pub. His father had passed away shortly thereafter, and Harley had remained in Sweetwater, their small hometown, to care for his mother, sister, and two nieces, who had all been falling apart at the seams. Though Harley and Piper hadn't been close when they were growing up, he'd become one of Piper's closest friends since he'd moved home. He made a habit of being a pain in her butt, giving her grief about one thing or another and scaring off her dates. Even so, she couldn't help but love the big, burly bartender.

He was one of the few guys outside of work who wasn't intimidated by her directness, her inability to put up with bullshit, or the way she'd dominated the male-driven construction industry, becoming one of the most sought-after contractors in the area. She spent more evenings hanging out with Harley and their friends at the pub watching sports or eating dinner than she spent at home. She couldn't imagine her life without Harley in it, and the thought of him not recognizing her caused a crushing feeling in the center of her chest.

She sat on the edge of the bed and took his hand in hers. She couldn't reconcile her large-and-in-charge friend with this man who seemed so lost. "You don't recognize me? Do you remember your family?"

He shook his head, his eyes turning serious. "Wait, are you my girlfriend? Have we knocked boots? Because I'm sure I'd remember a sweet little darlin' like you in my bed."

"*God*, even with amnesia you're a pain in my ass." She dropped his hand and said, "I'm going to find a nurse and figure out what's going on."

She pushed to her feet, and he snagged her wrist, yanking her down so their faces almost collided. An arrogant grin slid across his lips, and he said, "Maybe if you kiss me, I'll remember the rest. Or even better, what do you say we make a few *new* smokin'-hot memories?"

He winked, and she tore her wrist free, anger simmering inside her. "You ass! I should let you stay here and rot!"

Laughter rumbled out of his mouth, and he smacked the mattress. "I got you *good*, Trigger!" He called her Trigger, or Trig, because it didn't take much to get her fired up.

"You're lucky I don't have a gun to *pull* the trigger," she snapped. "I thought you had seriously forgotten *everything*. I was worried about you, and you're playing games!"

"Aw, come on, Trig," he said with a softer tone. "Admit it was funny."

"How about we see how funny it is when I hit you so hard you *actually* lose your memory?"

"Uh-oh," a pretty dark-haired nurse said as she walked into the curtained-off area. She wore light blue scrubs, and her hair was pulled up in a high ponytail, like Piper's. "It sounds like Mr. Dutch didn't listen to my advice. You must be Piper. I'm Felicity, and I've had the pleasure of helping your boyfriend."

"Thank you for taking care of him, but he's *not* my boyfriend. He's like a stray dog I made the mistake of feeding and refuses to go away." Piper scowled at Harley, who was still chuckling, and said, "But since he's already here, can I knock him around a bit?"

"I'm sorry, but I can't allow you to do that," Felicity said lightly.

"Told you she was *wild*," Harley said a little slowly. He waved a hand at his body. "She wants *all* this."

Piper rolled her eyes. "That's enough, Casanova." She was used to his teasing. He joked around like that all the time.

"You want me. Doesn't she look like she wants me, Felicity?"

"That sounds like the pain meds talking. I think I'll stay out of this conversation." Felicity handed Piper a couple of papers and said, "These are Harley's discharge papers and his prescription. He's going to be on pretty heavy pain meds for the next two or three days, so you might want to prepare yourself if you're going to be taking care of him."

"Oh, that's not the pain meds talking. That's straight-up *Harley*, and I will *not* be taking care of him."

"She will be," Harley said casually.

"I have a *life*," Piper reminded him. "And it doesn't include playing nursemaid to a man who has refused stitches more times than I can count."

"Don't make me come over there." Harley sat up and shifted his legs over the edge of the bed, swaying a little.

"Whoa, slow down." Felicity put a hand on his arm as another hospital worker pushed a wheelchair into the curtained room. Then the woman left the room, returning a minute later with a walking boot and crutches.

"Thank you," Felicity said as the other woman walked away.

Harley pointed to the wheelchair. "Who's that thing for?"

"That's for you," Felicity said. "The doctor doesn't want you putting any pressure on your ankle for a few days." She looked at Piper and said, "He has a splint on under the wrap."

"I hate the splint," Harley said like a rebellious boy.

"You need it for stability," Felicity said sternly. "You can use the walking boot when you feel more stable, but you shouldn't try to use the crutches while taking the heavier pain medications over the next couple of days. I'd like to show you how to use the crutches."

"I know how to use them. I had a football injury or two back in the day."

"Okay. If you have any trouble, you can see your primary care doctor for a follow-up appointment." She went over instructions with Piper for his medications and how to care for his injury.

Harley looked pleadingly at Piper and said, "See, Pipe? I can't walk Jiggs. Not only do *I* need you now more than ever, but he needs you, too."

Piper had a soft place in her heart for the pit bull Harley had rescued three years earlier. Harley spoiled Jiggs rotten, and Piper swore he was needier than her six-month-old niece, Emerson. "I'll walk Jiggs, but you can take care of yourself. Can we please stop wasting Felicity's time and get on with this? I have to get back to work."

"She means she has to take me to pick up my nieces," Harley said a little groggily.

"Shoot. I forgot you were taking care of Delaney's girls." He'd been taking care of Jolie, who was twelve, and Sophie, who was ten, since Delaney's surgery. Piper glanced at the clock and said, "If we leave now, I'll have just enough time to get you home and then pick the girls up and get your prescription."

"Let me help you get him into the wheelchair," Felicity said, moving to Harley's other side. As they helped him into the wheelchair, which was like putting an enormous, floppy bear into a high chair, she said, "Before he took the pain meds, Harley and I were talking and he said you know my brother, Porter Lawton."

"That delicious-looking man is your brother? I met him through my friend Remi Divine." Remi was an actress and had recently gotten engaged. She and her fiancé, Mason Swift, had just purchased a home in Harmony Pointe. Mason owned the private security and investigation company Porter worked for as a bodyguard. Porter had looked after Remi last year when she'd had issues with a stalker. He was also Mason's best friend—and insanely *hot*.

"He's a great guy, and he's *single*," Felicity said softly. "He's great with my son, Lucas, too."

"Um, *hello*. Bad ankle here. This isn't an episode of *Love Connection*," Harley said a little drunkenly.

Piper patted his shoulder, grinning at Felicity. "Don't you *love* my built-in cockblocker? Even drugged up, he tries to protect my virtue."

Felicity chuckled.

"Your brother is gorgeous, and Lucas is so sweet. I met him at the birthday bash for foster children Remi and Mason held in January—"

"We have to go," Harley interrupted. He grabbed the wheels of his chair and tried to spin around but ran directly into the bed. He uttered a curse.

Piper folded the papers Felicity had given her and shoved them in the back pocket of her jeans. She grabbed the handles of the wheelchair and said, "I think I'd better drive. Thanks for thinking about me for Porter—"

"You're going to be *way* too busy for a while with me and the girls to even *think* about him." Harley pointed to his ankle and said, "I can't drive, and we really have to go. Thanks for everything, Felicity."

"The man thinks he owns me," Piper said. "Thanks again for helping him."

Felicity handed Harley the crutches and walking boot and said, "My pleasure."

As Felicity pushed the wheelchair out of the curtained area, Harley flashed a cheesy grin over his shoulder at Felicity and said, "Told you she'd take care of me."

Felicity stopped in the waiting room to say something to the woman behind the desk. When she walked away, Piper lowered her voice and said, "Why are you such a pain? Do you know how hot Porter is?"

"I know the man is built like he treats his body like a castle and you'd last about one night feeding him nachos or pizza."

As Felicity headed back toward them, Piper said, "Then it's a good thing one night is all I'm looking for."

Harley was so loopy from the pain medication, he couldn't help but chuckle as Piper, and all of her buck-ten pounds, tried to wrangle his six-three, two-forty body from the wheelchair into her double-cab truck. She'd excused Felicity the second she'd brought the truck around with a curt, *Thanks for wheeling him out, but I've got him.*

As always, the front seat of her truck was covered with what looked like remnants of a fast-food party.

"Wait," Piper said as he used her as a crutch. She reached into the truck and swept a pile of empty food wrappers and cups onto the floor.

"You know, if you learned to cook, you'd save loads of money." He was only giving her shit. He knew damn well that if cooking were the only way to eat, Piper would find a way to survive on air. She was *that* determined.

She glowered at him as she put the crutches and boot in the truck. "Get your ass on the seat and be careful of your ankle."

"Really? My *ass*? Is that how you sit in a vehicle?"

"Okay, smart-mouth. Get yourself in the truck. I'm going to bring the wheelchair back inside." In true Piper style, she ducked from beneath his arm and stalked away, leaving him to wobble like a drunken flamingo.

He grabbed the door and climbed into the truck.

Piper walked out of the hospital like she was on a mission, which was the only way she knew how to move. Only *Piper* could look as hot as sin in dirty jeans with tears in the knees that she'd probably been wearing for a decade, a Dalton Contracting T-shirt, and tan work boots. Her light blond hair was pulled back from her gorgeous face in a ponytail, and as she climbed into the driver's seat, Harley fantasized about tugging that ponytail back and devouring her sass-talking, sexy mouth. His medication-addled mind ran down a dark and dirty path, playing with thoughts he was usually much better at pushing aside. He imagined how incredible her soft, supple body would feel lying naked beneath him and the sinful sounds she'd make as he touched and tasted every inch of her, driving her out of her mind. He got hot all over thinking about how it would feel to have her feminine yet strong hand wrapped around his—

"Are you listening to me?" she snapped, dragging him back to reality.

He shifted in his seat, trying to get comfortable with a raging hard-on.

Piper stopped at a red light, and her gorgeous green eyes trailed over his face. "Geez, you *are* drugged up. Look at that goofy grin. How's your . . . ?" Her eyes moved lower and her jaw dropped. "Oh my God! No *wonder* you're smiling. Geez, Harley, what are you doing? Fantasizing about that nurse?"

"That nurse isn't in this truck."

"*Ugh!*" The light turned green, and she gunned the engine. "Do *not* think of me like that." She glanced at him and said, "Turn your head!

Look out the window. I'm glad I'm taking you home before I get the girls. They can't see you like this."

"There's no time," he said, still grinning, because damn, he was high as a kite and she was so angry it made her even hotter. "Just head to the school."

She shot him a death stare. "I told you to stop looking at me."

He chuckled and tipped his head back, closing his eyes.

"And *stop* smiling!"

Piper barked orders like a drill sergeant, gave him as much grief as he gave her, and rolled her eyes so often he was surprised they didn't fall out of her head. She also swore like a sailor, loved sports and beer, and she was the most organized, hardworking, and *ornery* woman Harley had ever known. Her brilliant mind was always *ticking*, planning a project, or thinking of her family and friends. According to Piper, who was never too embarrassed to say what was on her mind, she also loved good, hard sex and wasn't looking for more. Harley wasn't sure he believed the latter part of that claim, but either way, he'd been utterly captivated by her for the last few years and considered himself lucky to have Piper in his life.

She drove to the middle school, ranting about him getting control of himself. "They probably mixed up your meds and gave you Viagra by accident."

"No little blue pill, Pipe," he said with a laugh. "You're hot and I'm a dude, so . . ."

"Okay, *enough* of this," she said with a huff. "What happened to you? And how'd you get to the hospital?"

He turned his head, watching her drive. "Got into a fight with three guys."

"Bullshit, not on a Wednesday afternoon." Her lips curved up sassily.

"Wrestled a bear?"

"Nope." She turned into the school parking lot.

"Come on, Trig. Let me man it up a *little*."

She glanced at his crotch and said, "I think you've done enough manning up for one day."

"That was *your* fault."

She gave him the narrow-eyed give-me-a-break look she'd perfected as a teenager.

"I fell, okay? No big deal. Jasper was busy, so a customer drove me to the hospital." Jasper Lennox was one of Harley's employees. He managed the bar in Harley's absence. Harley pointed to the line of cars in front of the side doors to the school and said, "That's the pickup line."

Piper pulled to the end of the line and said, "A customer drove you?"

"Yeah. She was pretty cool about it. Thanks for coming to get me. I appreciate it."

"No worries." She took out her phone and started thumbing out a text.

"Who are you texting?"

"Nosy much?" She continued typing and said, "I need to let Kase know I'm not coming back today."

Kase seemed like a good guy, and Piper trusted him, which was what Harley cared most about. Piper was as tough as nails, but Harley still worried about her every time she started a new project, working with new clients and subcontractors. He'd seen her hold her own at the pub, and when she was going out with a guy for the first time, she always met him at the pub. She claimed it was a good way to weed out the weak from the strong, since Harley was quick to size them up and get rid of the assholes. But Harley had another thought on why she met them there. Piper was bullheaded enough to bring them by just to get Harley's goat. She'd never shown any interest in Harley beyond their friendship, but he was sure that was because she simply wouldn't allow herself to go there. His asshole younger brother had taken care of her trusting men with her heart years ago, much less trusting a Dutch in that way.

He watched her typing furiously, her thin brows knitted in concentration as she sent one text and began typing another. She was completely in control of her life now, but his mind reeled back to a night when she hadn't been. It was spring of her sophomore year of high school, and she'd been dating Marshall for five or six months. Harley had been home for the weekend, working at the pub. It was dark when he'd left work, and he'd seen the silhouette of a person huddled at the edge of the dock in the marina by the rowboat Piper and Marshall had built. He'd gone to investigate and had quickly realized it was Piper. The image of her shaking with sobs was etched in his mind, as was the mortification on her face when she'd looked up and seen him approaching. He'd also never forget the overwhelming urge to protect her that had instantly consumed him, or the rage that had stormed through him when he'd learned the reason she was crying. His brother had cheated on her, breaking her tender teenage heart. Harley had made sure his brother paid the price for his actions.

Just thinking about that painful night brought a rush of anger and a surge of protectiveness. He tried to push the painful memories away, focusing instead on how Piper had pulled herself up by her bootstraps. She'd lifted her adorably pointy little chin that awful night, glaring at him like he was the enemy as she'd risen to her feet, and said, *What the fuck do you want?* She'd stormed off without giving him a chance to respond. From that day forward she'd never let anyone drag her down—but just in case, Harley had always had her back. He'd returned to college and had eventually moved to New York City, but he'd come back often and had always checked on Piper, even when *she'd* gone away to college. It wasn't until he'd moved back home when his father had taken ill and he and Piper had become closer that his feelings had begun changing from protective friend to *interested man*. Given Piper's well-armored heart, he had a hell of a time figuring out what to do with all those feelings.

The school bell rang, pulling him from his thoughts.

Piper shoved her phone into her back pocket and said, "They won't know my truck." She threw open her door and stood on the running board. When she spotted his nieces, she whistled. "Jolie! Sophie!" She waved her hands, causing *all* the kids to look over. "I'm holding your uncle hostage! Get your heinies in the truck; we've got things to do!"

Sophie ran toward the truck, waving.

Jolie's momentary grin quickly settled into a frown, and she trained her eyes on the sidewalk, skulking toward them.

The girls looked like Delaney, with big blue eyes and long brown hair. But while they'd once shared her easygoing demeanor, recently Jolie had become sullen. Their father had skipped town the day Delaney had graduated from law school in New York City, leaving Delaney pregnant and with a baby to care for. She'd moved home to live with her parents while she found her footing and started over. Those first few years were hard on them, and Harley had come home and stepped in as often as he could to help Delaney, and maybe more importantly, to show the girls that they were special and loved and they were *not* the reason their father had disappeared. But he worried about the changes he'd seen in Jolie lately, some of which were normal for an adolescent girl, but as to be expected, her unhappiness had amplified with her mother's cancer diagnosis. Her diagnosis had terrified all of them. It had taken several weeks for Harley, Delaney, and their mother to come to grips with it, and they'd done everything they could to help the girls understand that their mother's diagnosis wasn't a death sentence. But convincing his young nieces of that was like claiming there weren't wars going on in the world when it was all over the news. Luckily, Delaney's cancer hadn't spread to her lymph nodes, and the surgery had left her with clear margins, which meant they had eradicated the cancer and she would not need radiation. Harley had hoped Delaney's excellent prognosis would ease Jolie's bad moods, but he was still having trouble connecting with her.

Sophie rushed into the back seat, bright-eyed and chattering as she crawled across the bench. "Hi, Uncle Harley. Hi, Piper! Why is Piper here?"

"Because she's Uncle Harley's girlfriend," Jolie said flatly as she climbed in.

Piper's head whipped in Harley's direction, and she glared at him. "I am *not* his girlfriend."

"Then why does he have two pictures of you guys on his fridge?" Jolie asked with enough snark to put Piper's sass to shame.

"One of you guys dancing at Ben and Aurelia's wedding," Sophie added. "And one of you on his shoulders playing basketball. He said he lost the game but won the girl. Right, Uncle Harley?"

The shock on Piper's face made him chuckle. Although, he was pretty high, so she could very well look *annoyed*, not shocked. He really couldn't tell.

"Your mother gave *my* mother the picture from the wedding, and I asked for a copy. Can you blame me? We looked hot together." He ignored her eye roll and said, "And your mother gave me the basketball picture. It was from—"

"The pickup game at Willow's last summer. She gave me that one, too. I remember being on your shoulders."

Harley looked at the girls and said, "See? I won the girl."

Piper smacked his arm. "You're going to confuse them." She glanced into the back seat and said, "He did not *win* me. We were a *team*, and I'm *not* his girlfriend."

"Whatever," Jolie said, bored with the conversation.

Sophie bounced in her seat. "Guess what? I got an A on my math test."

"That's great, Soph," Piper said. "Congrats."

"Attagirl, squirt!" Harley held a hand up, and Sophie high-fived him. "Buckle up, peanut. How was your day, Jo?"

"Fine," she mumbled. "Can we go?"

Piper looked over her shoulder at Jolie and said, "What's up with the long face?"

Jolie rolled her eyes, and Piper glanced at Harley.

He shrugged. "You're the queen of eye rolls. This should be right up your alley."

"I think I've got competition for my crown." Piper glanced at Jolie again and said, "Hey, Jolie. Do you need me to kick some kid's butt?"

Jolie's expression softened. She shook her head and looked out the window.

"Did you kick Uncle Harley's butt? Is that why his ankle is wrapped up?" Sophie asked.

"Darn right I did," Piper said as she cruised out of the parking lot.

When Piper stopped at the pharmacy to get Harley's medication, Sophie went with her, skipping through the parking lot, while Jolie stewed in the back seat. Harley tried to figure out new ways to communicate with the females in his life. He was as determined to get through to Jolie and help her deal with whatever was bothering her as he was to prove to Piper that not all the Dutch brothers were destined to break her heart.

But the way his head was swimming, he was pretty sure none of that was going to happen today.

CHAPTER TWO

ON THE WAY to Sweetwater, a short drive from Harmony Pointe, Harley answered dozens of Sophie's questions about his injury. He made up a story about hurting himself while rescuing a bear from a trap, and Sophie ate it up. Jolie, on the other hand, stared absently out the window. Piper adored Harley's nieces, and while she worried about both of them, at the moment her mind was on Jolie, who was obviously struggling.

As she drove past the marina and pub, she spotted Harley's truck in the parking lot and made a mental note to walk up and drive it back to his house. Harley lived only about a mile down the road, on three private wooded acres on Sugar Lake.

When they arrived at his house, the girls piled out.

Harley opened his door and said, "Jolie, take the keys."

Jolie doubled back to get them. Piper grabbed the pharmacy bag, her mind spinning with lists of things she had to do for work and for Harley. The girls ran up to the door, and Piper had a feeling she'd be adding the girls' needs to her to-do list. She helped Harley out of the truck and handed him the crutches. He took one and draped his other arm around her neck.

"You have *two* crutches for a reason," she said as they made their way up to the porch.

"You have shoulders for a reason, too."

"I can see it's going to be a long night," she said under her breath.

He tapped his head lightly against hers and said, "And you're lucky enough to get to spend it with me and the girls."

"You *are* three of my favorite people," Piper admitted.

The girls opened the door, and Jiggs barreled out, barking and jumping up on Sophie.

"Jiggs, down," Piper hollered.

"He's okay," Sophie said, giggling as she tumbled to her butt. Jiggs crawled all over her, soaking her face with sloppy kisses.

Jolie stepped around them and went inside.

"Jolie's having a hard time processing what's going on with her mom, huh?" Piper asked.

"Yeah. I can't get her to talk to me. I don't get it. We used to be so close, but now it's like I'm the bad guy or something."

"She's at that age, but she's probably scared, too." She helped Harley up the steps, and Jiggs barked and ran over, knocking into Harley's sore ankle and jumping up on him.

Harley clutched the railing and winced, but he bent down and loved up his dog, letting Jiggs lick his face. "That's my boy. Daddy's home, but you've got to watch my ankle."

Jiggs whimpered and licked him again.

"Come on, Jiggsy!" Sophie yelled as she darted into the house.

Jiggs took off after her, barking up a storm. The happiness on Harley's face told Piper there was no pain big enough to keep him from seeing that dog and those girls happy.

They headed for the couch in his living room while Jiggs and Sophie played chase. The sounds of Sophie's laughter, Jiggs's barking, and feet and claws dashing across the hardwood floors filled the room. Piper dropped the pharmacy bag on the coffee table and helped Harley down to the couch. She let out a breath and wiped her brow. The heavy tools she used and loads she carried at work were nothing compared to this. The guy was *heavy*.

"Uncle Harley, I'm hungry!" Sophie hollered as she ran past with Jiggs on her heels.

"Apples are in the drawer," he said, waving a hand in the air.

Sophie and Jiggs bolted into the kitchen. Sophie pulled open the fridge and Piper said, "Soph, maybe you and Jiggs can play chase out on the deck. Jiggs hasn't been out yet. I'm sure he needs to go to the bathroom."

"In a minute!" Sophie called out as she ran through the kitchen.

Harley closed his eyes and sighed.

Piper was so used to seeing him take charge. He had to be either hurting or flying high as a kite to be so laid-back. She hoped it was the pills, because the thought of Harley in pain made her ache inside. She pulled the medical instructions out of her back pocket and said, "Okay, let's see. We need to elevate your ankle." She grabbed a pillow and placed it under his foot. "You need to rest it, as Felicity said, ice it three times a day for twenty to thirty minutes, keep it wrapped to compress it, and—"

Jiggs jumped over the back of the couch with his leash in his mouth and landed on Harley's stomach. Harley let out a loud, "*Argh!*"

"Jiggs!" Piper tried to shoo him off, but Jiggs buried his face in Harley's armpit and Piper swore the dog was clinging to Harley for dear life. Jiggs looked like he had a French manicure on his big, stubby toes. He was all gray with a white chest, a streak of white down his snout and around his nose, and white tips on each toe.

"It's okay," Harley ground out, shifting Jiggs's feet away from his crotch, wincing as he repositioned his leg. Jiggs licked Harley's face, and Harley scratched his dog's head with both hands, kissing his snout.

Lucky dog . . .

Holy cow. Where did that come from?

Harley patted the dog's back, smiling groggily up at Piper.

"You spoil him rotten," she snapped, more harshly than she meant to. But they were both so damn cute, she struggled to keep her worries about those unexpected thoughts in the forefront of her mind.

He winked flirtatiously and said, "I'd spoil you, too, if you'd let me."

She rolled her eyes and turned away to put the instructions and papers on the coffee table and try to figure out *why*, when he'd said things like that a million times, she was suddenly thinking a little harder about his words. This was ridiculous. She was just feeling bad that he was hurt and had so much on his plate right now. That had to be it.

She put a hand on her hip and said, "Just don't complain when Jiggs does it again and lands on your ankle—or your *junk*."

A spark of heat flamed in his eyes, and he opened his mouth to speak.

She held up her hand and said, "*Don't.* I don't want to hear any more loopy snippets from you. Got it?"

He closed his mouth and looked at Jiggs, whispering, "She loves me. She's just fighting it."

"Dream on, Dutch." Piper looked up as Jolie skulked down the stairs.

Jolie stood on the bottom riser, holding on to the railing as if ready to flee. "Uncle Harley, did you go to the store today?"

"Crap," Harley said. "Sorry, honey. I didn't have time, but there should be more apples in the drawer."

"Gross," Jolie said, and she moped back up the steps.

"Let me guess," Piper said. "You need me to go to the grocery store?"

"Only if you don't want the girls to starve."

Jiggs pushed his snout into Harley's cheek, and Harley petted him.

"Should I let him out before he pees on you?" Piper asked.

"You can try, but he won't go," Harley said, stroking the dog's back. "He's used to going on an afternoon walk."

As if on cue, Jiggs lifted his chin, the leash hanging out of his mouth, and he whimpered. Both he and Harley looked at Piper with pleading eyes.

"Of course he is," she said with a sigh.

"And an evening walk before bed." Harley stroked Jiggs's back and said, "Right, buddy?"

Piper rolled her eyes. "I *really* need to have a talk with your mother about how you were raised. Remind me to warn your future wife to be prepared for spoiled kids *and* dogs."

Jiggs barked and crawled across Harley's stomach, staring up at Piper with his big dark eyes, his floppy, pointed ears adding another pleading dose of cuteness. When he cocked his head to the side at the same time Harley did, she had to laugh.

She grabbed the leash and said, "What have I gotten myself into?"

A few hours later they ordered pizza, eating around the coffee table so Harley wouldn't have to hobble to the kitchen. Piper made a list of their schedules and realized there was going to be a heck of a lot more to helping Harley than she'd thought. At least she'd remembered to pick up his truck when she'd taken Jiggs for his walk, so that was one less item for her list. But it was the little things that were giving her more of a hard time. Harley had asked her to help him to the bathroom earlier, and when she'd handed him the crutches, he'd said they were annoying. He hadn't liked her snappy comeback: *They're not the only thing that's annoying.* He'd grabbed the crutches and hobbled to the bathroom, but she'd felt guilty, and when he was done, she'd helped him back to the couch. It was strange seeing Harley unable to fend for himself. She wanted to tough-love him back to his strong, capable self, but knew she couldn't do that when his ankle was so messed up, which meant she was stuck with feelings she wasn't sure what to do with.

"My soccer sleepover is Saturday night." Jolie looked at Harley and said, "Can I still go?"

"Why wouldn't you be able to go?" Harley asked. "Are you planning on robbing a bank between now and then? Going to get thrown in the slammer?"

The triumphant light in Harley's eyes, and Sophie's giggle, told of the *funny-uncle* status he thought the comment would add to.

Unfortunately, Jolie's shoulders slumped. "I mean because I need a ride there and back and you can't drive."

"But I can," Piper said, and she added *Jolie's soccer sleepover* to her list.

"You don't mind?" Jolie asked tentatively.

"Of course not. I'm happy to pitch in. Harley, do you have a sleeping bag she can use?"

"Sure do," he said.

Jolie looked horrified. "Nobody brings *sleeping bags.*"

Piper looked at Harley, who shrugged. "Okay. No sleeping bag," she said. "What time is the party?"

"Right after our last game, which is at two," Jolie said.

"Two o'clock soccer game and then the party—got it. This will be fun. I haven't been to a school soccer game in . . . well . . . *ever.*"

Harley chuckled, and then his expression turned serious. He turned his glassy eyes on Piper and said, "Piper was too busy fixing people's drywall and helping the church paint over graffiti, and whatever other repairs needed doing that a teenage girl could handle."

Piper was stunned. How did he know about the things she'd done while he was away at college? It wasn't like they'd hung out together back then. And *why* was he looking at her like he could see her thoughts? She tore her gaze away, picked up a slice of pizza, and chomped into it, wondering what kind of superpowers were in those pain meds.

"Jo, can you get me a phone number to touch base with the parents who are hosting the party?" Harley asked.

"Okay," she said in a resigned voice.

Piper felt Harley watching her as she added the soccer game to her list. He wouldn't be able to drive until he could put pressure on his ankle, which the doctor had told him could take anywhere from a week to several weeks, depending on how much he stayed off it. When he'd taken off the wrap to ice his ankle before dinner, his entire foot was so swollen, it looked fluid filled. He'd taken off the splint and had refused to put it back on after he'd iced his foot. He'd claimed it bothered him too much to wear it. She was determined to keep him off that foot and help him heal.

"Sophie, are you in any sports or other extracurricular activities?" Piper asked.

Sophie bit into her slice of pizza and shook her head. "I don't like sports."

"Then after Jolie's game, you and I can do something fun." Piper wrote *Sophie?* next to *Jolie's soccer sleepover.*

"Pipe, if you need to work, I'm sure I can bribe one of the guys to help me out with the girls this weekend," Harley said.

Harley hadn't asked for help the whole time he'd been taking care of Jolie and Sophie, and he was always willing to help everyone else. Piper didn't mind helping the man who never asked for a damn thing. In fact, she wanted to.

"It's okay. Kase can handle things Saturday." She scanned the list, seeing her work hours dwindle with each item. She knew her crew could handle the project, but as much as she loved the girls, she might lose her mind if she had too much downtime. She was used to working with her hands, swinging hammers and using power tools. It looked like she'd have to find another outlet for a while.

"Thanks, Piper," Harley said, grabbing another slice of pizza.

"It's okay. Let me know if anything else comes up that I should put on the schedule." They'd spoken to Delaney before dinner, but they hadn't said anything about a visit. "When am I taking the girls to see Delaney?"

"Friday after school," Sophie answered.

Harley nodded. "That's right."

"Got it." Piper scrawled *Girls to Delaney* beneath their school pickup. It looked like she'd have Sunday free. She'd catch up on work then. The girls went to school in Harmony Pointe. Even though it was a short drive from Sweetwater, it would take forty-five minutes or longer each way because of the lines in the school parking lot. At least she was working in Harmony Pointe. She wondered how Harley had taken care of all these things with the girls and still managed to run Dutch's without asking for help.

Jolie finished her pizza and fed the crust to Jiggs, who was sitting between her and Sophie on the floor in front of the couch. Jiggs would eat anything. When Harley first adopted him, he'd eaten an entire jigsaw puzzle that Harley had left on the coffee table.

Jolie put her paper plate on the table and headed for the stairs.

"Hold on, Jo," Harley said. "Plate in the trash, please."

Jolie's shoulders sagged again, but she came back and grabbed her plate.

"Get started on your homework," Harley said as she headed into the kitchen.

"I *know*," she said with an air of frustration.

"Hey!" Harley hollered loudly, but not unkindly.

Jolie threw out her plate and looked over.

"Love you, Jo." Harley blew her a kiss.

Jolie rolled her eyes and hurried up the stairs, but not before Piper saw the smile appear on her pretty face.

Harley reached down with both hands and gently tipped Sophie's face up. He leaned over her and said, "Love you, too, kiddo."

"Love you, Uncle Harley."

Jiggs put both paws up on the couch beside Harley and whimpered. Harley kissed Sophie's forehead, then petted Jiggs. He sat back and winked at Piper. "We've got a lot of love in this house."

It was strange to feel like he was including her in this, especially when she was still flipping out over seeing her pictures on his refrigerator. Sure, she had framed the same picture of them playing basketball and put it up in her living room, but she had *lots* of other pictures of family and friends there. The only other things hanging on Harley's fridge were the girls' school pictures, a picture of Delaney and their mother, one of Harley and his father, and a Polaroid of Harley sleeping with his arm around Jiggs in what she assumed was Harley's bed. She hadn't even known they made Polaroid cameras anymore, and she didn't want to think about *who* had taken that picture. Probably one of the *ladies* he dated.

Jiggs jumped onto the couch, landing on Harley's chest, his back feet in Harley's crotch. Harley doubled over and moaned, but those big, strong arms were wrapped around Jiggs like he didn't want his dog to jump off.

Sophie laughed. "Jiggsy!"

Piper couldn't do anything other than stare at the man who glowered threateningly at her dates and fought like a pro with his fists, as he loved on his dog despite being curled in pain.

"Jiggs," Harley croaked. "We have to work on your aim."

She was right.

Harley was all *cuddly cub*.

Thank God.

If she was going to be subjected to Harley's flirting, which was totally different when he was under the influence of pain medication than it was normally, she needed *big, uncrossable* barriers to remember why she wasn't taking him up on his innuendos. *Cuddly cubs* were a big *no* for her. The last thing she wanted was a man who was looking to settle down.

She tried to figure out what had changed besides the addition of the pain medication. Usually when Harley said something flirtatious, he was reacting to a guy hitting on her or to their friends joking around about sex or relationships. But they weren't with any of their friends now.

Oh shit . . .

She realized they were *always* in a group, doing *guy things*—watching sports, drinking at the pub, playing basketball. She stole a glance at him, catching him watching her with a *darker, hungrier* look than she'd ever seen. That new look called to the animal in her, sparking flames deep inside her. God, she loved the feeling of lust simmering hot and anticipatory, just waiting to ignite. Apparently even when it was coming from Harley. She couldn't tear her eyes from his, despite knowing she couldn't afford for their flames to become an inferno.

Sophie popped to her feet and said, "I need help with math."

"I'm great at math!" Piper grabbed Sophie's hand and dragged her away from Harley before Piper caught fire—or Harley noticed her momentary slip into Hornyville.

CHAPTER THREE

HARLEY HAD FORGOTTEN how much he hated pain medication. Piper had given him another dose at nine, and by nine forty-five he was high as a kite again, which made focusing on his phone conversation with his sister difficult.

"Soph got an A on her math test." He was sitting on the couch with his foot propped on a pillow on the coffee table, and Jiggs was lying beside him. He scratched Jiggs's head, trying to remember if the girls had said anything else worth mentioning.

"She told me. Are you sure you're okay? You sound out of it."

"I'm fine. Piper's here, and she's like a whirlwind of badass energy. She's putting the girls to bed now."

"Ah, now I see what's going on," Delaney teased. "You're drunk on *love*."

Harley chuckled. "Drunk on pain meds, maybe. But I'm fine, sis. How are you?"

"Recovering. Not fast enough, but *appropriately*. They took the drains out today. I shouldn't look too scary to the girls Friday, but I'll look tired."

Delaney was an attorney, and like Harley, she wasn't used to not being in control. She had opted to have immediate breast reconstruction, and Harley had learned that *immediate* didn't mean they reconstructed her breasts at the time of surgery. It meant they started the process, putting in an implant during the mastectomy. It would be weeks before the reconstruction was complete.

"I've got weeks of discomfort ahead of me," she said. "But I want *details*, Har. Is Piper pampering you? Are the girls being nice to her?"

Harley was taking care of the girls until a week from Friday, when Delaney should be well enough to have them come home. He didn't want her to worry about Jolie seeming withdrawn when she needed to rest and relax, so he said, "The girls are fine, they're nice to Piper, and Piper's taking great care of me. She's not really a pamperer, but I've got no complaints. She's *perfectly Piper*. We're in good hands."

He rested his head back. Piper had switched into *work mode* right before his eyes, a mode he knew she found much more comfortable than hovering over children and a man with a bum ankle. She'd helped the girls with homework and then made sure they had everything they needed for school tomorrow. Then she'd gotten them to take showers and made a grocery list of all the things they liked to eat. He had no idea what she'd do with those things once she bought them, since according to just about everyone who knew Piper, she could burn water, but she got an A for effort in his book.

"Oh boy," Delaney said. "I'm getting the feeling you're high on *Piper* more than the pain meds."

"Yeah," he said sleepily, and then he processed what she'd said and backpedaled. "High on *meds*, sis. Sorry. I'm loopy as shit." He heard Piper coming down the stairs and said, "I'd better go. I'm glad you're doing okay. Tell Mom thanks for asking Piper to pick me up today."

Piper walked into the room as he ended the call. She'd let her hair down, and it fell straight and shiny to her shoulders, with a little wave from being in a ponytail all day. His nieces' hair did the same thing.

"The girls are in bed," she said softly. "Sophie fell asleep reading on her iPad when I was with Jolie, and Jolie is probably texting, but she looked pretty tired. I'm worried about her, Harley, but I can't even think straight without some sugar."

He couldn't help puckering up.

She laughed. "Does that *ever* work for you?"

"Apparently not."

"What do you have that's sweet? And *don't* say apples. Seriously, Harley. Little girls need ice cream and cookies sometimes."

"I've got a *banana*," he said in a way he hoped was coy, but his head was swimming, and he had no idea how it came out.

"I don't remember seeing any bana—" She groaned, finally catching his meaning, and stalked off toward the kitchen.

"Hey, Trig," he called after her.

She stopped and cast a deadpan look over her shoulder. Most women would jump at the chance to make out with him, and he loved that Piper wasn't a pushover. But he wasn't giving up.

"I'm really glad you're here for me—*us*, me and the girls. I appreciate it. I know it's an imposition."

"It's not an imposition. It's fine," she said.

"Good, then turn around and get your sweets so I can watch your hot little ass."

Her eyes warmed, softening the tension in her beautiful face, and his heart beat faster. Maybe he'd finally gotten through to her.

"No more pain pills for you," she said in a singsong voice, then sauntered into the kitchen.

She returned with a half gallon of pralines and cream ice cream and two spoons and plunked down on the couch beside him, handing him a spoon. When Jiggs lifted his head, she said, "Sorry, Jiggsy, but you'll have to share with your daddy."

Harley petted Jiggs's head, and his pooch settled back down with his chin on his lap.

"The girls are pretty great," Piper said as she dug into the ice cream. She filled her spoon and tilted the container toward him.

"Yeah, they are." He scooped out some ice cream.

She sucked her spoon clean, and his foggy mind went straight to a darker place, one he'd thought about an embarrassing number of times even when he wasn't on pain medication.

"I'm worried about Jolie," she said, snapping him from his fantasy.

"That makes two of us. I've been trying to get her to open up, but she won't."

"Do you know what's going on with her?"

"I think she's worried about Delaney." He filled his spoon and held it out to Piper. She held up her spoon as if he might have forgotten she had her own. He shook his head and ate the ice cream.

"I know she's worried about her mom. That was obvious by how quickly she left the room when I asked about seeing her. But is there anything else going on? Is everything okay at school? Is she having trouble with boys? Friends?"

"Got me. She hasn't said anything."

Piper's brows knitted as she dug out another spoonful of ice cream and ate it. "When your dad first got sick, you must have been scared, right?"

A chill flared in his chest. His father had run Dutch's Pub for as long as Harley could remember. Frank Dutch was big and beefy like Harley, and stable as the day was long. He'd been Harley's rock, and he'd supported Harley's choice to move to the city and work on Wall Street the same way he'd supported Delaney's desire to go to law school and Marshall's dream of becoming a smoke jumper. When they were growing up, their father had been strict about grades and responsibilities, more so for Delaney and Harley than Marshall, but he was loving and kind to all of them. Harley couldn't remember a day going by that his parents hadn't told them they loved them. That was just one of the many reasons he had a hard time with Marshall turning his back on their family the way he had.

But that was a thought for another day, when his brain wasn't foggy and Piper wasn't sitting beside him waiting for an answer. It would be easy to minimize how he'd felt when he'd gotten the call about his father having cancer since he hadn't talked about it with anyone but Delaney. But he wanted to be honest with Piper.

"I was pretty terrified," he admitted. "One online search told me how aggressive pancreatic cancer was, and they'd caught it late. I remember thinking about how unfair it was to him, to my mom, my siblings, his grandkids. I went numb, I think, going through the motions to make sure everyone was holding up okay, which they weren't, of course. And after he died, I went from numb to sad, and then I got angry, but you remember how awful I was then."

"You weren't awful. You were a son grieving his father." Piper put her hand over his, lacing their fingers together, and said, "It was unfair to you, too."

"What?" He met her gaze, and the empathy in her eyes was inescapable.

"You mentioned everyone else, but not yourself. I'm just saying it was unfair to you, too."

"I guess . . ." He gritted his teeth against the pain burning in his chest.

"You must miss him so much. When I was little, I used to love seeing your dad at the Strawberry Festival or some other event. He'd swoop me off my feet, hold me over his head, and say something like, 'Put some meat on those bones, Builder Girl, or a bird's going to pick you up and carry you away.'"

Harley laughed. "I forgot how he used to call you that. And he'd call your sister Talia *Bookie*. He loved his nicknames." He turned his hand over to hold Piper's, but she pulled away and pushed a strand of hair behind her ear.

"Anyway," she said abruptly, and put the carton of ice cream in his hand.

She stuck her spoon into the carton, and then she put space between them, turning to face him on the couch. She fidgeted with the seam along the back of the couch. Was she nervous? He'd never seen Piper nervous. Maybe the meds were playing tricks on him.

She squared her shoulders and put her hand in her lap. "Maybe that's what Jolie is feeling. She lost her grandfather soon after finding out he was sick, and even though she's been told her mom is out of danger, she's still probably terrified of losing her."

Harley's brain was moving slowly, and he was still trying to decide if Piper had been nervous. He blinked a few times to clear his head and said, "I think you're right."

"If she's scared, she's probably also angry. I bet she feels like the world is pretty unfair right now, just like you did."

"I agree." He scooped some ice cream and let Jiggs lick it off his spoon. "I didn't mention her mood to Delaney. I don't want to worry her."

"That might be smart, or maybe she knows what Jolie needs better than anyone. I don't know what's right in this situation since Delaney just had surgery, and her crisis includes the girls' well-being. You know she's got to be as worried about them as they are about her. My gut tells me Jolie needs someone to talk to, and Soph might, too, even though she seems okay. Some kids keep everything bottled up, and you can't tell what they're really feeling. But I think Jolie definitely needs to get whatever it is out of her system. I love my family, but at her age, I wouldn't have been thrilled to talk with them about personal stuff, or something that I considered bad or confusing. I think she should talk to someone who's not family. Someone she feels safe with. Does she have a teacher or a counselor at school that she trusts? A friend's mom, maybe?"

"I honestly don't know. I can ask Delaney." He rested his head back again and closed his eyes. That horrible feeling in his chest was now accompanied with an extra ache for Jolie. How had he pushed aside how very desperate he'd felt when his father had gotten sick? He should be the one suggesting these things for Jolie. Piper might not be the pampering type, but she cared about everyone. The question was, could she ever care about him the way he cared about her?

"Okay," she said. "I'll nose around tomorrow and see what I can find out, too."

"You don't have to do that. I can take care of it."

"Lord knows what'll come out of your mouth with those pain pills in your system. How about if you focus on icing your ankle and getting better?"

"Thanks, Pipe. I appreciate that. Would you be willing to try talking with her?"

"Me?" She shook her head. "I'm used to dealing with the guys at work. When one of them gets crabby, I have to snap them out of it fast or it causes everyone's attitude to take a nosedive. I think Jolie probably needs someone with a softer touch."

"Don't sell yourself short."

"I'm always *short*," she said sassily. "I'll ask my sisters for advice. I'm meeting Willow at the bakery tomorrow morning. But don't worry—I'll be back by seven to get the girls ready for school. I'll ask Bridgette to meet us. She's the sweetest person I've ever known, and she lost her first husband, Jerry, remember? She'll know what to do for Jolie."

He remembered all too well. Piper's youngest sister had quit college and married a musician. She'd gotten pregnant right away, and then her husband was killed in a car accident right after their son, Louie, was born. The Daltons had rallied around them and helped Bridgette get back on her feet. She'd even opened a flower shop called the Secret Garden, next to their sister Willow's bakery, Sweetie Pies. Now Louie was almost seven years old, Bridgette was remarried to Bodhi Booker, and last fall they'd welcomed a beautiful baby girl, Emerson.

"I wish Talia could meet us, but her mornings are too busy." Talia, Piper's oldest sister, was a professor at Beckwith University, a small private school in Harmony Pointe. She and her husband, Derek, had recently opened Our Friends' House, an adult-daycare center. "She has a soft touch. She probably has good advice. I'll call her if Bridge can't help."

"Piper, not every person needs a soft touch. You should consider talking to Jolie. She likes and trusts you," Harley said, wishing Piper would give herself some credit. Sophie had loved working on her homework with Piper. She'd giggled more than she ever had while doing homework. And Jolie might be having a hard time, but when the girls came down to say good night before bed, Jolie had hugged him and she said she was glad Piper was there.

"Right now I'm considering all the things I should do before heading home," Piper said as she pushed to her feet. "Like getting you upstairs to your bedroom."

"Now we're talkin'!" He clapped his hands.

Jiggs bolted upright, jumped off the couch, and scurried away.

"Forget it. You're sleeping on the couch. How about something more comfortable to sleep in?"

He cocked a grin. "You're walking right into these, Trig. I sleep in my birthday suit."

Jiggs carried his leash into the living room and sat at Piper's feet.

Piper sighed. "Jiggsy, you're going to have to wait until I get your big daddy settled."

"*Big Daddy.*" He paused just to see her roll her eyes. "I'm not into girls with daddy issues, but I'm sure we can figure out another name for you to call me."

"Get over yourself before I smack your ankle. Do you want to *sleep* upstairs?"

"No. The couch is easier."

"Perfect. Considering your nieces don't need to see Uncle Harley's *Harley*, how about a pair of basketball shorts to sleep in?"

"Okay, but I wasn't thinking about my nieces." He took her hand, pulling her down beside him, and said, "I was thinking about my sexy nurse."

"I'm sure Felicity would appreciate that." She pushed to her feet.

"The sexy *blond* nurse standing before me."

"Yeah, okay. Whatever. I'm going to grab your toothbrush and find those basketball shorts." She headed for the stairs.

"I know you love me," he called after her.

"I'm going to rummage through your drawers!"

"Then get back here so you can reach them!" He chuckled as her footsteps faded. "We might have to milk this injury, Jiggs. I'm digging having Piper around."

Jiggs cocked his head.

"You too, huh?"

Piper came downstairs a few minutes later with the blanket and pillow from Harley's bed, his toothbrush, toothpaste, and a pair of shorts. She tossed the shorts to him and said, "Put those on." She dropped the blanket and pillow on a chair and held up a sheet. "I found this in the linen closet. You're incredibly organized for a guy. I'm going to put it on the couch after I put your toiletries in the bathroom down here."

As she walked out of the room, Harley pushed himself up on one foot and shoved his jeans down to his knees; then he sank down to the couch.

"You can shower down—" Piper stopped cold, looked at him sitting in his boxer briefs, and frowned.

"That's not the response I was hoping for," he teased.

Her eyes narrowed. "Why aren't you putting those shorts on?"

"I need help getting my jeans off." He pointed to his ankle. "My ankle and foot look like Fred Flintstone's. Sprained ankle. Ring a bell?"

"*Fine.*" She came around the couch and held out her hand. "Give me your good foot."

He lifted his leg, which caused him to lift both, since his jeans were at his knees. Piper looked at his feet; then her eyes drifted up his legs to his crotch, and his cock twitched. She scowled, her eyes flicking up to his.

"*You* were looking. It's your fault," he said through a laugh.

"I wasn't looking—"

He scoffed.

"I didn't *mean* to! It was right there!" She pointed at his crotch and then waved her hands. "I was trying to figure out the best way to get your pants off without hurting your ankle!"

He chuckled.

Jiggs looked at Piper.

"Shut up," she snapped. She pushed the coffee table back and sat on the floor, gently guiding his pants down his legs. "You okay?" she asked as she maneuvered the stiff denim over his sore ankle.

"Yeah. I'm digging this view."

She scowled, mumbled something about *jackass*, and finished taking off his jeans. She put his shorts over his feet and pulled them up to his knees. "You can do the rest." She stood up and said, "You can't take another dose of pain meds until three o'clock. Do you want me to set an alarm on your phone?"

He hiked his shorts up, using one foot for leverage. "No. I'm sure I'll wake up if it hurts." His eyelids were so heavy, he had doubts about anything waking him up once he allowed them to slam shut. "Take my extra keys so you can get in tomorrow morning. In case you're early or we're still asleep."

"Okay. I need you to stay standing up for one sec." She spread the sheet on the couch, and as he sat down, she said, "The instructions said to stay ahead of the pain. Are you sure you don't want me to set an alarm?"

"I can handle pain."

She helped him prop his ankle on the other end of the couch, then put the pillow behind his head and handed him the blanket. She moved the coffee table closer to the couch, got a bottle of water from the fridge, and put it with the pill bottle on the table.

Jiggs whimpered, the leash still hanging from his mouth.

She crouched in front of the pup and petted his head. "I know, Jiggs. I've got you."

As she hooked Jiggs's leash on his collar, Harley thought about Piper walking down his secluded road. "Piper, he can skip his walk."

"No he can't. Daddy spoiled him. He can't pee without a walk, remember?"

"Then just walk him down to the water so I can see you from the deck." He sat up, and she put her hand on his shoulder, pushing him back against the pillow.

"I'm a big girl, Harley, and I've got this ferocious dog to keep me safe. Your job is to get better, not tell me what to do. I've lived in Sweetwater all my life and nobody's ever attacked me. I think I can handle walking your dog."

"Damn it, Piper. Why are you so stubborn?"

She shrugged. "Part of my charm, I guess." She opened the door, then pointed to him and said, "I will walk him down by the water, but if you get up from that couch, I will not come back to help you tomorrow. Close your eyes and chill, okay? I promise not to get raped or pillaged."

Piper made her way down to the water, trying not to think about Harley. The trouble was, she couldn't *stop* thinking about him in those damn boxer briefs. She tried to shift her thoughts to work, but they kept circling back to Harley—his laugh, the heated look in his eyes when she was taking off his jeans, his thick thighs, and that enticing package pressed against his thin cotton boxer briefs. She didn't know what was worse, that she was thinking about all those things or that he suddenly had unnecessary protective instincts. She walked along the edge of the grass, waiting for Jiggs to do his business, and gazed out at Harley's dock. The dock was built in a U shape around the covered slip where he kept his cabin cruiser. She and their friends had helped him build the slip when he'd first bought the place about a year after he'd moved back to Sweetwater. They'd had fun working with their friends that weekend, and swimming in the lake when they were done each day. She gazed past the slip at the moonlight glistening off the inky water, and her mind traveled back to the horrible night all those years ago when Marshall had broken her heart and Harley had found her at the end of the dock at the marina.

A chill ran down her spine with the painful memories she rarely allowed herself to think about. She'd felt Harley's presence behind her on that cold, dark night before he'd made a sound. When she'd looked over her shoulder and he'd seen her tears, his face had gone from concern to rage. She was used to her older brother, Ben, protecting her and getting angry on her behalf, but not Harley. She'd been mortified that he'd seen her like that, and in the space of a second that mortification had brought the harsh realization that there were things in life nobody could protect her from. That realization had shocked and momentarily paralyzed her with fear. But the embarrassment of Marshall's brother seeing how badly Marshall had broken her had propelled her to her feet, giving her the strength and determination to protect her heart at all costs, and she'd never looked back.

As she gazed out at the water, she wondered what Harley might have said to her then if she'd given him the chance. Would he have given her sage advice? Tried to make her feel better about herself and feel safe, as he did with his nieces? Or would he have just been like most college-aged guys and not known what to do?

Jiggs nudged her with his nose, and she realized she'd zoned out.

Irritated with herself, she said, "Sorry, Jiggs. Let's get out of here." *The faster the better.* She was obviously losing her mind, doing so much thinking about Harley. As they made their way up the steps to the deck and around to the front door, she told herself she was just out of sorts because of the way Harley was acting, and because he was hurt.

And maybe also a *little bit* because she was bothered by some of the things that Harley and the guys at work had said. Harley had said that not every person needed a soft touch, but Piper didn't believe that. Maybe guys like Mike didn't, because he'd be with a dude if he had a vagina. But guys like Harley definitely needed, or liked, a softer touch. Darren's voice whispered through her mind as she climbed the porch steps. *My girl is always hanging on my every word and giving me foot rubs. I just can't see you doing those things.*

"Neither can I," she muttered as she walked inside. Harley was sacked out, head back, mouth wide open, one arm hanging off the sofa. The blanket was on the floor beside him. Her heart squeezed, and she told herself to ignore it as she crouched beside Jiggs and whispered, "Your daddy is sleeping." She unhooked his leash but held on to his collar. "You need to be really gentle with him tonight, okay? No jumping."

Jiggs cocked his head. She swore Harley must have taught him that look and exactly when to use it. She scratched Jiggs's head the way Harley had and said, "How about if I make you a doggy bed beside the couch? Okay?"

She held on to his collar just in case he got the urge to snuggle his daddy as she pushed the coffee table closer to the end of the couch where Harley's head was. Then she took the cushions from the armchairs and love seat and spread them out on the floor by the other end of the couch.

"I can't believe a spoiled dog like you doesn't have a doggy bed," she whispered. *Why would you? You probably sleep on his bed every night.*

She led Jiggs up on the cushions and whispered, "Stay." Then she picked up the blanket and spread it over Harley, tucking it between him and the back of the couch. She gazed down at him and pulled the blanket over his chest, letting her hand linger there, feeling his heart beat against her palm. *Harley Dutch, what are you doing to me?*

He shifted, and she snapped her hand away, feeling like she'd been caught with it in a cookie jar as his eyes fluttered open and his lips curved up.

"You know I love you, right, Pipe?" he said groggily.

She swallowed hard, knowing it was the medication talking, and stood stock-still as his eyes closed. She exhaled with relief.

Those pain pills were going to kill *her* before Harley even had a chance to heal. She just knew it.

CHAPTER FOUR

THERE WERE THINGS Piper had always counted on, like her family having her back, work bringing more satisfaction than any man ever had, and her younger sister Willow's baked goods making everything in life seem better. She was exhausted after staying up all night wondering why she'd been attracted to Harley, and as she climbed from her truck and headed for the back door to the bakery, she was counting on the promise the baked goods held.

As she pulled open the door, country music and the scent of sugary goodness wafted out of the kitchen, easing her tension. The counters were covered with cooling racks filled with baked goods. The work space in the middle of the kitchen was littered with bowls and baking accouterments. Willow stood at the counter across the room with her back to Piper, talking on her cell phone. Her thick blond hair hung in a pretty braid down her back. A sense of comfort embraced Piper. She had breakfast with Willow several times most weeks before work, and today it was exactly what she needed to remind herself of her *own* reality. What she felt last night for Harley wasn't reality. It was guilt, or empathy for his being hurt. But it wasn't *real.*

Willow turned and held up a finger, listening to whoever was on the phone. She looked cute in cutoffs and a long-sleeved shirt. She had a body like Marilyn Monroe and was the curviest of her sisters, while Piper had a body more like Kristen Bell *before* she had babies.

Willow mouthed, *I'll be right off.* Then she turned around and continued working at the counter. She spoke so softly into the phone, Piper couldn't make out anything she said. There was a time when Piper had wished for all the things her sisters had that she didn't, like Willow's voluptuous body and overly peppy outlook, Talia's height and academic prowess, and Bridgette's sweet, patient demeanor and ability to talk anyone off a ledge. But those desires had waned around the same time Piper had realized she needed to be in control of her own well-being. She'd not only accepted her thin straight hair, narrow, boyish hips, small breasts, and enjoyment of working with her hands, but she'd *embraced* them all. She imagined it was easier to be taken seriously when men weren't ogling her body and trying her patience. She liked things just as they were.

Or at least she *had* until her siblings had each fallen in love, leaving Piper as the last unspoken-for Dalton. She told herself she wanted it that way, but her crew's comments had drudged up the insecurities she'd been trying to ignore. The time with Harley had magnified all of it, leaving her even more confused.

Willow ended her call and spun around with a plate of baked goods in her hands. She arrived at the bakery most mornings between four thirty and five o'clock to start baking for the day. "Bridgette texted and said you SOS'd her, needing advice about Harley and his nieces, so I made you all your favorites." She put the plate on the counter between them and pushed it across to Piper.

Piper tried not to drool over the pastries: a Boston cream doughnut, a cinnamon roll, and a chocolate croissant with powdered sugar on top. "You're a goddess!" She grabbed the doughnut and took a big bite. Sweet chocolate and creamy custard melted in her mouth as Bridgette came through the door.

"Sorry I'm late." She put her purse on a chair and said, "I see Willow hooked you up. I texted Talia, Aurelia, and Remi last night, but Talia and Aurelia were both slammed this morning, and Remi and Mason left for the city last night."

"I don't need the cavalry. I just need a little advice." Piper took another bite of the doughnut, then carried the plate of goodies to her usual spot on the counter and hoisted herself up to sit on it.

Bridgette walked around the kitchen eyeing the freshly made goodies and said, "Your text said to get my ass to the bakery in the morning because you needed girlie advice. I figured the more the better."

It dawned on Piper that she hadn't told Bridgette *why* she needed advice. "Willow, how'd you know I wanted to talk about Harley and the girls?"

Willow and Bridgette exchanged a look that told Piper her sisters had a secret, and that annoyed the shit out of her.

"Someone better start talking, because I'm in no mood to be fucked with." Piper buried her irritation in another bite of sugary goodness.

"Bodhi's mother told him that Mom told *her* that Harley's mother said you picked up Harley from the hospital and you were helping him with the girls," Bridgette explained.

"Sweetwater gossip at its finest." Piper finished her doughnut and picked up the cinnamon bun. Some aspects of small-town life sucked, but there was nowhere else Piper would want to be than near her family. "Did she also tell you that she gave Harley a picture of the two of us dancing at Ben's wedding? He's got the damn thing on his refrigerator."

Willow laughed. "You know Mom. She loves to make people happy. She made healing lotions for Delaney after she got the news about having cancer, hoping they would help, and last weekend she made a love potion for Doris Pilcheck."

Their mother made organic fragrances, shampoos, body washes, soaps, and lotions and sold them in stores around town. But she was best known for the *love potions* she claimed to put in some of her wares. She swore she was responsible for at least half of the love connections in town.

"Doris is seventy-five years old," Piper said.

"And still in her prime, according to Mom." Willow glanced at Bridgette, who was still pondering the sweets, and said, "You need to actually pick one up and eat it. Despite how it looks when Piper scarfs them down, they won't leap into your mouth."

"I have another ten pounds to lose, so I'm just going to get drunk on their delicious aromas and savor the sight of them. I'm carrying five pounds here." Bridgette patted her butt in her pretty floral dress and said, "And five pounds here." She grabbed her boobs.

Piper rolled her eyes. "You look great and Bodhi adores you, so choose one and eat the damn thing already."

"That's easy for you to say. You can eat anything and not gain a pound," Bridgette said.

"Which translates to there's no natural way for me to grow bigger breasts or a rounder ass." Piper took another bite.

"You don't get it." Bridgette leaned her hip on the counter and said, "Being pregnant with Emerson changed my *whole* body even worse than when I was pregnant with Louie. I have all this loose skin on my stomach, more stretch marks that I swear look like road maps, and my boobs are starting to look like an old lady's."

"Whatever. You have a beautiful baby girl and you see things about your body no one else does. You're still hot, Bridge. *Own* those curves," Piper encouraged her.

Bridgette looked at Willow.

"Don't look at me. I'm on team eat-the-sweets," Willow said. She went to the other end of the counter and began frosting a cake. "I'm also on team give-me-all-the-details, so spill, Pipe. What's up with you and Harley? Why do you need advice?"

She finished a bite of the cinnamon bun, trying to figure out if she should lead with Jolie or Harley. Jolie was easier, so she skipped right over the hot, confusing one and said, "I need advice about Jolie. She's in that sullen, eye-rolling, preteen stage, and I'm worried about her because of everything her mom is going through. I think she should talk to someone, but I'm not sure it's really mine or Harley's place to ask a teacher or counselor to talk to her. Sophie, on the other hand, is her normal happy-go-lucky self. I think that's good, but what do I know? I deal with grown men who have more testosterone than emotions. What would you guys do?"

"That's a tough one," Bridgette said, looking longingly at the cake Willow was frosting. "Did you tell Delaney?"

"With everything Delaney is going through, Harley doesn't want to worry her. On one hand I think he's right. But on the other, what if he's wrong?"

Willow looked up from the cake and said, "Have you or Harley tried to talk to Jolie?"

"Harley said he did, and I tried last night a little, but you guys know I'm not great at tiptoeing around subjects." Except for right now, as she avoided talking about Harley. "I'm afraid I'll say something too harsh."

"You're great with Louie and Emerson," Bridgette pointed out.

"You're not harsh with kids, Pipe; you're *direct*. There's a difference." Willow finished frosting the cake and handed Bridgette the spatula. "And *you're* not *fat*. So happy licking."

Piper smirked. "That's what Bodhi says."

"Don't tell Bodhi this," Bridgette said with a mischievous grin, "but this tastes *way* better than *that*."

They all laughed.

"That's why you need to put the frosting *on* Bodhi," Piper suggested.

"Or whipped cream. *Mm*." Willow pulled a tray of croissants out of the oven.

Piper finished her cinnamon bun and said, "Or the icing Will puts on the cinnamon buns. *Anything* sugary would make it better." Her mind tiptoed back to Harley sitting on the couch in those tight boxer briefs. He probably wasn't into *icing the spatula*, but every guy was into having a woman lick it clean.

"Don't drool over there," Willow teased.

Piper realized she was licking her lips and staring off into space. She shook her head to clear her mind, but Harley was *lodged* there, and he refused to budge.

"Geez, what were *you* fantasizing about?" Bridgette asked.

"Nothing," Piper snapped. "Let's get back to Jolie. What should I do?"

"Talk to her," her sisters said in unison.

Piper slid off the counter and paced. "Did you not just hear me say I'm not used to dealing with this kind of thing? It's as foreign to me as taking care of Harley, who, by the way, is a wicked flirt when he's high on pain meds. Which brings me to my other issue. What the hell happened to me when they were handing out *wifely* genes? I swear I must have been standing in the badass-single-broad gene line and missed out completely. Don't worry—I'm not looking to get married. Nothing has changed in that regard. The last thing I need is a guy who thinks he knows everything telling me what to do or how to act. And that's a good thing, because I don't have what it takes to be a wife anyway. I don't know how to be sweet like Bridge or careful like Talia. I can't dole out peppy tidbits of advice like Willow. I have no business even *helping* Harley and the girls. If I were a better friend, I'd recruit a chick who cooked and cleaned and didn't roll her frigging eyes—"

Willow touched Piper's arm, startling her out of her rant. She'd been talking so fast, she lost track of what she was saying.

"Where did all that come from?" Concern swam in Willow's eyes. "Do you really feel like that?"

Piper looked at Bridgette and saw the same worry gazing back at her. "No," she snapped, falling into self-protection mode. She looked up at the ceiling feeling conflicted and vulnerable, fighting the urge to keep her feelings to herself because she desperately wanted to figure out how to help Jolie—and maybe even herself. *Time to pull up my big-girl panties.*

She lowered her chin and said, "*Yes*, okay? I do feel like that. You guys know how I am. *Who* I am."

"You're right, we do. You're an amazing sister and a loving aunt and friend," Willow said vehemently.

"Who intimidates every man I come across."

"Only the weak ones are intimidated." Willow pointed at Piper and said, "You don't want *them* anyway."

"And even though you don't want to get married," Bridgette said as she came to Piper's other side, "you *would* be a good wife *and* mother. I don't even know how you can question those things. Who cares if you're different from us? We're *all* different from each other. And you might think you're harsh, but you're really not that way when it comes to kids. Don't you remember when Ben and Aurelia first found Bea on his porch? They didn't know what to do with her. You showed up with everything they needed, and you taught them how to swaddle her. You're a natural mother, Piper, even if you don't want to be one right now. I'll always be grateful for how you handled Louie when I first had Emerson and Louie was having a hard time. You took him outside with his tools and had him work out his frustrations on the treehouse. Remember? When he came inside he was a whole different kid. I couldn't have done that. Even Bodhi didn't know what to do. If you ask me, it's a darn good thing you and I are different."

"Yes, but I was flying by the seat of my pants, *hoping* I was doing the right thing. Nine times out of ten you guys inherently *know* what to do for your husbands and for the kids," Piper said.

"Oh, *bull*," Bridgette exclaimed. "We're all flying by the seat of our pants."

Willow nodded in agreement. "We're all just *hoping* we're doing things right. The most important thing is that we aren't doing them so wrong we cause them harm or hurt feelings."

Piper sighed. "I don't know. Poor Harley's ankle is so swollen, it hurts me just to look at it. Most people's first instinct would be to coddle him and make sure he was comfortable. But mine?" She couldn't believe she was going to admit the truth, but if she didn't, it might eat her alive. "In the hospital I felt horrible when I first saw him. My heart ached in a way it never has toward the big lug. But then he pretended to have amnesia, and I was *pissed*. By the time we got to his house, I wanted to tell him to just get over it already and hobble around. Harley didn't deserve that. The guy gave up his career and his entire life in the city to come back and be with his family. I mean, that's huge, right? And there he was, one of my closest friends, who has never asked for a damn thing from anyone, loopy from pain meds, while caring for his nieces. I should *want* to take care of him. But it wasn't until he was hobbling around and clearly uncomfortable that I started to *feel* like that, and even then, when I was feeling guilty for not being nurturing enough, *that* guilt kind of annoyed me."

"Because you were mad at him," Willow said.

"Or maybe because you aren't used to seeing him like that, and it scared you," Bridgette said carefully.

That was just *one* of the things Piper had been up all night picking apart. "I don't think that's it." *Is it?* And what about all the other feelings he'd sparked in her?

"It's okay to be scared, Piper," Bridgette said softly. "Harley's your friend, and he's a big, strong man. Seeing him hurting *is* scary. It makes him go from the indestructible guy you hang out with at the bar who isn't afraid to stand up to troublemakers and the sports partner who can play for hours to being a mere *human*. Seeing this more vulnerable side of him has got to throw you off-kilter. I think I'd worry more if it didn't make you feel weird. And I don't think I've ever seen you react to bad things with anything *but* anger. Remember when Jerry died? We were all a mess, crying our eyes out, and you wanted to *kill* him for hurting me and Louie. And last year when Caroline showed up at Ben's door, you were ready to go to her hotel room and kick her ass for abandoning Bea." Caroline was Bea's birth mother.

"Bridgette has a point," Willow said. "Plus, you're around construction guys all day. You're not really *allowed* to be nurturing or soft. You're the boss, leading rough and gruff men. You have to command respect. I would imagine that showing any weakness is a no-go in your position, and that has to carry over to other aspects of your life. Not in a bad way, but it's not like you can work construction all day and come home and throw on a frilly dress, get your nails done, and turn into sweet Suzy Homemaker. Just because you're more direct doesn't mean you can't talk to Jolie about a sensitive subject or take care of Harley."

"I get all that, but it doesn't help me figure out what to do. I don't want to screw up Jolie or make Harley think I don't care if he's hurt."

Bridgette sighed. "I'm sure you're fine with them, but don't you remember how your tough love pulled me through my grief? While everyone else was telling me they'd be there to take care of everything and that I'd figure out how to move on for *Louie's* sake, you reminded me of how brave and strong I was to have gone against everyone's advice when I ran away to marry Jerry. You made a list of all the things I needed to do each day and gave me something other than Jerry's death to focus on. Remember? You said it was normal to be sad and torn up, but to 'suck it up, buttercup,' because I had a baby who needed a mother. I needed that more than you could ever know, Piper. And when you took me to the Mad House, that was genius."

The Mad House, ten wooded acres with an old stone house and several outbuildings in various stages of disrepair, had been in the Dalton family for many generations. It was where Piper went to work out her frustrations by wielding a sledgehammer and doing as much damage as she could before wearing herself out.

"Wait a sec. I never knew you said that *buttercup* stuff to Bridgette. I'm glad it helped. But more importantly, you took her to the Mad House?" Willow asked, wide-eyed.

"Yes, she took me there," Bridgette said. "Why?"

"Because she took *me* there the first time I came home from college freshman year." Willow narrowed her eyes in Piper's direction. "She told me to let it be our *little secret*."

Piper shrugged. "Guilty as charged. I didn't want your friends getting wind of it and turning it into make-out central. You both needed to go there. It was either that or listen to you sob into your pillows."

"Did you ever take Talia there?" Willow asked.

"No. She would have launched into a diatribe about destroying property. Talia works through things in her own way. She confronts her worst fears head-on, which is funny since she's the most timid of us all."

"I know," Bridgette said. "That is weird. But taking me to the Mad House worked so well. It felt amazing to smash that outdoor firepit. I have never felt so powerful or in control. I hurt all over the next day. I remember thinking I'd never be able to use my arms again, but it did the trick. You knew just what I needed. And you know what else, Piper? Harley knows *exactly* who you are and what you're capable of. He wouldn't ask you to help with the girls if he didn't think you could handle it. And as far as all that flirting goes, the man is crazy about you."

"That's true." Willow looked over a tray of tarts and said, "That man likes everything about you, construction boots and all. I think you're worrying about nothing."

"I don't know how many times I have to tell you that he's *not* really into me," Piper snapped. "He just wants everyone to think that he is because he gets his jollies cockblocking me."

"But—"

"Don't go there, Willow," Piper warned. "Harley and I are *not* happening." Maybe if she said it enough times she wouldn't have any more of those weird feelings when she saw him later.

"Didn't you go out with his brother when we were kids?" Bridgette asked.

"Oh my gosh, that's right! Marshall made you a rowboat, didn't he?" Willow asked.

"Hardly. *I* built most of it while he checked out my ass and dicked around with his friends. But he did finish it when I got sick with the flu."

Willow began mixing something in a bowl and said, "What happened to that thing?"

"It got ruined in a storm," she lied. She'd taken that vibrant blue boat with winter-white stripes to the Mad House and beaten the hell out of it.

"Well, I still don't understand why you don't want to go out with Harley. It's not like Marshall was the love of your life or anything. I don't even remember you being upset when you two broke up."

Of course she didn't. There was only one person on earth who knew that secret, and Piper intended to keep it that way.

"It's because I *like* Harley and I don't want to ruin that by screwing him. You've seen the women he dates. They're *ladies*. I'm . . . *me*. He needs a wife, kids, and a little picket fence around his lake house. You should see the way he spoils his dog. You are well aware that Harley is the marrying type, and I'm *not*." Piper picked up the chocolate croissant and tore off a piece, popping it into her mouth. "Can we get off the Harley-and-Piper train now? I'm not looking for a husband. You don't have to sell me on being a wife. I just need to figure out how I can help Jolie without screwing her up."

"None of that will matter if you keep eating like that. You'll keel over from a sugar coma before you leave the bakery," Bridgette teased.

"I've been eating like this my whole life, and so far, no sugar coma." Piper shoved half of the croissant into her mouth and tore a hunk off with her teeth.

"We just got off track. We're not trying to sell you on being a wife. We're just showing you that your type of tough love isn't a bad thing. But you know what I'm wondering?" Willow began frosting a tray of cupcakes. "You said you were annoyed about feeling guilty for not being nurturing enough toward Harley. But you *did* start to nurture him more, right? How did *that* make you feel?"

Piper tore off another piece of the croissant and put it in her mouth, mulling over the question. "Surprisingly, I didn't hate it. But it kind of bothered me that I *didn't* hate it, which shows you how effed up I am."

Her sisters exchanged another secret look.

"Maybe you feel something for him," Bridgette offered.

"Can we please stop with *that* and focus on what I should do? I have to be at his place by seven to get the girls ready for school."

Willow gasped and pointed the spatula at Piper. "I've got it! You think you're too harsh to help Jolie, which means you *want* to be more nurturing. You're taking care of Harley! Use him as a test."

"You've lost me."

"A *test*!" Willow exclaimed. "Whatever you think you need to do to help Jolie, try it out on Harley first. If that means be softer, try it. It might not feel like you, and then you know not to try it with Jolie."

"Oh, I like where this is going! I'm not sure what you think is wrong exactly, but maybe you could try to be more patient? Use fewer curse words so things come out less forceful?" Bridgette suggested.

"I guess I could try that," Piper agreed. "What else?" She finished her croissant as her sisters looked curiously at each other.

"*We* don't think you have a problem," Willow pointed out.

Piper rolled her eyes. "Come on, you guys. If you can't give it to me straight, who can?"

Bridgette shrugged. "I've got nothing, Pipe. Sorry."

"This isn't a lot to go on, but I'll try those things." She glanced at the clock. "I've got to run. Willow, can I take a few doughnuts for the girls? And can you throw in two blueberry scones for Harley?"

"Sure. I'll box them up."

As Willow put the goodies in a box, Piper said, "I still don't know exactly what I should do about Jolie."

"Talk to her!" her sisters said emphatically.

Willow handed her the box. "You've got this, Pipe."

"But what if I say the wrong thing?" She headed for the door.

"You won't," Bridgette said. "We have faith in you."

Willow hugged her. "I'm excited for your test! Watch out, Harley Dutch, because Piper is going to blow you away."

"I'm not *blowing* Harley!" Piper laughed as she pushed through the door.

Her sisters' laughter followed her out to the truck, but much to Piper's dismay, it was quickly overridden by thoughts of *blowing Harley.* She climbed into the truck, mumbling about how ridiculous she was being. As she drove out of the parking lot, she rolled down her window, hoping the crisp morning air would clear her head. And just in case that didn't help, she mentally chanted a mantra—*I will not fall for Harley Dutch. I will not fall for Harley Dutch*—and continued all the way to Harley's house.

By the time she arrived, she was breathing easier and felt more in control. She let herself in and found the girls watching television in the living room, still in their pajamas. The sheets and blanket were folded neatly and piled on an armchair. Jiggs darted over to greet her.

"Hi, Piper," Sophie called out.

Piper petted Jiggs, holding the box out of his reach. "Hi, Soph. Good morning, Jolie."

"Morning," Jolie said, not too sullenly, which gave Piper hope that she might have a good day.

Piper held up the box and said, "I brought doughnuts."

"Doughnuts!" Sophie hollered, and the girls hurried to the table.

Piper put the box on the table and peeked into the open bathroom door looking for Harley, but the bathroom was empty. "Where's Uncle Harley?"

"Upstairs," Sophie answered.

Piper got the girls settled with plates and drinks and said, "I'm going to check on him. I'll be right back."

When she got to the top of the stairs, she heard a loud *crash* and a *thud* and took off running toward Harley's room, her heart racing. "Harley?" She ran through the open door, her eyes sweeping over a pile of folded clothes on the bed, to the open bathroom door.

"Piper?"

Harley's pained voice sent her bolting through that door into a ridiculously small bathroom, and she froze. Water rained down on Harley, sitting cockeyed and naked on the tiny shower floor, one knee bent, his right leg sticking straight out of the shower, and part of the curtain bunched in his fist. The curtain rod lay on the bathroom floor.

She needed to move, to help Harley, but Lord help *her*. She couldn't tear her eyes away from him, and she had no idea why he suddenly looked exceptionally beautiful, but he did, with a thick, muscular chest covered in a dusting of hair, which led south to the monster between his legs.

And he was groaning in pain.

Pain? Oh shit! Shit, shit, shit. "Harley! Are you okay?" she asked frantically.

"No," he ground out between gritted teeth. "I think I broke my *ass*."

The sound of the girls ascending the steps sent panic through Piper. She grabbed a towel and threw it at Harley, then ran out of the bathroom, pulling the door closed just as the girls and Jiggs raced into the room.

"Is Uncle Harley okay?" Jolie asked, fear written all over her face.

Jiggs jumped onto the bed, sniffed the folded clothes that were piled there, then jumped off and scratched at the bathroom door.

Piper put an arm around Jolie, trying to act calm despite her whirling thoughts, and said, "Yes. The shower curtain fell. But he's fine, I promise." At least she hoped he was, because she sure as hell wasn't.

"Are you sure?" Sophie asked.

"Yes. Why don't you girls get dressed and brush your teeth so you're ready for school, and run Jiggsy out back so he can pee before we go. I'll help Uncle Harley get himself together, okay?"

"I'll walk Jiggs!" Sophie said as she ran out of the room with Jiggs on her heels.

Jolie was staring absently at the bathroom door. Piper moved in front of her, looking directly into her worried eyes, and said, "I promise he's okay. The shower curtain fell, that's all." She gave herself a pat on the back for being patient, considering it a *win*, but that win was quickly overshadowed by worry about Harley.

Jolie nodded and left the room.

Piper's hand flew over her panicked heart. *God, I suck at this. Jolie's freaking out, and I have no idea how to help her, and Harley was sprawled out on the floor and I stood there staring like I've never seen a naked man before.*

Not that she'd ever seen a man as magnificent as Harley Dutch. She looked at the bathroom door, wondering how she would be able to look into his eyes after everything she'd just seen.

"Harley?" she called through the closed door. "You okay? Do you need any help?" *Please say no.*

"Yeah, if you don't mind."

The pain in his voice cut her to her core.

What kind of advice would Willow and Bridgette give her now? *Patient* and *nurturing* had been booted out the door by *Holy fuck, look at that!*

She was definitely failing this test.

Piper opened the door and peered around it, her hand over her eyes, cheeks flaming red, and said, "I'm so sorry. Are you okay?"

He didn't know it was possible for Piper to blush, and he liked that look on her so much, it distracted him from the pain in his ankle and his ass. "I'm covered. You can look. Although I'm not sure why you are trying not to. You already got an eyeful."

"That's not my fault!" she said angrily, her eyes moving to the holes in the wall where the curtain rod hardware should be. "What were you doing? *Acrobatics?* Usually it takes *two* people in precarious positions to rip a curtain rod out of the wall."

"Have you ever tried to shower standing on one leg?" His mind immediately placed *her* in a very precarious, erotic position. "Don't answer that," he said sharply.

It was a good thing he'd fallen when he had because he'd been planning on relieving the sexual tension that had been building inside him, heightened from the fantasies he'd had about Piper last night. If he'd started, this would be playing out very differently.

He held the towel around him with one hand and reached up with the other. "Give me a hand, will you?"

She averted her eyes as she helped him up. "What actually happened? How did you fall?"

"I dropped the bottle of body wash, and when I reached for it, my head hit the wall. I forgot about my ankle." He lowered himself to sit on the toilet lid, and Piper turned off the shower and began gathering the shower curtain. "I put weight on my foot and immediately jerked it up and lost my footing. I guess I grabbed the shower curtain." He cocked a grin, though Piper couldn't see it as she placed the shower curtain and rod against the shower wall and began inspecting the holes in the drywall. "I've got to admit, this isn't how I imagined being naked with you in the shower."

"How long do you have to take those pain meds?" She turned to face him, but the second their eyes connected, she turned away again and said, "I'm not sure I can take much more of *high* Harley flirting."

He snaked his arm around her wrist, tugging her to his side and earning an eye roll that rocked the room. "Look at me," he said firmly.

She huffed and put one hand on her hip, meeting his gaze. She looked hot in her work clothes and boots, scowling even as a flush rose on her cheeks, and she snapped, "What?"

He was kind of digging this new, embarrassed side of her. Her guard was down, which made it the perfect time to put his cards on the table. "I haven't taken any pain meds other than Motrin since you left last night. This is all me, Pipe."

She didn't even crack a smile. "In case you haven't noticed, there's no one here to cockblock me from, so you can cut the crap."

She tried to pull free, but he gripped her wrist, holding tight, wanting her to finally hear his words for what they were. "The last thing I want to do is block you from the only cock in this room."

"Harley, cut it out," she scolded him. "I've got to get the girls to school so *I* can get to work. I don't have time for this. And don't try to fix your shower. I'll do it when I bring the girls back after Jolie's soccer practice. Do you want help getting into the bedroom so you can get dressed?"

What he wanted was to pull her onto his lap and kiss her until she forgot whatever fear or frustrations were keeping her from taking him seriously.

"Piper," Jolie called from the bedroom. "We're ready to go."

"I'm coming! Make sure you have your soccer stuff. I'll be right down." Piper pulled Harley up and said, "Come on. They can't be late." As she helped him out of the bathroom, she said, "How'd you get in here, anyway?"

"Didn't you see the crutches by the door?"

"No, I was a little *distracted.*"

"Pipe, listen—"

"No, *you* listen," she said sharply, giving him a nudge down to the edge of the bed. "I just saw you naked. Don't make this any weirder."

He grabbed his boxer briefs and said, "Why does it have to be weird at all? If I saw you naked, it would make things *better*, not worse." He leaned forward to put on his briefs and his towel fell open. He couldn't stop a chuckle from falling out.

"I'm *out of here!*" Piper stormed from the room and hollered, "Girls, let's go!"

"*Damn it.*" Harley looked down at his cock and said, "This is the first time *you've* scared a girl off. Thanks a lot. She's the only one I want to stick around."

He dressed as fast as he could, listening to the girls and Piper as they got ready to leave and wishing he could haul ass downstairs to talk to her. But by the time he got his shorts on, the house was silent and empty, other than Jiggs, who wandered into his room. Harley hopped and hobbled to the window just in time to see them driving away. *Damn injury.* It hurt like a bitch, but he'd rather deal with that than be light-headed around Piper.

He'd said his piece, *uncapped the bottle.* It was time to tip it back.

He grabbed his phone from the dresser and thumbed out a text. *At least now I know you'll be thinking of me today.* He sent it to Piper, pocketed his phone, and hopped into the bathroom to retrieve the crutches. After making the girls' beds, he went downstairs and found a box of doughnuts on the kitchen table. Beside it was a plate with two blueberry scones. His favorite.

Smiling, he sat down and broke one of the scones in half, giving half to Jiggs.

Half an hour later his phone vibrated with a response to his text from Piper. *Get over yourself. I have BIGGER things to worry about.*

Like hell you do, he thought. He scratched Jiggs's head and said, "That's our girl, Jiggsy. She's stubborn as an ox, but one day she'll get out of her own way and realize she loves us."

CHAPTER FIVE

MOTHERS MUST HAVE superpowers. Piper had no idea how they had time to breathe, much less work. Not that she minded helping Harley with the girls, but the morning had been an eye-opener. She and the girls had fun on the way to school. Jolie was in a better mood and looking forward to soccer practice, and although Piper and Sophie had to make a quick trip to the grocery store while Jolie was at practice, Sophie was excited to go to Aurelia's bookstore afterward. Being with the girls was a great distraction from the burly man Piper was trying *not* to think about naked.

Or at *all*, really.

But the minute she was alone in the truck, every one of her thoughts led straight back to Harley. She saw everything more clearly now, the pain in his eyes when he'd been laid out on the shower floor, the heat and sincerity in them when he'd said he didn't want to cockblock her from *himself*, and his disappointment when she'd shut him down.

Her chest ached at that last part. Why did he have to say that crazy shit to her?

She struggled to push those thoughts aside as she drove to the job site. By the time she arrived, it was almost nine o'clock—two hours later than usual. She'd thought work would bring her solace, but from the moment she'd arrived right up until now, as she packed her tools to pick up the girls from school, her every move was shadowed by thoughts of Harley. She'd wrestled with the urge to call and check up on him all day. What if he fell again? What if he tried to take Jiggs out and was lying injured on the side of the road? She told herself that the shower incident was a fluke and he was a big, smart man who didn't need her to babysit him. Cognitively, she knew that was true, and she had no idea why she couldn't shake those weird feelings.

She was taking off her tool belt when Kase and Mike came outside. "Working banker's hours, boss?" Mike asked.

"I've got to get Harley's nieces from school. I'll see you guys in the morning." She tossed her tool belt into the back of her truck.

"Are you meeting us later for drinks at the pub?" Kase asked.

"I don't know. I've got to see how much help Harley needs." He'd made it up the stairs this morning on his own, and she imagined he'd made it down since he hadn't called for help. Maybe he wouldn't need her help at all tonight. An odd sense of disappointment washed through her with the thought.

"Look at Harley's little homemaker," Mike teased. "Guess Kase might've been wrong about you putting on an apron after all."

Piper walked around the truck to the driver's side and started to tell him to fuck off, and then remembered Bridgette's suggestion to stop swearing so much. She flipped him the bird and climbed into the truck, considering that a *win*.

Two wins to one big, fat loss? She guessed they sort of evened each other out.

After school, Piper saw Jolie with her teammates on the field while waiting in the pickup line. She looked happy enough, and Piper hoped that meant she'd had a great day.

Sophie climbed into the cab of the truck in a mood as bright as her aqua top and white capris. "Can we get purple hair dye at the store?"

"That's an interesting request."

"It's crazy-hair day at school tomorrow and all my friends are dyeing their hair."

As Piper drove out of the parking lot, she said, "I think I'd better check with your uncle and make sure your mom won't mind first."

"Okay. Also, when we go to the bookstore, can I get my mom a book? I can pay you back. I have savings from my allowance."

Piper's heart warmed. "Sure, but you don't have to pay me back. Do you know what she likes to read?"

"Mm-hm. Anything with a man on the cover. Her bookshelf is filled with them."

"Okay, one hot-guy book coming up. But first we have to go to the grocery store."

"Can we get gummy bears?" she asked excitedly.

"I think we can pull that off."

They drove to the grocery store. Sophie was singing along to the radio.

"I'm just going to make a quick call." Piper stepped outside the truck and called Harley.

"Hey, Trig. Miss me?"

How can I miss you when I've done nothing but think about you? She decided to skip over his question. "Hi. I'm at the grocery store with Soph, and she asked if we could get hair dye for crazy-hair day at school. I wasn't sure if Delaney would mind."

"Nah, she's cool. They did that last year. I think Jolie had pink streaks for a week."

She looked in the truck window at Sophie, who was fiddling with the radio, and said, "Great. Are you okay? You didn't fall and mess up your other ankle or anything, did you?"

He chuckled. "Not yet, but my ass has a nice bruise on it. It might need some attention tonight."

"*And* that's my cue to end this call."

"Why? Because now you're thinking about my ass?"

"Goodbye, Harley," she said, humored by the big lug's cockiness.

"Hey, Pipe?"

"What? And no, I won't massage your ass."

"Sure you will."

"*Goodbye*, Harley."

"Wait!"

"Harley! You have ten seconds. I'm on a tight schedule, and Sophie's waiting."

"Give Soph a squeeze from her uncle Harley, and I just wanted to tell you that Jiggs missed you today."

She felt herself smiling.

"And I might have, too," he added.

Her stomach flip-flopped as it had that morning when he'd said he didn't want to cockblock her from *himself*. Darn it. She couldn't afford to be flustered when she was with Sophie. "You're just bored. I'm glad you're doing okay, though."

"Well, other than a certain throbbing appendage—"

"*Harley!*"

He laughed and said, "I meant my *ankle*. Damn, Trig, get your mind out of the gutter."

"That's a little hard to do when you can't keep your clothes on!"

"I *knew* you thought about me all day."

"*Ugh!*" She ended the call and shoved her phone in her pocket. Maybe she'd meet the guys at the pub tonight after all. It was either that or deal with a roller coaster of emotions that made her want to smack—and *kiss*—Harley.

When Piper grocery shopped for herself, it took ten minutes and her list was only seven or eight items long. She and Sophie shopped for almost an hour and bought *six* bags of groceries. Sophie was a great helper, checking items off their list and chatting the entire time, which was a lot more fun than Piper's solo trips—and a great way to keep Piper's mind too busy to think about Harley's confessions.

When they arrived at Chapter One, Aurelia's bookstore, Aurelia was ringing up a customer. Aurelia had purchased the Harmony Pointe bookstore last spring, and Piper and her crew had renovated it for her. The bookstore was thriving, and Piper was sure it had a lot to do with the literary-related events Aurelia held, like readings and children's story times. Chapter One had a warm and welcoming vibe. Aurelia and Willow had partnered to bring books into Willow's bakery and baked items into the bookstore, and Aurelia had decorated each area of the store to match the genre it housed. The children's section boasted a large mural, and the classics section was decorated with ornate moldings, rough-hewn wooden shelves, and antique furniture. Even the reference and nonfiction areas carried their own theme—classic library style with heavy wooden furniture and leather reading chairs.

"Soph, why don't you go pick out a book for yourself, and I'll see if I can find one for your mom," Piper suggested.

"Okay." Sophie waved to Aurelia as she passed the register.

Piper headed for the romance section, stopping on her way to look through a display of journals. She had kept a diary when she was younger, and she wondered if that might be something Jolie would like. It might give her a private place to vent. She wasn't sure what Jolie's favorite color was, so she chose a simple red leather diary with a heart-shaped lock, and then she went in search of a book for Delaney.

Piper scanned the titles, though she had no way of evaluating them because she didn't read romance. That was Bridgette's thing.

"Uh-oh," Aurelia said as she approached, looking cute in a pair of jeans and a T-shirt that had REAL-LIFE WIFE. FICTIONAL POLYGAMIST written across the chest. "Piper Dalton in the romance section. Has hell frozen over?"

"Possibly. There's some strange shit going on in my life right now. But this isn't for me. Sophie wants to find a book for her mom, but you know, I have no clue what I'm looking for. My romance comes in the form of a football game, a cold beer in my hand, and a bunch of guys to bet on the game with. Do you have any idea what authors Delaney likes?"

"You're in luck. I have just the thing. We just got in two of her favorite authors' new releases: Charlotte Sterling and Emma Chase." As Aurelia searched the titles on the shelves, she said, "I heard Harley hurt himself and that you were helping him with the girls. How is he feeling? How's everything going?"

"He's doing okay. His ankle's pretty bad, but the girls are great. I just hadn't counted on seeing Harley naked."

Aurelia whipped her head around, eyes wide. "You saw Harley *naked?*"

"Yup, and everything Heaven Love said about him is spot-on. The man's got a beast of a *blissmaker* between those thick thighs." A streak of jealousy shot through her. Piper had grown up with Heaven and her siblings, Everly, Echo, and Magnolia, in Sweetwater. Heaven had once made out with Harley, and she'd deemed him the *Muff Marauder.*

"Damn. You shouldn't have told me that. Now I'll blush every time I see him."

"Tell me about it," Piper mumbled.

Aurelia pulled a book from the shelf and said, "So have you two . . . ?"

"No. What is with everyone wanting me and Harley to hook up? He fell in the shower and I had to help him up."

"Yikes. Is he okay?" She handed Piper two romance novels, and just as Sophie had suggested, they had hot guys on the covers.

"Yes, but *I'm* not. I think seeing his pocket rocket broke me or something." She glanced at the books without really seeing them, because the image of Harley sitting on his bed and the towel slipping off his waist blurred her vision. "I've always had a fond appreciation for lust. It's the most amazing feeling in the world. It belongs on a pedestal right beside orgasms. But now the big, burly oaf has ruined that for me."

"Wait, wait, *wait*." Aurelia waved her hands excitedly. "Are you telling me that you're *lusting* after Harley Dutch?"

"*No!* Yes? *Ugh!*" She pressed her lips together and looked across the store at Sophie, who was sitting on the floor reading. "I don't know what happened," she said in a quieter voice. "But I think whatever switch he flicked inside me was flicked last night, *before* I saw him naked, and seeing him naked this morning just made it irreversible. But it's more than that. Do you know what he *said* to me?"

"No, but I'm dying to!"

"*Stop it.* You can't get all excited about this. It's *not* a good thing."

Aurelia laughed. "Says *who*, exactly?"

"Me! Harley said he didn't want to cockblock me from the only man in the room—and it was just the two of us."

Aurelia grinned so hard Piper was sure she'd pop a blood vessel.

Piper gave her a deadpan look. "I can see you're not going to be any help." She handed Aurelia the books and the diary and said, "Just ring these up. And don't say a word to my brother about this."

"Wait. You can't leave me hanging! And don't worry. I'd never tell Ben any of this, but he knows Harley's been after you for years."

"He has *not* been after me," she said for what felt like the millionth time. "This is *new*, trust me."

"Why are you upset over this? You guys are great together."

"*Because* we're great together. Never mind. Nobody understands what it's like to be me."

Aurelia eyed her and said, "Hot, smart, and tough can't be too difficult of a way to go through life, Piper. You're not getting any sympathy from me."

"Seriously? You know men are intimidated by me, and the ones who aren't think they can change me."

"Not Harley."

"Because we're not *dating*," Piper explained. "Just don't say anything, okay?"

"Okay, but I have to say this: I think you're being foolish. Don't shut him out."

Piper arched a brow. "That's great advice coming from a woman who bought a bookstore and moved out of town to escape her crush on my brother."

"That was different. I'd loved Ben *forever* and I didn't think he was interested. You aren't in love with Harley. *Wait.* Are you?"

"God, everyone's lost their minds. No, I'm *not*. I never even *thought* about him like that until he hurt his ankle. He's a freaking *switch flicker!*"

"I wonder what other switches he can flick . . ." Aurelia waggled her brows.

Piper didn't want to think about *that*. It would only make her think about him naked again.

Great. Now she was doing just that.

"Can you please *stop*?" Piper pleaded. "The minute you sleep with a man, they change."

"Not always. Why can't you just give him a chance? Give *yourself* a chance," Aurelia asked as Sophie headed in their direction. "Ben and I took a chance, and look how happy we are. I'm married to my best friend, and I can tell you that sleeping with him only made things better."

"*Ew.* I don't want to know anything about my brother's sex life."

"Fine, whatever. But I'm telling you, we're ridiculously happy. I can't believe it's been more than a year since Bea came into our lives," Aurelia said as Sophie joined them. "Hi, Sophie."

"Hi. I was hoping you had Bea with you today," Sophie said. "I haven't seen her in a while."

"I loved bringing her to work with me, but I don't bring her with me that often anymore," Aurelia said. "She's too curious, and into everything. She pulls all the books off the low shelves. She'd love to see you, though. *Hey*, I have an idea. Why don't you and Jolie come for a visit

Saturday after I get off work? We'll give your uncle and Piper a few hours to take care of some grown-up things."

Before Piper could shut down her matchmaking, Sophie said, "Jolie has a sleepover after her soccer game, so she can't come, but I'd like to."

"Actually, I have a better idea." Aurelia had a scheming look in her eyes. "Ben and I could use a break from playing with baby toys. I'd love to have a mother's helper like you around for an evening. Why don't you come spend the night Saturday, Sophie? We'll have dinner, go to the park, maybe get some ice cream. What do you say?"

Sophie turned pleading baby blues on Piper and said, "Can I? *Please*, Piper?"

Piper realized if the girls weren't with Harley, he shouldn't need her around Saturday night. She could go to the pub, hang out with the guys, and get her overactive hormones under control. *Then* things would go back to normal.

Her annoyance quickly turned to gratitude as she said, "I have to ask your uncle, but I'm pretty sure he won't mind."

"Thank you!" Sophie exclaimed.

Looking overly pleased with her scheming, Aurelia said, "Great! Now that that's settled, Sophie, did you find a good book?"

Sophie held up the book, showing them the cover. *Dork Diaries 8: Tales from a Not-So-Happily Ever After.*

Piper snagged it from her hands. Life had enough hard knocks, as Sophie had experienced firsthand after losing her grandfather and now with her mother's cancer diagnosis. "Soph, are you sure you want to read something with a sucky ending? Shouldn't you be reading a book with a happy ending?"

"I've read seven of this series already. They have happy endings," Sophie said, as bright-eyed and undeterred as ever.

"Piper is just trying to protect you from getting your heart broken," Aurelia said reassuringly. "Read the back, Piper. These are great books for kids her age. Each one teaches a valuable lesson."

Piper scanned the description and said, "I see that. Lessons about mean girls and boy crushes. But shouldn't girls Sophie's age be learning about how awesome they are all on their own, without boy crushes?"

"I *know* I'm awesome," Sophie said proudly. "I'm smart and I have lots of friends. But I can put it back if you don't want me to read it."

She had even more confidence than Piper at the moment. Piper knew she was pretty cool, but she was also well aware of her weaknesses. Wasn't this the perfect time to fix one of them and use a softer touch?

"No, it's fine, honey. You should read it if you enjoy them." *Another win!*

"Thank you. My mom says books like this teach us how to deal with things that are hard and confusing."

Piper put her arm around Sophie as they walked to the register with Aurelia and said, "Maybe I should read it when you're done."

CHAPTER SIX

JOLIE LOOKED CUTE with her hair pulled up in a ponytail, chatting with the other girls as they walked off the soccer field. Piper tried to read her expression, but she didn't look particularly unhappy *or* cheerful. The other girls didn't, either. Maybe Jolie's attitude wasn't so far out of the norm for girls her age after all.

Jolie climbed into the back seat, and Piper said, "Did you have fun?"

"Yeah. My friend Trish hurt her foot and her mother had to come get her, but she thinks she'll be fine by Saturday," Jolie said.

"I hope so." Piper handed her a cookie and said, "We figured you might be hungry."

Jolie's eyes lit up. "Thanks!"

Piper made a mental note to tell Harley to ditch the apples and bring on some sugar.

"Uncle Harley usually brings fruit or granola bars," Jolie said around a mouthful of cookie. "This is so much better."

Oops . . . Harley was probably doing what Delaney had asked him to.

"Guess what?" Sophie said excitedly. "I might spend the night at Aurelia's house and play with Bea Saturday night!"

"Good for you," Jolie said in the same bored tone she'd used yesterday.

Sophie chattered on about the things she wanted to play with Bea if Uncle Harley let her spend the night—and she didn't stop talking until she climbed out of the truck at Harley's house.

The front door flew open as Piper grabbed grocery bags from the back, and Jiggs darted out to greet the girls.

"Our girls are home, Jiggsy." Harley stepped onto the porch using the crutches, his ankle neatly wrapped. He was wearing a pair of basketball shorts and his navy hoodie, zipped up to the center of his chest. The sexy dusting of chest hair peeking out told her he wasn't wearing a shirt beneath it.

Their eyes connected, and the crazy lust she'd been trying to outrun ricocheted inside her. She felt her cheeks burn, and he cocked an arrogant grin.

Damn switch flicker!

Jolie tried to walk past him, but he swept an arm around her, hugging her as he kissed the top her head, and said, "How was soccer?"

"Fine. How's your ankle?" she asked.

Jiggs rubbed his body against Harley's leg.

"Good. Thanks for asking." He released Jolie, and as she walked inside, Sophie put her arms around her uncle. Her backpack slipped from her shoulder as she hugged him. "Hey, squirt. Did you have a good time with Piper?"

"Yes! I got a new Dork Diaries book, and Aurelia invited me to spend the night Saturday. Can I? *Please?* I want to play with Bea."

"Sure." Harley arched a brow in Piper's direction and said, "A sleepover on Saturday sounds like a great idea."

Piper stumbled over her own feet, and he chuckled.

"Thank you!" Sophie gave him another quick hug, then headed inside.

Harley set his eyes on Piper again as she ascended the porch steps, sending sparks searing beneath her skin. Her arms were full of groceries, and his arms were open wide, as if greeting her in this fashion were totally normal. She had to think fast because she did *not* trust herself right now. Not after thinking about him in all sorts of compromising positions all day.

"Don't even think about it, Dutch," she said as sternly as she could, thankful for the paper grocery bags. At least she had a buffer between them.

"Oh, I'm definitely thinking about it." He stepped in front of her and wrapped his arms around her, his frustratingly handsome face peering down at her from above the groceries.

If he kept looking at her like that, the paper bags were liable to catch fire.

"How was your day, Pipe? Still thinking about me?"

"No. Definitely not. In fact, I thought about everything else *but* you."

"You suck at lying. We could put those sucking skills to much better use."

Holy crap. Maybe you're not a cuddly cub after all.

He waggled his brows like he was teasing, but his seductive tone told her he was dead serious. She opened her mouth to speak, but nothing came out, which made him grin even more arrogantly. That riled her up enough to find her voice.

She thrust the grocery bags at him and said, "Since you're up and around, you can get the rest of the groceries. I'm going to fix your shower. I told Sophie I'd dye her hair, and then I'll get out of yours." She stalked back to the truck.

"I'd rather you got *tangled up* in it," he called after her.

"Dream on, Dutch." Was he *really* hitting on her like this? Or was this the same way he always teased her, and she was just losing her frigging mind?

She retrieved the bag from the bookstore as he hobbled inside. Harley came outside as she was collecting the supplies she'd brought with her to fix the bathroom and joined her by the back of the truck. He moved surprisingly swiftly on those crutches.

"Are you going to wear your tool belt? I have a thing for hot women in tool belts."

She wondered what—besides her seeing him naked—had happened today that had turned him into a flirt machine. Then the answer dawned on her, and it finally made sense.

"You ended up taking those pain meds, didn't you?" She hoped so. Then she could blame all this craziness on them.

"What do you think?" He winked and grabbed two paper grocery bags, slipping the handles over his fingers. He hung the remaining bags from his other hand.

I think you look hot as hell carrying those heavy bags all cocky and one-footed, maneuvering with the crutches like a pro. She grabbed her toolbox and headed inside without answering.

Sophie was digging through the grocery bags in the kitchen when Piper entered the room. She set Sophie's book on the counter.

"Thanks. Can you tell Aurelia that Uncle Harley said I could sleep over on Saturday?" she asked as Harley hobbled through the front door.

"Sure. I'll text her," Piper said, avoiding Harley's gaze as she walked upstairs. She had a feeling she'd set a new record for the fastest drywall patches ever made.

She found Jolie sitting on her bed looking at her phone. Piper set down the toolbox and supplies and knocked on her open bedroom door. "Hey there."

When Jolie looked up, Piper walked in and handed her the diary. "I got you this at the bookstore."

"Thanks." Jolie fidgeted with the heart-shaped lock.

"I had a diary when I was your age." She sat on the bed and said, "It was nice to have a private place to write things down and get them out of my head."

Jolie's eyes remained trained on the diary as she asked, "What kind of things did you write about?"

"I wasn't really into boys at that point, so I think it was mostly stuff that I was upset about, like fights with my sisters or if I wasn't allowed to do something or go someplace. There were a few mean girls in my classes, and I remember writing about them, which was a good thing because otherwise I probably would have said or done some not-so-nice things."

Jolie's lips curved up.

"Hey, listen. I'm not very good at knowing the right things to say, but if you ever want to talk about what your mom's going through, school, or anything, I'm a pretty good listener."

Jolie's gaze hit the diary again. "I'm good, thanks."

Piper knew a dismissal when she heard it. She pushed to her feet and said, "Okay."

"Thank you, anyway," Jolie said as Piper collected her tools.

Piper headed into Harley's bedroom feeling good. She'd gotten an extra thank-you, which she counted as another *win*. She might not fail this test after all.

As she passed Harley's bed, she remembered that damn towel slipping off. She gritted her teeth and walked into the bathroom. Harley's masculine scent assaulted her. *When will this nonsense stop?* Her eyes swept over the holes in the wall and the curtain rod leaning against the shower wall. The image of Harley naked and soaking wet slammed into her. She closed her eyes against the assault, but that made it even worse, like she was watching him on a big screen.

We could put those sucking skills to much better use.

Her eyes flew open. She needed to flick that switch off. *Stat!*

What had he done to her? She'd always been able to flirt with any guy and forget him three seconds later.

She told herself to focus on the work she needed to do. She would get lost in the project and shut out the world, like she always did. It was a good plan. *An excellent plan.* She set her toolbox and the bucket of supplies down and started organizing her tools, but then she remembered the way he'd swept her against him right there in the bathroom earlier that morning, rooting her in place with an enticing look in his eyes. She struggled to push the feelings and images away, but Harley was *inescapable.*

She sat down on the toilet lid, breathing deeply, wondering when Harley Dutch had become louder than the rest of the world.

Jiggs trotted into the room holding his leash in his mouth and dropped it at her feet.

"Are you kidding me? You've been home with Harley all day and you want *me* to walk you?"

Jiggs rested his head on her lap, gazing up at her with his big, dark, pleading eyes.

"He trained you to do this to me, didn't he?" She sighed and hooked the leash to his collar. *Fine.* She'd walk him. It wasn't the dog's fault Harley was wreaking havoc with her sanity.

But she was going to walk right outside, and when she came back in, she wasn't even going to *look* at Harley.

Harley put the groceries away, surprised to find a box of bones for Jiggs among them, and then he started cooking dinner. As he seasoned and browned ground beef for nachos, he thought about Piper. She'd stalked right past him to take Jiggs for a walk a little while ago, which had surprised him, since she was working on the bathroom. He hadn't expected her to stop working to walk Jiggs. But she had a huge heart, and Jiggs was a tough guy to turn down. Harley just hoped he hadn't pushed her too hard today with all his innuendos. But he'd tried dropping small innuendos and scaring off her dates. He'd even asked her out a time or two, but until this week, she'd never looked at him like she was interested in more than friendship. Then again, Piper rarely looked at anyone like she wanted anything from them. She talked a big game about wanting this or that type of man and having her way with men. That's why he figured he'd try to be as in-her-face as she was about most things.

He'd spoken to Delaney earlier, and he'd admitted how much he liked having Piper around. He didn't tell his sister that he sensed Piper's walls coming down or that their dynamics were definitely changing. But he must have said all the right things, because his sister, whom he trusted implicitly with just about everything, told him to stop dicking around and let Piper know exactly how he felt about her.

He also didn't tell his sister he'd finally done exactly that.

Piper hadn't said a word when she'd come inside after walking Jiggs and headed upstairs. She was probably pissed at him, but at least now he'd seen the truth in her eyes, heard it in her voice. She was *definitely* into him.

"Okay, Uncle Harley," Sophie said. She was sitting on her knees on a chair at the table, spreading nacho chips over a baking pan that was covered with tinfoil. "Did I do it right?"

Nachos were Piper's favorite meal. He was sure she'd eat them for breakfast if she weren't such a sugar fiend. Luckily, the girls liked them, too.

"That's perfect." He put the meat in a bowl and said, "Now spread the cheese over the chips. I'll cut the tomatoes."

"Heavy on the cheese," she said, parroting what he'd said a million times when they made nachos or pizza.

"That's my girl." He put a cutting board on the table and stood beside her, halving cherry tomatoes. "Missed a spot," he teased.

"I'm not done!" She snagged a tomato and popped it into her mouth. "Are you trying to make Piper your girlfriend?"

"*What?* No, why?" He hated lying, but on the off chance he'd read Piper wrong, he didn't need his niece knowing he'd blown it.

She shrugged, spreading cheese over the second pan of chips. "I wish you would. I like her."

"I like her, too, squirt." He pushed the cutting board over to Sophie and said, "You can do the honors of adding the tomatoes while I get the olives, the corn, and the beans."

"Ricky Ciccarelli gave Jenny Johnson his Cheetos and now they're boyfriend and girlfriend. Maybe if we make these good enough, Piper will be your girlfriend."

"If only it were that easy," he said as he brought the rest of the ingredients to the table. "It's a little more complicated than that with adults."

"Can I do the meat?" She peered into the bowl.

"Absolutely."

After they finished layering ingredients on the chips, Harley put the trays in the oven and Sophie ran upstairs to tell Jolie to start her homework. The girls did their homework while dinner cooked and Harley cleaned up. When the girls sat down to eat, he realized Piper had been upstairs a long time. Taking a hint from Sophie, he stuck a bottle of beer in the pocket of his hoodie, realizing he had no way to carry a plate of food upstairs without spilling it.

"Hey, girls, I need some help. I'd like to bring this up to Piper, but I can't carry a plate upstairs without spilling it. Who wants to be the waitress?"

Sophie's arm shot up. "Me!"

"Jolie? You want to help?" He tried to get her involved since she seemed to be connecting with Piper, and he'd like to keep that line of communication open.

Jolie shrugged.

"I could use you both." He pulled the beer from his pocket and said, "I would rather send the alcohol up with you since you're older."

Jolie grinned. "Okay."

"Great. Soph, you carry the plate and tell Piper it's a peace offering. She's going to give you one of these looks." He wrinkled his nose and furrowed his brows, making the girls laugh. "When Piper does that,

Jolie, you hand her the beer and say, 'Enjoy!' and then come down and finish dinner. Sound good?"

They both nodded, and he said, "Okay, go ahead."

"I hope it works!" Sophie said excitedly as she headed for the steps.

"What works?" Jolie asked.

"I think Uncle Harley wants to ask Piper to be his girlfriend."

Jolie looked over her shoulder at Harley wide-eyed and smiling. Harley shrugged, palms up, and the girls giggled the rest of the way upstairs. He grabbed his crutches and limped up behind them. He listened to them delivering Piper's dinner, and they came out laughing. Sophie high-fived him on her way downstairs.

He found Piper sitting on his bedroom floor, hunkered down over a pad of paper, the beer and nachos on the floor beside her. She'd worn her hair down today, and it curtained her face.

She looked up with a furrowed brow, her hair dusting her shoulders. "The girls were cute, but what was that all about?"

"I figured I pissed you off earlier and needed a peace offering." He lowered himself to the edge of the bed.

"Forget that." She grabbed the plate of nachos and sat beside him on the bed, with the plate on top of the pad. "I want to show you something. I hung your shower curtain a little higher temporarily, so I could patch the holes in the wall, but that bathroom is way too small for you. Why haven't you ever renovated it?"

"I don't know. I guess I never really noticed it until I hit my head."

"You're such a *guy*. I had an idea. I checked out your unreasonably large walk-in closet to see if you could expand your made-for-tiny-humans bathroom. It looks like you only use about a quarter of the closet, which is great because I have not-so-nice thoughts about guys who have more fancy clothes than I do."

"Why doesn't that surprise me?"

"Because you know me." She popped a nacho in her mouth. "These are delicious. Thank you."

She lifted the plate and set the pad on his lap. He scanned it and quickly realized that while he'd been worried that she was upstairs stewing, she'd been redesigning his bathroom. As if she weren't *already* doing too much for him? He wanted to wrap his hands around her and kiss her to show her how much she amazed him, but he knew better.

"I think we can use several feet from your closet to create a much bigger shower." She pointed to the design. "See this alcove? That's where the new shower would go, with glass doors so you're not messing with a shower curtain. We can expand your single pedestal sink to a vanity, which would give you storage space. By moving the original shower, we gain enough space to put a small linen closet in this corner of the bathroom. That way you won't have to keep your extra toilet paper and towels in your bedroom closet."

Her expression was serious as she studied the design he *should* be looking at, but he couldn't take his eyes off her. *God*, she was beautiful, speaking passionately about doing the work she loved.

She tilted her head to meet his gaze, catching him looking at her instead of the designs. He'd never met a tougher woman, or a smarter one than the green-eyed stunner looking at him like he'd grown a second head. She had such delicate features, she could be a model. Without thinking, he reached up and tucked a lock of her silky hair behind her ear.

"Don't get weird on me," she said a little shakily, which surprised him.

The last thing he wanted was for her to pull away, so he said, "I just wanted to see your face while we're talking. You can do whatever you want to my bathroom, as long as *you* do the work, not one of your guys."

Her gaze rolled slowly over his face, and then she looked down at the drawing and said, "My guys are very good at what they do."

"But you're the best, Pipe. I won't settle for anything less."

She met his gaze again, brows still knitted, as if she was considering what he'd said. He didn't look away, didn't soften his expression, wanting her to know that he meant it with regard to *all* aspects of his life. Her gaze softened, and that minuscule change felt like a huge step.

"I can do that," she said.

"Great, so when you're done at Windsor Hall, put me on your books and let me know what I owe and when to cut a check."

"First of all, you're not paying for my time. Windsor is going to take weeks. After the main house, we're renovating the carriage house. I'm going to do your bathroom in the evenings since I'm here anyway."

"What about after the girls go back to Delaney's? Evenings are supposed to be your time off. I don't want to put you out any more than I already have. This can wait."

"Harley, the last thing I need is to be hauling your butt out of that tiny-ass shower the next time you drop the soap." A tease rose in her eyes, and she said, "I'll be sure to install a handicap bar in the shower."

Forget backing off. He freaking loved her snarky comments. "Just make sure the shower's big enough for two, and I want dual showerheads."

"Plan on having a shower party?"

He leaned closer and said, "I'm thinking of something much more intimate than a party."

Her fingers curled around the plate in her lap, but he swore she leaned in, too.

"Piper" came out as soft as it did rough.

She licked her lips, her expression turning hungrier, and *not* for nachos.

Thank Christ.

He could finally get the kiss he'd been thinking about for too damn long, *finally* hold Piper in his arms. He lifted his hand to draw her closer, expecting her to pull away, but she seemed just as mesmerized as he was. His fingers grazed the back of her neck, and she inhaled sharply. He wanted to hear that sexy, needful sound again. He pressed his fingers to her warm skin and was granted his wish just as Jiggs ran into the room and barked, sending Piper to her feet, clutching the plate. Harley ground out a curse, glowering at Jiggs as Sophie barreled into the room.

"Can we do our hair now?" Sophie held up two boxes of hair dye.

"Yes," Piper said breathily, her skin flushed. She didn't look at Harley as she ushered Sophie out of the room and said, "Let's do it in your bathroom."

Jiggs jumped up on the bed and shoved his wet nose into Harley's face. "Your timing sucks, buddy." Then he realized if Sophie had caught them kissing, things might have been even more awkward. He scratched Jiggs's head and said, "Wanna be a good wingman? Next time keep Sophie downstairs."

CHAPTER SEVEN

HARLEY CLEANED UP from dinner and iced his throbbing ankle while Piper helped the girls dye their hair. He'd seen Piper with her nieces and nephews and knew she was good with them, but Jolie was much older, and at a tough age. With all Jolie was going through, she could be hard on people. Harley also knew that Sophie was so easygoing and upbeat, it would be easy to let Jolie stew alone in her unhappiness, but Piper had come downstairs and convinced Jolie to let her do something fun with her hair, too. To his surprise, between the sounds of the shower running and the hair dryer blowing, he'd heard *Jolie* laughing a *lot*.

He was sitting on the couch with Jiggs when the girls finally came downstairs. They were wearing their pajamas, talking excitedly as they ran around the couch and stood in front of him. They were so stinking cute, their fingertips touching like they used to do when they were little and excited or nervous about something. It was wonderful to see them so happy together.

"Do you like it?" Sophie asked.

They both turned in a circle. Sophie's hair had wide purple streaks in the front and a pink stripe down the center of the back. The bottom two or three inches of Jolie's hair was bright pink all the way around, and they were both grinning from ear to ear.

"Wow! You guys look *great*," he said. "You'll have the coolest hair at school."

"Do you like Piper's hair?" Jolie asked, reaching for Piper's hand as she came into the room, pulling her in front of him. "She let me and Sophie do it."

Why did that endear Piper to him even more?

Piper wore an expression he couldn't read. It was a little cold and a little cocky, with an undercurrent of trepidation—a combination only Piper could pull off. He'd hoped for more of the lust he'd seen and felt earlier, but this was Piper Dalton, and she did not like anyone else having control. He wondered if she was that way in bed, too, because if she was, they were going to have a very interesting sex life.

He was banking on it.

Her hair looked freshly washed, shiny and beautiful, parted on the side, with a purple streak at the front, where her hair often fell over her eye, and a second streak a little farther back.

"I *love* it," he said. "The guys at work will probably give you a hard time tomorrow, huh, Pipe?"

"Let 'em try," she said with a bite in her voice. "The girls did an awesome job, didn't they?"

"Yeah. Who knew they were so talented."

"Thanks, Uncle Harley." Sophie flopped down beside him and put her head on his shoulder. "Can we watch a few minutes of television before bed?"

"Sure."

"I've got to get my tools together." Piper headed for the stairs.

"Can I say good night now?" Jolie asked. "I want to write in the diary Piper gave me."

He waved her in for a hug and kissed her temple. "Love you, kiddo."

"Love you, too," Jolie said.

After she went upstairs, he said, "Piper bought Jolie a diary?"

"Mm-hm. A pretty red one with a lock on it. Can Piper tuck us in tonight?" Sophie asked. "I want to show her something in the book we bought today."

"Why don't you ask her when she comes back down?" he suggested. A *diary*. Why hadn't he thought of that? His sister had written in a diary when she was younger. Harley and Marshall used to steal it and tell her they were going to read it. They never did, but she used to get so mad she'd chase them around the house.

A familiar pang of sadness and regret washed through him. *Sadness*, because until Delaney had been cleared of cancer, he'd been terrified they'd lose her, and regret always accompanied thoughts of Marshall. Well, that and anger. He hadn't even heard from Marshall since he'd stormed off after his father's funeral. Harley couldn't really blame him, since Harley had given him hell for showing up stoned, or drunk, or both for the funeral, and for disappearing on them when their sister and parents had needed him most.

A little while later Piper came downstairs and set her toolbox and the bucket of supplies by the door, avoiding his gaze. *Damn it.* She was planning on bolting.

Sophie popped to her feet and said, "Can you tuck me in before you leave?"

Piper's eyes darted to Harley, but she wasn't seeking approval. Even from across the room he could see she was wondering if he'd put Sophie up to it.

"She wants to show you something," he said, trying to figure out how to convince her not to leave without scaring her off.

"Okay. Are you ready now?"

"Uh-huh." Sophie hugged Harley. "Good night, Uncle Harley. I love you."

"Love you, squirt." He watched them go upstairs, and then he petted Jiggs and said, "She's *not* taking off. Not without talking to me first."

He grabbed the crutches and made his way to the door to wait for her. When Piper came downstairs, she looked annoyed at seeing him standing by her toolbox, but thankfully, she didn't appear angry.

"Girls okay?"

"Fine," she said.

"Thanks for doing so much with them today."

"It was nothing. I had fun." She reached for her toolbox. "I'm going to the pub for a drink."

He grabbed her wrist in one hand, holding the crutches in the other, and said, "After we talk."

"*Harley*," she complained as he dragged her through the living room.

Jiggs followed them, racing from side to side, like he didn't understand what was going on.

Join the fucking club. Harley's life had been uncorked by the sprightly blonde.

"Sit your fine ass down and talk to me." He sat down and hauled her down beside him. Her foot hit his ankle and he winced, cursing through gritted teeth.

"Oh God!" She jerked her wrist free, worry written all over her face. "Are you okay? I'm so sorry."

His ankle throbbed, the pain cutting so deep it radiated up his leg. "It's *fine*." Jiggs poked his nose at Harley's ankle, and he put his hand between the dog's nose and his foot.

"Bullshit. You look like you're going to kill someone. Let me see it. Did you even elevate your ankle today, or were you hobbling around all day?"

"Piper, *stop* changing the subject."

Her eyes shot silent daggers. "Let me see your ankle, or I promise you, I will walk out that door without saying another word."

"You're so damn stubborn." He threw a pillow on the coffee table and propped his foot on it.

She began unwrapping his ankle. It was black-and-blue and horribly swollen all the way up his toes. "Oh, *Harley*." Her pain-filled voice slayed him. "You poor thing. That has to hurt."

"It hurts like a son of a bitch, but I've had worse."

"Maybe you should take those pain pills. Did you ice it?"

"I don't like how they make me feel. And yes, I iced it three times today."

"Did you elevate it most of the day?" she asked in a less-empathetic voice.

When he didn't answer, she said, "Harley, you're never going to get better. I'm going to have to hire you a babysitter. What could *possibly* be so important that you had to hobble around after falling in the shower?"

"I'm going stir crazy sitting around here all day," he admitted. "I'm used to being at the pub, surrounded by people, *working*." He wasn't about to admit that he'd started hobbling up the road on the crutches, so deep in thought about Piper, he was halfway there before he realized he shouldn't have brought Jiggs with him. The bar rarely got rowdy in the afternoons, but he didn't want to chance it with Jiggs. So he'd turned around and hobbled home.

"I understand that. I'd probably lose my mind, too," she said empathetically. "Why don't I drop you at work tomorrow when I take the girls to school and pick you up before I get them and we go see Delaney. But you have to promise to elevate your ankle after a couple of hours *and* ice it. Wait, is that too early for you to go in?"

"I have work to do in the office before we open. That'll be great. Thanks. But I hate having you come all the way back to Sweetwater when you're already in Harmony Pointe."

"I have to go home and shower before I pick up the girls anyway. I don't want to show up to see Delaney gross from work." Her eyes narrowed, and she said, "I'm calling Jasper to make sure you ice and elevate at lunchtime."

"Fine. I'd like to go with you to see my sister anyway. Now can we talk about us?" He leaned back, pulling her beside him to get the focus off his foot—and because he liked having her close. "You never look gross, by the way."

"What has gotten into you?"

"You have, Pipe. For three years I've been trying to get you to go out with me."

"You have not!"

"I have, just not as aggressively as I should have. I figured eventually you'd get sick of dating losers and realize there's a reason you meet dates at my pub and hang with me there after work."

She rolled her eyes and crossed her arms. "Because I like it there."

"Yeah, because *I'm* there."

"You're not there tonight, and that's where I'm going."

He gritted his teeth and turned toward her. "Damn it, Piper. Be straight with me. I saw the way you looked at me upstairs when we almost kissed. You're into me. I know you are. So why are you denying it?"

"I'm not your type, Harley. You just like acting like I'm yours, and you get off on scaring guys away."

"Seriously?" He couldn't stifle a laugh. "You think I get off watching you bring other guys into my pub? I've got news for you, Trig. I've never *acted* like you were *mine*. You'd know it if I did, and if you'd give us half a chance, you'd never look anywhere else. I'm all the man you need, and if you'd open your damn eyes, you'd see I'm the *only* one you want."

She scoffed. "A little sure of yourself, aren't you?"

He leaned closer, tracing his fingers along her jaw and down her neck. Her eyes widened, then softened, growing darker. "I know you, Pipe. You won't settle for anything less than a man who knows exactly what he wants, and I want *you.*"

She was breathing faster, and for a second he thought she might agree. But in the next breath, she said, "I'm not your type."

"You're *exactly* my type. I've had my eyes on you since the first Christmas after my father passed away, when you and I sat at the bar toasting him. Remember? That was the night you told me about how much you missed your grandmother because she was so much like you. You said she was tough and smart, and she hated wearing dresses because it made her feel weak. And then I walked you home, but you wouldn't let me inside."

"You didn't *walk* me home. You gave me a piggyback ride." Her lips curved up, and she said, "I can't believe you remember that conversation after how much we drank that night."

"I'm a big guy. It takes a lot to get me drunk enough that I can't remember things. I'm the guy you want to go out with, Piper. Stop holding back and just go with it."

"I've seen the girls you go out with. They're the polar opposite of me."

"Of course they are. You think I want to go out with a second-rate version of Piper Dalton? Not a chance. Nobody can ever replace you, but come on, Pipe. Do you really think you're the only one who needs to satiate an urge now and again?"

A challenge rose in her eyes. "So you just want to sleep with me."

"Hell no. I want to *be* with you. I want to be the guy you come to see at Dutch's each and every time. I want to go out with you as a *couple*, with other couples, and do more than play basketball. I want to spend time together at night doing normal things people do when they're in a relationship, like having dinner and talking about what they want out of life. I want to go out on my boat with you, go fishing and swimming, and make love to you under the stars." He paused to let his words sink in. That hungry look in her eyes returned with a vengeance, unleashing his tethers even more. "And then I want to take you home and make you feel incredible"—he put his mouth next to her ear and said—"with my *mouth*, my *tongue*, my *fingers*." He bit her earlobe and said, "And my *cock*." He gazed into her eyes and said, "And then, *yes*, I'd like to fall asleep with you in my arms. That look in your eyes tells me this isn't the first time *you've* thought about it, either."

Her tongue swept across her lips, and "Harley" fell out, a half-hearted warning he was not about to heed.

He pushed his hand to the nape of her neck, drawing her closer. Her sweet scent combined with the tiny anticipatory sound she made as he crushed his lips to hers. In an instant, years of anticipation, of *fantasies*, collided with reality, and *sweet Jesus*, his fantasies hadn't even come close to this incredible moment. Piper kissed him with fervor, clinging to his arms as he angled her mouth beneath his, taking the kiss deeper. He'd waited so long for this, for *her*, everything magnified, her enticing scent, the feel of her tongue tangling with his, her fucking *sinful* taste . . .

Harley's big hand palmed the back of Piper's head, holding her exactly where he wanted her as his tongue delved and explored, his whiskers deliciously scratching her cheeks. His lips were soft, but the kiss was rough and visceral. His other arm snaked around her, pressing her against his hard chest. His hand pushed into her hair, fisting there, causing a titillating sting on her scalp. Fire scorched through her veins. Harley wasn't a cuddly cub at all. He was a demanding, powerful bear of a *man*, and she freaking loved it. He wasn't just kissing her—he was *consuming* her, *claiming* her. His grip on her hair tightened as he took the kiss impossibly deeper, like he couldn't get enough, and she was right there with him, desire storming inside her. Every swipe of his tongue took her higher. She could barely breathe, couldn't think, could only *want*. His grip eased, and she mourned the roughness as his kisses turned softer. As if he'd read her mind, he trapped her lower lip between his teeth and tugged, sending spikes of lust skating through her core. Just when she caught her breath, he crushed his mouth to hers again, as if he'd been trying to hold back and lost the battle. She had never gotten lost in a man, but she felt herself floating away, lost in the overwhelming sensations, and she didn't fight it as he devoured her mouth, nipping at her lips, rubbing his beard along her cheek, and then took her in another plundering kiss.

He continued ravaging her for so long, she lost track of space and time. Her world blurred together. Eventually he slowed his efforts, kissing her softly, making one appreciative noise after another, and it was so luxurious, being in his arms, being kissed by him, it was like icing on the most delicious treat she'd ever had.

When their lips finally parted, hers tingled and flamed, and it was all she could do to try to remember to breathe.

Wow . . .

She thought she'd had great kisses before, but holy cow, she'd been *so* wrong.

He brushed his beard along her cheek. "Say you'll go out with me, Pipe," he said in a gravelly, lustful voice, bringing her down from the clouds.

"I . . . *wow* . . . that was some kiss."

"I was saving it just for you." His lips curled up in a sexy, playful grin.

She laughed softly. "Harley . . . I like our friendship, and I'll ruin it."

"You can't. I won't let you."

"You can't stop me. I'm not right for you. You might think I am *today*, but in a month, or a year, or *five*, you'll feel different, and then you'll sleep with some chick who comes into the bar, and I'll be left with a broken heart, hating you. I don't want to hate you, Harley."

He pressed his hands to her cheeks, making her eyes meet his, and said, "What are you talking about? The only reason I've gone out with *anyone* else—and you know it hasn't been often—is because I'm waiting for you to see the light."

She sat up straighter, facing him. "You know I'm not a forever girl. I'm not looking for a husband. You're a family guy, Harley."

"I'm not asking you to marry me, Piper. I'm asking you for a date."

"You're willing to risk our friendship when you know this can't lead to anything?"

"That kiss tells me it can."

"Harley, I'm being serious."

"What are you so damn afraid of? That you'll fall in love with me?"

She rolled her eyes, but that was her way of trying to pull herself back to reality. Her heart was racing and her senses were reeling. She wasn't thinking straight, or maybe she was thinking the clearest she ever had. She didn't know, *couldn't* know, because even though she was saying all the things she believed, that kiss was tempting her, begging her to give them a try. But her walls had been up for so long, she was afraid of what letting him in might bring. So she let the truth come out. "It's not what I'm *afraid* of. It's what I *know*. Every guy I've ever gone out with has eventually—after one date or *three*—done or said things to try to get me to change, and I *like* who I am. They'd say my nails would be pretty if I grew them longer or got manicures. One guy literally ordered food for me at dinner because he didn't think I ate healthy enough. Oh, and the best one? The guy who suggested I find a career that was less physical because I was such a pretty girl, it was a shame I wasn't more feminine. Another guy bought me a gym membership, as if my job isn't physical enough?"

"They were assholes," he said adamantly, his eyes locked on hers.

"No *shit*. But don't you see? It wasn't just one or two guys. It was almost every one of them, including your brother, who I was stupid enough to try to change for. Did you know I was going to sign up for cheerleading because I noticed how much he liked to watch the cheerleaders?"

Amusement sparked in his eyes, but it quickly turned to something darker.

"I know. I was an idiot, right? In my defense, I was only sixteen. But I actually considered giving up the work I was doing after school—the work I *loved*, helping people with renovations—to try to be who I thought Marshall wanted me to be. I will never do that again."

"I'd never ask you to, Piper. I like who you are."

"I know, but I'm afraid to risk it. If we take our friendship to another level, eventually you'll realize you don't want me to be so . . . well . . . *Piper*. That would be worse for me than Marshall cheating on me."

He leaned closer, his breath coasting over her lips as he brushed her hair from in front of her eyes. "I like that you know how to wield a hammer and that your hands have little calluses on them. I find everything about you insanely sexy, from your badass attitude to the way you're not afraid to own up to liking beer, football, and sex. Give me a chance to prove that to you."

He pressed his lips to hers in a tender kiss, and her whole body arched forward, wanting to experience more of his earth-shattering kisses. He threaded his hands into her hair, taking her in another thrillingly rough kiss. As he intensified his efforts, blood pounded in her ears and her consciousness ebbed and flowed. He made a raw, primal sound, and she knew she'd hear it in her dreams. She came away breathless and a little dizzy.

"God, Harley," she panted out. "You make this so hard."

His eyes flamed, and a wolfish grin spread across his handsome face.

"Don't *even* . . . I don't need to have *that* in my mind right now."

"Don't kid yourself, Trig. You already do."

Her head tipped back against the cushions, and she closed her eyes for a second to try to wrap her head around the fireworks exploding inside her. He waited patiently, without pushing for more, or for answers. His hand rested on her thigh, and it felt like he was branding her through her jeans.

"You know, until you got hurt, I had no issue being around you." She met his gaze and said, "But ever since, it's like I see you differently."

"Because you care about me."

"No. I've always cared about you. You're my friend. It's because you got all weird and aggressively flirty with me. And now you've ruined everything. Between seeing you naked and those kisses, nothing will ever be the same between us." She pushed to her feet, swaying a little, her heart racing.

Jiggs was lying on the floor. He lifted his head, watching them.

"Good." He took her hand, bringing her back down beside him on the couch. "I'm done dicking around. We're going out, Piper. You and me. Saturday night."

"There's a playoff game Saturday night." It was hockey season, and they never missed the playoffs.

"*Jesus* . . . As I said, we're going out Saturday night."

"You're a pain." She pushed to her feet again.

Jiggs jumped up and lumbered out of the living room.

Harley was still holding Piper's hand, amusement dancing in his eyes.

"Let go, Harley. I have to leave."

Jiggs trotted back with his leash in his mouth and sat in front of her.

"Jiggsy, didn't we talk about timing?" Harley shook his head.

"He's your dog." Piper sighed and hooked his leash to his collar.

"I'll take him," Harley said.

"No. You'll elevate that ankle, or I'll be stuck taking care of you forever."

He smiled so big, she had to laugh. "Again, I'll take him out."

She pointed to Harley and said, "Sit." Then she tugged on Jiggs's leash. "Come on, spoiled one." She felt Harley's eyes on her as she headed out the back door and crossed the deck to the yard. She'd lost her mind. She shouldn't even consider going out with Harley. She never should have let him kiss her.

But oh man, those kisses . . .

She looked out at his boat, remembering what he'd said he'd like to do to her in it. Her insides flamed. Making love with Harley under the stars sounded perfect to her.

It was the aftermath that concerned her.

On their way back up to the house after Jiggs did his business, she saw Harley leaning on the doorframe of the doors that led to the deck. Jiggs ran to him.

"You don't listen very well," she said as they went inside.

He followed her on crutches. "See? We're a perfect match."

"You're setting yourself up for heartbreak, Harley Dutch." As she picked up her toolbox and the bucket of supplies, she had a feeling she was talking to herself as much as she was to Harley.

"I'll take my chances."

"I'm serious. I'm worried about this. You're a warm-hearted guy, and I've got mine packed in ice. I just want to go on the record as saying I told you so *now*, in case you hate me later. Maybe we should have a funeral for our friendship."

"Toast it? Have a few beers?"

"Yeah, that sounds about right. Now I need a drink."

He leaned down and looked directly into her eyes. "How about instead, we celebrate how great we'll be together?" He pressed his lips to hers and said, "You heading to the pub?"

She lifted her chin and squared her shoulders. "Yes, and don't make the mistake of telling me not to."

He laughed. "Remember me? *Harley? Not* the assholes you've dated? Have fun, Trig. Tell the guys I said hello."

Was he for real? She knew that would soon change now that they'd kissed. Guys were worse than women when it came to jealousy. Not only was he a *switch flicker*, but now she felt a time bomb ticking in her head, counting down the end of their one-in-a-million awesome friendship.

She put her things in the truck and climbed into the driver's seat, trying to keep her emotions at bay. But her head was spinning, and her body was still humming from his kisses. She didn't want to ruin their friendship, but *God*, Harley had gotten under her skin.

As she drove into the pub parking lot, she wondered, if he kissed like that, what would he be like in bed? The animalistic sounds he'd made came back to her, and her entire body shuddered. She threw the truck into park, fighting the urge to turn around and go back to his house, to take everything she wanted tonight just in case she woke up smarter tomorrow. She gripped the steering wheel so tight, her knuckles blanched. She stared up at the sign over the door of Dutch's, and no part of her wanted to go in. She *always* went to the pub on Thursday nights. What was wrong with her? Mere kisses had never affected her like this before.

Irritated with herself, she threw the truck into drive and turned around, stopping at the edge of the parking lot. Her pulse sprinted as she gazed down the dark, wooded road toward Harley's house. "Fuck it."

She'd never been one to take the safe route. But with her friendship with Harley on the line, she sped out of the parking lot toward home, knowing it was the right thing to do.

CHAPTER EIGHT

HARLEY WOKE UP feeling like he had a new lease on life, despite knowing he had to be careful with how he handled things with Piper. She might have built walls around her tender, needing-to-be-loved heart long ago, but it was still in there, and he knew she'd fight him tooth and nail to protect it.

"Let's go, girls!" Harley called upstairs as he put the lunches he'd packed for the girls in their backpacks. He hadn't wanted to inconvenience Piper any more than he already was by leaving the girls' school preparations to her, so he'd taken care of things himself and texted her to let her know she didn't need to be there until it was time to leave for school.

"Uncle Harley, will you give me one ponytail on the side for crazy-hair day?" Sophie asked as she flitted down the stairs in a pair of pink shorts and a sweatshirt. She held her new book under her arm and was waving a comb like a flag.

"Sure, but it's got to be quick. Piper will be here any minute." He took the comb as she turned around. "Do you have a hair tie?"

She nodded. "And a ribbon in my pocket."

"Attagirl." As he parted her hair and made the ponytail, he remembered the hours Delaney had spent teaching him how to make ponytails, braids, and buns. She had needed to attend a conference in New York City, where Harley was living at the time. Their parents had been running the bar, and Marshall had already gone AWOL. Harley had let Delaney stay at his place, and he'd gone to stay at her house with the girls for the weekend. Jolie had been five and going through a very girlie phase, which had included frilly dresses and socks with lace and braids or ponytails with ribbons and bows, all so different from her tomboy attire of late. He'd arrived on a Thursday, and by midnight he was a hairstyle pro. His friends had given him a hard time, but he'd have done anything to see his nieces happy.

He tied Sophie's ribbon around the hair tie as Jolie came downstairs wearing a pair of denim shorts and a long-sleeved shirt with a picture of a soccer ball and JUST KICK IT! across the front. She was carrying her diary. He took it as a good sign that she put the diary in her backpack. "Want me to do anything funky to your hair, Jo?"

She shook her head.

"Do you like my hair?" Sophie asked.

Jolie looked at her. "Yeah."

She sounded bored, but at least she didn't pick a fight with Sophie. When Harley had worked on Wall Street, his best buddy, Ralph, used to tell him cringeworthy stories about the way his three young daughters were always at each other's throats. The stories were reminiscent of the way he and Marshall had butted heads, and he wouldn't wish that on anyone.

He heard the sound of Piper's truck out front and said, "Okay, let's go, girls."

The girls grabbed their backpacks and ran out the door. He followed them out on his crutches. Piper was just getting out of her truck when Jiggs bolted out and ran straight to her. She crouched to love him up, and Jiggs licked her face, earning a laugh that lit up Harley's morning.

"Do you like my hair, Piper?" Sophie exclaimed. "Uncle Harley did it for me."

Piper looked at him curiously as she rose to her feet. "Yes. It's definitely crazy. And, Jolie, your color looks great this morning. Sorry I didn't have time to get doughnuts."

"It's okay. Uncle Harley made us pancakes," Sophie said as she followed Jolie into the back seat of Piper's truck.

Harley had wondered how Piper was going to act today, and in true Piper fashion, she was sending a strong nonverbal message with I SPEND MY DAYS BANGING STUDS written in white across the top of her black T-shirt above a picture of a woman holding a hammer and facing a wall. Below that it read AND MY NIGHTS BEATING THEM OFF, with a picture of three men running away from the woman wielding a hammer.

Did she really think that could scare him off? Over the last few years she'd given him enough sass to turn ten men away, but Harley saw it as part of her charm. He loved being able to be himself around Piper without any pretense. She didn't mind when he swore, gave him shit when he deserved it, and they had so much in common, she was always fun to be around.

As she made her way to the porch with Jiggs, he said, "Nice shirt."

"I think so." She eyed the crutches. "Have everything you need?"

"I do."

"Motrin, or whatever you're taking for pain?"

"Got it at the pub," he said, glad she cared enough to ask. "Would you mind telling me why you threw out my body wash?"

She looked away and said, "I'll get you a new one."

"I liked the way that one smelled. Your mom gave it to me."

"*Exactly*," she said sharply. "I'll get Jiggs inside while you hobble down to the truck."

He chuckled on the way to the truck. Everyone knew about Roxie Dalton's famous love potions, although her mother hadn't said anything about the body wash he'd been buying from her since he came back to town having any funky potions in it.

A few minutes later they pulled up in front of Dutch's. Harley peered over the seat at the girls and tapped his cheek.

Sophie unhooked her seat belt and kissed him. "Have a good day, Uncle Harley."

"Thanks, squirt, you too." He turned his other cheek and said, "Get over here, Jo. You know I'm not getting out of this truck until my cheeks are even."

Jolie rolled her eyes, sighing exasperatingly as she unhooked her seat belt and gave him a chaste kiss on the cheek. He'd take it. He was a firm believer that people needed to give and receive love in their lives. And after his father passed away, he swore he'd never leave the ones he loved without letting them know he loved them.

"Have fun at school," he said, "and remember, we're seeing your mom this afternoon."

"I know," they said in unison.

He winked at them, and then he turned to Piper and said, "How about a little sugar?" He puckered up, and the girls giggled.

Piper scowled and pointed to his door. "Out. *Now.* Before I slap that goofy look off your face."

Sophie and Jolie roared with laughter.

"She *burned* you, Uncle Harley," Jolie said.

"She loves me. She just has her own way of showing it. See y'all after school. Love ya." He stepped from the truck and grabbed his crutches. As he settled them under his arms, he grinned at Piper and said, "Love ya, too, Trig. Have a great day at work."

If looks could kill, he'd have been laid out on the pavement right then.

He chuckled as she drove off, then headed inside.

It felt good to be back at work.

His parents had purchased the pub when they'd moved to Sweetwater right after they were married, before they'd had Delaney. Harley had spent his youth helping his parents after school, washing dishes, doing inventory, and mopping the floors. It was at the pub where he'd first discovered his love of finances. He had always been good with numbers and had taken calculus in tenth grade and college-level math courses at Beckwith University for the remainder of high school. His mother had done the books for the business, and she'd taught Harley how to do them. His father, also a numbers guy, had been reading about the stock market in his office one day, and Harley had quickly become obsessed with the idea of investing in financial markets, how it worked, and the potential it held. By the time he went to college, he knew exactly what he wanted to do for a living, and he'd made it his life goal to work on Wall Street.

Now, as he sat behind the same desk his father had, going over inventory and receipts from the last day and a half, he didn't miss the all-consuming career he'd once enjoyed. He liked knowing he was car-rying on a family legacy, and he hoped one day to have children who might want to do the same, though like his father, he'd never push them into it.

The morning flew by, and he was knee-deep in work when Jasper poked his head into the office and said, "You icing your ankle yet?"

Jasper was a laid-back, good-natured guy, with Matthew McConaughey hair, a little long and curly in the back, and wily eyes. He'd lived in New York City for several years, working in restaurant and bar management, and had come to Sweetwater two years ago. He'd become a loyal employee and a good friend, and he was excellent at managing their part-time bartenders and waitresses.

Harley looked up from the report he was evaluating and said, "Who are you, my mother?"

Jasper strolled into the room, closing the door behind him, and dropped a bag of ice on the desk. "No, but Piper called and said to make sure you took your meds to stay ahead of the pain, and that if you didn't elevate your ankle and ice it at lunchtime, she'd have *my* ass." He carried the chair from the other side of the desk over to Harley. "I'm sure you'd eventually get around to taking care of this, but I do *not* want to get on that woman's bad side. I like Piper, but I've seen her take guys bigger than me to their knees with her sharp tongue." He pointed to Harley's sprained ankle and then he motioned toward the chair.

Harley put his leg on the chair and began unwrapping his ankle. "I *love* her sharp tongue." He also liked knowing she cared enough to check on him. "I'm surprised she called you after how pissed she was when she left to come here last night."

"You guys came here after hours?"

"No. She left my place and headed here for a drink."

"Then she never made it. Murph and I were here until closing, as you know." Murphy was one of their waitresses. "Kase and some of the other guys who work for her were here, and Willow and Zane came in for a drink earlier in the evening." Zane Walker was Willow's husband. "But I never saw Piper. I figured you finally wrangled her into an *after-party*."

Harley didn't know what to make of Piper not showing up. "She must've changed her mind."

"Guess you struck out, then, huh? I thought maybe she'd feel bad for you being hurt and, you know, give you a pity ride."

"She does feel bad for me, but I'm not trying to score. I'm interested in making her *mine*."

"This is Piper Dalton we're talking about, right? Little sexy thing with a mouth like a sailor? The one who's like those little dogs that don't know they're small? *That* Piper?"

"The one and only." Harley set his ankle wrap aside and pointed to the bag of ice. "Give me that, will ya?"

Jasper winced at the sight of Harley's bruised, swollen ankle and handed him the bag. "Damn, boss. You shouldn't even be here. No wonder she called. That looks awful. I'd have my ass on the couch for a week."

"I'd lose my mind." He put the ice on his ankle.

"I don't claim to know everything about Piper Dalton, but she makes no bones about not wanting to get married. Hell, I remember when she was a senior in high school and she turned down three different dates for the prom. She told them all the same thing—that she didn't *do* commitments. I get the impression she likes her life just as it is, and you've seen her in here with different guys. That's a woman who likes to have a good time, not the kind of woman looking to become anyone's permanent squeeze."

Harley sat back and said, "I'm well aware that she doesn't want to get married, and she's been trying to have a good time with all the wrong guys."

"You must be a glutton for punishment. I've seen you hit on her, and I've seen her laugh it off like it was a joke too many times to count. She's got you so deep in the friend zone, you'll never climb out."

Their kisses told him otherwise. "You know what my mother said when Delaney's husband took off? She told Delaney she needed to kiss a lot of toads before she found her prince."

"Probably because Delaney married the first guy she'd ever kissed. Piper's been kissing toads for years."

"Thanks for reminding me," Harley said sarcastically. "Hey, do you think Griff can pull a few strings and get me two seats to the playoff game tomorrow night?" Griffin Lennox, Jasper's younger brother, played hockey for the New York Ice Caps.

"I can call him, but you sure you want to do that? Your ankle looks horrendously painful. What's up? You going to see a buddy in the city or something?"

"Nope. I've got a date with Piper."

Jasper sat on the edge of the desk, rubbing his hands together. "Dude, you want to make this woman *yours* and a hockey game is your play? We seriously need to have a talk. Piper might drink beer and play basketball, but she's still got a *vagina*. Trust me on this—women are hardwired to need flowers and shit. It's like guys needing porn. Hardwired, man. *Hard. Wired.*"

"Thanks for the dating advice, but I think I know her pretty well. Would you mind making the call?"

Jasper pushed to his feet and held his hands up in surrender. "Hey, man, this is all you. I'll make the connection, but don't blame me if the only goals you see Saturday night are on the ice. And take your pain pills, will you? There is only one reason I want to get on my knees for a woman, and this ain't it."

The girls were in good moods when they arrived at Harley's mother's house, but within minutes Piper noticed that Jolie grew quiet and withdrawn. While Sophie was sitting close to their mother on the couch, talking animatedly about her day at school and last night's trip to the bookstore, Jolie slowly moved away, putting space between herself and Delaney. Piper's heart hurt for both of them. Delaney looked exhausted, although she had clearly put effort into looking as healthy and normal as possible for her girls. Her long, layered dark hair was styled, and her makeup was freshly applied. She wore jeans and a loose, soft-looking button-down cotton shirt, but Piper could see she had on a compression garment beneath. Surely to a watchful and insightful twelve-year-old girl who was used to a vivacious mother with endless energy, the fatigued and carefully moving mom before her was a little scary.

"Jolie, tell your mom about the party you're going to tomorrow," Harley encouraged. He'd been watching the girls and Delaney as closely as Piper was.

Only Piper was also watching him, finding it hard to breathe every time she allowed herself to think about their kisses and the things he'd said to her.

Jolie fidgeted with a seam on the arm of the couch and said, "Elizabeth is having a slumber party after our last game."

Delaney reached over to touch Jolie's hand, but she winced in pain and pulled her arm back. "You *love* the end-of-season parties. I can't wait to hear all about it."

"I'm spending the night with Aurelia and Ben, and I'm going to help take care of Bea!" Sophie exclaimed.

"Uncle Harley told me," Delaney said, her eyes running between Harley and Piper. "That's exciting. What are you going to do with her?"

Piper sat beside Debra on the other couch, gazing out the window that overlooked the front yard. It had been years since she'd been there, and she remembered how special she'd felt when she'd walked into their home as a high school sophomore, holding Marshall's hand. It turned her stomach to think of how naive she'd been back then. Marshall was her first real boyfriend. They'd been going out for only a couple of weeks when he'd asked her to come over and watch a movie, and she'd been a nervous wreck about *everything*—how close they should sit, what his parents thought of her, even though they'd known her for practically her whole life, and what *Marshall* thought of her.

She glanced at Harley sitting in an armchair a few feet away and realized she'd never wondered what *he'd* thought of her back then. He was a sophomore in college when she was seeing Marshall. He came home often on the weekends and worked at the pub or hung out with Ben and Zane and some of their other friends. But she hadn't had much interaction with him back then. Although sometimes she'd see Harley walking to or from work when she was fishing out on the lake in the rowboat she and Marshall had made. Back then Harley had just been Marshall's older brother. He'd come over to chat a few times after she'd docked the boat, though she hadn't thought much of those conversations, either.

Had he?

Harley glanced at her, catching her lost in thought, and goose bumps rose on her flesh. She shifted her eyes away, hoping his sister and mother hadn't noticed. Her eyes caught on a framed picture on an end table of Harley standing between Delaney and Marshall, with his arms around them, smiling like he'd never been happier. Harley appeared to be around seventeen or eighteen. He and Marshall looked nothing alike. Marshall's hair was lighter brown, like their mother's, and he was tall and athletic, but he'd never been thick-bodied like Harley. Piper had always thought Harley looked just like his father, but now she noticed his smile was all Debra.

They were all smiling in the picture, but Piper saw a hint of restlessness in Marshall's eyes. Why hadn't she noticed it back then?

Debra put a hand on Piper's forearm, startling her. She reminded Piper of Katey Sagal, with long, layered hair a shade lighter than Harley's and a slightly long face with high cheekbones.

Debra leaned closer, speaking in a hushed voice. "My Marshall broke a lot of hearts, mine included. But I have hope that one day he'll find his way back to us."

Piper had always considered herself lucky that Marshall hadn't returned to Sweetwater to build his life. She didn't relish the idea of seeing him on a daily basis. When his father got sick and he didn't come home, she'd written him off as an even bigger asshole than when he'd cheated on her. And when he came home for the funeral, she'd thought he was there to make things better and she'd been nervous about seeing him again. But she'd never had the chance. He'd taken off before the day was done, and she'd considered herself lucky once again. Now she realized how selfish that was. She might not want to see him, but Debra needed him. Did Harley? Delaney? How about the girls? Marshall had been such a troublemaker when they were younger, egging Piper on to streak down Main Street, getting her to sneak out at night, and going to parties all the time. When he'd disappeared, she'd assumed he was one of those guys who would never grow up.

But now that she saw the other side of what she thought had been luck, she felt guilty and said, "I hope he does."

"Don't hold your breath." Harley held Piper's gaze and said, "He's the least loyal person I know. There's a reason he was never able to hold on to a girlfriend."

Piper hadn't realized he was listening, and the irritation—*jealousy?*—in his eyes told her he'd heard every word and had taken them wrong.

"People change," his mother said.

Harley shook his head.

"Did Uncle Harley tell you he tried to get Piper to kiss him this morning?" Sophie asked with a giggle. "She wouldn't do it. It was funny."

"Oh boy," Piper said, cringing inwardly. Delaney didn't need to worry about her brother making moves on Piper while he was supposed to be taking care of her children. She had been through enough worries for one lifetime. Piper caught Delaney's eyes and said, "It wasn't like that."

"It was *exactly* like that, Dee," Harley said.

"All my children have a little mischief in them." Debra patted Piper's arm and said, "If he tried once, he'll try again."

Piper felt her eyes rolling and stopped them because everyone was looking at her. Her stomach knotted uncomfortably, but she managed to wink at Jolie and scowl at Harley, who had the nerve to chuckle, and said, "Uncle Harley is a big goofball, isn't he, Jo? He kisses everyone, even his *dog*."

Jolie nodded, and she even smiled a little.

"Maybe you went out with the wrong brother in high school," Delaney teased. "Harley would have been a safer bet. I'd choose a dog kisser over a cheerleader kisser any day." She laughed, then winced in pain, and her hand flew to her chest. "Ow, ow," she said softly.

The color drained from Jolie's face, and it took all of Piper's control not to go to her, but to let her family console her.

"Are you okay, Mom?" Sophie asked.

"I'm fine, baby," Delaney said. "Just a little twinge of pain."

Jolie pushed to her feet and said, "I'm going outside."

Delaney frowned. Piper felt her heart tearing right down the middle. She wanted to go after Jolie, to hug her and tell her everything would be okay, but just as she opened her mouth to speak, Sophie jumped up and yelled, "Wait for me!" and ran after her.

Piper couldn't hold back and leave those girls on their own to figure out how to handle this. She and Debra stood at the same time.

"I'll bring them some cookies. You stay and visit," Debra said.

Piper sat down, looking at Harley, who was having some sort of stare down with Delaney.

"What are you not telling me?" Delaney asked. "She hasn't been herself since she walked in the door."

"I didn't want to worry you," Harley said, moving to sit beside her.

"I'm *worrying*, Harley," Delaney said angrily. "Those girls are my *world*. I hate not being able to run after Jolie, to take her in my arms and make her feel safe. That's my *job*." Tears welled in her eyes.

"I know, Dee, but right now your job is to heal so you can take care of them," he said. "If you do too much, your healing will take longer. We're keeping communication open with Jolie, reassuring her about what's going on with you, and Piper bought her a diary, which she's using. She's going to be okay. We're not leaving her to fend for herself. The girls are going to be home for good in a week. Seven more days, Dee, then they're all yours."

Piper moved to Delaney's other side and said, "Harley's taking really good care of both of them. He's patient and loving with them, Delaney. I know Jolie is hurting and scared, and she's *twelve*. That's a hard age. Remember what it was like? Everything changes when you're twelve. Suddenly boys mean something, and friends form cliques, and every emotion feels new and big and overwhelming. *Yes*, it's harder for her with you recovering from surgery, but she's learning to get through it and we're both watching out for her and Sophie. Harley's right. You need to focus on getting better so she sees that you're okay."

Delaney wiped her eyes and said, "It's so *hard*. I used to worry about what effect my working as a single mom would have on them and whether I could do enough at work to maintain a leg up in the firm. Now everything's changed. I am fighting for my life—for *their mother's* life. I have no idea if cancer will come back someplace else. I'm terrified. How can they not be?"

A lump lodged in Piper's throat.

"Dee, you have *clear margins*," Harley reminded her.

"Tell *cancer* that," Delaney said, tears spilling down her cheeks. "Hey, big C," she said cavalierly. "You can't come back. I had clear margins." Her eyes narrowed, and she said, "Cancer doesn't give a damn about *margins*. It's a bully that I never saw coming. I swear I'll never take another second of life for granted."

Anger and sadness reared up inside Piper. She wanted to take away Delaney's fear, and she knew that was impossible, so she did the next best thing. "There's only one way to handle a bully, and that's to kick its flippin' ass. If it comes back, you'll fight with all you have to beat it, and we'll be there every step of the way."

"*Thank you*," Delaney choked out through her tears.

Harley put his arms gently around his sister, careful to keep his burly body from pressing against her chest, holding her as she cried. Piper felt tears welling in her own eyes and put a hand on Delaney's back. Harley put his hand over Piper's, his compassionate eyes holding hers. He pressed a kiss to Delaney's shoulder and said, "We've got the girls, Dee. Now, tell us what we can do for *you*."

"*This . . .*" she whispered.

Harley's words made Delaney cry harder. He was so selfless and took such good care of everyone, Piper had the overwhelming desire to take just as good care of *him*. She wanted to make him feel as safe and comfortable as he made everyone else feel, and she was going to make damn sure the girls were happy, so he would never regret asking her to help.

CHAPTER NINE

HARLEY CLIMBED INTO Piper's truck after Piper and the girls, feeling like his chest had been ripped open. Piper had a determined, angry look in her eyes, but sadness wafted off her like the wind. He looked into the back seat at the girls, and it took his pain deeper. Jolie was staring out the window frowning, like she wanted to curl up and cry, while Sophie was watching her sister. Their fingertips touched across the bench seat. Harley wondered if it was worse for Sophie to see her big sister, the girl she'd always looked up to, falling apart, or for Jolie, not having an older sibling to lean on. Harley had always looked up to Delaney as much as he'd protected her. But there was no protecting her from cancer or her daughters from the fallout. Talk about feeling powerless . . .

Sophie met Harley's gaze, her lower lip trembling.

He would not fail his sister or her daughters. One way or another, he was going to make sure they all made it through this without losing themselves.

"Your mom's going to be okay," he assured them. They didn't understand expressions like *clear margins* or how lucky their mother was that the doctors had eradicated all of the cancer. All they knew was that their mother wasn't *Mom* right now, and he'd give anything to fix that for them. He reached over the seat, taking their touching fingers in his hand, and said, "I promise."

"Buckle up, girls," Piper said, full of conviction as she started the truck. "We're going on a little adventure."

Harley put on his seat belt and said, "Adventure?"

"You'll see," she said as she pulled away from the curb.

They drove through town and kept on going, until the lake disappeared from sight in the side-view mirror. They passed the old water tower on the outskirts of town, and Piper turned onto a winding tree-lined road heading toward the mountains. Harley had no idea where they were going, but Piper seemed intent, and he trusted her explicitly. The road narrowed and the trees gave way to thick brush, the branches scraping the sides of the truck. She turned onto a dirt road, and after a minute they came to a chain blocking their way.

Piper put the truck in park and said, "Be right back."

She unhooked the chain and then returned to the driver's seat. She was smiling as she drove up what Harley realized was an overgrown, nearly indiscernible driveway—a long mound of earth between two rutted grooves, camouflaged by long grasses and weeds, hidden beneath an umbrella of trees.

"Where *are* we?" Jolie asked, sitting up taller, eyes wide as branches scraped the windows like nails on a chalkboard.

It felt like the start of a horror movie. Harley lowered his voice and said, "Are you sure this is a good idea?"

Piper smirked and glanced in the rearview mirror, eyeing the girls. "You can't tell anyone about this place. It has to be our little secret."

"I don't think I want to know this secret," Jolie said, worried eyes darting to Harley.

He winked and said, "It's an adventure, Jo. Just go with it. Piper would never take you anywhere that wasn't safe."

"What is this place?" Sophie said.

"The *Mad House*," Piper said as the woods fell away, revealing acres of overgrown pastures and fenced areas.

A large stone house sat crooked on a small wooded knoll up ahead to their right, partially hidden behind enormous trees. Ivy snaked up the stone, much of which was green with moss. Just beyond was an enormous barn in near-perfect shape, and another smaller barn, which looked like an old, decrepit, and withered version of the first. Piper followed another set of rutted, overgrown tire tracks toward the house, and several more outbuildings came into view, all in various stages of disrepair. One building stood crooked, with spriggy, leafy limbs growing out of the chimney; another was missing a roof, and the left side of an old summer kitchen was completely destroyed. Piles of rubbish littered the overgrown yard near each of the buildings. Boarded-up and broken windows gave the structures lifelike features, as if they were winking, blind, or all-seeing.

"Welcome to the Mad House, ladies," Piper said as she parked by the stone house. "I know it looks creepy, but trust me, when you leave here you're going to feel a whole lot happier than you do right now."

"I doubt that," Jolie said under her breath.

Sophie moved her face closer to the window and said, "I think I'll stay in the truck."

Piper took off her seat belt and turned around, perching on her knees and holding the back of the seat with both hands. Her eyes filled with mischief, and still, her underlying determination shone through. "This property has been in my family for generations. At one time it was a dairy farm. When I was a little older than Jolie, I went through some tough stuff, and I was so angry and sad, I couldn't stand to talk to anyone. My father took me here, and if you'll let me, I'd like to show you why. I promise nothing bad will happen." She nodded toward Harley and said, "Uncle Harley might be on crutches, but he's pretty badass. Even hurt, he could protect all of us like a superhero."

Harley searched for a hint of bullshit, but she appeared to believe her own words. That did funky things to his stomach, and he freaking loved it. He nodded reassuringly to the girls. "Damn right I can."

"Like the Hulk," Sophie said excitedly.

"Pretty much," Piper said. "You girls in?"

Jolie and Sophie exchanged a wary look.

"Come on, let's check it out," Harley said, and they all climbed from the truck.

"We need to start at the big barn," Piper said as they traipsed through the long grass.

The barn was set up like a workshop, with antique tools, machines, workbenches, and even an old tractor. The girls were mesmerized by the tractor, and after Piper did a visual sweep of the machinery, which Harley was sure was to check for unwanted critters or reptiles, she told the girls to climb in if they wanted to. They scrambled into the tractor, and the tension in the air came down a notch.

A flash of bright blue and white hanging on the wall caught Harley's attention, out of place in the rustic barn. He stepped closer, recognizing the sharp blue paint with a fine white line through it. He'd mixed that specific shade of blue for the rowboat Piper and Marshall had built together. A pang of jealousy shot through him. Had she kept it as a memory of his brother?

Piper grabbed goggles for each of them from where they hung above a workbench and called the girls over. She handed them to the girls. "Put these on."

Harley shook off the ridiculous notion about Marshall and focused on his three girls.

Piper handed them work gloves. "You'll need these, too."

As the girls put the gloves on, Harley realized what Piper had in mind and thought she just might be the most brilliant woman on earth. She took two small sledgehammers from beneath a workbench, handing one to each of the girls.

"Want one, Hulk?" Piper asked.

"No thanks. I'll stand watch."

"Suit yourself." Piper picked up a larger sledgehammer and rested it on her shoulder. "Let's go, ladies. Time to do some damage."

"Damage?" Sophie asked. "To what?"

Piper grinned. "Anything you want, as long as it's not structural." She pointed at the older barn and said, "There's furniture in there that you can destroy." She pointed across the grass to a courtyard behind one of the outbuildings. "The kitchen of that house could use a good demolishing." She pointed to two other outbuildings and said, "Those have a few walls that could come down."

"You want us to *break* things?" Jolie said in disbelief.

"Absofrigginlutely. That's what the Mad House is for, to get rid of all that pent-up anger, hurt, and frustration."

Jolie strode toward the barn with a devious grin. "This is *so* much better than the diary."

Sophie ran after her.

"The Mad House, huh?" Harley asked as they followed the girls.

"Some people aren't as good at talking things out as others."

Several hours, three destroyed walls, and lots of broken furniture later, they all left with lighter hearts. At Jolie's request, they stopped to say good night to their mother, and both girls came out looking like a great weight had been lifted from their shoulders. They went out for pizza and ice cream, and when they got home, everyone was emotionally exhausted. Harley went upstairs with Piper to tuck the girls in, and after sweet hugs from Sophie, Jolie gave Piper the longest, tightest hug Harley had ever witnessed.

"Love you, kiddo," Harley said as he pulled Jolie's door closed behind them. His head and heart were so full, he couldn't find the words to express all of the emotions he felt.

Jiggs raced ahead of them as they made their way downstairs. As Piper helped him through the living room, he said, "Thank you for everything you did for them today."

"It was nothing."

"It wasn't *nothing*, Piper." He couldn't keep from drawing her into his arms. "Don't minimize what you did. It meant the world to me, and I know it will to Delaney, too. You knew exactly how to help the girls when I was lost."

"You're never lost. And don't think I don't realize you're using me instead of a crutch right now."

"You don't have to do that with me," he said softly.

"What?"

"Act like you don't care, like you don't want to be in my arms."

She rolled her eyes.

"Admit it, Pipe. You like how *we* feel."

"I like big men. You're big." Her gaze slid to his mouth, and she licked her lips. "You know how to kiss pretty well, too."

The invitation in her eyes was inescapable, and his sister's words sounded in his head—*I'll never take another second of life for granted.*

Unwilling to waste a second of their time together, he lowered his mouth to hers, taking the kiss he'd been thinking about since last night. Her arms circled his waist, and she went up on her toes, pressing her soft, luscious body against him. He took the kiss deeper, earning a sexy moan that sent heat coursing through him, spurring him on. He lowered one hand to her ass, pushed the other into her silky hair, holding her body flush with his so she could feel what she'd done to him. She felt so perfect in his arms, kissing him fervently, writhing against him, it sparked an internal battle. He wanted to lay her down on the couch, strip her bare, and love her like she deserved—and then he wanted to love her like he knew she *craved* just as badly as he did. But Piper had spent years seeing men and sex as a means of nothing more than relieving tension, and there was no way he'd let her see him in that same light.

It killed him to break their connection, and he did it slowly, reluctantly, taking several tender kisses before finally pulling away. She gazed up at him with desire welling in her eyes, cheeks flushed.

He brushed his lips over hers, needing the connection, and said, "One day you're going to realize you're safe with me, Pipe." The way she was looking at him, he thought—*hoped*—she might admit it right now.

She lowered her gaze and stepped out of his arms. "You've been on your feet too long. Your ankle has to hurt."

She nudged his chest as if she could push him down to the couch, but he didn't budge. He couldn't believe how easy it was for her to go from eagerly kissing him to safely protected behind an invisible barrier.

She walked around him and said, "I'll take Jiggs for his walk. You rest."

He watched them go out the back door, wondering how long it would take Piper to admit what he saw in her eyes and felt in her touch. If only a sledgehammer could tear down *her* walls.

When she came back inside, he was sitting on the couch with his ankle propped on a pillow on the coffee table and Piper's favorite movie queued up on the television screen, hoping she'd stick around. Jiggs trotted over and licked his face as Harley loved him up.

Piper headed into the kitchen and said, "What can I get you?"

"An ice pack and *you* is all I need."

She didn't respond, but returned a minute later with the ice pack, a glass of water, and a bottle of Motrin. Her face was a blank slate, giving nothing away, and he wondered if she'd ever get tired of maintaining that tough facade. He put the ice pack on his ankle and took the pills. When she placed the glass on the coffee table, he reached for her hand, pulling her down beside him.

"I've got *Thor* all ready to go." He put his arm around her, pulling her tight against his side, and she made an exasperated sound. "Just go with it, Trig. It's been a long, emotional day. Let yourself relax and enjoy the moment."

"What if I have plans?" she said with feigned annoyance.

He touched the side of his head to hers. "Like the plans to hit the pub last night that never came to fruition?"

"I'm going to *kill* Jasper."

He chuckled and started the movie, holding her tighter. Jiggs jumped onto the couch next to Piper and rested his head on her lap.

"You're both needy and assumptive," she said more to Jiggs than to Harley as she stroked his pup's head.

Jiggs sighed and closed his eyes.

"I'm only staying for the eye candy," she said, eyes trained on the movie as she snuggled closer. "So don't think you're getting lucky tonight."

Maybe Harley wouldn't need a sledgehammer after all, just a good deal of patience.

"I wouldn't dream of it." He was already the luckiest guy in town.

CHAPTER TEN

BETWEEN JOLIE'S SOCCER game, dropping off the girls for their sleepovers, and spending an insane amount of time picking out an outfit for her date with Harley, Saturday had flown by—and Piper was a nervous wreck. She'd considered consulting her sisters about what to wear, but she didn't feel like dealing with all their girlie gibberish about the importance of choosing the *right* outfit for their first date. Even the term *first date* sounded ominous, like it was just waiting to kick her in the ass. She didn't have much luck with first dates, which was usually okay, because she wasn't often looking for a second.

But this date was with Harley, a man she'd envisioned by her side forever.

As a friend.

But now that he'd started climbing over her walls, like a boyfriend sneaking in for a clandestine tryst, she wanted more. She'd tried just about every nice outfit she owned, and everything felt wrong, like she was trying too hard or not trying hard enough. She had no idea how women did this shit. Harley saw her in work clothes every day and he'd *still* asked her out. Irritated with herself for overthinking, she'd finally thrown on her favorite ripped and distressed skinny jeans, a flowy, off-the-shoulder white gauzy top with scalloped edges, and low-heeled beige leather booties.

They'd been together for forty-five minutes, and her nerves still hadn't calmed down. "You're not taking me to one of those froufrou restaurants, are you?"

She'd been trying to guess where he was taking her. He'd told her to drive to the train station when she'd picked him up. All she knew for sure was that they were heading to the Big Apple. While she wouldn't want to live in the city, she loved the hustle and bustle of it in small doses, and she was blown away that Harley had planned a first date that was already very different from any she'd ever had.

"If I were taking you to a froufrou restaurant, do you think I'd be dressed like this?" Harley looked down at his black T-shirt and dark-wash jeans.

"Oh, *please*. You look hot in everything you wear." *Shit.* She hadn't meant to let that slip. It was true, but she was still feeling uneasy about going out with him. He wasn't worried about putting their friendship at risk, but despite their scorching chemistry, she still heard that ticking time bomb in her head.

"I'm glad you noticed," he said, grinning like a proud peacock. He put his hand over hers and moved it to his lap.

Her pulse quickened. He was always touching her now, holding her hand, putting an arm around her, pulling her in close. She hadn't ever been with a man as openly loving as Harley. He'd never made her nervous before, but all those touches had new meaning, and her stomach was fluttering so much she wanted to slap herself.

But she also kind of liked it.

"This is weird, right?" she asked. "You and me going out on a real date? Does it feel weird to you?"

"No. It feels *right* to me." He lifted their joined hands and kissed the back of hers.

She sighed, and it sounded absurdly dreamy, which made Harley beam and annoyed the heck out of her.

"Any more guesses about where we're going?" he asked.

"A Broadway show? That hardly seems worth missing the playoff game. I know most women like them, but all that singing and dancing . . ." She caught herself before she could roll her eyes, realizing how rude she sounded. What if he *had* planned to take her to a show? God, she sucked at dating. A show was a romantic date, even if she didn't think she liked them. Maybe she *would* with Harley. "I'm sorry. I sound like such a downer. A show would be nice."

Amusement rose in his eyes. "The only thing great about a show would be that you and I were watching it together. And knowing us, we'd spend the whole time picking it apart, making fun, and wondering when they were going to serve drinks."

"Oh, thank God," she said with a laugh. "I love that you get it. My sisters get all excited about that shit, but . . ."

"But you'd rather shoot yourself in the foot with a nail gun."

"Yes! *Exactly.*"

They both laughed, and her nervousness fell away, leaving behind a new curiosity.

"Do you miss living and working in the city?" she asked.

"Not really. Working on Wall Street was great, but stressful."

"Ben said you were really good with investments and that you still handle some of his. Is that true? I mean, he's an investor, so it seems weird that he'd have someone else invest for him."

"Ben has his hands full with business investments. I handle his stocks and bonds and such. I enjoy the hell out of the work, but the environment on Wall Street was like a pressure cooker. To excel, you need to live and breathe the business, and I saw many good men get dragged down."

"What do you mean? Fail at their jobs?"

"Fail, give up, become alcoholics, and worse." His eyes swept over the people around them on the train, and when they found Piper again, he looked a little distraught. "Right before my father got sick, one of my best friends came close to committing suicide. He had three young girls and a sweet wife, but he'd gotten too aggressive and made some bad financial decisions. He was on the verge of losing everything, and he couldn't see his way out. It was just dumb luck that I walked into the men's room before he swallowed the fistful of pills he was holding. It was awful. I didn't know what to do, so I called a suicide prevention hotline right there in the men's room and got him help. I found him a psychiatrist and called his wife, who met us at his office. I stuck around to make sure they had a plan and he wasn't going to be booted out the door and forgotten. It was hell, but with counseling and his family's support, he got out of the business and eventually turned himself around."

She couldn't imagine how difficult that must have been for Harley and for his friend and their family. "Thank God you found him in time. Do you still keep in contact with him?"

"Yeah. His name is Ralph, and we talk once a month or so. My dad got sick a few weeks later. Once I came home and saw how sick he was, I knew I'd never go back. Delaney was right yesterday about not taking a minute for granted. Time is a precious commodity, and we never know how much we have left." He brushed his thumb over the back of her hand and said, "Anyway, you asked if I missed living there, and the truth is, I never had time for much other than work. I don't miss it at all."

"So you're saying you didn't leave a string of brokenhearted bed buddies in your wake?" she said to lighten the mood.

"I've never been one to sleep around. Not that there's anything wrong with it," he added quickly. "I just need more of a connection than some people do."

Piper knew that he probably thought she'd slept with many of the men she went out with. She hadn't slept with *most* of them, but she'd been with her fair share of men over the years, and she wasn't going to apologize for doing what she wanted or needed.

He must have noticed something in her expression, because he said, "It doesn't bother me that you've been with other guys, if that's what you're thinking."

Harley had never judged her, even though he'd stopped her from going out with several men he'd deemed not good enough for her. She'd never felt a need to lie to him about her personal life, and she wasn't about to start now. "I'm glad, but I was just thinking that I don't regret the things I've done."

"And you shouldn't. Experiencing life is how we figure out what we really want."

"Lots of people feel otherwise," she said honestly.

"Who gives a damn? I'm a firm believer that nobody knows us as well as we know ourselves. I'm sure you were with whoever you felt was right at the time."

For the first time ever, she wanted to set the record straight. It felt important that Harley knew the truth, and that was a tad scary. She liked people thinking she took life by the horns, by her own terms, and she wondered if telling him she'd probably been with fewer men than he thought would make her seem weaker.

He squeezed her hand and said, "What is going on in that mind of yours?"

"Just thinking about how life is a tightrope. Lean too far one way or another and you lose all the advantage you've gained."

The train stopped, and people filed in and out.

"Is that why you snuck out in the middle of the night last night?"

She was hoping she'd get away without talking about that. She'd fallen asleep while they were watching the movie, and she'd woken up at a little after two o'clock in the morning, with her head on Harley's lap and his hand on her butt. They hadn't done anything more than share those heart-thundering kisses before the movie, but he'd looked so pleased, fast asleep with a small smile on his lips. And she'd felt an overwhelming sense of peace being there with him, being *held* by him. That had scared her, and she'd left before they could have an awkward conversation—and before he could wake up and ask her to stay, because she just might have done it.

"I didn't want the girls to find me there in the morning." It was the perfect excuse, though she didn't think the girls would think twice about her falling asleep watching a movie with Harley. When she'd hugged Sophie good night last night, Sophie had taken Piper by surprise and said, "Love you." Sophie and Harley seemed to throw their emotions around like confetti, as if they should be celebrated. When Jolie had hugged Piper good night, she'd held Piper for a long time, and then right before she'd let Piper go, she'd whispered, "I'm glad you're here." She had a feeling that she and Jolie weren't that different when it came to keeping the lid on their emotions, making Jolie's words that much more meaningful.

Harley didn't look like he was buying her excuse.

The train stopped at Penn Station, and Harley said, "Off we go."

Piper helped him get situated with his crutches, and they made their way off the train and up to the main level.

"I hate these crutches," Harley said as they stepped out of the building and onto the busy sidewalk. The scents and sounds of the city rose around them.

"Why?"

He gave her a perplexed look as they hurried along the sidewalk. "This is our *first* date. I want to put my arm around you or hold your hand, not hobble along beside you."

Why was it such a turn-on that he'd admit that?

"Possessive much?" she teased. "Where are we going, anyway?"

He stopped walking and reached for her hand, pulling her against him. "Happy first date." He pointed up ahead to the sign above the entrance to Madison Square Garden.

It took a second for her to understand what he was saying, and when she realized what he'd done, she shouted, "Are you freaking kidding me? You got tickets to the playoff game?"

"Just for you, babe."

"Harley!" She launched herself into his arms, sending him stumbling back on his hurt ankle.

He cursed, reaching for the side of the building to take the pressure off his ankle, knee bent, teeth gritted, as his crutches crashed to the ground.

Piper jumped back. "Oh my God! I'm so sorry!" Panicked, she scrambled to retrieve his crutches. "Are you okay? I'm sorry! I suck! What a crappy friend I am."

He shook his head, pulling her against him despite his obvious pain. He rested his forehead on her shoulder and said, "You don't suck. You're awesome. That was exactly the reaction I was hoping for, but this bum ankle tripped me up. If I didn't have it, I'd have caught you *and* that kiss I missed."

He lifted his head from her shoulder, and his eyes drilled into her without a speck of anger for what she'd done. She was overwhelmed with so many emotions for this incredible man, she didn't think past the one that gripped her the hardest—the desire to give him the best kiss of his life. She dropped the crutches against the building, went up on her toes as the crutches slid to the sidewalk, and took his handsome face between her hands. When she pressed her lips to his, his arm belted around her waist, holding her tight against him as he took control, deepening the kiss. She was right there with him, pushing her hands into his thick hair, taking and giving in equal measure. He kept one hand on the building, the other firmly around her. The sounds of the people and traffic fell away, and she became hyperaware of all of *him*—the tickling of his beard, the strength of his tongue, his sweet, manly taste, and the feel of his hardness pressing against her. She didn't want the kiss to end, and he was obviously in no hurry, as a guttural noise traveled up his chest and into her lungs.

She had no idea how long they stood there making out, but when their lips finally parted, she swayed against him, light-headed and a little giddy. She realized they'd been grinding against each other right there on the sidewalk. She should be embarrassed, or at least ticked off at herself, but it was hard to feel anything but pleasure when Harley was looking at her like she was everything he'd ever wanted and her lips were tingling from their kisses.

As she sank back down to her heels, she said, "I hope I didn't hurt you too badly."

He pulled his shirt over the bulge in his jeans and sang, "Hurt me, baby, one more time . . ."

"Oh Lord, my kisses make you delirious." She handed him the crutches and said, "Let's go, *Britney*, before you get *speared*."

The stadium was packed. Harley knew he shouldn't be jealous, but Piper had captured the attention of every male within a three-row radius, including a group of teenage boys. Luckily, along with jealousy came a boatload of pride, because she was there with *him*. She kept her hand in his or on his leg practically the whole game and leaned into him when he put his arm around her. Piper wasn't flirtatious with anyone but him, and her brand of flirtation wasn't blatant like other women's. She was all sass and challenge, but there was no missing the heat sizzling in her eyes or the lust in her innuendos.

He glanced at her as she discussed which players had the best stats of the season with the guy sitting on her other side. He didn't think it was possible to fall harder for her than he had over the last few years, but he was wrong. She'd been high-fiving, fist-pumping, and cheering like she did at the bar when they watched sports, but she was even more vivacious and spirited here at the game, which he didn't think was possible—and he was totally digging it. They'd eaten hot dogs and popcorn for dinner, and though Piper said she didn't want a beer, she drank half of each of his. And yeah, he dug that, too.

"That's what I'm talking about," she said as she reached for the cup on the floor between Harley's feet. She took a sip and hiked a thumb at the guy on her other side and said, "I love this guy. His wife is eight months pregnant. If they have a boy, they're naming him Griffin because he's his favorite player. If it's a girl, they're naming her Lennox. How cool is that?"

"Pretty awesome," Harley said as she took a drink. They were sitting in the front row, center ice, and he was getting more joy out of watching her than the game.

Piper took a drink and said, "If I ever have kids, I'm giving my girls boys' names."

"Why?"

"Because girls need something to overcome. It makes them tough. Do you think it was easy growing up with a name like Piper?" She handed him the beer, and as he took a drink, she said, "I've heard it all, from *Pied Piper*, to *come blow my horn*, to I must be a *plumber's daughter*. You're lucky—you have a great name. Harley is rugged and manly. Nobody messes with a *Harley*."

He put the drink on the floor and pulled her close, speaking directly into her ear as he said, "I'm hoping a certain someone wants to mess with a Harley."

She turned, bringing their mouths a whisper apart, and the world seemed to stand still. The game and the crowd turned to white noise, and as he leaned in, the guy beside Piper yelled, "You're on the kiss cam!"

They both looked up and saw their faces on the screen above the rink and yelled, "Nerd reel!" in unison.

They stuck out their tongues and made faces, wiggling their hands with the hang-loose gesture—thumb and pinkie extended, fingers curled down. They gave each other bunny ears, laughing like fools. Practically the whole stadium chanted, "*Kiss! Kiss! Kiss!*" But Piper and Harley continued their childish antics. They loved making fun of the people on the kiss cam, for which they'd coined the name *nerd reel*, because the kisses always looked forced and uncomfortable. They had a running joke that if they ever got caught on the nerd reel, they'd act even weirder than the kissers.

When the camera panned away, they fell into each other's arms, cracking up.

"I can't believe we were on the nerd reel!" she exclaimed. "This is the *best* date I have *ever* been on!"

That was music to his ears.

They laughed and joked, cheered and booed throughout the remainder of the game. When their team made the final goal and won the game, they shot to their feet—well, Piper shot to her *feet*; Harley shot to his one good foot—whooping and cheering. This time, when she launched herself into his arms, he was *ready*, and their mouths connected with a kiss so hot it could melt all the ice in the rink.

She jerked back, wide-eyed and panicked and so damn beautiful, she took his breath away. "*Oops!* I did it again!"

He laughed. "I was ready for you, Trig. I'll *always* be ready."

He drew her mouth back to his as he sank to his seat, bringing her down on his lap, and proceeded to kiss the hell out of her.

He continued kissing the hell out of her as they left the stadium—and from the minute they got back on the train heading home all the way until they hobbled across the parking lot and into her truck, where they were currently fogging up the windows. Thankfully, they'd parked in a dark corner of the lot and the truck had tinted windows, because Harley wasn't about to stop until they got their fill.

They lay across the front seat, devouring each other's mouths like they'd never get another chance. He was hard as an iron spike behind his zipper, throbbing as he thrust against her softness. He wanted to claim every inch of her, to feel her mouth on his body, see her sucking his cock as he buried his hands in her silky hair. But he'd been dying to get his mouth on *her* all night, and when he pushed his hand beneath her blouse, meeting her bare breast, heat seared through him. He loved her perfect little breasts and that she didn't always wear a bra. He teased her nipple, and she moaned, arching and writhing, driving him out of his mind. He'd never imagined their first time touching that way would be in a truck, but he wasn't about to complain. He was careful of his sore ankle as he tore his mouth away and moved lower, needing to taste more of her. He sealed his mouth over her neck, sucking hard. She dug her nails into his flesh.

"*Yes*," she said on a long, needy breath.

"Again," he growled, sucking hard again, trying to earn another sexy sound.

"*Harley!*" she cried out, and he eased his efforts. "Don't stop, *so good*," she whispered as he teased her nipple with his fingers. He lowered his mouth to her neck again, and she hissed, "*Yesss.*"

There was an art to loving Piper Dalton, and he was determined to become an expert. He licked and sucked, nipped and kissed down her neck, across her shoulders, and along her breastbone. He pushed her shirt over her breasts, baring her to him.

"Christ, you're *gorgeous*."

He pressed a series of tender kisses between her breasts, each touch of his lips earning a sensual, anticipatory gasp or murmur. When he lowered his mouth over one breast, she grabbed his head with both hands, holding him there. She bowed up beneath him, and he sucked harder. She cried out, but when he tried to pull back, she wouldn't release him.

"Again," she pleaded. "I like it hard."

Holy. Fuck.

She was his every fantasy come true.

He grazed his teeth over the taut peak, and when she panted out a plea, he sucked hard, then soothed the redness with his tongue. She drew in several sharp breaths, guiding his mouth to her other breast, which he gave the same lavish attention to. One of her hands slid from his head to her other breast, and she began caressing it. She was driving him to the edge of madness. He rose, moving her other hand from his head to her other breast, and watched her touching herself as he unbuttoned her jeans. She scooched up along the seat, resting her neck on the arm of the door, watching as he yanked her jeans down past her knees, all the way to her ankles, leaving her bare, save for a black thong.

"Off," she said urgently, lifting one leg so he could push her jeans off.

He took off her ankle boot and pulled one leg of her jeans off. Then he spread her legs and ran both hands along her outer thighs. He loved the heat of her skin, the dark look in her eyes as he kissed, licked, and sucked his way up her inner thigh. Every suck brought a sinful moan, every lick, a needy whimper. He couldn't resist teasing her until she was wild with desire. He lowered his mouth over the triangle of cloth between her legs and pressed his tongue flat against the thin material covering her center, teasing her through the damp cotton. Her eyes closed, her neck arched, and she ground her hips against his tongue. The scent of her arousal sparked fire beneath his skin. He kissed his way up her hip, across her stomach, licking her belly like he was going to lick between her legs.

She fisted her hands in his hair. "*Harley.*" She lifted her hips off the seat. "*Please!*"

He hooked his fingers in the strings of her thong, sliding it down her legs. She was shaved bare, save for a neat strip of blond curls. He was dying to unlatch his jeans and bury himself to the hilt. But that would have to wait if he wanted Piper to desire him for the man he was, not just for his willing cock.

"Touch yourself," he said, and she put her hands on her breasts again, eyes on him, dark and seductive.

"Down here, beautiful." He guided one of her hands between her legs.

Her eyes were dark and libidinous as he slicked his tongue along her glistening sex. Her essence spread over his tongue like sweet honey, and he thought he'd died and gone to heaven. He pushed his hands under her ass, lifting and angling so he could feast on her. He used his teeth and tongue, holding nothing back. Her hand moved faster over her clit, and she spread her legs wider, hooking one over his shoulder. He dragged his tongue over her fingers, taking them into his mouth, and held her wrist, slowly drawing her fingers in and out of his lips. Their eyes connected with the heat of a thousand suns. Her hips began moving to the same rhythm as her fingers in his mouth, and he moved his other hand between her legs. She moaned, holding his gaze, moving sensually against his thumb as her fingers moved in and out of his mouth, giving *all* his senses a feast of pleasure.

He drew her fingers out of his mouth, kissed her fingertips, and guided her hand to her chest.

"Touch your breast" came out as a guttural, greedy demand.

Her eyes flamed, then narrowed, and she moved her hand between her *legs*. Then she reached down with her other hand and brought *his* hand to her breast.

"You are a little vixen, aren't you? You want to play dirty?"

She arched a brow and said, "Is there any other way?"

"Not in my book."

He held her gaze, making her wait as she teased her sex, and he caressed her breast, rolling her nipple between his finger and thumb. He kissed her inner thigh, and she rocked up beneath him. He glided his tongue along the length of her finger as she teased her clit, and she whimpered. He did it again, and she closed her eyes, moaning as she arched up and brought her other hand between her legs, dipping her fingers inside her. Seeing her take her pleasure into her own hands was too much. He lowered his mouth to her center and pressed his wet thumb against her other entrance. She moved her hand to her breast, keeping the other between her legs. He quickened his pace, stroking faster, fucking her with his tongue. He squeezed her nipple, and her legs went rigid. In the next breath, she cried out, loud and unabashedly. Her body bucked and her sex pulsed as her climax tore through her. She dug her nails into his shoulders, and he stayed with her, teasing and devouring, taking his fill. As she came down from the peak, he pushed two fingers inside her and took her clit between his teeth, sending her spiraling over the edge again.

He rose, put his arm around her, and brought her up to a sitting position, facing him on the seat, her knees wide open. She reached for the button on his jeans, but he moved her hand away.

"*No*," he ground out, and captured her mouth in a penetrating kiss.

She didn't flinch at the taste of her own arousal, and it nearly pulled him over the edge. With one arm around her, his hand fisted in her hair, he kissed her rough and possessive, pushing two fingers of his other hand into her velvety heat and teasing her most sensitive nerves with his thumb. He fucked her hard and fast with his fingers, kissing her deep and rough. She came hard, and he swallowed her moans and whimpers.

When she went silent and soft against him, he lifted her onto his lap, cradling her in his arms, kissing her lips, her cheeks, her chin. He settled her head on his shoulder, and he knew in his heart this was new for her, allowing a man to hold her like this. Her breath was warm on his neck, her body jerking with aftershocks. He rubbed his hand along her thigh, up her hip, and around her back, memorizing the feel of her, the sound of her sated breaths, the scent of her arousal, her sweetness lingering on his tongue.

He held her for a long time, their heavy breathing the only noise cutting through the silence.

"All these years I had to listen to you give my dates shit, when you could have put that mouth of yours to *much* better use."

She sounded so peaceful, he could almost hear her walls chipping away. He bit back the reminder that she'd laughed off all of his advances. When she lifted her head and gazed into his eyes, the trust in hers nearly did him in.

"Don't get all weird on me," she said softly.

"I wouldn't dare." *Patience,* he reminded himself. He needed a boatload of it.

CHAPTER ELEVEN

"WHAT DO YOU think about moving the toilet and sink to this area and using this side for the shower?" It was Monday afternoon, and Piper was in her father's home office, going over the plans for Harley's bathroom with him.

Her father studied the plans, his dark brows furrowed in concentration. Dan Dalton was a tall, slim, serious man with close-cropped salt-and-pepper hair and sharp dark eyes. He'd retired from his position as a college professor to follow his dream of becoming a custom builder. He and Piper made a perfect team. She loved managing the jobs and doing hands-on work, and he enjoyed running the business and working on-site as time allowed. She hoped he'd never slow down. She couldn't imagine ever partnering with anyone else.

"I wouldn't change it. I like the way you've laid it out here, with the shower in the nook. It's a large shower, but you said he wants two showerheads, and this will accommodate that. How did this job come about? I saw Harley by the marina two weeks ago. He didn't mention anything about renovating his bathroom."

As she rolled up the plans, she said, "He hit his head in the shower while trying to pick something up and forgot he had a sprained ankle. He lost his balance, grabbed the shower curtain, and ripped the rod right out of the wall on his way down. The shower's only thirty-two by thirty-two. I wasn't about to let him continue showering in *that*. I'm still trying to work out how he ended up on his ass in that tight of a space."

Her father winced. "How is his ankle doing? Any better?"

"It's a little less swollen. He's back to work for a few hours each day."

"Good. He's getting around okay on crutches? Or do they have him in one of those boots?"

"Crutches. He's good with them." *Too good.* He'd gotten so adept with them, he chased her around, cornering her to steal kisses and gropes when the girls weren't looking.

She gazed out the window, thinking about yesterday afternoon. After picking up the girls from their sleepovers, they'd taken them fishing off Harley's dock. Jolie couldn't stop talking about the fun she'd had with her friends, and Sophie told them every detail about her time with Bea. It was nice to see them so happy. As the afternoon progressed, Piper was sure the girls would notice how much things had changed between her and Harley, because she felt it in every word they spoke, every furtive glance, and every hungry touch. But the girls didn't seem to notice. They'd enjoyed a fun afternoon, and they'd *all* begged her to stay for dinner. But after Saturday night, when Harley had blown her mind, anticipating *everything* she'd wanted, touching her so perfectly, *erotically*, and making her feel things she'd *never* felt before—things she didn't know what to do with—she'd had to escape the *perfectness* of it all. Being with Harley was *too* good. He made it easy to forget her emotional boundaries.

Her mother touched her arm, startling Piper from her thoughts. She hadn't heard her come into the office.

"Are you okay, honey?"

"Mm-hm. I was just thinking about the bathroom renovation for Harley," Piper said, putting on a smile for her always bubbly mother. Roxie was free-spirited and laid-back, with a mass of blond curls and a flair for bohemian fashion.

"I see," her mother said. "The *bathroom renovation*. That Harley is a smart man. He knows something special when he sees it."

"*Mom*," Piper warned. Her mother was always trying to matchmake.

"What? He knows you're good with your hands."

"Mom!" Her comment sent Piper's mind to *Harley's* hands. Hot dogs, hockey, and *Harley* were the perfect combination for an epic night out. She still couldn't believe he'd gotten tickets to the playoff game.

"Oh, honey, all I meant was that you're the best there is, and he knows it. Debra said the girls are doing well, and they really seem to have taken to you."

Piper looked at her father, sitting at his desk studying something on his computer and pretending not to listen, and said, "I took them to the Mad House after their visit with Delaney last Friday."

Her father looked over. "Did it do the trick?"

"Yes, at least for now." Both girls were in good moods this morning when she'd taken them to school, and Harley was in an especially good mood—as was she, which she was still trying to wrap her head around. Her pulse quickened every time he texted. It had been so long since she'd texted with a man, she'd actually felt her cheeks burning as she'd read his text late last night after she'd gone home. *My truck feels left out. I think we need to christen it.* She'd responded with, *I'm not buying the truck-envy angle.* Her phone had vibrated a minute later with the message, *How about bed envy? My bed is jealous of yours because you're in it.* They'd gone back and forth with silly jokes that turned dirty. Her blush had quickly faded, and she'd gotten lost in their sexting. He was as demanding over text as he had been in the truck, telling her where and how to touch herself.

The man had serious *game*.

Her mother's phone chimed, bringing Piper's head down from the clouds.

As her mother read the message, her hand moved over her heart and her face lit up. "Oh, goodness. Look at little Emma Lou. I can't believe she's a year old already. She's got such pretty dark hair, just like her daddy, and those blue eyes are going to bring Brindle a lot of heartache in a few years." Emily Louise, "Emma Lou," was Piper's cousin Brindle's baby with her husband, Trace. They lived in Oak Falls, Virginia, near five of Brindle's six siblings. Her rock-star brother, Axsel, was always on the road. Brindle's mother was Piper's aunt Marilynn Montgomery, Roxie's sister.

"Brindle would give you the evil eye for calling her Emma Lou and not Emily or Emmie. Let me see." Brindle thought Emma Lou was too *country* for her daughter, but her cowboy husband refused to call her anything else. Piper took her mother's phone, and her insides turned to mush at the sight of the precious little girl wearing tiny cowgirl boots and a pretty blue dress.

"She is too cute for words," Piper said as another message bubble popped up from Marilynn. "Mom, what does Aunt Marilynn mean by *Send the usual plus a little extra F?*"

Her mother took the phone from her, looking guilty. "Nothing."

Piper crossed her arms. "What kind of shenanigans are you up to?"

She heard her father chuckle.

"It's nothing. Aunt Marilynn is mad that I have more grandbabies than she does."

Piper spun around and said, "Dad? What's she *not* telling me?"

"Oh no, don't pull me into your argument." He hated conflict as much as Piper thrived on it.

"It's nothing," her mother insisted. "I send her lotions and body washes for the girls and soaps for Axsel each month. She wants something with a little *fertility boost*, that's all."

"Mom, seriously? That stuff doesn't really work. It's just timing, that's all."

"How can you say that? Look at you and Harley."

"*What?* How do you know about us?" Piper snapped. "We *just* started seeing each other!"

Her mother's eyes sparkled with excitement. "I didn't. But now I do. I need to tell Debra! It must be the combination of potions *and* matchmaking."

"*Ugh!* Matchmaking?"

Her mother pretended to zip her lips and throw away the key.

"You are shameless! This is unbelievab—*wait*. I threw out his body wash. See? Your *potions* had nothing to do with us getting together." She refused to believe her mother's famous concoctions had magical powers, even if just about everyone else in town believed in them.

"If you say so," her mother said lightly. "But you did use Bridgette's body balm over the winter."

"She said she got that online!"

"Really?" Her mother's eyes widened. "That was *clever* of her. In any case, Harley's been using the body wash for a few *years*."

Piper gave her an incredulous look, and her conversation with Harley came rushing back. She'd asked him what had gotten into him, and he'd said, *You have, Pipe. For three years I've been trying to get you to go out with me.* Her knees weakened, and she grabbed the edge of her father's desk.

Her mother looked amused as she said, "Oh, baby girl. You don't have to believe for love to work its magic."

"I'm *not* in love with Harley Dutch!" But she could hardly breathe as the emotions of the last few days rained down on her. She needed an umbrella made of steel to fend them off. "I have to go get the girls from school." She started to walk out of the office, but turned back, pointing her finger at her mother. "Stay away from Harley!"

Her mother lifted her hands, palms up, and said, "What's done is done, baby. Once love makes its mark, there's no going back."

"Love has *not* made its mark on me or Harley!" she seethed. "This is *lust*, Mother. Pure, unadulterated *lust*. Nothing more. You're fooling yourself if you think your potions are controlling us. I'll be over him as soon as he no longer needs my help with the girls."

"Sounds like I'm not the only one fooling myself," her mother said.

Piper stormed out of the room, trying to outrun the sound of truth ringing in her ears.

Harley followed the girls into his bedroom Monday evening, where Piper had been working since she'd gotten home with the girls after school. She worked tirelessly, without complaint, and seemed genuinely excited about the work she was doing in his bathroom. He'd cleared out his closet so Piper could tear down walls to allow the plumber to reroute pipes for the new shower, and based on the number of trips she'd made carrying drywall out to her truck, she must be making progress. He couldn't wait until his damn ankle was better. He hated not being able to help her, and he'd like to take some of the pressure off from helping with the girls and driving him to and from work. Although selfishly, he knew that once his ankle was better, Piper would have no reason to come by every morning and afternoon, and he hated that. If he had it his way, they'd be together more often, not less.

Piper was bent over, using a Shop-Vac to clean the bathroom floor, giving Harley a brief but glorious view of her ass before she turned off the vacuum and picked up a bucket of drywall mud. Their eyes met, and heat *zinged* through him. Her white tank top clung to her body, speckled with dirt and drywall dust, as were her arms and her right cheek, and she still looked like a million beautiful bucks. He'd come upstairs to sneak a few kisses when the girls were eating dinner, and they'd gotten so carried away, they hadn't heard the girls coming upstairs and had almost been caught with his hand down her pants. Luckily Jiggs had come into the room a few seconds before the kids, giving Harley and Piper time to fix their clothes *and* their expressions. Thank God for long T-shirts, because it had taken quite a while for his erection to deflate. And now the look in Piper's eyes told him she wasn't done with him yet. Man, he loved that look. She already had him half-hard again.

"Oh my gosh! Look, Uncle Harley!" Sophie exclaimed, pointing to the missing wall between his closet and the bathroom.

Piper flashed a killer smile and said, "It's getting there. It won't be too long before your uncle has a nice big bathroom, with real doors on his man-sized shower."

"Will it be done before we go back home?" Jolie asked.

They were going back to Delaney's Friday after school. He would miss having the girls staying with him, but he was definitely looking forward to having some alone time with Piper. Sneaking around was exciting at first, but now it was damn frustrating not to be able to put his hands on her whenever he wanted.

"It probably won't be done by then because I'm only working on it in the evenings," Piper said. "But it shouldn't take long. I'm sure your uncle won't mind if you come by to see it after it's done."

The girls grinned.

"By the way," Piper said to Harley, "the plumber should be here tomorrow afternoon."

"Perfect. The girls wanted to say good night before they brushed their teeth."

"Are you going to work all night?" Sophie asked.

Harley wasn't about to let her work any later than when the girls went to bed. He needed his *Piper time*. Their sexting sessions had been a first for him, and while it had filled a gap at a time when he desperately wished she'd stayed over, nothing could replace the feel of his girl in his arms.

Piper shook her head. "No. I'm cleaning up for the night."

Jolie put her hand on her hip and said, "You should just stay here since you come back in the morning anyway. Uncle Harley can sleep on the couch."

"Now, there's a *fantastic* idea," Harley said.

"Yes!" Sophie said, bouncing on her toes.

"I can't," Piper said, giving him a stern look. "Look how dirty I am. I don't have clothes or anything here. Besides, I have things to do at my house."

"Like what?" Sophie asked.

"Well, um . . ." Piper stammered.

"Do you have a dog who needs to be walked?" Sophie asked.

"No, but I have *other* things to do." Piper looked at the bucket and said, "Like bringing this drywall down to my truck. Good night, girls. I'll see you in the morning."

She glowered at Harley on her way out of the room, and he chuckled. The girls were way better wingmen than Jiggs, who was currently trotting downstairs after Piper.

After the girls were settled in bed, he went in search of Piper and found her in his bathroom closing her toolbox, which was resting on the sink. The bathroom was spotless; the only indication that there was work being done was the missing walls. He set his crutches by the door and put his arms around her from behind, kissing her neck.

"I would have helped you clean up." He set her toolbox on the floor and put his arms around her again, kissing her shoulder.

"It was my mess," she said, dismissing his offer.

"Yes, but I could have helped since you're fixing *my* bathroom." He slid his tongue along her neck, loving the way she pressed her ass against him. Thankfully, he'd changed into basketball shorts after work and didn't have to deal with his zipper pressing uncomfortably against his arousal.

"Did you tell Jolie to ask me to stay over?"

"No," he whispered next to her ear. "But I love the idea. I miss you." He dragged his tongue along the shell of her ear and slid his hand up her belly, cupping her breast. He kissed and caressed until she was breathing hard, clinging to the edges of the sink. "What do you say we finish what we started earlier?"

"I haven't showered."

"I like the taste of your salty skin." He sealed his mouth over her neck, sucking hard enough to earn another of those sensual sounds he loved as he unbuttoned and unzipped her jeans.

"What about the girls?"

"Their bedroom doors—and mine—are closed, and my watchdog is sitting in the hall."

He pulled her jeans and panties down past her knees, and then he brought his mouth to her neck again as he teased between her legs.

"Oh *yes*," she said breathily. She put her hand over his, pushing his fingers inside her.

"I love when you show me what you want," he said against her neck.

"I love when you touch me. Suck *harder*."

He sealed his mouth over the curve at the base of her neck, sucking harder as he pushed his other hand beneath her shirt and bra and gently squeezed her nipple.

"So *good*," she panted out, craning her neck to the side, giving him better access to devour her heated flesh.

He quickened his pace between her legs, earning a sharp gasp with every stroke of the secret spot that had her rising on her toes. "Stay with me tonight," he said into her ear.

"I don't do sleepovers."

He gritted his teeth against the sting of her response, wanting to be so much more than a good fuck. "You're safe with me, Pipe. You can trust me."

"I know, *but* . . ." She shook her head, pressing her ass harder against his erection, and said, "Just touch me."

He knew she felt their connection as deeply as he did. If only he could figure out how to make her feel safe enough that she wouldn't be afraid to acknowledge it.

Patience, he reminded himself as he kissed her shoulder, working hard to push those thoughts away, and sank his teeth into her flesh, giving her what she wanted.

"Harley" fell from her lips, followed by a low, hungry sound. She ground her ass against him as she rode his fingers and said, "Do that again."

He brought his thumb to her clit and bit down on her shoulder, squeezing her nipple with his other hand harder. She gasped and whimpered.

"I want your mouth," he demanded.

She turned her head, and he slanted his mouth over hers, swallowing her needful sounds. He ground against her ass, fucking her faster with his fingers. She was so wet and tight, when he pushed a third finger into her, her head fell back with a long, surrendering moan. He grabbed her jaw, bringing her mouth back to his as her climax took hold. Her sex pulsed tight and greedy around his fingers. He didn't relent. His tongue plundered to the same frantic pace as his fingers, until her jaw fell slack, and she collapsed forward, her trembling arms braced on the sink.

"I want your cock," she panted out.

"No." He turned her in his arms, taking her in another passionate kiss.

She tore her mouth away, eyes narrowed, skin flushed. "I said *I want your cock*, so unless you're not *clean . . . "* She licked her hand and pushed it into his briefs, palming his hard length. "I'm going to *have* it."

He was so hungry for her touch, to make love to her, his thoughts shattered as she stroked him, slow and tight. He gritted his teeth and grabbed the edge of the sink to keep his balance. *Fucking ankle.* If he weren't injured, he'd haul her ass into his arms and toss her onto his bed, taking her every which way to Sunday.

She held his gaze as she yanked down his shorts, dropped to her knees, and lowered her mouth over his shaft.

"*Christ*," he hissed out.

She grinned around his cock, and he shifted, leaning his butt against the sink, allowing him to stay off his bad ankle while burying his hands in her hair. When he thrust his hips, her challenging gaze hit him with the force of an earthquake. She let him lead, taking his cock to the back of her throat time and time again. Lust pounded through him as he watched his shaft moving in and out of her hot, willing mouth. When she cupped his balls, a loud groan escaped his lungs. She grabbed his thighs, pulling back and teasing the head of his erection with her tongue. The sight of her loving him with her hands and mouth sent heat searing through him. He grabbed the base of his cock to stave off his orgasm, wanting to enjoy every second of her. Her eyes narrowed, and she reached between her legs, touching herself as she loved him. *Holy. Hell.* She took them both right up to the edge of ecstasy.

"Keep going," he ground out. "I want to see you come while you suck me."

He wrapped his hand around his cock, stroking himself as her mouth moved along his length. She quickened her efforts between her legs, then slowed for both of them, and he didn't miss a beat, stroking in time to her lead. He could barely see, couldn't think, as she brought him to the brink of madness. The glimmer of achievement in her eyes made him go wild, thrusting harder and *deeper*. She grabbed his ass with both hands, pulling him in deeper. *Fuuck.* He gritted his teeth against his mounting orgasm. His chin fell to his chest, eyes trained on Piper as she wrapped one hand around his cock, dropping the other between her legs again, stroking them both as he fucked her mouth. She moaned around his cock, the vibration sending lust spiking down his spine, and he *lost* it. His body bucked, and he ground out her name as he came. She stayed with him, taking everything he had to give. When the last pulse moved through him, he closed his eyes, trying to catch his breath.

"Watch me," she practically *purred*.

His eyes flew open, hypnotized by her. He'd have stood on his head if she'd asked him to. She licked his half-hard length, touching herself until her head fell back, and she came loudly and unabashedly, her sinful sounds filling the bathroom.

"Jesus, Piper." He stroked her cheek and said, "You *destroy* me."

She didn't just destroy him. She *owned* him.

Body and soul.

She rose to her feet with a sultry and victorious look in her eyes, pressed her hands to his cheeks, and crashed her mouth over his. She thrust her tongue into his mouth, fucking it as he'd just fucked hers. She kissed him like she *knew* she owned him, and he realized that if he wanted her to trust him with her *heart*, to realize—or rather *acknowledge*—that he *wasn't* like every other guy, he needed to slow down and make sure she felt it.

When their mouths parted, her lips were wet and tempting. He kept her close, loving the feel of her bare skin against his. The last thing he wanted to do was slow down.

She kissed his chin and said, "I should go."

"Stay with me." He wanted to hold her in his arms, to spend time just being together, but he knew she'd balk at opening herself up emotionally, so he said, "I haven't tasted *you* in *days*. I need a hit of my girl."

Her brows lifted, and she said, "*Good.* At least now I know you'll be thinking of me today."

Her words sounded familiar, and as she hiked up her jeans, he realized it was exactly what he'd texted to her the morning she'd run out of his house after seeing him naked. He pulled up his shorts and hauled her back into his arms.

She gave him another scorching kiss, grabbed her toolbox, and with a sassy wink, she said, "I'll walk your *watchdog* before I go and lock the door when I leave, so you don't have to hobble downstairs."

His heart hurt for both of them. He went for another dose of honesty, hoping to break through her walls before she left the room. "Pipe, you don't need to play games with me or try to scare me off."

The sass in her eyes faltered.

"I'm not going to hurt you, Piper, and I'm sure as hell not going anywhere."

Her gaze hit the ground, and she gripped the handle of her toolbox so tight her knuckles turned white. She stood still for a few hopeful seconds before walking out the bathroom door.

"Piper."

She turned, and he saw a glimpse of something deep and meaningful in her eyes, but it disappeared as quickly as it had come. He wanted to ask her to stay *again*, but he knew he hadn't yet earned that rung on her ladder of trust, so he said, "We're bigger than sex, Pipe. You'll see."

Her mouth twitched, as if she liked the sound of that, but she turned away and said, "Good night, Harley," and left the room.

CHAPTER TWELVE

DUTCH'S WAS BUSY for a Tuesday afternoon. The local Kiwanis club was having its monthly lunch meeting, and the knitting club ladies had rescheduled their normal Wednesday-afternoon meeting to today. Doris Pilcheck, the leader of the knitting club, had a date later that evening with someone she'd met on a senior dating site, and her girlfriends were bringing her up to speed on the dating scene. Doris was a lovely woman in her midseventies who had lost her husband, Rodney, several years ago. She'd known Harley all his life, as had most of the gray-haired ladies around Sweetwater. Doris had pumped him and Jasper for advice for a long time after she and her friends had first arrived. At the top of his list of advice was to meet her date someplace public and to drive her own car, so she wasn't put in a compromising position. He watched them across the room, talking over their iced teas and salads, and wondered why it was easier for some people to open up than it was for others.

"You okay?" Jasper asked as he wiped down the bar. "Your ankle hurting?"

It had been six days since Harley sprained his ankle, and it was finally doing much better. He couldn't walk on it yet, but the swelling was coming down. The light throb in it was a reminder that he needed his next dose of medicine. He'd been able to go longer stretches without it, but as Piper had reminded him that morning when she'd come to pick up him and the girls and shoved a bottle of Motrin into his hands, being upright for several hours caused his ankle to swell. Piper was funny like that, keeping her emotions locked down tight, then taking extra measures to ensure that he was okay.

"I'm fine."

"How about Doris and online dating?" Jasper raised his brows.

"I just hope she doesn't get herself into trouble. I don't like all that online dating crap." And he was glad Piper wasn't on any of those dating sites.

"I heard two of her friends say they would show up wherever she went on her date as backup." Jasper chuckled. "Seems like not much changes as chicks get older."

Harley sure hoped that wasn't true. He didn't want Piper to change *who* she was, but he'd like to get that lock off her heart at some point.

As if he'd conjured her from his thoughts, his beautiful little spitfire strode through the door, rocking her construction boots like no one else ever could. Her lips curved up as she climbed onto a barstool, looking like a golden-haired gift from the heavens above. Unfortunately, he wasn't the only one checking her out. Just about every other man in the bar was, too.

"Stare much, Dutch?" she said casually.

"Hello to you, too, beautiful. It's been a few days since I've had the pleasure of seeing you walk in here." Since he wasn't working nights, he hadn't seen her in the pub since before he'd hurt his ankle.

She looked down at her keys as she set them on the bar, as if he'd embarrassed her.

When she looked up, he held her gaze and said, "You never come in for lunch, which must mean you missed me."

"What I *missed* was Dutch's famous chicken wings." She smirked. "I'll take an order of wings and a Coke, please."

"Ah, yes, the *wings*." He laughed and leaned across the bar, stopping within kissing distance, and said, "Missing me is a good thing, Trig. *Own* it, 'cause I sure missed you."

She tried unsuccessfully to school her expression. "Do you hit on *all* your customers?"

"Just the lucky ones."

"I'll get the wings for you," Jasper said, patting Harley's back as he passed behind him.

"Jasper's a good man," Piper said tauntingly.

He knew she was trying to rile him up, but he wasn't jealous. She didn't look at *any* other man the way she looked at him. "He *is* a good man. One of the best."

He got her soda, and she eyed him curiously as she took a drink. *That's right, Pipe, you can't scare me away that easy.*

"How's your ankle?"

Her switch to a safer subject did not go unnoticed. She'd tried to get him to use the walking boot this morning, but he hated that uncomfortable thing. He preferred to wrap his ankle and use crutches. "It's holding up. I'm glad you're here. It's nice to see you."

"You just saw me a few hours ago," she said a little dismissively.

He knew she was there to see him, but hearing the truth from her would make it that much better. "True, but nothing brightens my day like seeing you, Pipe."

She glanced at the door to the kitchen and said, "Where are those wings?"

She was adorable trying to keep her feelings under wraps, fighting a smile. He grabbed the crutches and went around the bar to sit beside her. He lowered himself to the barstool next to her and leaned the crutches against the bar. "It must be hard keeping all those emotions reined in. You don't have to, you know. You can trust me not to hurt you."

She rolled her eyes. "When did you become an armchair psychologist?"

"Isn't that what a bartender is?"

"I've known *bartender Harley* for a long time, and he doesn't dissect everything I do. Can we get that guy back?"

He shifted to the edge of the stool, putting one leg on either side of her, boxing her in. "Sure. But how about *boyfriend Harley*? Do you like that guy?"

Her eyes flamed, telling him just how much she liked that guy. She glanced over his shoulder and sat up straighter, schooling her expression just as Doris walked up to them, smiling warmly.

"Hi, Doris. Do you ladies need refills?" he asked.

"Oh no, sweetheart." Doris had short, layered white hair, pale skin that looked soft as butter, and naturally pink cheeks—probably from smiling so often. She patted his arm and said, "I just wanted to say thank you to Piper for helping me with my roof last week." She turned kind eyes to Piper. "I meant to make you my special raspberry brownies this past weekend, but I got a little busy."

"You don't have to do that," Piper said. "It was my pleasure."

Doris patted Harley's arm again and said, "Isn't she just the sweetest little thing?"

Piper arched her brow, as if she found Doris's use of *sweetest* funny.

"She won't take money from me," Doris explained. "But she loves my raspberry brownies."

"It's not a big deal, really," Piper said. "You don't need to make me anything."

"The way you help people is a *very* big deal. My Rodney used to say there weren't enough Piper Daltons in the world. It's a wonder you can make a living the way you help folks like me."

Harley recognized the struggle on Piper's face. Taking compliments was not her strong suit, but it only endeared her to him even more. Her generosity knew no limits, and he didn't think it ever had.

"At least you didn't fall and hurt yourself when you were working at my house," Doris said. "Poor Harley was fixing a flooding toilet in the ladies' room for our knitting group—you know how Martha is when she drinks iced tea—and look what happened to him. I felt so guilty the whole way to the hospital."

"That's funny," Piper said. "He told me he hurt his ankle wrestling a bear."

"Oh, goodness. Harley, I'm sorry to have outed you for embellishing," Doris said.

Piper smirked. "Don't worry. I'll never let him live this down. It was nice of you to take him to the hospital."

"Of course! I would have waited to drive him home, but when he was in with the doctor, I called Debra to let her know he'd been hurt and she insisted that *you* would want to pick him up."

Piper looked curiously at Harley.

"Don't look at me. I'm sure she just didn't want to keep Doris from her knitting club."

"Your mother is such a doll, Harley. Well, I'd better get back to the girls." Doris looked at Piper and said, "Maybe you can share the brownies with your new *beau*."

Piper's mouth dropped open as Doris walked away. "I'm going to *kill* my mother for gossiping about us."

"Maybe I should *thank* her," he said as Jasper returned with her wings and set them on the bar.

"Who are we thanking?" Jasper asked.

"Nobody." Piper snagged a wing and took a big bite.

Jasper looked at Harley and said, "Right. Anyway, I saw you guys on the kiss cam. It looked like you had a great time at the game, but you know you were supposed to kiss, right?"

"I've endured two days of harassment from the guys at work about that." Piper pointed her wing at Jasper and said, "I don't do nerd-reel kisses."

"Too bad for Harley," Jasper said as he walked away.

Harley was still stuck on Piper killing her mother. "You told your mom about us?"

She set the chicken bone on her plate and licked her fingers, her gorgeous green eyes narrowing again. "What do you think?"

That I love watching you lick your fingers. "I wish I could say I thought you told her, but I don't. So why are you going to kill your mother?"

She chomped on another wing, then pushed the plate toward him. "Want one?"

"What I want is a straight answer." He couldn't hide his amusement at her eye roll that followed his comment. "Pipe, you know everyone who was watching the game saw us on the kiss cam, and maybe we weren't kissing, but if your mom is telling people we're going out, then the whole town probably knows. You're going to have to pull up your sexy-as-sin big-girl thong and deal with it."

"Let's leave my thong out of this." She finished the wing and sucked her fingers clean again. "Stop looking at me like that."

Was it crazy that he loved the fact that she didn't eat daintily? "Get used to it. It's only going to get worse if you keep sucking on your fingers."

Her cheeks pinked up, and he knew she was thinking about what she'd done to him last night, just as he was.

She picked up another wing and said, "At least you're not embarrassed by the way I eat. Do you want one?"

"Nothing you do embarrasses me." He leaned in, putting a hand on her back, and said, "I don't want a wing, but I'd love a kiss."

She glanced around them and said, "I have sauce all over my lips."

"Nice try." He pressed his lips to her cheek. "There. Now everyone knows you're *mine*. Look at that. You didn't shrivel up and die."

"*Whatever.*" She set the chicken bone down and picked up another, biting into it without meeting his eyes.

He reminded himself that coming to the pub to see him in the middle of the day when she was working in the next town over was a *big* step for her. Knowing that patience was a virtue when it came to Piper and their relationship, he eased up on her and said, "How's work today? You said the guys were giving you shit. Want me to shut them down?"

She gave him a deadpan look.

He laughed. "Sorry. It was a gut reaction. I don't like the idea of anyone giving my girl shit."

"Your *girl?* You're really doing this, aren't you?"

"Hell yes, *we* are."

Her lips twitched again in a poor attempt to look serious. "Your girl can handle herself." She took another bite and said, "But thank you for wanting to . . . you know . . . be like that. And work is great. Thanks for asking."

He'd take that baby step, and any others she was willing to make. "Tell me about the project you're working on."

"I don't want to bore you."

"It's part of your life, Pipe. I want to know about it."

She seemed to consider that for a minute while she finished eating. Then she wiped her hands on a napkin and said, "I've wanted to get my hands on Windsor Hall for a long time, and I'm excited about the work we're doing there. The owner has had it rezoned as commercial property. The location is *perfect*, right off the main drag, by the park. Thankfully he's not tearing out everything. He wants to keep all of the original woodwork, which is gorgeous. We're touching up the intricate ceiling medallions, replacing missing balusters to match the original existing ones, taking out plaster walls, that sort of thing. You've seen the carriage house from the outside. It's even more magnificent inside. We're renovating that next."

Her passion for her work showed in the uplifting cadence of her voice and the brightness of her eyes as she described the property in more detail, telling him about ornate chandeliers, high ceilings, and stone fireplaces. "The space could be used for almost anything. I can imagine an event company hosting weddings and other fancy events, or a café on the ground floor, with offices or retail shops upstairs, a vet's office, or a community center. That would be cool. I can't wait to see who buys it. I hope they don't tear out the original woodwork."

"How about another Dutch's Pub, with a bigger restaurant?" he asked.

"I didn't know you were interested in expanding." Her eyes turned sharp, all business. "Are you getting tired of the same-old day-to-day routine?"

"I'm definitely not tiring of my routine, but I am an investor and always keep my eyes open. I was just thinking aloud. I'm not sure another bar or a big restaurant is the way to go."

"Because it's not a good investment?"

"That depends on a lot of factors, but that's not why. I want to have a family someday, and a new bar or restaurant would really eat up my time. I'm finally to the point with this one where I can work when I want to. It's been nice taking nights off to be with you and the girls."

"The girls go back to Delaney Friday," she reminded him. "Will you go back to working nights?"

"Not if I can help it." He held her gaze and said, "I have this great new girlfriend, and I don't want to cut into any of our time together."

"As much as I like hearing that, don't change your life for me, Harley." This time she didn't try to hide her smile. "In case you haven't noticed, I'm not the easiest chick on the planet." She pushed from her stool and said, "I have to go wash my hands."

He grabbed her hand and pulled her closer. "You're not a difficult person, Pipe, and whoever made you feel that way deserves to be pummeled for it. Just because you don't wear your emotions on your sleeve doesn't make you any less attractive to me. I like who you are and how you handle yourself."

She nodded and said, "That might change, but thank you."

He watched her disappear through the ladies' room door, hurting for her. It had to be awful for her, thinking nobody could love her forever for who she was. He wondered how many asshole men it took to make such a big lie stick like glue.

When she came out of the bathroom, she pulled her wallet from her back pocket and placed money on the bar.

"My treat," Harley said, pushing the money back toward her.

She didn't take it. "You don't need to do that. I earn a fine living."

"I know you do, but this is what boyfriends do for their significant others." He pushed the money into the front pocket of her jeans and said, "Just go with it."

"Fine," she said. "Thank you." She grabbed her keys from the bar and said, "I also wanted to say thank you for taking me to the game the other night. What happened *after* was pretty incredible, too. But the date was the best one I've ever been on."

Her confession felt much bigger than a baby step. He had the urge to do a fist pump, but he knew he had to be careful not to scare her away, so he went with, "I look forward to many more incredible dates."

She nodded, wordlessly taking a step away, some kind of internal battle simmering in her eyes. She looked down at her keys, then glanced sheepishly at him. In the next second that sheepish look turned confident, and she said, "Seeing you in the middle of the day was almost as good as the wings."

She turned to leave, but not before he saw the cheeky look he adored.

CHAPTER THIRTEEN

"CAN I LICK the spoon?" Sophie asked, looking up at Piper as she mixed a bowl of cookie dough.

It was Wednesday evening, and Piper was dubbing it the Night Everything Was Forgotten. When the girls were getting ready for bed, Sophie had remembered that she needed cookies for one of her classes and Jolie had remembered that she needed papers signed for an upcoming field trip.

Jolie dropped a handful of papers in the trash and said, "You only get the spoon if I get to lick the bowl."

"Deal," Sophie said.

"No deal. There's more dough left in the bowl than on the spoon. You two need to share," Harley said from his perch on the couch, where he was elevating his ankle. "I used to pull that on my younger brother all the time, Jo."

"*Fine,*" Jolie said, sifting through more papers from her backpack.

Harley had made dinner for the girls while Piper was working on the bathroom, and he'd finally gotten a chance to elevate his foot when the cookie adventure had come about. Luckily, Piper had already put up a vapor barrier and the cement backer board around the newly installed pipes for the shower. She'd just finished taping and mortaring the seams when the girls had run in asking for help. The timing was perfect for her to take a break so Harley could stay off his feet. Not that Piper knew the first thing about baking. The last time she'd baked anything was when she was probably around Sophie's age. All she'd had to do since then was ask Willow if she felt like baking, and a little while later she had sugary treats to eat. But how hard could it be to make a box of cookies?

"I found the permission slip." Jolie brought it to Harley.

As Harley and Jolie texted Delaney to make sure the trip to the aquarium wasn't a problem, Piper sprayed the cookie sheet.

"How do we know when the dough is ready?" Sophie asked.

Piper scanned the back of the cookie mix package. "Who knows. Good ol' Betty Crocker didn't include a picture."

"Once you get all the lumps out, it's ready," Harley called out to them.

Sophie giggled. "Thanks, Uncle Harley."

"I think it's ready," Piper said, peering into the bowl.

They scooped spoonfuls of cookie dough onto the cookie sheet, and as Piper put it in the oven, the girls snagged the bowl. Piper tossed the box in the trash and noticed a flyer for a seventh-grade father-daughter dance on top of the pile of papers Jolie had discarded. She wondered if Jolie had mentioned the dance to her mother, or if she just let things like that go like they didn't matter. Piper knew how much they mattered. She'd been proud to show off the father she idolized at her own father-daughter dance when she was around Jolie's age. Much to her sisters' disappointment, she hadn't worn a dress, but she'd still gone, and she would have been sad if she'd had to miss it.

Piper grabbed Jiggs's leash. "Harley, while the girls are scarfing down the rest of the cookie dough, why don't you and I take Jiggs out?"

A rakish grin spread across his face, and he reached for the crutches. "*Absolutely.* We'll be right back."

As they made their way down to the water with Jiggs, Piper asked herself if she was butting in where she didn't belong. For all she knew, Jolie could have already talked to Harley about the dance.

"I thought I'd have to wait another half hour to be alone with you," Harley said as Jiggs sniffed around the grass.

He put his crutches in one hand and swept an arm around Piper, pulling her into a mind-numbing kiss. When he deepened the kiss, she pressed her hands to his chest, pushing away with the need to get the dance off her chest.

"Hold those kisses. I need to talk to you about Jolie. Did you know there's a seventh-grade father-daughter dance coming up?"

"No. Should I?" he asked.

"*Yes*, I think. Or maybe not. Jolie threw a flyer for the dance in the trash tonight. Maybe Delaney knows about it, but what if she doesn't? Since Jolie didn't mention the dance to us, I wondered if that might be something else that's weighing on her."

He looked up at the house with a serious expression. "You think so?"

"Maybe? I know they don't see their father, but this kind of thing has to affect the girls. Don't you think?"

Harley's jaw clenched. "Yes, definitely. Every time I think about the girls having issues because of their dickhead father, I want to tear him apart."

"Luckily, they have Uncle Harley to show them how a man should treat little girls." She touched his hand and said, "Big girls, too. Maybe you should text Delaney and ask her about it?" She walked with Jiggs down to the water's edge. "For all we know, she and Jolie have already dealt with this kind of thing."

"I can do one better than that. I'll ask Jolie to be my date for the dance. I may not be her father, but I'm her uncle, and I'll proudly take her. When is it?"

She returned to his side and said, "It's a month away, so your ankle should be fine by then."

He put his arm around her, tugging her against him, and said, "You don't mind giving me up for an evening, do you?"

"I think I can handle it." He was so open and loving, she wondered how he'd stayed single for so long. Most women loved guys like that. Although she'd never been one of them, Harley made her think about wanting to be, and that desire to change made her a little anxious.

"I doubt those dances go on too late." He held her tighter and said, "I'll make it up to you afterward."

He lowered his lips to hers, kissing her anxiety away.

"Hey!"

Piper jumped at the sound of Jolie's angry voice, but Harley kept his arm firmly around her. Jolie stood on the deck with her hand on her hip and a scowl on her face. Sophie stood beside her, happily bouncing on her toes.

Jolie crossed her arms, her hip jutting out in pure preteen angsty fashion. "Why did you lie to us?"

"We didn't lie," Harley said.

"We're not . . ." Piper stopped herself from the knee-jerk reaction of saying they weren't boyfriend/girlfriend, when in fact that was exactly what they were. "This is new," she explained, hating that they'd done anything to upset Jolie when she was already dealing with so much.

Jolie huffed out a breath. "Uh-huh. How *new*?"

"Since the nachos?" Sophie asked. "I knew that would work, Uncle Harley!"

"We're not babies. We're old enough to understand that you're boyfriend and girlfriend," Jolie said vehemently.

"We don't think you're babies," Harley said, making his way to the deck swiftly on his crutches.

"Jolie, we don't think you're too young to understand," Piper said. "Things between us have changed since we told you we weren't together."

Jolie pursed her lips. "*What* changed?"

Sophie sat down on the deck to play with Jiggs and said, "Nachos. *Duh*."

"They were good nachos," Harley said.

Jolie rolled her eyes.

"The nachos were good, yes, but it was more than that," Piper said, wondering how to explain to a kid something she didn't even really understand.

"Like what?" Jolie challenged. "What could have changed in a week?"

"Watch your tone, Jo," Harley warned.

"Adult relationships are complicated," Piper added. "Harley and I *were* just friends, that was true. But feelings can change, and you don't always see it coming. I'm sorry, Jolie. Our lives are so busy. It wasn't like we thought to give you guys a relationship-status update. We're not *Facebook*."

Jolie's tough stance relaxed, and Piper breathed a little easier.

"We'd better get those cookies out of the oven," Harley said to Piper. Then, to Jolie, he said, "One thing you can count on, kiddo, is that I always try to tell you the truth."

"If you weren't a couple, then why did you have her pictures on the fridge?" Jolie asked.

"Because we've been close friends for a long time, and I really like Piper," Harley said as they all went inside. "Even though we were only friends, I hoped one day we'd be more, and seeing her picture with our family made me happy."

Piper glanced at Harley as she pulled the cookies from the oven, catching him watching her *adoringly*. She nearly dropped the pan. Between her impromptu trip to the bar yesterday and coming out to the girls tonight, her nerves were fried.

"They look perfect!" Sophie exclaimed.

Jiggs went paws-up on the counter, sniffing the cookies as Piper transferred them to the wax paper. "Jiggsy thinks so. Down, Jiggs." When Jiggs got down on all fours, Piper said, "You're an excellent baker, Soph."

Harley pressed a kiss to the top of Sophie's head and said, "Now that we're all set for tomorrow, you and Jo run upstairs, brush your teeth, wash your hands and face, and climb into bed. We'll come up in a sec."

Sophie dashed upstairs. Jolie wasn't quite so peppy on her way up.

Harley made his way over to Piper and said, "So the nachos helped, huh?"

"I had *no* idea what to say, but I didn't want her to think we had lied to her."

"What you said was perfect. So . . ." He put his arms around her as she set down the last cookie to cool and said, "Are you on Facebook? Do we need to change your status?"

She pushed playfully from his arms and said, "You know I'm not a social media girl. Get your nosy butt upstairs. Let's get the girls to bed."

As she followed him upstairs, he said, "But if you *were* on social media?"

"Then I'd have been on Tumblr before they banned the good stuff. Don't you have better things to do than ask me ridiculous questions?"

He looked over his shoulder and said, "As a matter of fact, I do. I have a little girl to ask to a dance. And then there's a big girl I'd like to kiss beneath the stars again."

She stepped onto the landing at the top of the stairs and whispered, "Play your cards right and you might even get lucky."

Fifteen minutes later Harley had a date for the dance, and both he and Jolie had a new light in their eyes because of it. Sophie heard Jolie's excitement and ran into her room.

"Can you take me to my father-daughter dance when I'm Jolie's age?" Sophie asked.

"You bet, kiddo."

Piper hoped she'd be around to see that.

Jolie called Delaney, and Piper could hear her excitement through the phone. Bedtime turned into quite an event, with extra time to write in Jolie's diary and extra hugs from both girls. It took them half an hour to calm the girls down and say their final good nights.

"They're lucky to have you," Piper said on the way downstairs.

"I'm pretty lucky to have them, too. What is that?" He stopped halfway down the steps and waved his crutch in the direction of the kitchen. There were cookie remnants all over the floor.

"Oh no!" Piper ran past him and found Jiggs sprawled out on the kitchen floor, his front paws trapping the waxed paper as he licked it clean. "Thank God we didn't make chocolate cookies! We need to make more so Sophie doesn't get upset. I hope he doesn't get sick."

"He's got a cast-iron stomach." Harley scowled at Jiggs. "Dude, you're eating up my make-out time."

Between long, steamy kisses and enticingly erotic gropes, the second batch of cookies took a little longer to mix than the first. Once the rest of the cookies were in the oven, Harley and Piper went out back with Jiggs. They left the door open so they could hear the girls and sat on the steps of the deck, looking out at the water. Harley had been riding high since Piper visited him at Dutch's yesterday afternoon. That telling visit, along with their admission to the girls, felt like they were finally making progress toward a *real* relationship.

Jiggs pushed his nose between them. Harley scratched Jiggs's head and said, "You really are the worst wingman, buddy."

"Careful, you'll give him a complex." Piper pushed to her feet, looking at Harley's right leg, stretched out along the steps. "I'll be careful of your ankle," she said, straddling his hips. Her arms circled his neck and she glanced over her shoulder at his ankle, which was resting comfortably on a riser. "Is that too much pressure?"

"No." He wrapped his arms around her and said, "You look beautiful tonight."

She brushed her fingers along the back of his neck and said, "Let me clue you in on something. I'm a sure thing. You don't need to say stuff like that."

He should have expected that response, but that didn't mean he'd accept it. "I don't say anything because I need to. I say what I feel. *Period.* So get used to it, babe, because it's not going to change."

"You never know . . ."

She lowered her mouth toward his, but he cradled her face in his hands, stopping her short, and said, "I *do* know, Piper. I've known for a long time."

"Then show me," she challenged.

He crushed his mouth to hers, their tongues battling for control. She ground against him, making him hard as stone. He grabbed her ass with one hand and pushed the other into her hair, angling her mouth against his. She opened wider, allowing him to take the kiss deeper, *rougher*, sending an electric current arcing through him. She felt so good and right in his arms, he lowered himself to his back, bringing her down on top of him without breaking their kiss. The wooden deck was hard on his back, but nothing could take away from the perfectness of Piper rubbing her whole body against him.

She made a sizzlingly sexy noise as he ran his hands down her sides and clutched her ass, rocking up as she ground against him. He wrapped her in his arms, holding the back of her head, and rolled them over, cradling her off the hard decking. She wrapped her legs around the backs of his thighs as they kissed. When he drew back, pressing several lighter kisses to her lips and cheek, she kept her eyes closed, making a soft, sexy sound.

He pressed his cheek to hers and said, "I could kiss you forever." He felt her stiffen a little and pressed a kiss beside her ear, whispering, "That's not going to change either, Pipe. I know you're worried, but you don't have to be with me."

She opened her eyes, genuine desire gleaming up at him. She used desire as a mask for her vulnerabilities so often, he liked to think he could tell the difference.

"Kiss me," she said softly.

He lowered his lips to hers, soaking in her eager kisses. He was captivated by the feel of her soft, feminine curves beneath him and the press of her hands on his back. He tried to keep from devouring her, but their connection was too strong, their desire too *alive*, and their kisses turned urgent and forceful. Jiggs pushed his nose against their faces, and Harley put his hand between them and the dog. But Jiggs whined and pawed at Harley's arm.

He tore his mouth away and said, "Jiggs. Lie down, buddy."

He reclaimed Piper's luscious lips, wishing he could carry her up to bed and sink into her. Jiggs made a strangled noise somewhere between a growl and a whimper, pushing his nose against their faces again, and barked. Harley snapped his head up, looking around, and Jiggs ran into the house, then bolted back out, whining, and ran back in again. Harley saw smoke coming from the kitchen, and his heart lurched.

"Shit! The cookies." He pushed up and grabbed the crutches as Piper shot to her feet, running in with him. Smoke billowed out of the stove. "Open the front door before the smoke alarm goes off," he said as he pulled the cookie sheet from the oven. The cookies were burnt to a crisp. "Damn it."

Piper ran around opening all the windows on the first floor. "Oh my God, poor Sophie." She ran into the kitchen and said, "I'll fix this. I promise. I'll call Willow. I'm sure she can help. Give me the hot pad and I'll take that outside."

He gave her the hot pad, and she carried the cookie sheet out the front door. When she came back in, she was talking on her cell phone. "Harley's dog ate the first batch, and we burned the second." She listened as she paced the floor. "Yes, I'm still at Harley's. Would you stop pumping me for information about me and Harley and *focus*? There's a little girl upstairs who's going to be very upset if she doesn't have cookies tomorrow morning."

Harley leaned against the counter, watching his girl save the day. He had heard her sisters try to pry information from one another on many occasions, and it was always entertaining. Knowing Willow was vying for info about *them* made him feel all kinds of good.

Piper turned away from Harley and lowered her voice. "No, I'm *not* staying here tonight. You know how I feel about sleepovers."

A wave of disappointment moved through him. Maybe they weren't coming along quite as quickly as he'd thought. *Baby steps*, he reminded himself.

"Thanks, Willow. You're a lifesaver. I'll pick them up tomorrow morning before the girls wake up," Piper said, sauntering toward Harley. After she ended the call, she said, "It's official. I do *not* belong in the kitchen."

He wrapped his arms around her and said, "Not to worry. I'm *very* good in the kitchen."

"And in the *truck*." Her arms circled his neck. "In the *bathroom* and on the *deck*—"

Her words were lost in the hard press of his lips.

CHAPTER FOURTEEN

TWELVE INCHES HEADING your way!

Piper's heart raced as she stood in the kitchen of Windsor Hall reading the text from Harley for a *third* time Friday afternoon. The sounds of her crew working competed with the rush of blood in her ears. This was *not* the place for her to be getting hot and bothered over the idea of *finally* getting down and dirty with Harley. Every time they were near each other, a magnetic pull sent them straight into each other's arms, and now that they'd told the girls they were seeing each other, Harley was always pulling her into his arms or kissing her cheek. She'd never been *insatiable* for a man like she was with Harley. She'd always enjoyed *sex*. But she'd never had any emotional ties to the men she'd been with, which meant sex was a means to a stress-relieving end. She knew it wouldn't be like that with Harley, but she and Harley weren't having *sex*. They were making out, which in and of itself was mind-blowing.

Making out had never been part of the equation for Piper. A little foreplay, sure, but *minutes* of it, not *hours*. Everything was different with Harley. She could make out with him for *days* and never tire of his kisses or the feel of his arms around her. And touching *him*? Her stomach got fluttery every time their eyes met. She greedily touched him every chance she got, and when they were apart he infiltrated her every thought—she heard his laughter in her head at jokes her crew made, and his expressions—naughty, appreciative, *and* adoring—flashed in her mind all the time.

But she wanted *more* with him, and every time she tried to take it, or thought they were heading that way, he stopped them. So why was he announcing the arrival of his beloved *blissmaker* with a text message *now*? She liked to take risks, but there was no place private enough for *that* at the job site. If he thought she was going to fool around in the truck anywhere near that place, he was dead wrong—even though she would like nothing better than to *finally* see if Harley was as incredible in bed as he was out of it. They were taking the girls to Delaney's after school this afternoon, now that Delaney didn't need full-time care, but that still didn't explain why Harley had announced a visit to her work as if they were planning a lunchtime tryst.

She thumbed out a response. *Dream on, Dutch. I've got a measuring tape. 8–9 inches max.* She sent the text, chuckling at her joke. She knew he'd laugh, too, and that was another thing she really liked about him. Their banter was just as fun as it had always been, except now their sexual comments were directed at each other, not generalized as they were when they were with a group of friends. She kept waiting for him to try to change her, but he wasn't, at least for now.

Unless she counted his unwillingness to take their relationship to the next level.

"Earth to Piper," Kase said as he walked into the kitchen. He tossed a sub on the counter. "Sorry to interrupt your thoughts, but this just came for you."

"I didn't order a sub."

He shrugged. "Well, someone did." He hiked a thumb over his shoulder and said, "Me and a few of the guys are going to eat across the street at La Love Café. Want to join us?"

"No, thanks. Apparently I have a sub to eat."

"Cool. At least whoever ordered it knows what you like. See ya."

As he walked out, Piper picked up the sub and turned it over. TWELVE-INCH MEAT LOVER was scrawled on the side of the wrapper with black marker. "Are you fucking kidding me?"

"Sounds like someone's in trouble," her sister Talia said as she walked into the room, her high heels clicking along the hardwood floor. "I just saw Kase; he said it was okay to come in. Am I interrupting?" Like Ben, Talia took after their father. She was tall, with dark hair and a careful demeanor. She was a professor at Beckwith University, not far from Windsor Hall, and the most even-keeled of Piper's siblings.

"Hey, Tal. Not at all. What's up?"

Talia pushed her glasses to the bridge of her nose, smiling like she knew a secret. "I keep hearing about you and Harley being a *couple*. Mom's all wound up about some big matchmaking scheme she and Harley's mother concocted, and Willow said you and Harley have been together every day for almost two weeks. I know how you feel about committing to more than one *date*, so I figured I'd come to the source and see if the rumors were true."

"Yeah. They're true." She handed the sub to Talia and said, "What do you make of this?"

"A sub?"

"A twelve-inch meat-lovers sub, which was delivered right after Harley sent me this text." Piper navigated to Harley's text message and handed her phone to Talia.

"I'd say Harley knows you like meat-lovers subs. Why?" She set the sub on the counter.

"No." Piper sighed. "I mean, *yes*, he knows I like them. But that text? If you didn't see the sub, what would you think?"

Talia bit her lower lip, her cheeks instantly turning pink. "Something *dirty*?" she said just above a whisper.

"Yes, something dirty! *Ugh.*" Piper paced. "I don't know what to think. Is there some new dating rule about not having sex until the hundredth date or something? Am I *that* out of the loop?"

"Because he sent you a sub?" Talia asked.

Piper glowered at her. "No! Because he *won't* have sex with me."

"Oh!" Talia's eyes widened in shock. "Wait. Really? Guys always want to have sex, especially with *you*."

"Well, not Harley. We've done everything else, and I don't know why he won't go there." They'd even had full-on phone sex last night after she'd gone home. It had started just as it had the other night. Their flirty texts had progressed to sexting. But last night when things started to get hot and hectic, Harley had *called*. She'd never had phone sex before, but with Harley she wanted to try *everything*. Even though that all-consuming desire had freaked her out, nothing could have stopped her from playing along with him. After days of his cutting her off before they could consummate their relationship, she'd been so sexually frustrated she'd held *nothing* back. He was even more demanding on the phone than he'd been during their sexting sessions, and he seemed to love that she was just as much of a control freak as he was. She'd given him commands as *explicit* as those he'd given her, and they'd ended up putting their call on speakerphone because they'd both needed the use of two hands. Harley's demands, the heat and control in his voice, and the thought of him touching himself had sent her over the edge. When he'd ground out her name in the throes of his own release, she'd come even harder. Afterward, when they were both sated, their voices raspy, he'd told her in explicit detail what he'd have done to her if he'd been in the room with her when she'd come, getting her hot and bothered all over again.

Talia tapped her finger on her chin, deep in concentration. "Do you think he knows you want to . . . *you know?*"

"Have sex? *Yes*, he definitely knows." Piper loved her sister and everything about her. But she often wondered how they could have been raised by the same parents and turned out so different. "But right when I think we're going to, he shuts me down and holds me or asks me to stay over, which he knows I won't do."

"I don't blame him. He *likes* you, Piper. He probably wants to hold you afterward, which I highly recommend you try if he ever gives you the chance. Have you tried to make the right *kind* of move? Undress him or something?"

Piper rolled her eyes. "What do you think?"

"I don't know. I assume you have, but maybe not. Look who you're asking for advice. None of this makes any sense. He's been crazy about you for years." Talia's brows knitted, her face pinched tight.

"Then why won't he get naked with me?"

Talia's eyes flew open wide. "Oh my gosh!" She covered her mouth, laughing softly. "I know what it is." Laughter bubbled out as she said, "I can't believe you don't see it!"

"See *what*?" Piper snapped.

"That *you* . . ." Talia doubled over in hysterics, holding her stomach. "This is too good!"

"Spit it out, Talia, because I'm about to lose my shit."

Talia stood up straight, trying to school her expression, but every time she opened her mouth to speak, more laughter bubbled out, and when she closed it, she made a grunting-laughing noise trying to hold it in.

Piper glared at her.

"I'm sorry." Talia waved her hand as if it would help her stop laughing. "But why can't *you* see it? You like—no, you *need*—control. But you also have this thing about wanting a *man* to take control. Don't you see, Piper? You've met your match. Harley Dutch has outwitted you. He's completely taken control of your relationship, or at least of your sex life."

"Wha—" *Holy shit.* Talia was right. *"Fuck that.* I'll see you later." She stormed through the house, texting Kase to let him know she was leaving, and flew out the front door.

"Wait!" Talia called after her, rushing to keep up. "Where are you going?"

"To regain control. *Nobody* one-ups me." She hurried into the parking lot.

"But you left your sub!" Talia exclaimed.

"You can have the damn sub!" Piper threw open her truck door. "This meat lover is getting the real thing."

Driven by her ego as much as the emotions wreaking havoc inside her, Piper blew through the doors of Dutch's Pub and scanned the room in search of a certain bearded male who had some explaining to do.

She stalked up to the bar, and Jasper's welcoming expression faltered. "Where is he?"

"Office." He pointed across the bar.

Piper spun on her heels and headed for Harley's office. The door was ajar, which was good, because she probably would have torn the damn thing off the hinges. She threw it open, and Harley looked up from his chair behind his desk.

"Hey, Pipe."

She closed—bordering on *slammed*—the door. "Don't give me that good-guy voice and those hauntingly hot eyes. What the hell kind of game are you playing, Dutch?" She didn't mean to yell, but she'd stewed the whole way from Harmony Pointe, and she was *livid* . . . at her own vulnerability and at *him*.

He grabbed the crutches and stood up. "What are you talking about?"

"You know *exactly* what I'm talking about!" She paced in front of his desk. "You tell me I can *trust* you, that you're not going to *hurt* me, and then you withhold *sex* just to gain the upper hand? Talk about a control freak!"

He came around the desk, his features strained. "What the hell, Piper? You think I'm withholding sex to gain the upper hand?"

"It sure as hell looks like it." She stopped pacing and crossed her arms.

His features hardened, and his words flew furiously between them. "Have you ever thought that maybe I don't want to be just another notch in your bedpost? That I've spent three years not just liking you, but fucking *falling* for you?"

Shock hit her like a slap to the face. "Is *that* what you think? That we'll have sex and you'll be just another guy to me?" Her voice escalated with hurt and anger. "I have rearranged my entire *life* to help you with your nieces and to spend every damn minute at your place just to ensure you take it easy so you don't fuck up your ankle even more! I walk your dog, *and* I'm renovating your damn bathroom! If that doesn't scream 'I'm crazy about you,' then I don't know what does!"

"What that screams," he said in a calmer, though still angry voice, "is that you're a great friend with a big heart."

"A great friend who *blows* you? Who lets you do all sorts of dirty things to my body?" Hurt lodged in her throat. She turned away, her hands curled into fists, and she gritted her teeth, unwilling to fall apart in front of him.

"That's not what I meant," Harley said evenly.

She faced him again, struggling against the pain rattling inside her. "I might not be touchy-feely or good with words like you are, but damn it, Harley, those things I'm doing mean something to me. Something *huge* that I've never felt before. But all of this just goes to prove what I told you when we started this crazy shit between us. I can't be whatever it is that you're looking for." Tears welled in her eyes. She willed them not to fall as she reached for the door and said, "And for your information, my bedpost hasn't seen a fucking notch in months."

"You've never said you were crazy about me before."

She froze at the strain in his voice, still holding the doorknob. He was standing behind her, and she was glad he couldn't see the tears in her eyes.

"I don't play games, Piper," he said firmly. "But I know you. I know when we're close, every snarky comment you make is to protect your heart.

I get that you have built iron-clad walls around yourself, and I respect that. But guess what? Yours is not the only heart that needs protecting."

His words hit her like bullets in the chest. She could barely breathe. She was trembling, and the tears she tried to will away blurred her vision.

"If you want to walk out that door, go ahead. But that's on you, Pipe." He moved behind her, his presence as familiar as the hurt inside her was foreign. "I don't want to fight," he said in a gentler tone. "And I don't want to change you. I'm willing to wait however long it takes to earn your trust, but I can't read your mind. You have to clue me in to things sometimes, like what you feel for me. Otherwise I'm just spinning my wheels, trying to guess where your head is."

She inhaled a ragged breath, debating bolting. She lowered her hand from the doorknob, and without facing him, she said, "It would be easier to walk out that door and never look back, to just pretend we never happened, than it would be to do this." She turned toward him, tears spilling from her eyes at the pain in his. "But I could never pretend we didn't happen. Not after you've opened my eyes to all that you really are, to *us*."

His lips curved up, and he reached for her hand. "Then don't go."

"You don't get it, Harley. I *suck* at this stuff. I may never be good enough at it to be the person you need, no matter how much I might want to."

"That's a lot of pressure to put on yourself. Ever heard of baby steps? So you'd rather give the shirt off your back than confess your true feelings? That's not so bad. I just need to know what those feelings are so I know if I'm misinterpreting us."

A choked laugh came out, drawing more tears. "Don't you get it? I don't know what to do with everything I feel for you. It scares the crap out of me. It's like I was a perfectly maintained playing field, and you came in and trampled all over it, kicking up so much dust I have no idea which way to turn."

♥ ♥ ♥

Harley knew, could feel, how difficult that confession was for Piper to make. Her words sank beneath his skin, rooting in his heart. "I know you're scared," he said softly. "I'm scared, too. What we have is so strong, Pipe. Stronger than anything I've ever known."

She nodded vehemently, tears wetting her cheeks.

He framed her face in his hands and brushed away the wetness with the pads of his thumbs. "What you just said is *everything*."

"What?" Confusion glimmered in her eyes.

She really didn't get it, and that only made him love her more. "In your own Piper way, you just told me how much you feel for me. That's all I wanted, babe. I wanted to know I wasn't alone in all of this. I don't have any interest in ever one-upping you in the bedroom, or any other aspect of our lives. I'm no expert in self-sabotage, but I have a brother who is. I know the signs, and I'm not going to let you push me away when what you really want is to hold on for all you're worth."

More tears flooded her cheeks, and her body rocked as she tried to hold back sobs.

"I want to *love* you, Piper, and I want to know that you'll let me." He gathered her in his arms, but hers remained limply by her sides, her body trembling. "I'm going to tell you this until you not only hear it but believe it. *You can trust me.* I'll never let you down." He kissed the top of her head and rested his cheek there.

He ran a soothing hand down her back, willing his strength to become hers as she struggled to regain control. He didn't know how long they stood there, but eventually her breathing steadied and her tears stopped, loosening the knots inside him. When she finally put her arms around him and fisted her hands in the back of his shirt, her knuckles pressing into his skin with the force of her embrace, he knew they'd crossed a rickety bridge together. He was glad they'd made it to the other side still in one piece.

"I'm sorry," she whispered.

"Don't be. This is what couples do. They figure out the hard stuff together. It's new for both of us, and it's going to take time to work out the kinks."

"Let's keep the *kink*," she said with a strained tease in her voice. "Oh, Harley," she whispered. She pressed her hands flat against his back, holding him tighter. "I don't want to hurt you, or to make you feel like I don't care about you, because I *do*. But I might never be able to say the right things like you do."

"I know, and I don't expect you to. Just toss me a bone every once in a while."

"And then you'll give *me* one?"

He heard the lightness in her voice, and it made him feel better, too.

"Anytime you'd like. I never wanted to hurt you, either, but I obviously did. I'm sorry, babe. I should have just told you why I wanted to wait, but I didn't want to put any pressure on you to say something if you didn't feel it, or to show me you're committed to us if you didn't want to be." He tipped her face up to his, aching at her red-rimmed eyes and tear-streaked cheeks. "I thought waiting to make love to you was the hardest thing I've ever done. But I was wrong. Seeing you sad is so much worse."

He pressed his lips to hers in a tender kiss.

"Sorry I yelled," she said softly.

"No you're not," he said, earning the sweetest smirk he'd ever seen. "That's how you get it all out, Trig. If I wasn't cool with it, I would never have asked you out in the first place."

"You aren't going to hold this fight against me? Because guys do that."

"*Assholes* do that. You just told me how you feel about me. The only thing I want to hold against you is my body."

She pressed a kiss to the center of his chest, and when she gazed up at him again, a wicked glimmer shone in her eyes. "You know twelve inches was an overshot, right?"

And . . . his girl was back.

CHAPTER FIFTEEN

"PIPER, WILL YOU come shopping with us for a dress for the dance?" Jolie asked when Piper and Harley dropped the girls off at home Friday afternoon. "Can she come, Mom?"

Piper glanced at Delaney for approval, not wanting to intrude on her time with her daughters. Delaney had more energy than she'd had the last time Piper had seen her, and the brightness in her eyes had returned, though she said she still got worn out quicker than she had before the surgery, and her activities would be limited for a while. But it was easy to see how happy she was to be back home with the girls.

"It's fine with me, as long as Piper doesn't mind," Delaney said.

"I'd love to," Piper said. She wasn't much of a shopper, but she'd do anything to help Jolie keep today's sunny disposition. "When are you thinking of going?"

"The week after next, I think," Delaney said. "I want to heal a little more. Shopping can be exhausting, especially when you're looking for a perfect dress for a special occasion."

"Sure. The only thing I have on my agenda other than work is finishing Harley's bathroom, which should be done—or close to it—by then. Which reminds me, if you need help driving the kids around, getting groceries, or running errands, just let me know. I'll be working at Windsor Hall for a few more weeks."

"They can take the bus to and from school now that Jolie's soccer is over, and my mother is going to be helping to run errands. But thank you. I appreciate the offer," Delaney said as Harley draped an arm over Piper's shoulder, leaning on her instead of one of his crutches.

This was the first time he'd openly claimed her like that, and it was a strange—and good—feeling. Piper had wondered if things between them would be awkward after their argument. They'd both had to go back to work, but throughout the afternoon, they'd exchanged a few sweet texts, which quickly turned flirty and then dark and dirty. They were two peas in a pod when it came to their sexual desires. She only hoped she wouldn't disappoint him as his *girlfriend*.

"Let us know what day you want to go shopping as soon as you know," Harley said. "Now that we're a couple, we'll be fitting dates and other *stuff* into our schedules."

Sophie giggled and sang, "*Uncle Harley and Piper sitting in a tree—*"

"Okay, that's enough, Soph," Delaney said with a nudge. "I'm pretty sure they're not kissing in a tree."

"They kissed on the *deck*, and we caught them!" Sophie exclaimed.

Delaney's brows lifted in surprise. "Did you? Real *cool*, Uncle Harley," she said sarcastically.

"Don't look at me." He pointed at Piper and said, "This one's all lips," sending Sophie and Jolie into hysterics.

Piper smacked him in the stomach. "That's *not* true!"

"It was Uncle Harley! I saw him pull Piper into his arms, doing this." Sophie puckered up and made kissing noises.

Harley grabbed Sophie and tugged her into a one-armed hug, while still leaning on Piper. "Love you, too, squirt."

He kissed Sophie's head and tickled her ribs. Sophie squealed and jumped out of his reach. Piper squirmed out from beneath Harley's grasp and handed him one of the crutches as he snagged Jolie, hauling her in as his next victim. He doled out the same kiss, *love you*, and tickles that he had to Sophie.

"Uncle *Harley*! *Stop!*" Jolie pushed out of his arms and hid behind Piper. "Don't let him get me."

"Sorry, sweets, but you're going to have to pull up those big-girl panties and fight back. The man has only *one* good foot," Piper pointed out. "You and Soph could do some damage tickling him."

Sophie and Jolie exchanged a conspiratorial glance and then went at Harley with both hands, tickling and giggling. Harley played right along.

"You are *definitely* a keeper," Delaney said, watching them play.

"So is *he*," Piper said, chuckling as he threatened to *take the girls down*. "Are you sure you're okay with the girls?"

"Yes, and even if I wasn't, I need to be with them. I thought it would be easier to have space to recover without the chaos of taking care of the girls every day, but I missed them so much I think it was harder not having them around. Besides, I'm going to be sore and bruised for a long time as they increase the size of the tissue expanders for the reconstruction. It's so weird to be able to choose what size breasts I want to have."

"I'm cool with my itty-bitties."

Delaney nudged her and said, "So is my brother."

It felt funny to joke about something like that when Piper had spent her life disconnected from the relationship world, but she'd just have to get used to it.

"Are you worried about the reconstruction?"

Delaney wiggled her hand as if to say, *A little*. "I'm trying not to think about it too much. I just want it to be done, and for a year to pass with a clean bill of health."

"We all do. You know we're here for whatever you need, even if you want us to just take the girls out for a couple of hours here and there." She glanced at Harley, hugging his nieces, and said, "He gave the girls a long talk about not fighting and twenty bucks to help around the house and do their own laundry."

"I still can't believe he hired At Your Service to bring dinners for me and the girls for the next two weeks. He spoils me." Delaney glanced lovingly at Harley and said, "He's such a good guy, always going above and beyond for everyone else. I'm glad he's finally doing something for himself, and by that I mean getting involved with *you*. He's husband material—you see that, right? It doesn't get much better than that man right there."

Piper didn't want to say she wasn't looking for a husband, much less that she wasn't sure she was *wife material*, so instead she said, "He's a great guy, but don't go marrying us off yet. We've only just started seeing each other."

"I know. I was just bragging about my little brother."

Piper scoffed. "There is nothing *little* about your brother."

"I don't want to know *that*," Delaney said, and they both laughed.

Half an hour later, they said goodbye to the girls and Delaney climbed into the truck. Laying all her cards on the table had been the most difficult thing she'd done in a very long time, but they were stronger for it. Harley had to be the *most* patient man on earth, and though patience wasn't Piper's strong suit, at least he'd been well aware of that from the get-go. Tonight she was going to show him that she was willing to try to let down her guard in an even bigger way so he would know she meant what she said.

"Why are you grinning like you won the lottery?" he asked.

She reached across the seat, and for the first time *ever*, she took a man's hand in hers because she just wanted to feel closer to him. "Because of *you*." She drew in a deep breath, her pulse beating wildly as she took a leap of faith and said, "Willow called earlier. She and Zane are meeting Remi and Mason at Dutch's for drinks tonight. Do you want to go hang out with them?"

He squeezed her hand, an irresistibly devastating grin curling his lips. "Are you asking me on a *date*?"

She caught herself as she started to roll her eyes and said, "Yes. A triple date, actually."

"Like, in *public*?" he teased.

"*Harley*," she warned.

"I just want to be sure I understand what you're asking. You, me, as a *couple*, out in public on a Friday night?"

"Yes! Now stop being weird." She tried to pull her hand away, but he tugged her across the seat, bringing her face so close to his she could practically taste him.

"Can I kiss you while we're there?"

"Yes."

"Put my arm around you?"

"Yes," she said with a little laugh.

"Dance with you?"

"On *one* foot?" Her stomach fluttered like an infatuated teenager's.

"I'm a hell of a dancer," he said arrogantly.

She sighed, feigning annoyance. She knew how great a dancer he was, and she also knew it would be different dancing as a couple rather than friends, and she couldn't *wait* to experience it.

"You can hold my hand, put your arm around me, kiss me, and dance with me." She felt vulnerable saying all those things, but it also felt good. So good, she lowered her voice seductively and added, "Play your cards right, and you might even get to drag me into your office and have your way with me."

His eyes flamed, causing her entire body to sizzle.

"If you think the first time I make love to you is going to be on a couch or a desk with dozens of people right outside the door, you're sorely mistaken." His lips brushed hers as he said, "Play *your* cards right and you'll be in *my* bed tonight." His tongue swept slowly over her lower lip, and he whispered, "We both know you'll *never* want to leave."

CHAPTER SIXTEEN

HARLEY AND PIPER sat across the table from Willow and Zane, chatting as they waited for Remi and Mason, who were running late. Dutch's sure felt different from the other side of the bar. Or maybe it was the new twists in Harley's relationship with Piper that had him seeing the pub in a whole new light. The atmosphere was more festive, the beer was tastier, and *Harley* felt more alive than ever. Piper had picked him up almost an hour ago, and he still couldn't take his eyes off her. She was always beautiful, but tonight she wore an olive miniskirt, a black off-the-shoulder shirt, a slim leather choker, and sexy black boots. Her hair was parted to the side, shiny and beautiful, with a lingering hint of color covering one smoky eye. He could count on one hand the number of times he'd seen Piper in a skirt, much less wearing makeup. But it wasn't the clothes or the makeup that held his rapt attention. It was the way Piper had been looking at him like he was *hers* and giving off a definitely back-off-bitches vibe. He'd wanted her to feel that way for a long time, but he'd never imagined how incredible it would feel to experience it.

Willow sipped her wine and said, "Traffic coming back from the city must be really bad for Remi and Mason to be this late. We need to convince Aiden to move closer." Aiden Aldridge was Remi's older brother and Ben's business partner. He'd recently returned to the city after spending several weeks overseas for business, and Remi and Mason were on their way back from visiting him.

"You don't seriously believe they're stuck in traffic, do you?" Piper shook her head, giving Harley a get-a-load-of-her glance. "They're *totally* banging."

Harley couldn't resist leaning in and kissing her. She pulled back a little too quickly, her eyes darting across the table to her sister. He'd anticipated Piper's nervousness around her sister and Zane. He curled his hand around her shoulder, pulling her closer, and kissed her temple, whispering, "Just go with it."

Zane nudged Willow. He was an actor-turned-screenwriter with a playful, cocky attitude and classic Hollywood good looks. His debut screenplay, *Beneath It All,* was currently in production to become a major motion picture. More importantly, he adored Willow, and it showed in everything he did.

"Can I just say, *wow?*" Willow said with appreciation. "I have waited so long to see my big sis this happy with a man."

Piper rolled her eyes. "*Don't* go there, Willow."

"Aw, come on," Zane teased. "I want to know what Harley has that every other guy who has tried to win you over doesn't."

"Isn't it obvious?" Willow waved her hand across the table. "Check out the way he's looking at her, like there's no one else in the entire pub."

Piper's beautiful green eyes rolled leisurely over Harley's face, slowly moving down his body. She took her time, openly admiring his chest and lingering on his groin so long he felt the heat of her gaze blazing through him. Could the others tell how badly he wanted to drag her out of there and make good on his earlier promises?

When Piper finally looked at Zane, she slid her hand to Harley's thigh under the table and said, "It's not because of *what* he *has*. It's because of *who* he *is*."

Willow and Zane looked as astonished as Harley felt. He drew Piper close again and pressed a kiss beside her ear. Then he rested his forehead on the side of her head, taking a second to wrap his head around how hard that must have been for her to admit, before whispering, "Are you trying to make me fall so hard for you I'll never recover?"

"Sorry we're late!" Remi exclaimed, startling Harley and Piper apart. "Whoa! It's really true. Harley and Piper are a couple! Look at you guys, whispering sweet nothings and getting all lovey-dovey. Remember last year when you guys came over to help me and Mason slip out of town? I told Mason that night that you two would end up together."

Remi was an actress, and she'd had issues with a stalker last year. Mason had wanted to take her out of town without the stalker realizing she'd slipped away, and Piper and Harley had taken part in the ruse. Harley had made no bones about wanting Piper. She, on the other hand, had brushed him off just like she'd always done.

Thank God he'd finally forced himself out of the friend zone.

"Stop gushing and get your scrawny ass over here." Piper pushed to her feet, pulling the Natalie Portman look-alike into a hug.

Harley rose to shake Mason's hand, using the table for balance. "Hey, man. How's it going?"

Mason was a formidable man, standing eye to eye with Harley. "Couldn't be better." He nodded toward the girls and said, "Guess you might say the same?"

Hell yes. "Better than ever."

"Piper, look at you in that skirt! You have killer legs!" Remi pointed at Piper's legs and said, "Look, Mase! Doesn't she look hot?"

"She does," Mason agreed.

"My girl *always* looks hot," Harley said, pulling Piper into his arms.

Piper's eyes narrowed, and he readied himself for a hefty dose of snark. But a second later she sighed and said, "Thank you."

Laughter bubbled out before Harley could stop it. "Sorry, Trig, but this day is going down in history."

"Get over yourself," Piper said, pushing out of his arms to hug Mason. "Good to see you, *hottieguard.*"

Piper had coined the term *hottieguard* when Mason was Remi's bodyguard, and Harley supposed it fit. Mason was tall, dark, and muscular, with steel-blue eyes and perfectly manicured scruff. Harley had wondered if Piper had been into him when he'd first met the guy, but he'd quickly realized she'd just been sizing Mason up. She was always watching out for her friends, making sure they were treated well. Harley had heard rumors about Piper threatening the men her sisters and friends had gone out with, including the ones they'd eventually married. If the gossip was true, she'd told the men that if they hurt whoever she was watching out for at the time, they'd have *her* to deal with. He had no doubt she'd done just that. Remi was among her honorary sisters, which meant Mason had likely encountered the same treatment.

When Harley had first moved back to town, he'd noticed Piper's protective nature over her sisters and friends hadn't changed much since before he'd gone away to college, and he'd wondered who'd had her back while he'd been living in New York. It hadn't been a conscious decision to step in again when he moved back home. In fact, until this moment, he really hadn't thought about it much. He supposed some things were simply meant to be.

Mason chuckled. "You, too, Piper. I see you came to your senses and gave the big guy a chance."

"For now," she said teasingly.

As everyone took their seats, Willow asked how Aiden was doing. Remi looked at Mason, and the flush on her cheeks told Harley that Piper had been right about where those two lovebirds had been.

"He's good, and going out a little more often now," Remi said.

Aiden was twelve years older than Remi, and he'd raised her after their parents were killed in a car accident. He was a brilliant businessman, a self-made billionaire, and in addition to Ben's business partner, Aiden was also Remi's manager, although she was currently taking a hiatus from acting. Now that Remi and Mason were engaged, Aiden's role in her life had changed, and it had taken some time for him to get used to not always living in the same location as his sister or watching over her every move.

"A little?" Zane scoffed. "That man's been on daddy duty forever. I'm sure he's finally sowing his wild oats."

"I don't think Aiden's a 'wild oats' kind of guy," Remi said.

Piper's eyes shot to Remi's. "I hate to tell you this, naive one, but I'd put money on the fact that your brother has a red room tucked away in one of his many mansions."

Harley's ears perked up. *Hm.* Was his girl into that?

"Ew." Remi wrinkled her nose.

"I hope not," Mason said. "I'm thinking about setting him up with Krista." Mason had spent several years in the military and then as a covert operations specialist. Krista Bishop was a single mother and the widow of one of Mason's military buddies. "Did you see how close they were at the last birthday bash?"

Mason and Remi had recently partnered with Parker Collins-Lacroux of the Collins Children's Foundation to help foster children feel grounded and special, and to give them a sense of family no matter how many times they were moved to different foster homes. They hosted quarterly birthday parties as part of that new program, which they called "bashes," for all of the foster children in Sweetwater and Harmony Pointe, and on the children's birthdays they provided birthday boxes filled with gifts. Many children carried their belongings in garbage bags from one home to the next. Through this program, every foster child received a duffel bag filled with personal items. Remi and Mason worked with major corporations to provide the items for the birthday boxes and duffel bags, and they hoped to take the programs national within the next year.

"Krista said Aiden hasn't asked her out," Mason explained. "I thought I'd give him a nudge in that direction."

"But I still think we should set him up with Shira," Remi said. Shira ran Hearts for Heroes, the nonprofit organization that Bridgette's husband, Bodhi, had founded.

"How about Delaney?" Piper suggested.

Harley snapped to attention. "Whoa, what? My sister?"

"Why not?" Piper asked. "She's smart, gorgeous, and has two kids who could really use a loving stepfather in their lives."

"Yes!" Willow exclaimed. "Aiden would be *perfect* for Delaney. He took great care of Remi, even if he was overprotective. He had to be. Remi was in the limelight and Aiden's instincts were right. After all, he found Mason. He'd be amazing with Jolie and Sophie."

Remi cuddled closer to Mason and said, "He did find me the greatest man around."

"Want to duke that out, princess?" Piper wrapped her hand around Harley's arm.

"No way. I like my face just as it is," Remi teased. "You're right about Delaney and the girls, but Krista's daughter, Brooklyn, could use a daddy, too."

"What is this? An episode of *The Bachelor*?" Zane asked.

"Don't you think Aiden might want to have a say in his life?" Harley asked.

Mason put his arm around Remi and said, "As my soon-to-be wife says to me often, 'spoken like a true man.'"

The guys chuckled, and the girls went on about the ridiculous things men say. Piper was the ringleader of that conversation, and she had the girls in stitches.

"Don't even *try* to tell me that Zane and Mason haven't given you guys the old 'I could have gone all night, but you know, babe, I figured you were tired,'" Piper said in a baritone voice.

"Yes!" Willow and Remi said in hushed whispers, as if their men weren't able to hear them.

"Well, my man has never told me that," Piper said with a proud lift of her chin and a wink in his direction.

He nuzzled against her neck, kissing her there. "Damn right, and I never will," he said.

"Or when the dishwasher needs emptying and they coincidentally walk into the kitchen when you're almost done emptying it and say, 'I was just about to do that!'" Willow patted Zane's shoulder and said, "My man is famous for that. But I told him he didn't have to be good in the kitchen as long as he's *excellent* in the bedroom."

Zane bumped fists with Mason and Harley.

"Before we have too many drinks and I forget, can we count on any of you to help put together duffel bags and birthday boxes again? We're shooting for two weeks from this coming Tuesday at six o'clock in our barn." Volunteers gathered once a month to fill the birthday boxes and duffel bags with the donated items.

"I'll be there," Harley and Piper said in unison.

Harley had no doubt Piper would be there every time they needed help. Her generosity with her time was just one of the many things he admired about her.

"Us too," Willow said. "We'll be there."

Remi clapped. "Thank you! Now catch me up with what I've missed since we last saw each other, and *then* I'll tell you our big news."

"You're preggers," Piper said as she reached for Harley's glass.

Willow gasped, Mason shook his head, and Zane laughed. But as the others chatted about Remi and Mason's real news, their plans to foster children soon after their wedding, which was taking place in August, all Harley could think about was Piper drinking his beer. He didn't know why she hadn't ordered her own drinks when she'd always done so at the pub. But he loved that she was sharing his, as she had done at the hockey game. He chalked it up as another way she was telling him that she was into *them* as a couple without having to actually say it. Another *Piperism*. Like those alluring looks she was giving him.

"That's wonderful. Do you plan on having your own children, too?" Willow asked Remi, drawing Harley from his thoughts.

Mason looked lovingly at Remi as she said, "At some point, yes. But since Mason went through the foster care system, we really want to foster kids and give them the fantastic experience he missed out on. We might even foster to adopt or foster several children at once. We're trying to figure out how we can make the most difference in kids' lives."

"I love that idea," Willow said. "You guys will be great parents."

Harley brushed his lips over Piper's temple, wondering if she wanted children. She smelled like sunshine and unspoken promises. She slid her hand over his thigh, holding tight, and lifted her eyes to his. He had the urge to pull her into his lap and tell her how much he adored her, but she was finally letting him in, and he worried about pushing too far.

"Speaking of having children"—Piper looked around the table and said—"you girlies better watch yourselves around Mom. Apparently there's a baby war going on. Aunt Marilynn is upset because her kids aren't giving her grandchildren fast enough. They're keeping *score*. One Montgomery grandchild to three Dalton and Booker grandchildren."

"So?" Willow wrinkled her brow.

"So our mother is dabbling in *fertility* potions, not just love potions." Piper pointed around the table as Jasper approached, and then she pointed at him, too, and said, "None of y'all are safe. Grace and Morgyn are married, but they haven't had any babies. Our mother is sending enough *fertility boosts* for Pepper, Amber, *and* Sable, too. Heck, she'll probably send some for Axsel, even though he's gay. You know how our mother is when she gets a bug up her butt about something."

"I dated a woman named Grace who had sisters and a brother by those names," Jasper said. "There's no way there's more than one family with daughters named Sable *and* Pepper and a son named Axsel. Do you mean Grace *Montgomery*?"

"You dated Grace? The playwright? She lives in Oak Falls, Virginia?" Piper asked incredulously.

Jasper nodded. "We went out on a couple dates when she lived in New York City, before she moved back home. She's smokin' hot." He shrugged. "But we had no chemistry."

"That's insane," Willow said. "She's our cousin. She's married now to Reed Cross, the guy who was her dirty little secret in high school."

"I still can't believe good-girl Gracie had a delicious dirty little secret like Reed," Piper said with a smirk.

As Willow and Jasper continued their conversation, jealousy spiked along Harley's skin. He leaned down and spoke into Piper's ear, "Wishing you had Reed? Because I have no problem kicking his ass."

She slid her hand along his thigh and said, "Why would I want anyone else when I have you?"

Damn, he loved that answer. He kept her closer and whispered, "Does it bother you that I'm no longer *your* dirty little secret?"

She brushed her fingers over the bulge in his jeans, drawing back just far enough to look into his eyes with a sultriness that made his body ache for her as she said, "Harley Dutch, you could never be a dirty *little* secret."

"Damn, woman." He pressed his lips to hers, and to his surprise, she didn't pull away.

"Looks like these two are going to continue getting drunk on each other," Jasper said. "I guess when the boss is away, he likes to *play*."

Harley glowered at him.

Jasper chuckled. "Mason, Remi, what'll it be? The usual?"

"We'll have whatever Harley and Piper are drinking," Remi said with a giggle.

"Two Harley specials coming up." Jasper winked at Harley and headed up to the bar.

"Oh, my sweet Remi . . ." Piper dipped her finger into Harley's drink and licked the alcohol off it. "You can't handle what's in our glass."

Mason eyed Harley and said, "Wanna bet?" He took Remi's face in his hands and kissed her hard.

Zane and Willow laughed.

"*Nobody* shows us up." Harley pushed his chair out from the table, hauled Piper onto his lap, and proceeded to kiss the hell out of her.

Thank God she loved a good challenge as much as he did; she ground against him, making him hard as stone.

Cheers and applause sounded around them, and he heard Mason laughing. But Piper was on Harley's lap, kissing him like she never wanted to stop, and he wasn't about to let her down.

"Geez, you guys," Willow said. "Get a room."

Piper laughed against Harley's lips, her eyes shimmering with desire.

"That sounds like a great idea to me," Harley admitted. He was having a good time, but he needed Piper naked and in his arms. "What do you say, Trig? Is it too early to get out of here?"

Willow and Remi yelled, "Yes!"

"Seriously? We *just* got here," Mason reminded him.

"This is my sister's *first* triple date, *first* kiss in Dutch's Pub, *and* she's with her *first* boyfriend in forever," Willow said. "You are *not* stealing her out of here just yet."

Piper hopped off his lap and said, "I see I have a new cockblocker. Thanks, sis. At least we won the smoldering-kiss contest."

Harley put his arm around her, grinning like a lovesick fool. "That's my badass babe."

"We didn't know it was a contest." Remi pouted.

"It's always a contest," Piper said.

Remi gave her a deadpan look. "You get a boyfriend and turn even bossier?"

"I guess so. I'm going to the ladies' room." Piper leaned down and whispered in Harley's ear, "Before you show me your moves in the bedroom, you better show me your moves on the dance floor."

She sauntered off like the sassy chick she was, leaving him to try to figure out how he was going to dance with a bum ankle and a hard-on.

CHAPTER SEVENTEEN

THE EVENING FLEW by in a flurry of hearty laughter, lustful whispers, steamy kisses, and illicit touches. There was no hiding Piper's desire as she danced with Harley. She was sure it was oozing from her pores. She should be nervous about being so transparent and *free* in a local bar where everyone knew her, but no man had ever made her *want* to lower her guard before. She knew she couldn't hold back with Harley, and no part of her even wanted to try. She'd never realized that letting her guard down could heighten all of her senses, amplifying the feelings that had been building inside her for who knew how long.

And she was by no means *unguarded* at the moment.

But she was definitely opening up in ways she never had, and even though it was scary, Harley had gotten under her skin. Most guys had great moves in only one place, and it usually wasn't in the bedroom *or* on the dance floor. It was on a basketball court, in a boardroom, at a poker table, or in some other male-oriented business or sport. But even with a crutch in one hand, as they bumped and grinded, Harley touched her possessively, and his intoxicating mouth skimmed along her shoulders and neck without ever missing a beat. She already knew how good he was at sports and business, and although they hadn't made out in an actual *bedroom* yet, she knew just how exquisite he was going to be in that domain.

The music slowed, and Harley drew her against his chest, moving sensually to the slower beat of "Rumor" by Lee Brice. Piper had never liked anything cheesy like pickup lines or slow dancing. But when Harley held her close and touched his cheek to hers, singing every lyric to her, it was utterly irresistible. Every word he sang made it harder to breathe. She had no idea she could feel this way, and she didn't want it to end. She closed her eyes, soaking in his manly voice, and her thoughts skittered away. She held tight to the back of his neck, his body cocooning hers. Anticipation mounted inside her as the music rose and fell, and eventually the sound, and the people around them, faded away, until the only things that existed were the two of them and Harley's deep voice serenading her. She had heard this song dozens of times, and she knew it by heart, but never had it sounded so good or so *true*.

Before the very last word fell fully from his lips, she said, "Let's go, Harley."

He gazed into her eyes, and she swore she saw right into his soul. Her heart thundered, nervous energy and anticipation swirling inside her as they made their way back to the table to say goodbye to everyone.

"Want to stay at your place tonight?" Harley asked.

"Piper's place?" Willow said. "You're staying at Piper's place?"

Piper felt Willow's eyes boring into her before she'd even turned her head to meet her gaze.

"I thought you had a no-men-allowed rule," Remi said.

The night had been so perfect, Piper didn't want to admit to her rule and ruin it. Her rule just proved how weird she was compared to other women, and that would just screw up all of the amazing energy between her and Harley. She had to get out of there before the girls said anything more.

"We're going to *Harley's*." She heard the urgency in her voice. "It was good seeing everyone. See you at the bakery, or on Mother's Day, or *sometime*. Let's *go*, Harley."

She ushered him toward the door, silently chastising herself for rambling. Mother's Day wasn't for another *two weeks*. Her heart was racing as they pushed through the doors and the cool night air hit her warm skin.

Harley stopped on the steps, gazing at her with a serious expression, sending her nerves into overdrive. Anticipating an accusatory question, she felt her walls stacking up again. *No! Please don't!*

But then his lips curved up and he said, "First triple date, first Dutch's kiss, and first boyfriend in forever? I don't think I'll ever forget those words. I am, without a doubt, the luckiest man on the planet."

Piper knew he could find a warmer, sweeter, marriage-seeking girlfriend in a heartbeat. But he wanted *her*, and because of that she knew he had been wrong. He wasn't the luckiest person on the planet. *She* was.

"I think it's the other way around," she said softly.

He leaned in and kissed her just as he had a hundred times tonight, and the worries gnawing at her disappeared as quickly as they'd come. He hadn't *accused*, hadn't looked at her any differently than he had when they were on the dance floor, and that made her want him even more. It also made her feel *grateful*, which was another new feeling toward a man. He'd been her friend, her *sidekick*, the man she could be herself with, for so long, hope fluttered in her chest that maybe they'd last for a while.

Or maybe you'll never ask me to change.

She was far too smart to pull the wool over her own eyes. She kicked that hope to the side, but it still fluttered in the periphery of her being like a butterfly unable to take flight and unwilling to give up.

They hobbled and kissed their way to the truck.

The drive home was slow but titillating thanks to Harley, who leaned across the seat, driving her out of her mind with his mouth on her neck and shoulders and his greedy hands on her inner thigh. By the time they made their way into his house, Piper was wet, wild, and unable to think straight. He dropped his crutches the second they stepped inside and backed her up against the door, grinding and kissing her so forcefully she was sure they'd break the door off the hinges and they'd go flying onto the porch.

But they were still upright when it slammed closed and Jiggs pushed his nose between them. Piper was too lost to slow down as Harley's rough hands pushed under her sweater and he cupped her bare breast. A rumbling groan vibrated from his lungs to hers, setting her entire being aflame. Jiggs jumped beside them, whining too loudly to be ignored.

Harley tore his mouth away and said, *"Dude!* You're the *worst."* But even as he said it, he reached down with one hand, loving up his beloved buddy. "There's *got* to be wingdog training classes somewhere on this fucking earth."

Piper buried her head in his chest, laughing. He was so . . . *Harley.* She looked up at his strained expression, the air between them crackling with sexual tension. She didn't want to move, but one glance at Jiggs's pleading eyes brought a wave of empathy, and she said, "It'll take you longer than me to get up the stairs, so why don't you hobble up, and I'll take Jiggs out really quick."

"Hear that, Jiggsy? I knew she loved us." He pressed his lips to Piper's, and then he glowered at Jiggs and said, "No messing around, you hear me? You go out, do your thing, and come right back in."

Jiggs must have listened well to his handsome daddy, because they took their fastest walk yet. When they got back inside, Piper pulled off her boots and socks by the front door before heading upstairs. She heard soft music coming from the bedroom, setting those fluttery wings into motion again. Jiggs walked beside her down the hall, slowing when she did as she stripped off her sweater and skirt. Piper left on the lace panties she'd picked out just for Harley. She'd changed her clothes a million times before leaving the house this evening, but in the end, she'd wanted to throw Harley a well-deserved *bone.* She wasn't great with words, but she hoped he'd realized how special he was to her by her choice of clothing.

She stood one step away from his bedroom door, her nerves rattling. She drew in a breath and blew it out slowly, wondering what the heck was going on. Sex had never made her nervous. Granted, she hadn't had it in *forever*, and her best male friend was waiting in that room. The man who made her feel things she'd never expected, who brought *tears* to her eyes because she'd thought she might lose him.

Oh my God . . .

This isn't going to be just sex.

She backed against the wall, palms flat, heart thundering. What had he done to her? She'd never been with a man when it wasn't *just* sex. What if it felt wrong? What if she froze? What if they didn't click in the bedroom after all?

Holy shit.

She couldn't breathe.

Her hand covered her racing heart, and she told herself to calm down. *Yeah, right.* How did people do this? Feelings changed *everything*.

She looked past Jiggs, who was standing between her and the doorway, watching her expectantly. *Give me a second!*

She eyed her clothes on the floor, and then she glanced at the stairs, the thought of bolting clawing at her. But she didn't *want* to bolt. She just didn't want to be nervous with Harley of all people. She closed her eyes, giving herself a pep talk. *Suck it up, buttercup. He likes who you are. Just go in there and take control. All these confusing feelings will disappear the minute he touches you.*

She was the queen of taking control.

I've got this.

She opened her eyes, feeling better, and pushed from the wall. She straightened her spine and strode into the bedroom with all the confidence of a woman on a mission. But the second she saw Harley, her knees weakened and her heart stumbled. Candles danced in the darkness, casting a romantic glow on him as he sat on the edge of the mattress, shirtless and beautiful in his dark boxer briefs. His jeans were off one leg, bunched above his sore ankle on the other. She'd forgotten he'd been wearing shorts lately because his ankle was still swollen and sore, which made it hard to take off his jeans without causing pain.

He lifted his face, meeting her gaze, and all of the emotions she thought she could escape came rushing forward in an unstoppable wave. She didn't try to dodge them, didn't want to escape the impact. She wanted to get swept up in them—in *him*—and experience the power and the grace of this magical thing between them.

She didn't know if she was even capable of letting go like that, which made her even more nervous. Harley's gaze slid appreciatively down her body, igniting the inferno that had been simmering inside her all evening.

"You're so fucking beautiful," he said in a husky voice that drew her to him.

She wanted to tell him that he was even more beautiful than she was, but her voice was lost to her racing heart as she knelt by his feet and carefully guided his jeans over his sore ankle. She was too overwhelmed to think clearly, but the desire to *show* him just how special he was took over. She lifted his sore ankle and pressed a kiss just above the bandage. He caressed her cheek, bringing her eyes to his, and cradled her face, looking at her like he couldn't believe she was there. She came forward, running her hands up his calves and kissing his knee, his thigh. He gently lifted her face, guiding it closer, and pressed his lips to hers in a warm and wonderful kiss. She didn't know what to do with *warm* or *wonderful*, but as it turned out, she didn't need to, because Harley gripped her rib cage with two hands, lifting her up, and laid her on the bed. He moved over her.

"Your ankle," she whispered.

"I'm on my knee. I'm good."

His eyes drilled into her, a predator salivating over his prey, as he drew her wrists over her head, trapping them there with one strong hand. His other hand skimmed down her torso, lighting flames beneath her skin. He gripped her hip so hard she knew it might bruise. And she welcomed it.

She wanted *everything* he had to give, including the rush at seeing his marks on her body the next day.

"Fucking hell, Piper. You're finally in my bed." The dirty fantasies Harley had mentally prepared to live out with Piper got lost between the lust in her eyes, the wicked grin on her lips, and the feel of her near nakedness beneath him. Thank God they had their underwear on, because if his cock touched her hot skin, he'd drive into her so deep they'd both lose their minds, and he'd waited too long to rush through this.

Jiggs put his chin on the bed beside them, and Harley growled, "Go lie down, boy."

Jiggs slinked away.

Harley set his eyes on Piper again. The air between them pulsed with lust and greed, but there was something much more powerful winding around them, binding them together. Piper arched beneath him, straining against his grip on her wrists and his weight pressing down on her. She craned her neck to reach his mouth, breathing his name in a desperate plea.

"*Harley . . .*"

Fuuck.

Even her voice did him in, but he forced himself to go slow, determined to love her better than anyone ever had, and he was in no mood to rush.

He raked his eyes over her gorgeous face, contemplating her luscious, welcoming mouth. She licked her lips, and his cock twitched in his briefs. His gaze slid down to her breasts, and her breath hitched. Oh yeah, *that's* where he was starting.

"You have so many perfect parts," he said hungrily. "I'm going to love every damn one of them until you come, until you're so *hot*, when I finally get my cock inside you, you'll explode around me."

Her eyes flamed. "*Yes—*"

He dipped his head, slicking his tongue along the underside of her breasts, feeling her breath quicken. He licked between them, over her creamy globes and around her nipples without touching them. She writhed against him, making one needy sound after another as he tasted and teased, loving every second of her gasps and whimpers.

"Touch me," she pleaded.

"*No*" came out harsher than he'd intended, but the smoldering flames in her eyes told him she craved his gruffness. His entire being burned with the need to see that look in her eyes grow even hotter. He grazed his teeth over the swell of one breast, earning a sharp inhalation. "I'm going to make you come with only my mouth on your breasts."

"I can't. I've never . . ."

"Oh, but you *will*," he promised.

He lowered his mouth over the side of her breast, sucking hard enough to brand her, and she cried out. Fearing he'd hurt her, he released her sensitive skin, his gaze darting to hers, but in her eyes he found only approval.

"*Again,*" she panted out.

He held her gaze as he did it again, sucking longer, knowing he was leaving a mark. She moaned, making his entire body throb. He dragged his tongue over the dark spot he'd caused and kissed his way up to the taut peak.

"*Suck it,*" she begged.

He grinned, but he wanted to draw out her pleasure, and he didn't obey her request. He tightened his hold on her wrists and hip as he moved to her other breast, loving it thoroughly, making her pant and beg and suck in quick, sharp breaths. When he finally lowered his mouth over the hard peak, he felt her wrist muscles flexing and knew she was fisting her hands. Her legs tensed beneath him, and her eyes slammed shut. He eased his efforts, licking and blowing cool air over the wetness he'd left, earning one mewling sound after another. The needy sounds spurred him on. He feasted on her breast, sucking and licking, grazing and nipping, before lavishing her other breast with the same attention. Her heels dug into the mattress, and her muscles corded tight, on the cusp of release. He held her there, worshipping her body until it vibrated like a string strung too tight, and then he quickened his efforts and she lost control, bucking and crying out with pleasure.

He released her hands and hip and claimed her mouth, capturing those sexy-as-fuck sounds. She wrapped her arms around him, holding tight as she pushed his hands beneath her ass, angling her hips so he could grind his erection against her center and draw out her climax. Even through the thin sheen of their underwear he felt her sex pulsing, sending fire through his loins. She scratched and clawed at his head and shoulders as her orgasm tore through her. It was the most exquisite pain he'd ever felt. When she went soft beneath him, he cradled her head in his hands, kissing her tenderly. He reveled in this softer side of her, soaking in her sweetness.

He pressed several kisses to the edges of her mouth. Then he touched his cheek to hers, breathing her in as she caught her breath.

"*Harley*," she whispered.

"Hm?"

Her hands moved down his back, and she grabbed his ass. He felt himself smiling.

"Can we do that again?"

His heart turned over in his chest at the softness of her voice and the emotions it carried. He was happy to comply, but they didn't stop there.

As she came down from the crest of another climax, he kissed a path down the center of her body. She watched as he slipped off the pretty lace panties that had caused his thoughts to fracture when he'd first seen her looking vulnerable, eager, and mind-blowingly beautiful.

He dangled her panties from his fingers and said, "Piper Dalton in lace has just become my favorite thing."

She bit her lower lip, desire swimming in her eyes as he tossed her panties aside. He lowered his mouth between her legs, determined to keep his promise, and proceeded to devour *all* her perfect parts until they were *both* on the verge of madness.

The candles cast dancing shadows over the dips and curves of her body as he retrieved a condom. She lay with her fair hair fanning over his pillow and her green eyes conveying the same depth of emotions he felt. He'd waited so long for this moment, his emotions hung on the tip of his tongue, threatening to leap out. He went up on his knees and tore open the condom wrapper, trying to rein in the words that he knew would scare her.

Piper rose with him, holding his gaze without a hint of challenge, snark, or rebellion. *Trust* was the overriding emotion hanging between them as she took the condom from his hands and set the wrapper on the nightstand. She held his gaze as she sheathed his erection. Her fingers played over his pecs, and she pressed her lips to the center of his chest, holding them there. He stroked her hair as her eyes met his in such an overwhelmingly intimate moment, he sensed that everything was changing for her, too, but knew better than to say it aloud.

They lay down, and he kissed her sensually as he aligned their bodies. His heart hammered, and he felt hers beating wildly, too. He had to draw back to see her beautiful face. He'd thought the first time they made love would be wild and reckless, but as he held her in his arms, gazing deeply into her eyes as their bodies came together, there was nothing reckless about it. He didn't want to miss a single hitch in her breath or the flicker of surprise in her eyes as her body stretched to accommodate his girth. He reveled in the feel of her clinging to him like she needed to remain grounded to combat the intensity of their connection. He was right there with her, adrenaline coursing through his veins, his thoughts whirling as he pushed in deeper, taking her slowly.

"*God,*" she said in one long breath as he buried himself to the hilt.

He filled her so completely, her body squeezed around him like a vise. His head dipped beside hers, and for a moment he could do nothing more than be *part* of her.

She was so feminine and small, and he was so big all over, he worried he'd hurt her, and lifted up.

"Don't." She clung to him, unwilling to allow any space between them. "Kiss me. I want all of you."

She couldn't possibly know how much that meant to him. He lowered his mouth to hers, and as they began to find their rhythm, he knew they were made for each other. They moved slowly at first, giving her body a chance to get used to him, but they quickly got lost in each other, grinding and thrusting, groping and caressing. Every move, every touch, kiss, and sound, strengthened their connection. He made love to her mouth, his tongue sweeping forcefully over hers as he cradled her head with one hand. He pushed his other hand beneath her ass, angling her hips so he could take her deeper. He wanted to possess *all* of her, to take away all of the hurt she'd ever felt, to make her feel safe. To make her *his* in every sense—heart, body, and soul. She wound her legs around his, her heels digging into the backs of his thighs. He quickened his efforts, pressure mounting inside him like a storm building power with every thrust.

He tore his mouth away and said, "Squeeze me tight."

Her legs clamped tighter around him, sending bolts of heat to his cock. He pounded into her faster, but it wasn't rough and dirty; it was intense and *miraculous.* Sexy sounds escaped her lips with every thrust.

She shifted her legs higher, near his hips, and he drove in deeper. She cried out, "*Yes! Right there, don't stop.*"

That's it, baby. Let go.

The pleasure was so immense, he gritted his teeth to stave off his own release. Her thighs squeezed him so tight, he knew she was hanging on by a thread. He moved his hand between the globes of her ass, teasing over the entrance he had yet to breach. She was so wet, his fingers quickly became coated with her arousal.

"*Don't stop,*" she panted out, and pushed against his fingers, allowing them to breach that entrance. "Oh God, *Har-ley*! *Yes!*"

He reclaimed her mouth, swallowing her erotic sounds, his senses reeling. Her body pulsed, hot and perfect, around his hard length. She broke their kiss and sank her teeth into his neck. Pure, explosive pleasure raced down his spine, and he lost all control, driving into her as he ground out her name, his climax tearing through him with the force of a hurricane. She clung to him, lifting off the mattress with his every thrust. Sounds of flesh against flesh and their cries of passion created a chorus of lust and greed and unspoken emotions. Their pleasure went on and on, carrying them up to the clouds.

When their muscles went slack, the room spun. Harley felt himself drifting, unaware of time, space, or anything other than the woman in his arms as their mouths came together, their slick bodies tangled like a braided plait. He'd never felt anything like this. He couldn't even name the whirlwind of emotions coursing through him. Was he alone in them? He tried not to wonder as their breathing calmed, and he rolled them onto their sides, kissing her adoringly. He didn't want to leave her to take care of the condom. What he felt was too big to deny. He was afraid those all-consuming emotions might scare her, and if he went into the bathroom she might not be there when he came out.

He pressed his lips to hers, and her eyes fluttered open. He tried to read her expression, but it was one he'd never seen before, and he was afraid to believe it meant what he thought it did. She sighed, snuggling into the curve of his body, and then she closed her eyes, burying her face in his chest.

"*What* was that?" she whispered, a little panicky.

"Mind-blowing sex?"

She shook her head. "No. I mean, *yes*, it was, but it was . . ." She looked up at him, her cheeks pink and her eyes wide. "I have no idea *what* that was. I've never felt *anything* like it."

God he loved the panicked honesty she was sharing with him. She was probably terrified, but she was looking out over her own walls, and instead of scrambling back to safety, she was trying to understand what she saw.

He kissed her lips and said, "Don't be scared, Pipe."

"Too late. How can I not be *terrified*? You've done something to me with your magic blissmaker, and I don't know what to make of it or how to handle it."

He chuckled, stuck on *magic blissmaker*. "Just don't freak out on me and disappear."

"You think you know me," she said sassily, reverting to her safe place.

"I wish I could say I didn't." That was a lie. What he really wished for was that she wanted this as much as he did.

"No you don't," she challenged. "You like knowing me better than any other man ever has. You get off on it, and don't try to deny it."

"Can't get anything past you, can I?"

"Do you really want to?"

She was doling out one challenge after another. He rolled her beneath him and gazed down at her smiling face. "What I want to know is if I go into that bathroom, will you still be here when I get back?"

Hurt washed over her face. "You think I'd leave like that? After everything . . . *Wait. Ohmygod.* No wonder women lose their minds after sex. Does it feel like *that* all the time with you and other women?"

She wiggled, trying to get out of his arms, and he realized she truly had no clue how much this meant to him. How much *she* meant to him.

"Harley! Let me *go*. I just realized how much of a freak I a—"

He pressed his lips to hers, silencing her insecurities. At least verbally. He kissed her until she went soft beneath him again, and then he kissed her longer, hoping to buy himself a long enough period once they stopped kissing to explain what he'd meant before her brain started playing tricks on her again.

When their lips parted, he said, "If you call my girlfriend a freak again, I'll have to spank you."

"*Stop*," she snapped. "I feel ridiculous and stupid for not realizing—"

"Whoa, slow down, Trig. It's never been like this for me, either." He stroked his fingers down her cheek as his words sank in and said, "I always knew we would be good together, but I never imagined *this*." He saw disbelief rising in her eyes. "It's true, Pipe. I'd never lie to you, especially about this. You've always gotten to me, but making love to you? Babe, we rocked *my* world, too."

Trepidation and happiness battled in her eyes, and he waited her out, praying she wouldn't want to run. He brushed his nose along her cheek and whispered reassuringly, "You're not alone in these new feelings." He was thankful that *he* wasn't alone in them, either. "Just go with it, Piper. I'm right here."

She looked a little frightened, but then the edges of her lips twitched up, and she said, "I sure hope there's a twelve-step program for this, because damn, Dutch, this could be addicting."

There's my take-charge girl. "Hell yes, it not only could, but it *is*. Does this mean you'll consider spending the night?"

"No."

His heart sank. He really thought they'd crossed another bridge.

"But I'm pretty sure the overnight bag in my truck does," she said softly.

His head fell between his shoulders. She was going to be the death of him. "You were planning on staying?"

"I knew how much it meant to you." She trailed her fingers down his arms. "But beware, I'm not used to sharing my bed. I toss and turn all night. You probably won't get any sleep."

"I think I can handle it." He kissed her, and as he sat up, he said, "Thank you for staying over."

She rolled onto her stomach and crossed her arms under her head, gazing up at him with a telling smirk. "Thank you for the orgasms."

He chuckled as he grabbed the crutches and headed to the bathroom.

After taking care of the condom, he brushed his teeth and caught sight of the scratches and bite marks on his shoulders and neck. A thrill rushed through him.

He snagged the crutches and opened the bathroom door, surprised to see Piper lying beside Jiggs on the bed, one arm around his furry pup, the other tucked beneath her pillow, tripping up his heart even more. His sneaky dog wasn't allowed to sleep on his bed.

Harley made his way across the room, and Jiggs opened his eyes, gave Harley a once-over, and then closed them again. "Come on, Jiggsy," Harley whispered. When Jiggs opened his eyes, Harley pointed to the floor.

Jiggs crawled to the edge of the bed on his belly, his big brown eyes pleading with Harley. Harley shook his head. "Sorry, buddy, but I've waited too long to share this night with you."

Jiggs jumped woefully off the bed and skulked away.

Harley climbed into bed, and Piper snuggled against him, nestling into the curve of his hips, her back against his chest. He pulled up the blanket and wrapped his arm around her. She sighed and drifted off to sleep.

He lay awake for a long while with Piper safely tucked within the confines of his body, sound asleep. Holding her like this was better than sex, better than anything he'd ever known. He'd thought she'd already wrecked him in all the best ways, but now he knew she hadn't *wrecked* him at all. She made him whole.

CHAPTER EIGHTEEN

PIPER WAS WRAPPED in the warm cocoon of Harley's body when the morning light trickled over her closed eyelids. She moved her hand, grazing his arm, which was belted around her. He felt *amazing*, and she felt *different*. *Good* and *happy*, which sent her mind in another direction. She was always happy, wasn't she? She loved her job, her family, her *life*. Yes, she was definitely a happy person. She sighed with relief not to have discovered a life-shattering revelation about herself. But could this be another *level* of happiness? Could there have been more to happiness than what she'd always accepted? That was too deep to ponder this early in the morning. She pushed those thoughts away for now, focusing on how *else* she felt. *Weird*, definitely *weird*. She was lying naked in Harley Dutch's arms. If that shouldn't make her feel weird, she didn't know what should.

Harley tugged her closer. He was so warm, like a big, cuddly bear. *A cuddly bear with a fully erect blissmaker pressed against my ass.* She took stock of her emotions.

Weird, happy, and cuddling? Okay, I think I can deal with this.

Cuddling is so girlie.

God, I'm a mess. What woman doesn't like to cuddle?

Harley kissed her shoulder. "You must have liked sleeping with me," he said in a gravelly voice that sent heat down her spine. "You didn't move all night."

Her eyes flew open, and she sat up, her heart racing.

She hadn't moved all night? What did *that* mean? She was a wild sleeper, tossing and turning all night. Sometimes she awoke tangled up in her sheets, or with the sheets and blankets on the floor. She looked down at her nakedness and snagged the blanket from around her legs, pulling it over her chest.

Jiggs lifted his head from the dog bed in the corner of the room. He looked at Harley, and then he lay back down and closed his eyes.

Seriously? He taught you to sleep in on weekends?

Harley's arms circled her from behind and he kissed her back. "I thought I might get a few more minutes before you freaked out."

"Harley, you just said that I didn't move all night. I have no idea what that means. Isn't this weird to you? You, me, *naked*? It's Saturday morning, and it's—" She glanced at the clock on his nightstand. "Seven o'clock?" She never slept this late! "This is crazy. *I'm* crazy. You've *made me* crazy."

She moved to get off the bed, and Harley dragged her down to the mattress on her back, grinning at her. "Why are you looking at me like that?" And why, after all these years, did she suddenly see how gorgeous he was every damn time she looked at him? Had she really never noticed that his eyes weren't just blue, but they were rich and delicious. They were *blueberry blue*. And for the love of God, *why* did that make her all tingly?

"I just can't believe how beautiful you are when you freak out." Harley pressed his lips to hers.

She rolled her eyes. "*Harley . . .*"

"You asked if this was weird. It's not weird. It's perfect to me, Trig."

"Of course it is," she said sarcastically. "Well, it's weird to me. *I'm* weird to me right now."

His brows slanted. "You mean you want to bolt?"

"No. I don't *want* to."

"But . . . ?"

"I don't know, okay?"

"Did you hate waking up with me that much? Or is it because you're not in your own bed? We can try this at your place tonight."

"No, I *don't* hate this. That's why it's so weird. And we are *not* staying at my house. I just need a second. I thought I felt weird when I saw my pictures on your refrigerator, but this tops it. It's like . . . *weird* on steroids. I know people do this all the time, but I don't. This is the first time I have ever woken up in a man's bed. *Ever*, Harley. I need time to wrap my head around it."

"Okay." He shifted over her and kissed her cheek. "How about if I remind you *why* you decided to spend the night? Maybe then you'll feel less weird."

He slid his tongue along the shell of her ear and bit into the lobe, sending white-hot lust darting through her. He lowered his mouth to her neck, sucking and licking. She felt herself go damp and squeezed her thighs together.

His gaze darkened. He laced their fingers together and pressed her hands into the mattress beside her head as he nudged her legs open with his knees. The broad crown of his erection pressed temptingly against her center, causing her sex to clench.

He brushed his lips over hers and said, "It feels to me like you want to be reminded."

Did she ever . . .

He lowered his mouth to hers, taunting her with his cock, rubbing it along her wetness. She lifted her hips, wanting him so badly she was shaking. He sucked her tongue into his mouth, and she swore she felt it between her legs.

"Tell me you want me," he said heatedly.

"As if you don't already know." Her words dripped with sarcasm.

An arrogant grin slid across his face. "Oh, I know, Trig. I've always known. But I want to hear it."

How did he know exactly what she liked? "*Fine.* I want you, Dutch. I want your big blissmaker inside me, and I want you to fuck me hard."

"I like that dirty mouth of yours, and I'll fuck you, but then I'm going to take you so slow and make you feel so good, you'll want me to cherish you forever."

She swallowed hard, anxious to feel as close as they had last night. He reached into the nightstand and grabbed two condoms, tossing one to the other side of the mattress.

As he went up on his knees to sheath himself, she said, "After this we're going to the building-supply center to get the fixtures and tile for your bathroom. I need to get into my own headspace."

"It's a date," he said, coming down over her, nestling the head of his shaft against her center.

Her pulse spiked. "Do you have to feel so good? We'll never get out of this bedroom."

He chuckled and drove into her, burying himself to the root in one thrust.

"Holy *Harley*! Don't move," she said urgently, pressing down on his ass, as if she needed to hold him in place. "You feel so . . ."

"Incredible?"

"Uh-huh," she said breathlessly. "We're stopping at the bakery first. I'm gonna need sugar. *Truckloads* of it."

They walked into the bakery almost two hours later, and Piper was still blissed out. Willow looked up from behind the register where she was ringing up a customer. By the look of approval on her emotionally savvy sister's face, Willow had her *all* figured out.

The swelling and pain in Harley's ankle had eased, and he was regaining his range of motion. Piper had convinced him to try the walking boot. This was the first time since they'd come together as a couple that he'd stood beside her without assistance, and it brought a new thrill of awareness. He seemed even bigger and broader than usual, as if she'd gone through life wearing hot-Harley blinders.

He draped an arm over her shoulder and whispered, "Carb-loading is a good idea, since I'm going to convince you to spend the night again."

"Feeling a little overly confident?" she asked as she contemplated the treats in the display cabinet.

"Three orgasms and one 'I've missed three years of this?' gave me all the confidence I need."

She glowered at him and lowered her voice to a whisper. "You can't hold things I say in the bedroom over my head." If he could, she was in *big* trouble, because Harley had kissed and loved all of the marks he'd left on her body, and she'd said *wicked* things.

"I'm not holding them over your head." He pressed a kiss to her cheek as Willow finished with her customer and said, "I'm just taking stock."

Willow sauntered over from behind the counter, her thick blond hair framing her face. "I guess that well-loved look in my sister's eyes is the reason she didn't come hang out with us this morning."

Piper rolled her eyes.

"Damn right," Harley said.

Piper glowered at him, shaking her head.

He pressed a kiss to her temple and said, "Why hide the truth?"

"Because I don't need my sexual trysts burning up the Sweetwater grapevine." Anxious to change the subject, Piper said, "I'll take one Boston cream doughnut and a Loverboy. The kind that *doesn't* talk back."

Willow laughed as she grabbed a bakery box. "I think I need to give you a few tips on how not to scare a man off."

"She can't scare me off," Harley said, hugging Piper against his side. "I think she's perfect just the way she is, sassy mouth and all."

Willow glanced at Piper, brows raised.

"Don't get too excited, Will. He's vying for nooky points." Piper pointed at the brownies and said, "Can you throw in that big one, too?"

"And a couple of scones." Harley leaned over the display and said, "We're carb-loading for later." He winked.

Piper swatted him and said, "Didn't I just say I don't want to be the center of town gossip?"

Bridgette walked through the archway that connected the bakery to her flower shop and said, "Oh, it's too late for that. Heaven just called in an order to send her mom flowers for Mother's Day, and she said everyone's talking about you two. She and her siblings are making bets on wedding dates."

Piper tried to ignore the streak of jealousy slicing through her at the mention of their friend Heaven Love. She had planned on taking Harley to Heaven's father's furniture shop later to find a vanity for his bathroom. John Love was the most talented furniture maker around, and she knew Harley would appreciate his well-crafted, nature-inspired woodwork. Piper used his products in all of her custom homes. But now she was plagued by images of Harley and Heaven making out. It didn't matter that as far as she knew they'd hooked up only once, and it was when Heaven was a senior in high school. She hated the idea of any other woman's hands on him.

"Then Heaven and her wagering siblings are all going to lose their money." Piper planted a hand on her hip and said, "As you know, marriage is *not* in my future."

Willow's eyes darted to Harley as she put the scones in the box and set it on the counter.

"Don't look so worried, Willow. I know exactly how your sister feels about marriage." Harley pulled out his wallet and said, "How much do I owe you?"

"Nothing. It's on the house." Willow sounded as though she were apologizing for Piper's disinterest in holy matrimony.

Piper grabbed the box and said, "It's *always* on the house. Thanks, Willow." She headed for the door, trying to escape the pressure of her sister's comment and the niggle of guilt from what she knew might send Harley running for the hills. "Keep up, Dutch, or I might eat your scones."

"She loves my *scones*," Harley said to Willow and Bridgette on his way out the door.

Once they were out of the bakery, Piper tore the box open and shoved a Loverboy into her mouth. She had a feeling even a truckload of sugar wouldn't be enough to calm the chaos of confusion messing with her head.

Building-supply stores were as thrilling as they were calming to Piper. When she was in them, she got a rush of adrenaline, dreaming up future projects and concepts. She imagined that thrill was similar to what many women experienced in jewelry stores. And the sense of peace that came from being in her element was probably much like the sense of calm that flowery meadows brought to her sister Bridgette.

But even Piper had her limit, and she was coming very close to reaching it.

She and Harley had been at the store for more than an hour, and the only things he'd picked out were two showerheads and two sink faucets. The man did *not* make decisions lightly. She appreciated that about him, even if she didn't enjoy staring at towel racks until she was blue in the face. She had a feeling his careful decision-making wasn't reserved for household decisions. Three years was a long time to want a woman, and the more she thought about that, the more feelings it brought. She felt special, like she was precious to him and worth waiting for. *Precious* wasn't a word she'd use in the same sentence with herself, but he made her feel like maybe she should. She also felt *respected*, because Harley hadn't pushed during those years. He'd given her space, bided his time.

She didn't know if she deserved that kind of treatment, but she was glad he thought she did.

Given that he'd waited so long for her, she should cut him slack while choosing fixtures, but patience was not her strong suit.

"Hey, big guy. You've been looking at the towel racks for twenty minutes. Think you can pick one?"

He looked amused. "Got a date?"

"Yes, with a shower that needs to be tiled." She waved at a towel rack and said, "What's wrong with that one? It's about as masculine as a towel rack can get."

He pulled her into his arms and said, "Why are you so impatient?"

"Why do you take things so slow?"

"I like to savor the moment. It's not every day I get to go shopping with one-half of the infamous Dalton Contracting duo."

He was good at turning her complaints around. "You're quite the sweet talker."

"I seem to remember you liked other things I do with my mouth, too."

Shivers of heat trickled down her spine. "If you hurry up, maybe we'll have time for you to remind me."

"Maybe you should help me pick one out. You're good with *hard* things."

She cocked a brow. "That's a pretty wide net you're casting."

"Then let me narrow it down." He backed her up against the shelf with a rapacious grin, his eyes darkening. "I like the way you handle my cock, and I have a feeling I'll like the way you hold on to my towel rack while I take you from behind."

An image of Harley taking her from behind as she clung to a towel rack slammed into her. Lust pooled low in her belly. She wanted to do that with him, and so much more. She'd been trying not to think about christening his new shower when it was finally done, but they'd showered together in the guest bathroom this morning, and they'd had to be creative because of his ankle. They'd ended up with Harley lying on his back in the bathtub, the shower raining down on them as she rode him like the stallion he was.

She was definitely building a tiled bench in his new shower.

"You like that idea, don't you?" Harley asked, leaning in to kiss her neck.

Holy crap, Talia was right. He really was her *match*. If she wasn't careful, they were going to end up in a very precarious position right there in the store.

She forced her brain out of the gutter and said, "Unless you want two big holes in your wall, you'd better not try that. Let's get this show on the road." She took a step away, grabbed two of the highest-quality towel racks, and handed them to him. "Those are the best."

As he set them in the cart, she thought about him taking her from behind, and her whole body shuddered. Her mind took that thread and weaved a lecherous path to him bending her over the sink and pinning her hands against the wall as he drove into her. "If you like the way I rock your blissmaker in bed, wait until you see the things I can do with a sturdy vanity" came out before she could stop it.

He grabbed her hand and the cart and said, "What aisle are the vanities in?"

She'd never seen a person with an injured ankle walk so fast.

"We're only checking vanity height here and then getting your shower tiles. I know of a better place to buy your vanity. I think you'll like their styles better."

As they neared the vanity display, Harley said, "I definitely want a double sink. I have this awesome new girlfriend, and I'm hoping she'll decide to leave her toothbrush at my place for a while."

God, this man . . .

Skipping over his comment to save her sanity, she said, "Okay, let's talk vanity height. Most people go with thirty-two inches, but we can get one that's anywhere between thirty and thirty-six inches."

"My girl likes things *big*," he said with a waggle of his brows. "But this is one measurement we need to get just right." He lifted her up, her feet dangling in the air.

"Harley!" Piper whispered, half laughing half chiding as a couple walked into the aisle. She ducked her head beside his and said, "Put me down before someone we know sees us!"

He set her bottom on a vanity and wedged himself between her legs, despite her scowl, which *might* have been broken by a smile.

"And end up with a vanity that's not the perfect height?" He scoffed. "No frigging way." As the couple walked by, he said, "My girlfriend has a thing for vanities."

Piper's jaw dropped.

"Don't look so surprised, sweetheart." He put a hand behind her ass, hauling her to the edge. "I made you a promise never to let you down. That includes pleasuring you in the bathroom." He looked down at their impeccably aligned bodies and said, "Looks like we've found the perfect height."

"*Ohmygod.*" She pushed to her feet. "You are impossible. How do you get anything done?"

He swept her into his arms and kissed her. "You love the way I *get things done.*"

He had her there, and as he lowered his lips to hers, she let him have that, too.

An hour later they walked out with almost everything they needed to finish the bathroom, including the paint and new light fixtures. She had no idea how they made it out so fast with all the debauchery Harley had tried to coerce her into. She'd never gotten so hot and bothered in a supply store before. She'd nearly lost it when he'd asked her to stand in front of a shower tile display, and then he'd stood back, openly assessing her with a lecherous stare. Just seeing him looking like he wanted to devour her had turned her on. When she'd asked what he was doing, he'd said he was trying to decide which tile would look the best behind her when she was wet and naked. She'd been ready to drag him into the warehouse and have her way with him.

She'd never look at the store the same again.

As they drove toward John Love's woodworking shop, which was on the grounds of his family's orchard, Piper's stomach knotted up, quashing all those wonderful feelings. She knew the chances of Heaven being at her father's shop were small, but Heaven and her father both made jewelry, and Piper knew she spent time there.

She glanced at Harley, and he blew her a kiss. He was so patient with her. She didn't like the jealousy gnawing at her. It made her feel small, but she didn't know how to get rid of it without facing it head-on.

Facing it head-on meant admitting a weakness. A big one.

"I've never been in John's shop," Harley said. "I'm glad you suggested it."

She nodded, stewing over the images of Harley and Heaven she'd invented.

He reached across the seat and ran his hand down her arm. "Why do you look pissed?"

"If I tell you, I might have to kill you."

He laughed. "I kind of like being alive."

She glanced at him quickly as she drove, then focused on the road. "I like you alive, too."

"Wait. Do you hear that?" He cupped his ear and tilted his head. "I think I heard a wall crumbling down."

She laughed softly and said, "Don't push your luck, Dutch."

"Oh, I'm pushing it." He took her hand and pressed a kiss to the back of it. "I'm going to push it *good*."

She turned down the driveway toward Loves' Orchard, her nerves rattling more as she drove past the fruit and vegetable stand, nearing his shop. Two of the Loves' dogs were sleeping beneath the shade of a large tree. She followed the road past a row of fruit trees, telling herself she was being juvenile even thinking about Harley and Heaven. But when she turned down the road that led to John's shop, she felt like she might burst.

She pulled over and put the truck into park before reaching the shop, turned in her seat, and blurted out, "This will make me sound pathetic and jealous, and maybe I am, but I have to know. And I realize this is stupid, but it is what it is, and all this couple stuff is new for me, so I'm just going to say it. Did you and Heaven hook up?"

An incredulous sound fell from his lips, and he shook his head. "What? When?"

"When she was a senior in high school."

"Seriously?" Amusement rose in his eyes.

"I know how pathetic it is for me to ask, but you've fucked with my head, Harley. I can't stop picturing you doing all the things to her that you did to me. And that's your right. You can mess around with anyone you want to. I just think if I knew for sure, I could put it away, you know? Compartmentalize it in my head so I could stop thinking about it. So, did you hook up with her?"

"Define *hook up*."

"Please don't fuck with me, Harley. She calls you the *Muff Marauder*. I guess I should have known you had. Forget it."

"Whoa. She calls me *what*?"

"The Muff Marauder because you have such a big dick."

"Holy . . . I thought only guys made up shit like that." He turned toward her with a serious look in his eyes, holding her gaze. "I've got nothing to hide. One weekend when I was home from college, I met your brother and Zane at a party. She was there, and we got to talking. I gave her a ride home, and we made out, but I never even felt her up. She was looking to get laid, and I told you before, I'm not into meaningless sex and I wasn't back then, either. She got pissed and stormed out of the car. I had no idea she'd said we did *anything*."

"Well, she didn't explicitly say you had sex . . ."

"It doesn't matter whether she implied it or you jumped to that conclusion. I want to clear it up. I made out with girls when I was in high school, but I've only had sex with two women from Sweetwater. One of them moved away when I was a senior in high school, and I'm looking at the other. Like you, the people I've slept with aren't living in our gossip-filled town. I've dated a few women from—"

"Don't tell me any more. I only wanted to know about her because she's my friend. How do you know the people I've slept with don't live here?"

"Because I have ears and eyes, and if you think the Sweetwater gossip is only prevalent among the women, you're treacherously wrong. The pub is like a feeding ground for gossipers. Besides, I didn't know a single one of the guys you met there for your dates, except Zane's assistant the year he was filming that movie in town before he gave up acting. That shaggy-haired, chisel-faced, tatted-up guy."

"Patch Carver," she said, remembering how she'd gone to use the bathroom that night, and when she'd returned, she'd heard Harley in his office telling Patch that if he laid a hand on her he'd kill him. After Patch had left, she'd called Harley out on what he'd done. He'd said Patch wasn't good enough for her, and she'd told him to butt out of her personal life.

He hadn't butted out of her personal life, but he'd opened her eyes, and she'd been more selective about the guys she brought around, eventually stopping altogether. In fact, other than her date with Harley, she hadn't gone on a date since late last summer, when Harley had scared off another one of her *unworthy* dates.

Harley leaned closer and said, "It's not stupid or ridiculous that you're jealous. It means you dig me, Pipe, which I've known all along."

She scoffed, but the knee-jerk reaction felt wrong, and she closed her eyes, wishing she could take it back. When she opened them, Harley hadn't moved away. He was watching her with a small grin on his lips.

"This is all hard for you, isn't it?" he said compassionately. "All the things that go along with being in a relationship? The unexpected feelings? The way you suddenly see everything differently?"

She lifted one shoulder, feeling exposed.

"It's okay. It's hard for everyone. You just don't have much experience with it, so it feels bigger because it's so new." His gaze never wavered from hers as he said, "I appreciate you taking a chance with me, Piper, and I promise you won't regret it."

"How could I ever regret anything when you're so patient with me? Wait, actually, there is one thing I regret."

He braced himself with one hand on the door and the other on the seat and said, "Okay, lay it on me."

"I probably deserve that," she said lightly, and they both chuckled. What she was about to say wasn't light at all. The butterflies in her stomach must have spread, because as she reached across the seat and took Harley's hand in hers, she felt them fluttering in her chest, too. "I regret all the time I wasted when I could have been with you."

The minute they'd arrived at Harley's house after spending the afternoon shopping, Piper had raced upstairs to start working on the bathroom. She'd claimed to want to get a jump on the project, but Harley knew better. Her confession about regretting the time she'd wasted had been a giant leap, blowing baby steps right out of the water. He'd realized afterward that *neither* one of them had expected that reveal. He was sure she'd rushed upstairs because she was once again trying to climb back into her own headspace. She hadn't achieved that in the building-supply store, no thanks to him and his wandering lips. And John had been busy with a customer when they'd arrived at his shop, which gave Piper the perfect excuse to kick herself out of the holy-shit-did-I-really-say-that mode she'd gotten stuck in after her confession and switch to work mode. In the blink of an eye she'd gone from stealing nervous glances to being in full control, schooling Harley on the hallmarks of well-made wooden furniture and things to consider when buying a vanity, like storage and accessibility. By the time John had gotten to them, they'd already picked out a gorgeous maple vanity with three center drawers and two shelves beneath each sink. It was being delivered next week. But she'd been quiet on the drive home.

As Harley walked Jiggs down by the water, he wondered if Piper would ever *fit* into her old headspace the way she had before they'd come together. Being with her had changed him, but he'd expected it would. He'd had three years to think about those types of things. But he'd blindsided Piper with the depth of his emotions, and he felt a little bad seeing how it rattled her. That didn't mean he'd back off. Piper was strong. He didn't think there was anything she couldn't handle—and he knew she *wanted* to handle him.

He petted Jiggs, happy to be walking him again, and then they headed up toward the house. He made a quick call to touch base with his mother, and then he checked in with Delaney to see how she and the girls were doing. He'd already texted with Jasper, and he knew the bar was being attended to, which meant he had the rest of the weekend free to be with Piper. There was no other way he wanted to spend it.

The second he unhooked Jiggs's leash, his pooch sprinted up the stairs ahead of him. He hadn't imagined his dog falling as hard for Piper as he had, but he was glad.

Country music floated out of the bedroom, and he found Jiggs in the bathroom, watching Piper tile the shower. She was crouched on the floor, humming to the music as she pressed a tile to the adhesive. She'd already finished a few rows, and they looked fantastic. She'd changed into a tank top that had I BUILD COOL SHIT. WHAT'S YOUR SUPERPOWER? printed on the back and a pair of work jeans and boots she'd had in her overnight bag.

She didn't turn around as she said, "How long are you going to stare at me?"

"Hours. Days. *Years*, if you'll stay," he said, scratching Jiggs's head.

"You have a thing for watching women do manual labor?"

"I have a thing for *you*, and it gets bigger every time we're together."

She glanced over her shoulder with a heated look in her eyes. "*Bigger*, huh?"

He chuckled, and she went back to work, pressing another tile in place. "Want some help?"

"Have you tiled before?" she asked as she positioned another tile. "No."

"I can show you how, but I think crouching might be hard with your ankle, since we have to start at the bottom."

"That's probably true. How about if I wrangle up some dinner? Maybe by then you'll be closer to the top and I can help."

She remained crouched and swiveled around with a curious expression. "It really doesn't bother you that I do this type of work?"

"I'm proud as hell of the work you do. Does it bother you that I work at the pub?"

"No. I like spending time with you there."

He shrugged. "Then why would you ask if your work bothers me? Do I act like it bothers me?"

"No. It's just . . . Never mind." She turned back to tiling.

He went into the shower area, sat behind her, and pulled her onto his lap. "I'm not those other guys, babe, and I won't ever become them."

"I hope not. But we'll see." She started to get off his lap, but he pulled her back down. "*Harley*, the adhesive will dry."

He released her, and as she went to work, he said, "I wish I could go back however many years it would take to erase all that shit from your past so you wouldn't worry. But since I can't, I'm going to just keep being me, and hopefully one day you'll see that *this guy*, he's the real thing. The only people who change on you are the ones who are pretending in the first place."

Her hands stilled, her head bent forward, and her back rose with a deep inhalation. She set down the tile and moved onto his lap again. Her arms circled his neck, and she said, "You're a pretty kick-ass guy."

"You're just realizing that?"

"I've known it for a long time. I don't hang out with losers." She brushed her fingers through his hair and said, "I'm crazy about you, Harley."

The emotions in her voice made her words even more powerful.

"I don't think I've been pretending to be one thing or another my whole life," she said softly. "But I hope I can make a few changes, because I want to be able to tell you how I feel without fighting the walls that stack up inside me every time I think about it. I obviously have shit to work through."

"Like not spending time together at your place?"

She frowned. "I'm sorry. It's not you."

"Pipe, it's okay. I saw you cringe when I mentioned it this morning, and I heard what the girls said about your house. I'm okay with it. I'll never pressure you to do anything you don't want to. When you're ready, we'll spend time there, or we won't. That's up to you. I *adore* you, and I know I said I needed you to throw me a bone once in a while, but maybe that means *I* have some changing to do, too. I don't want to ever make you feel like you have to say things you're uncomfortable with. Just going out with me and letting us be a couple is *huge*. Having you stay over last night was like Christmas came early, and seeing you fall asleep with Jiggsy? I'm embarrassed to say that I was jealous of my own dog."

They both laughed.

"I love being with you, and *yes*, hearing you say you're crazy about me makes my entire world brighter," he said honestly. "But if you never say it again, it won't change how I feel about you."

She nodded. "In my heart, I believe that. But my heart has been wrong before."

"The great thing about hearts is that with the right care, they can heal." He pressed a kiss over her heart and as he kissed her belly, her stomach growled.

She covered it with her hand.

He moved her hand and kissed her there. "I'd better go make you dinner." He kissed her slow and deep, then said, "Don't worry about saying the right things. Just do what you feel and you can't go wrong."

CHAPTER NINETEEN

"HEY, HARLEY, I need a round of Sam Adams for table ten." Murphy Daly was from New England, and Harley came out as Ha*ah*ley. She was a few inches shy of six feet tall and as outgoing as she was beautiful. She was always doing different things with her long blond hair, and today she wore it in four thick braids, secured in a thick mass at the base of her neck.

"Coming right up." It was late Wednesday afternoon, and Harley's ankle was significantly better. When he spent too much time on his feet, he had twinges of pain, but for the most part, he was doing well and was glad to no longer need the walking boot or the crutches.

Murphy leaned on the bar, watching him as he filled the order. When he set the drinks on the bar, she collected them on her tray, her hazel eyes sailing over him. "I like this new look on you."

Harley rubbed his beard, which he'd trimmed that morning after leaving too many whisker burns on Piper's thighs.

"Not the *beard*," she said. "Although I do like the trim. I meant the I'm-way-too-happy-for-my-own-good vibe you're giving off these days. Piper must not only be good *to* you, but good *for* you."

"That she is," he said, and as Murphy went to deliver the drinks, he thought about Piper. She'd spent the night Saturday and Sunday, but Monday she'd insisted on going home to *find her own headspace* again.

Harley was learning that *finding her own headspace* really meant she was scared and needed to try to rein in her emotions. *Good luck with that*, he'd thought at the time. He knew there was no going back for *him*, but he hadn't been quite as certain about Piper when she'd shown up at the pub last night with Kase and a few of the guys they worked with and had barely given Harley a kiss hello. She sat at the bar watching the playoff game and joking with the guys as Harley tended to customers, just like old times. He'd started to wonder if she was making a statement, drawing some sort of line in the sand between work and their relationship. But he needn't have worried, because he'd *felt* the difference through her sexy glances and stolen touches across the bar. When she'd excused herself to the ladies' room, the secret invitation in her eyes had been seen only by him. They'd barely made it into his office before their mouths had collided. They were insatiable in the bedroom and out, but last night they'd kissed for only a minute before she'd said she missed him and Jiggs and that it had felt weird to sleep without him. She said she'd found her headspace and was free later if he wasn't too tired to see her.

As if that were even a consideration.

He'd realized that when she'd come into the pub, it hadn't been a line she was drawing in the sand that had her keeping her lips to herself. She'd been finding the courage to jump over that line.

Their insatiability had bled into all parts of their lives. They craved time together for more than just sex. When she'd come over last night, they'd taken Jiggs for a walk and then they'd driven out to an overlook on the edge of town and sat in the back of his truck on a blanket talking and kissing for hours. It was then that he'd realized there was no going back for her, either.

His cell phone rang, startling him from his reverie. Delaney's name appeared on the screen. "Hey, Dee. How are you feeling?"

"Good. It's going to take a while for the pain and fatigue to subside, but I'm better every day."

"I'm glad to hear it. Not a day passes that I don't thank God for *clear margins.*"

"Me too," she said. "Want to hear something weird? I was sitting outside with the girls. Jolie was kicking a soccer ball around and Sophie was playing songs she thought I'd like on Spotify, and suddenly I was hit by this overwhelming feeling of gratitude. I've been grateful every day—you know that—and the doctor had warned me that I'd go through a range of ups and downs, but this was overwhelming. I hadn't expected it to hit me so hard."

"Do you want me to come over?" Harley asked.

"No, I'm good, thanks. It was an incredible feeling. I'm *so* lucky, Harley. I get to see my girls grow older and see you fall in love. Hopefully the cancer won't come back anywhere else, so Mom won't have to bury her daughter."

"Aw, sis, don't talk about that." Harley walked around the bar and sat down at a table. After losing their father so quickly, they all knew just how lucky Delaney was. He'd been petrified when he'd learned of her diagnosis, and he hadn't been able to breathe right until after the surgery that cleared her.

"It's *big*, and I knew that. But now it's *real.*" She sniffled, and he knew she was crying.

"You sure you don't want me to come over?"

"Yes. These are happy tears. But it made me miss Marshall. What if I hadn't gotten lucky? I could have died without ever seeing him again."

"That didn't happen, and it's not going to."

He wanted to remind her that their brother had abandoned *them* a long time ago, and that he hadn't even been man enough to come back when their father had gotten sick and they'd needed him most. And although he'd never mention to Delaney that Marshall was probably the biggest reason Piper didn't trust men, the thought ate away at him with a vengeance.

"I know," she said. "It's just all so sad. When I was staying with Mom, she talked about him a lot. She misses him, and I think she worries that she'll grow old and die without ever seeing him again."

His mother never spoke of Marshall to Harley, and he knew it was because she had heard their argument the day of their father's funeral. What Harley wasn't sure of was whether she blamed him for Marshall leaving and never returning after their fight. That wasn't a conversation he wanted to have.

He didn't regret a word he'd said to Marshall.

"I don't know what to say about that." Harley pushed a hand through his hair.

"Neither do I, but I didn't call to bum you out. I wanted to ask if you sent me a gift in the mail."

"No. Why? Do you have a secret admirer?" he teased, knowing someone would have to go to a lot of trouble to keep a secret in Harmony Pointe or Sweetwater.

"I hope so." She laughed. "I just received a beautiful rose-gold warrior bracelet in the mail. There was no card and no return address, and the bracelet was wrapped in purple tissue paper." Delaney wrapped every gift she gave in purple tissue paper. "I bet it was one of the girls at work."

"Probably," he agreed.

"One last thing—can you be at Mom's a little early next Sunday for Mother's Day?"

"Sure. I ordered both of your presents a month ago. They're all wrapped and ready to be torn open."

"You're always so good about gifts. You know you don't have to get *me* anything. I'm not your mother."

"Yeah, whatever." Harley had picked up where her no-good ex had left off. He wasn't about to let a single Mother's Day pass without celebrating his sister as one of the best mothers he knew. "Why are we getting together early?"

"Mom said she wanted to go out to brunch instead of having us make it. I figured it's her day, might as well do things her way."

They talked for a little while longer, and then Harley got back to work. There was a steady flow of customers, which made the time pass quicker. When Ben Dalton walked through the door with his adorable daughter, Bea, in his arms, he was glad to see them. They hadn't played basketball in a few weeks, and Ben rarely came around the pub now that he had a daughter. Like his father, Ben was tall, dark, and serious, but he had a snarky side his father didn't, and he usually had a smile at the ready. But Ben's eyes were locked on Harley, and his face was all business. He wondered what was up. He'd checked the stock market that morning, and he knew he hadn't caused Ben any bad investments.

"How's it going, Ben?" Harley said as he came around the bar.

"It's going a'right," Ben said.

Bea bounced in Ben's arms, her chubby cheeks split by her babbles, "*Ha, Ha*," which was what she called Harley.

Harley tickled her chin, earning muffled giggles as she buried her face in Ben's neck. "And how are you, sweet thing?"

Bea was precious, with her daddy's big brown eyes, and wispy light brown hair that curled at the ends around her ears and the collar of her beige red-black-and-white checked dress. She had Ben—and Harley—wrapped around her tiny finger.

"I meant to get here a week ago, but kids have a way of screwing with even the best-laid plans." Ben kissed Bea's forehead. "Totally worth it, you know."

"After spending a couple weeks taking care of my nieces, I get it."

"I never got to thank you for letting Sophie spend the night. Bea had the time of her life, and Soph is just incredible. She acted like a big sister." Ben brushed another kiss to Bea's forehead and said, "There's something awesome about seeing your own child making friends."

Harley was looking forward to doing that one day. "Sophie had a blast. She's still talking about it. Piper and I appreciated the break, too."

Ben's face turned serious again.

"What's up, Ben? Is something wrong?"

"Just doing my brotherly duty," he said in a voice Harley imagined took control in many boardrooms. "You know how this goes down."

Harley chuckled. "You're here to give me *the talk*? Shake down the new boyfriend? Man, I did *not* see this coming. Isn't that usually Piper's job?"

"Yeah, but someone's got to have her back."

"I'm sure you know *I* do and *have* for a long time. Hell, everyone in this damn town knows how I feel about her. It just took your sister a while to realize it."

"She's a stubborn one," Ben said.

"She is. But I've got to tell you, Ben, bringing a cute little sidekick takes down your alpha cred. Give me that little princess."

He reached for Bea, and she thrust out her grabby little hands. "Ha, Ha."

"That's right, princess. Come to Uncle Harley." Harley loved children of any age, but he missed when his nieces were that small. He settled Bea in one arm and lifted her hand to his mouth, covering it with kisses. She giggled, pulling her hand away, then pushing her hand back to his mouth, urging, "*Muh, muh!*" which was little-girl speak for *more*.

"As you were saying," Harley said to Ben, noticing Murphy watching them from across the room.

"Just a minute." Ben stretched his neck from left to right, rolled his shoulders back, and crossed his arms, lowering his chin with his eyes trained on Harley.

It was all Harley could do to pretend his chuckles were all caused by Bea's playfulness as she tried to tug on his beard.

"Listen up, Dutch. Piper might seem tough, but she's more sensitive than you think. I can only remember seeing her cry once, and that was when we were little kids. I killed a caterpillar and she bawled . . . for like a minute. I was only about six, which means she was around five, and I remember thinking that was the worst minute of my life, because she never cried. But that wasn't the worst, because after those tears, she turned stone cold and beat the crap out of me. I haven't seen her cry since, but I know she's got tear ducts."

Harley laughed, then looked at Bea. "Your daddy is not very good at this shakedown stuff."

At hearing the word *daddy*, Bea reached for Ben. "*Dada, Dada!*"

"In a minute, Bea. I have to finish." His jaw clenched as he eyed his daughter. "Aw, hell. Give her to me."

Harley handed Bea over. "I get it, Ben. Don't mess with Piper's feelings, or I'll have you to deal with. I respect that. But I also respect Piper. I'd never purposefully hurt her, and we both know that if I did, she'd have my balls in a vise before I knew what hit me."

"You've got that right."

"Anything else you need to say? Because I've got a surprise planned for your sister, and I'd like to roll out of here in a few minutes."

"Yeah," Ben said with that snarky grin Harley knew so well. "If anyone asks, I rattled you, maybe shook you up a bit, left you thinking about things, like how you're determined to treat Piper right."

Harley nodded. "Of course."

Murphy came up behind Ben and said, "I'll back you up on that, Ben. You were freaking *badass*. I saw Harley shaking in his boots."

"Traitor," Harley teased.

Murphy turned her palms up. "Hey, he has hot single friends."

Harley looked at Ben and said, "I think this one needs both of us looking after her, or she's going to get herself in trouble."

"Maybe that trouble can be with Fletch." Murphy waggled her brows. "Or that big, broad, and broody guy who came in with you a few weeks ago, Porter."

"Don't you have customers to tend to?" Harley said, remembering the way Piper's face had lit up when Felicity had brought up Porter in the hospital.

Murphy tapped Ben's arm and then backed away, making the call-me signal with her hand to her ear.

Ben shook his head and said, "Please tell me we weren't ever like that."

"I was gone for years and have no idea what *you* were like then, but since I've been back? No way. We both knew who we wanted. We just had to play the game until they came around." Harley thought about that for a second and amended his comment. "Well, *I* had to. You got in your own damn way, waiting for the right time to suddenly make itself known before coming clean to Aurelia about how you felt. If it hadn't been for Bea, you might still be waiting."

"And if you hadn't hurt your ankle, you'd be keeping me company."

Harley cocked a grin and said, "Let's hear it for babies and bandages."

Piper's phone rang on her way to Harley's house early Wednesday evening, and Talia's name flashed on the screen. Piper knew exactly why she was calling. Her sister liked things tied up in pretty ribbons with perfect little bows, while Piper was cool with frayed edges and knotted strings. They'd disagreed often when they were younger, but her oldest sister didn't *argue*—she *reasoned*—while Piper's approach was more visceral and usually involved a loud voice. Their disagreements almost always ended with Talia looking at Piper like she was some type of alien with whom she simply couldn't relate and walking away. They'd gotten better at communicating with age.

She answered on Bluetooth. "Hi, Tal. What's up?"

"You *know* what's up," Talia said, sounding exasperated. "Every time I text you about how things went with Harley the other day, you reply with ridiculous texts that I don't understand."

Piper chuckled. As Piper had matured, she'd learned how to argue more rationally, but Piper would always be *Piper*, and in addition to frayed edges and knotted strings, she liked to rile up her siblings from time to time.

"Come on, Talia. I thought 'Can't text, I'm in a meat coma' was very clear."

"Yes, if you're on the *keto diet*!" Talia complained. "I know you guys worked things out, but did you find out why Harley wasn't sleeping with you?"

Piper turned onto the road that ran past the marina and realized if it weren't for Talia, she might still be stuck in a quandary with Harley.

Either that or she would have tied him to the bed and had her way with him.

"Yes, I did, but it wasn't because he wanted to take control of me. He wanted to know that he was special to me and not just another guy I banged." She glanced at the gift on the passenger seat and said, "That's kind of sweet, right?"

"That's really sweet, and he is special, right?"

"Yeah, Tal. He definitely is." She expected to feel a shiver of weirdness with the admission, but nothing tainted the happiness she felt.

"Oh, Piper. I'm so happy for both of you! Harley has been in love with you for a long time, and I always knew you'd fall in love despite yourself."

"Whoa, let's slow the *love* train, sis." She didn't know if Harley was *in love* with her, but she had no doubt that they were falling for each other in a big way. She'd been experiencing all of the characteristics of falling for a guy that her sisters had drilled into her head over the last couple of years—the fluttery feeling in her stomach, heart palpitations when they kissed, wanting to be with him every second, and feeling *off* when they were apart. But she didn't need the pressure to get married that she knew would come if her family got wind of how powerful her feelings were. She turned down Harley's street and quickly changed the subject. "How are things with Derek and Jonah? Will they be at Mom's for Mother's Day next weekend?"

"They'll be there, and they're doing great. I'm so glad we opened the center. Jonah has friends now that he sees every day, and in his lucid moments, he enjoys them. It's turning out to be everything Derek had hoped it would."

"That's wonderful. I know how hard he worked for this." When Talia met Derek, he'd been on the cusp of making his dream come true. He'd been working as an erotic dancer and bartender at a club in Harmony Pointe to earn money to care for his father and to start the adult-daycare center. Though Derek hadn't sought out investors, Ben had seen potential in the business, and he'd offered to invest as a silent partner, which had allowed Derek to remain in control and not deplete his savings. Piper and their father had handled the renovations to bring his dream to fruition.

Piper pulled into Harley's driveway and cut the engine. "I have to go, Tal. I just got to my *boyfriend's* house."

"I still can't believe that you have a real boyfriend. You haven't had one since . . . Oh my gosh, Piper! Since *Marshall*? Can that be right?"

A flutter of discomfort rattled her. She'd been trying not to think about Marshall, mainly because he wasn't a happy memory for her, but also because she wondered if her having dated Marshall bothered Harley. He'd mentioned his brother the other day when he'd spoken of self-sabotage, and that had stung. But he'd quickly soothed that sting by using his experiences with Marshall to understand how Piper's mind worked and help her understand, too. That he thought she was *anything* like Marshall bothered her, but there *was* an element of truth about her pushing people away. She was working on that.

"Yes," she answered. "But don't make a thing out of it."

"What? That you have now run through all the Dutch men in Sweetwater?" Talia laughed at her own joke. "I'm just kidding, but it's *true*."

"*Goodbye*, Talia." She ended the call and grabbed the gift from the other seat, wondering if she should bring up Marshall with Harley and kick that big old elephant to the center of the room.

She chewed on that thought as she climbed from the truck with the gift for Harley in her hand. A lantern glowed from the top step of the front porch. As she approached, she noticed a note tucked under a rock behind it. She set the rock to the side, scanning Harley's distinctly *male* handwriting. The note was written in pencil. Although each letter was perfectly crafted with tall, strong vertical strokes and perfectly rounded elements, the words were half-printed, half-cursive, as if he'd been in a hurry.

Pipe, you know where this half of our coupledom will be waiting. H

Piper usually hated games, and she had no idea what Harley was talking about, but a thrill tiptoed through her. She looked around for clues of where he was waiting. His truck was there, which meant he was on the property, and he'd left a lantern, which she assumed meant she needed to walk somewhere. She sat on the steps, mulling over her dilemma, and ruled out the obvious choice of Dutch's Pub.

Her mind drew a blank. She and Harley didn't have a special place.

That realization bothered her. Didn't most couples have special places? She guessed the pub was sort of their special place. It was where they'd spent so much time together, where they'd found each other . . .

She glanced at her truck and debated driving there, but quickly nixed that idea because he wouldn't have walked there. She read the note again, and her mind sifted through their conversations about being a couple.

I want to be with you . . . Check. They were together every night.

I want to be the guy you come to see at Dutch's . . . Check.

I want to go out with you as a couple, with other couples, and do more than play basketball. She thought of the night they'd gone out with Willow, Zane, Remi, and Mason and mentally checked that one off, too.

I want to spend time together at night doing normal things people do when they're in a relationship, like having dinner and talking about what they want out of life. Their hockey date was always on her mind. It was a night she'd never forget. Check.

I want to go out on my boat with you and go fishing and swimming and make love to you under the stars. Checkmate!

She shot to her feet, grabbed the lantern, and ran down the path toward the dock. As she passed a tree that had a beach towel hanging from a branch, she snagged it without slowing down. Her heart raced as she came to the crest of the hill behind his house and looked out at the dock. She clutched the towel to her belly, taking in strings of pretty blue lights trailing from post to post, illuminating a number of indiscernible items on the dock that formed a trail to the boat. Misty light rained down on Harley from a lantern hanging from the roof of the slip. His eyes caught hers, and her heart turned over in her chest, kicking her legs into gear. She ran down the path, nearly tripping over a small rosebush in a pretty blue container at the entrance to the dock. A rosebush! She'd never loved cut flowers because they died, and she couldn't remember if she'd ever mentioned that to Harley, but she must have. She picked it up and hurried to the next item on her trail to the best boyfriend in the world, a bottle of wine in a wine caddy built to look like a contractor, complete with a metal shirt, a toolbox in one hand, and a hammer in the other. She wasn't big on wine, but she loved this so much, she'd drink wine every day just to remember this moment.

She was wrong about hating games. She *loved* this game!

She rushed to the next item, picking up a fishing pole, and a few feet from there she retrieved a box of condoms. She was grinning so hard her cheeks hurt as she arrived at the boat juggling all her goodies.

"Oh my God, Harley!" She thrust her arms, full of goodies, toward him and said, "*Takeittakeittakeit!*"

He laughed as he took the plant from her arms and set it behind him.

"I don't know what to say! Thank you doesn't seem big enough," she said as he took more gifts from her hands. "Nobody's ever done anything like this for me before! *Hurry!* Get me *in* there! I need to be with you!"

He lifted her into the boat as if she were light as a feather and set her down beside a picnic basket and a thick blue blanket. She set the rest of the gifts down as fast as she could and launched herself into his arms, crushing her mouth to his. He tasted like new adventures, breezy evenings, and heart-thundering happiness.

"Thank you," she said between kisses.

As her toes touched down again, he said, "I brought dinner. Bacon burgers and cheese fries, just the way you like them."

"Oh, Harley!" she said, suddenly getting all choked up.

He pressed his lips to hers again and said, "In case you're wondering, that's beer in the wine bottle. I couldn't find a six-pack caddy that looked like a contractor. I hope that's okay. I'll personally refill the bottle with beer as many times as we need to."

She couldn't stop smiling. "I love the wine caddy and the towel and *everything*. You got me a *rosebush*! How did you know that I don't love cut flowers?"

"You don't remember the guy who brought you a bouquet when he met you for a date at the pub?"

"That was ages ago." She remembered it clearly, because it was the last date she'd had before she went out with Harley.

"I'll never forget the way you looked at him like he'd lost his mind. You told him you didn't appreciate gifts that *died*, and later, after I sent him packing, you bitched about it being bad enough that your sister made a living killing plants and flowers."

She loved that he'd remembered, but that joy was chased by guilt at what she'd said about Bridgette. "Thank God Bridgette wasn't there to hear that. She's so good at what she does, and she loves it. I must have been having a *really* bad day to have admitted it in public like that."

"You said you were ready to give up on men." He brushed his thumb over her cheek and said, "I remember hoping you meant it about all men *except* me."

"I did" slipped out. "I mean, I didn't know how I felt about you then, but that was the last time I went out on a date until you came along and turned my world upside down. Now kiss me again before all this sappy stuff gets to me."

"I kind of like the sappy stuff getting to y—"

She went up on her toes, silencing him with the press of her lips.

A long while later, after anchoring the boat in the middle of the lake and enjoying dinner, they sat side by side in the moonlight with their fishing lines in the water. They were drinking beer straight from the wine bottle because Piper's incredible boyfriend who remembered everything they needed for dinner and a night of lovin' beneath the stars forgot to bring glasses. Sweetwater was a distant glimmer of lights on the horizon, and Piper couldn't imagine a more perfect evening.

She tightened the slack on her line and said, "Remi texted earlier about the volunteer day to put together the duffels and birthday boxes. It was supposed to be two weeks from yesterday, but they had to change it to two weeks from today. Do you think you can still make it?"

"Absolutely. Jasper wants extra hours, and my two part-time bartenders are always happy to take on more."

"Good. What they're doing for foster kids is so important. I love being a part of it. It's like fate dropped Mason into Remi's life at the perfect moment. They're so similar, and it's great that they both want to foster children and maybe have their own."

"How about you, Pipe?"

"Me? I'm afraid Mason's out of luck, because fate already dropped a man into my life at the perfect time, and I have no plans of swapping him out."

"I'm damn glad about that, even though it's not what I meant." He leaned in and kissed her. "I know you aren't looking to get married, but you're great with kids. Do you want a family one day?"

"That's a hard question."

"Why?" He held her gaze, and she sensed that he might not let her out of answering.

"Because I want a family, but I also want my career. It might be hard to be several months pregnant in my line of work, or even a few weeks pregnant, because my crew might treat me different." She shrugged. "I don't know the answer, but since I don't want to get married, I might just be Auntie Piper forever."

He wiggled his fishing line and said, "Lots of mothers have careers. Look at our sisters. I know your job is different, but that doesn't mean you have to give it up if you want to have kids. Would it be so bad to manage projects instead of working hands-on for a few months?"

"I don't know. It's too much to think about right now."

"Okay, but I just want to throw out there that getting married isn't a prerequisite for having children."

"Just ask Ben, right?" She lifted her line, reeling in the slack, and hoped he would accept the subtle change in subject.

"Exactly. Speaking of Ben, he paid me a visit at the pub today."

"Oh yeah? How is my big brother?"

"He's good. He came to make sure my intentions were honorable."

Piper snort-laughed. "*Ben* did? I'd like to have been a fly on the wall for that conversation. You've got fifty pounds on him."

"It's not about size, babe."

"Here's a hint. Women lie." She arched a brow and said, "It's *always* about size."

He chuckled. "Let me rephrase that. Making a point is not about the size of the man; it's about respect. He did good by you. You should be proud of him."

"I'm always proud of him. I could never do all the things he does. Ben is a financial genius, and though it hasn't been easy, he's stepped up for Bea and handled fatherhood like he handles everything else—with humor, heart, and a boatload of patience. Like you do."

The appreciation in his eyes warmed her all over.

"Thanks, babe. Your brother's good with numbers, but so are you. You're also good with tools, with your body, my body . . ."

All her best parts sizzled with the smoldering look he was casting her way, and she leaned in for another kiss.

When their lips parted, he said, "Ben brought Bea with him."

So much for sizzling. "To give you a stern talking-to? That must have been hilarious."

"She's a doll." He gazed out over the water for a long moment, and then he said, "You'd make a great mom, Piper. It would be a shame for you to miss out on having a family of your own."

She didn't want to get into a heavy discussion when they'd had such a wonderful night, so she said, "What would be a shame is if we don't catch any fish tonight." They hadn't caught anything, and she didn't care. Just being with Harley was enough for her.

Harley's face turned serious as he reeled in his line. "Feel like swimming?"

"I kind of love sitting here with you. Unless you want to swim?"

"Nope." He rebaited his line and cast it out again. "I'm loving this, too. I hope you don't feel like I was pressuring you just now."

"I don't. You know how I feel about marriage. It's right for a lot of people, but it scares the hell out of me. I don't want to get married and wake up one day and find that my marriage has fallen apart because I'm not good at the whole wife/mother thing. I'm happier than I've ever been right now, with *you*, Harley. Please don't make me think about things that are hard to figure out."

Moonlight reflected in his eyes as he leaned in for a kiss, stopping with his lips a breath away from hers, and said, "How about hard *things*? Is that an appropriate topic for tonight?"

"Absolutely. But you should know that I like doing *this* with you, too—talking, fishing, having dinner. It's so peaceful out here, it's impossible to be stressed about anything. Kind of like being with you."

"You'd better be careful; that's two pretty big reveals you've made tonight."

"That's okay. Anything said out on the water stays on the water. And I'm counting on you sticking to that because I have one more thing I want to say, but if you make a big deal out of it, I can't guarantee how I'll react."

His lips tipped up with warm, loving acceptance. "I won't say a word."

"Okay." She looked out at her fishing line and said, "The reason I spent so much time at the pub after you moved back to Sweetwater is because I like being with you." She pressed her side against his and said, "I think I hid it even from myself, but ever since you moved back, at the end of a long day, you're the person I've wanted to spend time with."

He peered around her back, then glanced to his left.

"What are you looking for?"

"Making sure no one has a gun to your head."

She pressed a kiss to his shoulder and said, "No gun, just all this weird shit going on in my head that needs to get out. *Anyway*," she said loudly, letting him know they were *done* with that conversation, "it's been a long time since I've been out on the lake fishing at night. I miss it."

"You used to go out in your rowboat and fish, didn't you?"

"That was a *long* time ago." She reeled in her line, rebaited it, and cast it out again. She leaned over the edge of the boat and rinsed her fingers. "Can I tell you a secret?"

"You can tell me anything."

"The boat Marshall and I started building together wasn't destroyed in a storm. I smashed it at the Mad House."

"I wondered about that." He looked over and said, "I saw a piece of it in the barn when we were there with the girls. That bright blue paint gave it away."

"Why didn't you say anything?"

He shrugged. "I didn't want to pry."

"Harley, we're in a relationship and the whole town is talking about us. I think it's okay for you to pry."

"Maybe there are some things I don't need to know."

They fished in silence for a little while, each lost in their own thoughts. But the need to clear the air about Marshall got the best of her, and she said, "Does it bother you that I went out with your brother?"

Harley's chest expanded as he inhaled a long breath. He shook his head as he exhaled. "You were just kids."

"I know, but so were you and Heaven. Does it bother you?"

"The fact that you went out with him doesn't bother me, but it bothers me that he hurt you."

"Well, that makes two of us. The only reason I kept that piece of the boat was because I had worked so hard to build it."

"You mean you and Marshall worked hard," he corrected her.

"*No.* Marshall spent most of the time checking me out, trying to look busy, or talking with his friends. I have no idea how he finished building it when I had that flu. To be honest, it kind of pissed me off that he could pull his shit together over those five days while I was sick, when for two months he'd barely lifted a finger. But I was thankful he'd finished it. I think it was the only good thing that came out of our relationship." She reeled in her fishing line and set the rod aside. "That's not true. Destroying the boat was good, too. And having that constant reminder in the barn about why I don't want to change who I am is a good thing for me."

"How did you two even end up together? You're so different."

"On a dare," she said, remembering the way Marshall had challenged her to one date. "'One date,' he said. 'Give me one date and see what happens.' What happened was that I kept trying to be the person he wanted, and it was a big mistake."

"He's a fool. I love who you are, Pipe." He turned his handsome face toward her and said, "When I look at you, I see the brazen blonde who strutted into the pub those first few weeks I was back and took the time to ask about how my family and I were doing. The girl who showed up with a plow on the front of her truck after every snowstorm because she said she was in the area and thought she'd clear the parking lot—and then proceeded to go to my mother's and sister's houses to make sure their driveways were clear. I see the woman who helped me see the light on some of my saddest days after I lost my dad and wasn't sure I'd ever be happy again."

She was getting all choked up again.

"I see the woman who has spent three years giving me hell about everything from sports to the way I pour her drinks. The woman who I thought was kidding when she told me she was going to join me and the guys for a game of basketball, then proved why she was damn near better than all of us." His gaze moved slowly over her face, and then he said, "When I look at you, I can't see past you. You're *all* I see."

The emotions in his voice and in his eyes felt as tangible as the man beside her. She wrapped her arms around one of his and rested her head on his shoulder. "Your brother never saw *me* at all."

He pressed a kiss to her head and reeled in his fishing line.

"Thank you again for tonight, and for all the gifts, and dinner, and talking. I *love* this night. If I were the type of girl to dream about romantic nights, this would be on the top of my dream list. You did good, Dutch. Like our first da—Oh my *gosh*! You never opened your present."

"Present?" he asked, setting his fishing pole aside.

"Yes! I totally forgot I brought you one!" She jumped to her feet to retrieve his gift, and he moved to the bench seats.

She stood before him, nerves tingling as she fidgeted with the gift. "When I got you this, I didn't expect to find you on the boat with a big surprise planned. It seems silly now, but in my defense, I'm new at choosing boyfriend gifts."

He pulled her down to his lap, and his strong arms circled her. She *loved* how he always wanted her *right there* with him.

"Babe, you got me something and it's not my birthday. You can't possibly know how much this means to me, no matter what it is."

"Oh yes I can," she said, looking at the rosebush and all the wonderful gifts he'd given her. "You say that now, but this gift isn't nearly as good as all the things you gave me."

She handed him the gift and held her breath as he opened the framed picture of them from their first date, when they were on the kiss cam. They were sticking out their tongues and wiggling their hands with the hang-loose hand gesture. She'd written *World's Best First Date* on the frame with a Sharpie, and she'd used Photoshop to add *Piper + Harley* and the date to the picture.

Laughter bubbled out of him. "Babe, this is *fantastic!*"

She was elated by his response. "Since you have those pictures of us on your fridge, I thought you should have one of us now that we're a couple."

"I can't get over this. It's *awesome!*" He was smiling so hard, his whole face brightened. "How did you get it?"

"I found the nerd-reel footage on YouTube and took a screenshot. Then I added our names and the date using Photoshop."

"I *love* it, and I *love* that you took the time to find the picture, added the text, and wrote on the frame. I want another one for my desk at Dutch's and a big one to hang up behind the bar."

"You are *not* doing that," she said with a laugh. "Nobody wants to see us being fools."

"Oh, I'm doing it." He set the picture down and said, "Right after I do *you*."

In the next breath she was lying on the bench, pinned beneath his big, delicious body, and he was gazing down at her with a wicked glint in his eyes, like he wanted to gobble her up.

And *boy*, did she want him to.

His mouth swooped down, capturing hers urgently, igniting the inferno that was always simmering between them. He made guttural, appreciative noises, each one amping up her arousal. His hands moved roughly over her body from breast to hip and back up again, touching her like he couldn't get enough and was powerless to hold anything back. He rocked his hard shaft against her center, creating exquisite friction that had her angling her body and bowing up beneath him to catch every second of it. He broke their kisses off and stripped off her shirt, groaning at the sight of her bare breasts. She'd never tire of the way he adored her breasts. His desire sent fire and something bigger through her veins, and she pushed at his shirt. He stripped it off and lowered his mouth over one breast, sucking so hard she felt it between her legs.

"Oh, *Harley*—"

"Fuck, baby. When you do that it makes me want to tear off your clothes and take you hard."

"Do it," she demanded.

He reached between them and struggled with her button-fly jeans. They were an old pair, and difficult to undo. She took over, and they both stood and stripped off their clothes. He grabbed the box of condoms. As he opened the box, she pushed his chest, sending him down to his ass on the bench. Every second seemed like an eternity as he tore open the condom. She stood before him, knowing how much he loved seeing her touch herself, and put her hand between her legs as he sheathed his length. He reached for her, curling his big hand around the curve of her hip, drawing her to him. His eyes flamed as she straddled him. She didn't even try to stifle the moan that escaped as she sank down on his thick cock. He grabbed her ass with both hands as she rode him hard and fast. When his mouth clamped down over her breast, she nearly came, but she held back. She loved riding him, taking him so deep the mix of pain and pleasure sent electricity arcing through her. Her thoughts fractured as he sucked and fucked until she was barely breathing. Her entire body felt like one raw nerve. He brought one hand between them, expertly stroking the spot that sent the world careening away. She bucked and thrust as he clamped his hands around her waist, helping her move faster along his shaft, extending and magnifying her pleasure. Her vision blurred, their moans and groans filling the air as he took control and sent her soaring again. She cried out his name and he was right there with her.

"Piper, *fuck, Piper*..."

They rode out their pleasure to the very last shudder and collapsed in each other's arms. Their breathing was erratic, their hearts pounding frantically as they lay bound together in the blissful aftermath of their lovemaking.

Sometime later, when her vision finally cleared, Piper rested her head on Harley's shoulder, their bodies still connected, as she panted out, "Where have you been all my life?"

"Right here, Pipe." His hot breath swept across her neck. "Always right here."

Lord help her. She didn't just love that night.

She was falling in love with Harley Dutch.

CHAPTER TWENTY

MOTHER'S DAY MORNING arrived with sunshine and the promise of a warm day, and Piper's family was celebrating with brunch at Willow and Zane's house. Everyone was there, including Bodhi's mother, Alisha, and Aurelia's grandmother, Flossie, who had stepped in to raise Aurelia after Aurelia's mother had died during childbirth. Remi and Mason, honorary members of the Dalton family, were also there. Piper sat at the patio table with Emerson on her lap, feeling Harley's absence like a missing limb. He would get a kick out of Bea toddling across the yard after Louie, who was blowing bubbles. Every few steps, Bea plopped onto her bottom, giggling. It had been a week and a half since their romantic night on the boat, and in that time Piper's feelings had taken root and blossomed so completely, she was having trouble keeping them in check.

Being around her family and friends, who literally *emanated* love, wasn't helping.

Piper pressed a kiss to the top of Emerson's head, inhaling her sweet baby scent. Her light brown hair was fine as silk, and she had Bodhi's serious dark eyes. Piper had been thinking about what Harley had said about having children. She knew how badly he wanted a family, but until he'd come into her life as *the man in her life*, she hadn't thought too much about wanting children of her own. She loved babies and children, but fitting them into her busy life would be complicated. That used to be enough to stop her from thinking about it. But now she couldn't stop analyzing her feelings on the topic. Every time she thought about having children with Harley, she imagined him with their babies in his arms, the joy she knew he'd exude, and her insides fluttered. She hadn't realized how easy it was to get carried away with a fantasy when her heart was involved. She was getting way ahead of herself.

She tried to push away those thoughts and focus on the conversation around the table. Flossie was talking a mile a minute, sharing stories about her favorite Mother's Day moments. Across the table, Ben and Aurelia fed each other grapes, stealing kisses between bites. This was Aurelia's first Mother's Day as Bea's adoptive mother, and Ben had given her diamond earrings in the shape of the letter *B*. Piper had enjoyed teasing her brother about who that *B* actually stood for. His love for Aurelia and their daughter was an incredible thing to watch.

And . . . Now she was thinking about Harley and kids again.

Remi sat on Mason's lap in the chair next to Ben, and across the yard, Derek and Talia sat shoulder to shoulder at a picnic table beneath a big oak tree with Derek's father, Jonah, chatting with Bridgette, Bodhi, and Alisha. Bodhi had his arm around Bridgette, and their heads were touching, as if they were sharing secrets. Piper thought of Harley and the way he often touched his forehead to hers or rested it on her shoulder when he was still perched above her after they made love. She liked those intimate touches, and damn it, he should be there with them. He was her other half, just as important as Zane, Derek, Bodhi, or Mason. He felt like family, too. She should have invited him, or gone with him to celebrate with his family. She would not make that mistake again.

Willow laughed, drawing Piper's attention to the blanket where she and Zane were lying, holding hands and looking up at the sky. Zane leaned over and kissed her, driving Piper's longing even deeper.

"And then there was the time Aurelia made me a special Mother's Day shirt in second grade with finger paints." Flossie looked around the table with an impish grin.

Flossie was tiny at just under five feet, but her personality and flair for fashion made her seem bigger than life. Today she wore a pair of black culottes with a bright yellow blouse and a colorful fabric belt tied around her waist. Her makeup was perfectly applied, and her long silver hair was braided and secured in a bun on the top of her head. Piper couldn't imagine putting all that energy into clothes, hair, or makeup, but Flossie made it look easy.

"All the other mothers were wearing shirts with colorful streaks all over them, but not me," Flossie said, eyeing Aurelia. "I was the talk of the town when I wore *my* shirt with a bright green handprint over each breast. It was spectacular, and I wore it proudly."

Everyone laughed.

Aurelia covered her face and said, "I will *never* live that down."

"Nonsense, bubbelah." Flossie reached across the table and patted Aurelia's hand. "You mean nobody else's child will ever live *up* to your *perfect* artwork."

Piper's father cleared his throat. He was sitting at the head of the table, looking at Ben. "There was a time when Ben tried his hand at painting."

"Do *not* go there, Dad," Ben said sternly.

Aurelia said, "Now you *have* to tell us."

"*Dad*," Ben warned, glowering at their father.

Their father held up his hands in surrender. "The man has spoken, and he can withhold a grandchild if I don't listen."

Piper rolled her eyes and said, "Ben and Zane got into Dad's paints in the basement. They stripped naked and painted the walls, the floors, *and* each other."

Everyone laughed, except Ben, who looked like he wanted to scalp Piper.

"What's so funny?" Zane asked as he and Willow joined them.

"We were just talking about the day Piper streaked down Main Street," Ben said with a victorious grin.

Piper scowled at him. She'd only recently learned that her mother had known about that particular indiscretion, but by the wide-eyed look her father was giving her, he must have been kept in the dark. "It was on a *dare*, and it was dark out. I'm sure no one saw me."

Willow crouched in front of Piper to play with Emerson and said, "Except Marshall."

"Whatever," Piper said.

"Does Harley know about this naked street romp?" Ben asked, pulling his phone from his pocket. "I bet he'd like to."

"It was not a *romp!*" Piper exclaimed.

"*Benjamin.*" Their father shook his head, and Ben set the phone on the table.

Piper had no idea if Harley knew about her streaking, or if he'd care after all these years. All she knew for sure was that after nearly a month of spending every free minute with him, it sucked being apart. Those feelings made her a little anxious, and snappy. She snagged two of Emerson's toys from the table—a plastic horse and a noisy cloth doll that made different sounds depending on where she touched—and said, "On that note, I think I'll take a walk with Emerson."

She sauntered over to Ben and bent to speak in his ear. "The only reason I'm letting that comment go is because you had my back with Harley. Watch yourself, because I know your secrets." She didn't, but the worry in Ben's eyes was exactly what she'd hoped for.

"Ben, remember that girl you kissed behind the stage in sixth grade? The one who ran away laughing?" Zane teased as Piper walked away.

Piper strolled around the yard with Emerson, trying to weed through her thoughts, which was difficult with her adorable, apple-cheeked niece pulling on her hair and making sweet baby noises. "Can't you be annoying or something? It's hard to stop thinking about babies and futures when you're so freaking cute."

She crossed the yard and set Emerson on the blanket Willow and Zane had abandoned, settling in across from her. Emerson was adorable in a pink shirt and white leggings. Her pudgy little feet were bare, and Piper couldn't resist tickling them. Emerson's giggles filled the air.

"Uncle Harley would sure get a kick out of you."

Uncle Harley . . .

She kept telling herself she didn't want to change, but she wasn't sure she had control of that anymore. She never thought she'd want to disregard her steadfast rule about keeping her home *man-free*, but the night she and Harley had gone out on the boat, she'd been *this close* to inviting him to stay over. But when she'd tried, she'd gotten nervous and had let it go.

She'd thought about asking him every single day since. She *wanted* to, but their lives were so in sync, she didn't want to take a chance of rocking the boat. Staying at his place had become a *given* rather than an exception, and she liked it that way. She liked having her things there, showering in his new bathroom—which was gorgeous and a much more reasonable size for Harley—and knowing she'd wake up in his arms. She felt herself smiling as she thought of the way they slept, tangled up like they were one being. It seemed impossible that she'd gone from thrashing around in her bed to snuggling a man all night long.

Impossibly wonderful.

But it was not only possible; it was *real*. She couldn't imagine her life without Harley, or even Jiggs, in it, but if she invited him to spend the night at her house, in her *bed*, it would take away the only place she could hide if things went bad between them.

She saw her father heading her way and wondered if she and Harley could ever be as lucky as her parents were. To wake up thirty-plus years from now to grayer, wrinkled versions of themselves who were even more in love than ever. She swallowed hard, her pulse quickening with the thought.

"Mind if I sit with you?" her father asked.

"Not at all."

He sat beside her and waved at Emerson, who was chewing on her plastic horse, watching them. "She sure has changed, hasn't she? Sitting up, curious about everything. I swear they change fast at this age. Look at Bea, already walking. Time sure flew by." He motioned toward the picnic table, where Bea was toddling around the table, stopping at each person and patting their legs. Louie was sitting on Jonah's lap waving his hands like he was telling a story.

"When do all those fast changes stop?" Piper asked. "It seems like we go through our lives, changing this way or that, but one day we wake up and we know exactly who we are. Like everything is suddenly set and we know what paths we're supposed to take and where we'll end up. When is that, do you think?"

"I think it's different for everyone. You changed a lot in high school, but Bridgette, for example, knew exactly who she was from the time she was a little girl. She found different parts of herself as her life changed, but she's still the risk taker who ran away to marry a musician, and she always will be."

"But she's given up so much of herself and her freedom to be where she is."

Piper didn't feel like she'd given up a thing to be with Harley, and she felt lucky because of it. Their friendship had given them a rock-solid foundation, putting them years ahead of most couples, who learned about each other while dating. By the time they'd come together as a couple, they already knew what they had in common, how they differed, and what they liked—*loved?*—about each other. But they didn't have children, and she knew that would change everything.

"Don't be so sure," her father said. "I'd imagine when Bridgette's children are all grown up, she and Bodhi will go on some exciting adventures together and rediscover all the parts of herself she put aside to raise their children."

Emerson stuck her hands out, reaching for Piper. Piper picked her up and nuzzled against her cheek, kissing it repeatedly, causing the munchkin to squeal with delight.

"I totally get it, you know, the appeal of raising tiny humans," Piper said, settling Emerson on her lap with the noisy doll. "But do you think Bridgette regrets that she no longer has all that freedom *now*?"

"You tell me."

She followed her father's gaze back to the picnic table, where Bodhi was helping Bridgette to her feet. His arm circled her waist as he lowered his lips to hers. After a kiss, Bridgette headed their way with a dreamy expression on her face. Piper knew her sisters were happy, and they loved being wives. Bridgette loved being a mother, and she was good at it. She'd given up freedoms, but Harley was right—she hadn't given up her career to make it happen, and neither had Delaney or Aurelia. Although Ben had made major changes to his life when Bea and Aurelia had become part of it.

"I think you're looking at things from a builder's perspective," her father said. "You see the changes in Bridgette as tearing out the old and rebuilding with new, different stock."

"Because it seems that way to me. She might be the same person she was inside, or some version of that, but she's no longer a musical groupie."

"She's grown up, sweetheart. That would have happened with or without marriage and babies."

"I guess. But it seems like everyone's life changes a *lot* when they get serious enough to get married. Look at Ben. He moved from an enormous house to a two-bedroom apartment in the next town over to be with Aurelia. He completely revamped his workload, delegating travel and numerous responsibilities so he could be there for her and Bea. I think he did the right thing, and he's obviously happy, but what if one day he resents them for that?"

"Honey, your brother and sisters are stronger than you give them credit for. Ben built a billion-dollar business from the ground up. He gave it everything he had, and he still does, but what he has to give a business has changed. Do you really think he'd ever make changes he didn't *want* to make? Bea came into his life, and suddenly he had a chance to love the daughter he never realized he'd had, and to love and be loved by the *only* woman he'd ever wanted as his wife." Her father paused as Bridgette approached.

"I came to borrow our little one long enough to nurse her before we have brunch," Bridgette said.

"*Mamamamama.*" Emerson bounced on Piper's lap.

Piper smothered her chubby cheeks with kisses and handed her over to Bridgette, saying, "Thanks for sharing her."

"Anytime." Bridgette rubbed noses with Emerson and said, "Did you have fun with Grandpa and Auntie Piper?"

After Bridgette walked away, her father said, "Honey, about Ben. He didn't change because Aurelia asked him to or because the courts demanded it for his daughter. He discovered parts of himself that had *always* been there, and he rearranged his life in such a way that would allow him to become the man *he* wanted to be for them."

"I guess that's true." Her mother's laughter sailed loudly through the air. "Did you change when you met Mom?"

Her father laughed. "Believe it or not, you and Bridgette are a lot like your old man."

"That's weird, because Bridge and I are nothing alike."

"Hm. I'm not so sure. But I never thought I'd settle down. I used to love to have fun and run around with women before I met your mother. I was pretty wild."

Piper tried to stifle her disbelieving chuckle.

"I *was*. Just ask your mother, or better yet, don't. I don't want to relive those years. You asked if I changed when I met her, and the answer is yes, but my changes came from within. When I looked in the mirror, I didn't see the man she deserved. It was simple. I loved her, and I wanted her to be proud to be with me."

"Did you want Mom to change when you met her?"

"Never. She was the brightest star in the sky, and I wanted to reach her so badly, I'd have climbed mountains, swam across oceans. I needed your mother's earthiness in my life. She centered me in a way I never knew I needed. We had wild times together, and as the years passed, I found a more serious and responsible side of myself. An undiscovered part of myself that had always been there, just like Ben and the rest of your siblings have. I just lost touch with that responsible side of myself for a while when my father lost his job and things got hairy, which was about the time I met your mom. But we don't need to talk about that. Here's a bit of reality for you, pumpkin. If your mother told me she wanted me to get out of the contracting business and move to Africa, or take a flight to the moon, I'd do it, because other than our children and grandchildren, she's all that matters."

"You'd give up contracting?" Piper couldn't imagine that.

"In a heartbeat, and here's why." He glanced lovingly at her mother; then he looked thoughtfully at Piper and said, "I was worried about retiring from my position with the university to start Dalton Contracting. Starting a business is risky, as you know. We had to take those loans, and there was always the chance that we could fail. But your mother convinced me to take those risks. She made it clear that if we lost the house and had to start over, it wouldn't be the end of the world, because we have only one lifetime to fulfill our dreams. She said if I didn't try, I'd always wonder *what if* . . . If she wanted to travel, how could I leave *her* wondering *what if?*"

"So you'd change for her."

"No. I'd be the man *I* wanted to be for her. When you love someone, you want them to be happy. Does it take concessions? Sure. But that doesn't mean changing *who* you are. It means deciding whether you possess the qualities they need at that time, and shifting priorities. And sometimes *that* changes, too."

"That's what I'm worried about. I feel myself changing, and it kind of scares me."

"*Ah*, now I see where you were headed. We're talking about you and Harley."

She glanced around the yard and said, "I didn't expect it to be this easy."

"I don't imagine Harley thinks it's been easy."

"Dad! Am I *that* bad?"

"No, pumpkin. You're that smart and that strong. You won't put up with nonsense, and you demand respect. Those are good qualities. But if you think *any* of my girls are *easy*, you're wrong. It takes strong men to handle Dalton women."

"Come *on*. Bridge is as gentle as they come, and so is Talia. Even Willow is sweet, although she does have a mouth on her. I'm the only one who doesn't have a sweet bone in my body."

Her father's eyes narrowed. "I really don't like when you say things like that. You have spent a lifetime watching out for everyone else, making sure your sisters didn't get hurt, showing up to help everyone whenever they needed anything. You are a sweet, caring person, Piper."

"It's okay, Dad. I know who I am. I was just pointing out that my sisters are sweet, and that makes them much easier for relationships."

"You are tough by nature. I'll give you that. But you have to possess tenderness to be a bighearted, thoughtful person. You have to *care*. Look at how you jumped in to help Harley with the girls. Someone who isn't sweet wouldn't give up so much of their time to do that. Debra told your mother that Jolie raved about shopping with you for her dress, and we both know you hate shopping."

It was true, Piper wasn't a big shopper, but she'd had a great time Thursday afternoon shopping with the girls and Delaney. Jolie had been happier than Piper had seen her in a very long time, which Delaney had said was because she and Jolie had shared a good cry and Jolie had admitted how scared she'd been about losing her. Piper was glad Jolie was doing better, and she was glad to have been included in their shopping trip. The girls had been hilarious. Sophie picked out dresses, some of which were meant solely to make everyone laugh, and Jolie had been a great sport, trying on each and every one. In the end, they found a simple light purple dress for the father-daughter dance, and when Jolie refused every pair of sandals, Piper suggested ballet flats. Jolie had wrinkled her nose at that, too, just like Piper would have at that age. Piper went with her gut and suggested a pair of light purple Converse, earning a squeal and a hug from Jolie and an invitation to help Sophie shop for her dress when it was her turn to attend the father-daughter dance.

"Don't you see, pumpkin?" her father said. "The ease of a person doesn't have to do with if they're outwardly sweet or tough. Bridgette keeps the difficult stuff inside, and Bodhi had to work hard to unearth it. Talia is sweet, but you know she had a laundry list of things she wanted in a husband, and that wasn't easy for Derek to work around. And don't even get me started on Willow. Of all our children, I think Ben is the *easiest* when it comes to being in a relationship, but if you tell him that, I'll have to kill you."

She laughed. "We really are alike."

"Darn right. Listen, Piper. I know how your brain works. You think your sisters are easier than you. I know better than to try to change your opinion. But the bottom line is, *Easy* doesn't equate to *better*. Trust your gut with Harley. He knows exactly who you are, and he's a smart man. If he wanted *easy*, he'd never have pursued a Dalton."

"I guess you're right. Thank you for the perspective. But I'm worried about all this stuff I feel. I just saw him this morning, and I already miss him so much it hurts. Everyone has their significant other with them, and I didn't think to ask Harley if we could find a way to celebrate with both families. I'm *sucky* at this relationship stuff. But I want to try, Dad, which is new, and feels *crazy*, and you know I'm not a needy person. Is this the beginning of me changing everything about myself? Is this a red flag?"

"Dad!" Willow called from the patio. "Can you come here for a sec?"

Her father held up a finger in Willow's direction and said, "Sweetheart, I don't think you're changing who you are as much as you're finally letting someone get to you. In doing so, maybe you're discovering parts of yourself that have been hidden, too. And that can be scary."

"Tell me about it," she said as they pushed to their feet. "But good, you know? I like it. I like *him. A lot.*"

"Does he know that?" he asked.

The fluttery feeling returned, and she said, "Yes."

"Then you've opened that door. The question is, will you let him walk through it, or keep him out on the porch? What are you afraid of?"

For a second she wondered if her father knew she was worried about asking Harley to stay at her place, but quickly dismissed that idea. He designed and built homes for a living, of course he used similar metaphors.

"I don't know."

"The fact that you're scared at all tells me this man is important to you and you don't want to lose him. So you have to ask yourself, what's the worst that can happen? That he might track a little mud inside? He'll watch sports too loud?"

"I love sports, and I don't care about mud."

"Exactly. You know how to clean up messes, but broken hearts are a little more complicated." He winked and said, "Have a little faith."

Piper's head spun. Faith in who? Herself or Harley?

Maybe she needed to have both. Maybe she needed to take a giant leap of faith and just go with it. She pulled out her phone and called Harley, her heart racing. What if she was interrupting their brunch?

"Hey, babe. Everything okay?"

Just hearing his voice brought a wave of calm. "It's fine. I just . . . I wish I had thought ahead and found a way for us to be together and celebrate with both of our moms. I know that sounds clingy, but I miss you. I wish you were here."

"I miss you, too. Remember when I said I'd never let you down?"

"Mm-hm." He said it all the time, and she believed him.

"Turn around, darlin'."

Piper spun around just as Jolie and Sophie ran around the side of the house, heading for Roxie.

"Happy Mother's Day!" the girls hollered as they threw their arms around Piper's mother.

Harley came into view with Delaney and Debra, and Piper's heart nearly burst out of her chest. She ran across the yard and launched herself into his arms. He lifted her off her feet, kissing her as he spun them around like they were in a freaking Hallmark movie. Lord help her. She really was changing, because suddenly all that sappy Hallmark stuff seemed pretty damn good.

"*Uncle Harley and Piper sitting in a tree*," Sophie sang, sparking laughter as Willow and Remi joined her in singing the song, and Mason said, "Get a room!"

"Why are you here?" Piper asked, her feet dangling above the ground.

"Because our sneaky mothers conspired."

"I freaking love our mothers! I want you to spend the night at my house tonight," she blurted out before she lost her nerve.

Harley kissed her again as he sank down to the grass with her on his lap. "Say it again," he said. "I have to make sure I didn't make that up in my head."

"Don't push your luck. Just say you will."

"Oh, I will, baby, and you're never going to want me to leave."

Harley couldn't think of anything that could make the day any better. Brunch was delicious, the kids were entertaining, and the company was wonderful, but nothing compared to knowing Piper wanted him to stay at her place tonight. He glanced at her as she talked with Delaney, and his heart thumped a little harder. It felt good to be with Piper and her family today. This was the last place he'd expected his mother to take them when she'd said she'd chosen a place for brunch. But *man*, when they'd turned down Willow and Zane's street and Piper's truck had come into view, it was like a dream come true. He'd been missing her as badly as she'd missed him. He wasn't quite sure what was going on between their mothers *now*, as they sat at the other end of the table whispering like schoolgirls. They were definitely up to something, and if this brunch was any indication of what they could pull off, he was excited to see what else they had up their sleeves.

Harley felt a gentle pat on his leg and looked down to see a chubby little hand reaching for his plate. "Ah, sneaky Bea." He lifted her onto his lap, and she snagged a cookie from his plate.

"Watch out, Harley," Zane said. "Those adorable ones are contagious."

He kissed Bea's head, hugging her as he said, "I can think of worse things to catch." He gazed out at Jolie, Sophie, and Louie playing in the yard, and his mind took a perilous leap. He imagined Piper round with their baby, more of their children running around the yard. It was a dream he knew might never come true, but he couldn't help wanting it.

Willow nudged Piper and said, "Do *not* let him near Mom's new potions."

"Don't worry. I threw out Harley's body wash, and I never use her stuff." Piper narrowed her eyes, looking at Roxie, and said, "I'm onto our mama and her matchmaking ways."

"Doesn't Mom have a key to your house?" Talia asked.

"So?" Piper asked as she bit into a cookie.

Talia, Bridgette, and Willow exchanged a knowing look. Roxie pressed her lips together, but there was no squelching her smile or the guilt in her eyes as they darted away from her daughters.

"Oh no. *No, no, no*," Piper said. "I want my key back."

Roxie shrugged. "It already worked."

"No *it* hasn't," Piper said sharply. She hiked a thumb at Harley and said, "I've been showering with *him* for weeks. There's no way I . . ." She realized everyone was looking at her like she'd said something she shouldn't have. "Oh *shit*. I mean, I've been staying at his place. I mean . . ." She rolled her eyes. "Whatever. I'm a grown woman. I can stay wherever I want."

"So *that's* why Harley needed a bigger shower," Dan teased.

"With *two* showerheads," Aurelia chimed in.

Remi said, "I want two showerheads."

"We'll hire Piper to put them in," Mason suggested.

Piper's eyes nearly bugged out of her head. "How do you know we . . . *he* has two showerheads?"

Bridgette waved from the other end of the table. "That would be my fault. I didn't know the details of his bathroom renovation were a secret."

Harley couldn't stop smiling, but he knew better than to open his mouth and get in the middle of this.

"Okay, *enough*," Piper snapped. "Bottom line, *Mother*, is that we're safe from your fertility potions, *and* I want my key back."

"Why? Look how adorable Harley is with a baby," Roxie pleaded.

"She's right," Talia said. "He looks really good with Bea."

"Everyone looks good with Bea," Ben said.

"I would *love* more grandchildren," Debra said. "Ever since Sophie spent the night with Ben and Aurelia, she can't stop talking about wanting a baby, and Delaney has put her foot down."

"She's right," Delaney said. "I've done my duty."

Roxie and Debra looked around the table.

"Don't look at us." Zane leaned back and put his arm around Willow. "My wife and I have other things to focus on for the next year."

Emerson was fast asleep on Bodhi's chest. He patted her back and said, "We'll be happy to take some of that fertility potion in about six months. Until then, all we want are a few nights of sleep."

"Guess you're up, Tal," Willow said.

Talia reached for Derek's hand and said, "I don't think we need fertility potions. We weren't going to say anything yet, but we just found out I'm eight weeks pregnant."

The girls squealed and jumped up to hug Talia and Derek, while the guys cheered their congratulations.

"Oh, how wonderful," Flossie exclaimed.

Ben patted Derek on the back and said, "Get ready for sleepless nights."

"We're ready," Talia said.

"We're thrilled and nervous." Derek hugged Talia against his side and said, "We have a lot to figure out, but we're counting on Roxie and Dan, Bridgette and Bodhi, and Ben and Aurelia to teach us all the tricks of the trade."

"Happy to," Bodhi said. "You can start by babysitting next Friday night, if you'd like. Get up close and personal with two kids at once."

"We'd love that," Talia said excitedly.

"This is so exciting. Wait until I tell Aunt Marilynn!" Roxie whipped out her phone and thumbed out a text.

Ben put his arm around Aurelia and said, "I think you have double the news for her, Mom. We weren't going to say anything for another few weeks, but Aurelia just found out she's six weeks pregnant!"

"Oh, *goodness*! Two new babies!" Flossie's eyes teared up. "We are so blessed."

There was another round of cheers and hugs.

Piper put a hand on Harley's shoulder as she walked back to her seat after hugging Aurelia and said, "Auntie Piper is always up for babysitting, and I bet Uncle Harley would love to change a few diapers."

"I'm not afraid of dirty diapers," he said, wondering if she realized she'd referred to them as Auntie and Uncle. That might just be his favorite slipup ever, even better than her earlier slipup of *we* when she was talking about his shower, which he also thought of as *their* shower.

The conversation turned to baby showers and baby names. Bea wiggled off Harley's lap and toddled over to Ben, who scooped her up and smothered her cheeks with kisses. Bea shriek-giggled and squirmed out of Ben's hands, toddling across the lawn toward the other kids who were playing in the yard.

Ben stood up and said, "Who wants to celebrate with a quick pickup game of b-ball?"

The guys pushed to their feet, though Bodhi opted out so as not to wake Emerson.

Harley looked at Piper and said, "You coming, babe?"

"When do I ever say *no*?" she asked with a seductive glimmer in her eyes.

God, he loved her so damn much. As he gathered her in his arms, three very special words that had been vying for release for quite some time hung from the tip of his tongue. But she'd just taken a huge step by inviting him to stay at her place, so he held them back and said, "That's my girl."

"But what about your ankle?"

"It's been almost a month since I hurt it. I'm good, but I'll go easy."

She took his hand and said, "Like you even know what that means . . ."

They headed for the basketball court, and the kids ran over.

"Can we play, too?" Louie asked.

Harley lifted him over his head and said, "You want to go through the hoop?"

"Yes!" Louie squealed, kicking his legs. "Look, Mom! I'm flying!"

Jolie put her hands on her hips and said, "I'm really good, and Sophie's not bad."

"Hey!" Sophie mimicked her sister's stance and said, "I'm good, too."

"Absolutely," Dan said. "The more the merrier."

Piper's father reminded Harley of his own father, the way he loved his family. Harley set Louie on the ground, a pang of longing moving through him. Not a day passed when he didn't think of his father, but he liked to think he was watching over them.

As he took his position on the court, his thoughts tiptoed into a dark corner of his mind where he never allowed himself to linger, and he silently hoped his father was watching over Marshall, too.

Later that evening, after picking up Jiggs and all of his paraphernalia, Harley packed a bag and headed over to Piper's house. He briefly wondered if she'd change her mind about him staying over, but after how close they'd been, he thought it would take an act of God to keep them apart.

He parked in front of her adorably small stone house with a deep porch anchoring the left side. Above the porch was a three-window dormer. The right side of the house was taller, with a peaked roof. A picture window graced the second story, and below, the first floor boasted two circle-head windows looking out over well-manicured bushes.

Harley stepped from the truck, and Jiggs followed him out. As he walked up the front steps, the door opened. Piper stood before him, looking beautiful in the same jeans and T-shirt she'd had on earlier, nervously moving from foot to foot as he climbed the porch steps.

"Hi," she said, stepping out and pulling the door partially closed behind her. She crouched to love up Jiggs and said, "My house isn't very big, and it's not finished yet." She pushed to her feet and slid her fingers into the front pocket of her jeans. "I should have warned you about the state it's in."

"Baby, I wouldn't care if you lived in a tent as long as we were together."

"You might change your mind about that in a minute." She pushed the door open and they followed her into the living room, which was beautifully finished, with cream sofas and a peach armchair. Pictures of her family hung on the walls, and with them, a copy of the picture she'd given him on the boat. His heart swelled.

"I started renovating," she said. "But then you moved back, and it was more fun to have dinner at the pub and hang out with you than it was to do the work. This is the only part of the house that's completely finished. I'm sorry it's kind of a mess." She waved to a wall of exposed studs in the dining room. "The kitchen is behind that wall, and there's a den, but they're both partially renovated."

He dropped Jiggs's leash and gathered her in his arms, kissing her deeply. Jiggs went paws-up on their sides, pushing his nose between their bodies.

Harley reached down to unhook Jiggs's leash and said, "Jiggsy said he likes your excuse better than the one he heard."

"What . . . ?" Piper asked.

"A little bird told him that you spend more time helping people like Doris and me than you do helping yourself."

A tease rose in her eyes. "Maybe Jiggs needs to learn how to keep secrets."

"You put our picture up."

"Don't make too much of it," she said sassily. "I had to cover a hole in the wall."

"Uh-huh." Harley walked into the living room and teased, "Let's see that hole."

She ran in front of him and spread her arms out to her sides, blocking the pictures. "If you look, I'll have to kill you."

He laced their hands together and pressed his body against hers. "How about you kiss me and save us both all that pain?"

As he lowered his mouth toward hers, she said, "I'm glad you're here."

"There's no place else I'd rather be."

CHAPTER TWENTY-ONE

PIPER HAD RISEN before dawn for most of her life, excited to start her day and see what adventures might unfold. There was always a problem to be sorted out, a barrier to overcome, or a new job on the horizon to plan for. But she hadn't jumped out of bed for weeks. It was Friday morning, nearly two weeks after Harley had first spent the night, and she'd been awake for more than an hour, lying on his chest, listening to the steady and strong beat of his heart and the occasional sounds Jiggs made from his new doggy bed. She'd learned to enjoy these quiet stolen moments together. He'd turned her into a sound sleeper, and she usually woke up in the same position she'd fallen asleep in, which was always nestled against her grizzly of a man.

Once love makes its mark, there's no going back. Her mother's voice trailed through her mind, as it so often did on mornings like this.

Her mother had been right. No part of her wanted to go back to a time when she and Harley weren't together. She couldn't believe she'd been nervous about having him sleep at her house. Her house was *better* with Harley and Jiggs in it. Harley was patient and loving, and he knew how to deal with her insecurities. He'd become her best friend, her insatiable lover, and the person she wanted to share everything with—good days and bad, frustrations and fantasies. She didn't want a ring on her finger, but she definitely wanted this man by her side. And though they hadn't said they loved each other yet, she'd wanted to so many times, the urge to tell him was always on the tip of her tongue.

She moved her fingers through his chest hair, thinking about the walks they'd gone on earlier in the week with Jiggs. One evening they'd shared stories about things they never did in high school but kind of wish they had, like making out under the bleachers or skipping school to go to the movies. Another night they'd walked to the elementary school and sat on the swings in the playground swapping stories about when they were young. She loved thinking about Harley growing up and seeing him through new, loving eyes. The night on the swings, they'd ended up having a contest to see who could swing the highest— she won. He'd wanted to see who could jump farther, but she knew that was a recipe for disaster with his newly healed ankle. He'd insisted, and she'd finally won him over by promising if he *didn't* jump, she'd do dirty things to him beneath the bleachers at the high school.

Their walk the following night was *very* interesting.

Her love for him bubbled up inside her, and for the first time she didn't hold it back. She whispered, "I love you, Harley Dutch," and pressed a kiss to his chest. Joy and relief swept through her, and she closed her eyes, soaking in the incredible feeling of having finally said what she felt.

Harley's hand moved up her back. He kissed the top of her head and said, "I love you, too, Piper Dalton."

Her eyes flew open. She pushed off his chest, and a Cheshire-cat grin spread across his handsome face.

"You're supposed to be *asleep!*"

He chuckled. "*Supposed* to be?"

"Yes!" she said as Jiggs climbed onto the bed. "That was for *me*, not *you!*"

"You didn't mean it?" Confusion rose in his eyes.

"No. I mean, *yes!* I meant it, but I didn't mean for you to hear it like that, as a *secret.*"

"Do you want to take it back?"

She couldn't tell if he was teasing or serious, but it didn't matter. Her answer was the same either way. "No. I just hoped to one day look at you and say it, because . . ."

He cradled her face in his hands and said, "Because the million things you do for me and with me don't say it loud enough? They *do*, Pipe. I knew you loved me when you took care of me and the girls, and I knew you loved me more when you spent the night. By the time you invited me and Jiggs to stay here, I was pretty sure you had realized it, too. And that morning after we first slept here, when you spoiled Jiggs, buying him *two* doggy beds, boxes of treats, fancy food, and water bowls, and a leash with his name on it, I knew your love for us was solid."

Her heart melted. He really did *get* her.

She'd always known that, but even more so as they'd fallen into life as a couple, finding their routines, their *rhythms*, staying at his place the nights he worked late and at hers the other nights. They texted often, only now their dirty texts usually ended with them in each other's arms, living out their sensual fantasies. She continued to go to Dutch's for dinner when he was working, still hollered at sports and bantered with Kase and the guys from work. Only now she and Harley kissed across the bar, snuck into his office to make out or talk, and Harley stole food off her dinner plate.

"I've been wanting to tell you that I love you for a long time." He trailed his hand down her back and said, "But I was worried about scaring you off. Knowing that you want to one day say it to my face is huge. I can wait, Trig. We don't have to say it again until you're ready."

He was so good to her. "Harley—"

"No pressure, babe. Let's see how you feel after the father-daughter dance, when you get to my place and see me looking so hot I put all those fathers to shame. You might want to say it then."

She laughed. "Harley—"

"Oh, I know!" He whipped off the sheet, revealing his beautiful nakedness, sending her entire body into a frenzy. "How about now? Do you want to say it now?"

She climbed over him, straddling his hips, and Jiggs jumped off the bed. He'd turned into a great wingman after all. She laced their hands together and said, "Harley Dutch, I have no idea why you put up with me when you could have any other woman you want."

"I don't want any other woman, and I haven't for an embarrassingly long time. That's the power of my girl, right there."

"You're so crazy," she teased. "And I like your craziness, because it fits with mine so well. You have endless patience, which you need in order to be with me. You make me laugh every day, you have made me cry but only because it hurts to break down my walls, and you make me *cry out* in pleasure so often your love should come with a neon warning sign that reads BEWARE! ORGASM COMA AHEAD."

He laughed and blew her a kiss.

"You have accomplished the impossible, weaseling your way into my life, my *house*, and most importantly, my *heart*." She caressed his face, committing everything about the moment to memory—the joyful look in his eyes, his sexy smile, and how utterly perfect it felt to be in this amazing place with him. "I look at you and I feel things I never thought possible. I love you, Harley, and I'm going to say it *a lot*. Not just because it feels incredible to finally let it out, but because I want to see you looking at me the way you are right now every single day."

He swallowed hard, oceans of emotions welling in his eyes. He didn't say a word as he swept her beneath him and gazed down at her, blinking several times. "How about the way I'm looking at you now? Will you remember this as the moment you left me speechless?"

"*Yes.*" *I love you. I love you. I love you!*

"For someone who claims not to be good with words or feelings, you sure tripped up my heart. I love you, baby, and now I'm going to show you just how much in a way I know you'll understand."

He began kissing his way down her body, making her insides sizzle and her nerve endings tingle. But she needed to be in his arms, as close as two people could be.

"Harley," she whispered urgently, and he lifted his head. She beckoned him with her index finger, and he crawled up her body, perching above her again. "Be *here* with me. Make love to me."

He reached for a condom, and she touched his arm, stopping him. "I'm on the pill, and I just want to feel you, with nothing between us."

"Oh, baby," he said just above a whisper. He nuzzled against her neck, pressing a kiss there.

"Go slow. I don't ever want to forget this moment, either." She had no idea when she'd become so sappy, but she didn't care. Everything felt right with him.

His lips touched hers in dozens of tender kisses as their bodies came together, their eyes open, their love sparking like live wires around them. When he was buried to the hilt, the air left their lungs in unison, as if they'd both been holding their breath.

His head dipped beside hers as he cradled her beneath him, his heart thundering just as hard and fast as hers. They lay like that for a long, torturously beautiful moment, his hard length filling her completely, their breaths coming faster by the second. Her inner muscles flamed, pulsing around his cock, craving their magnificent friction. She felt his back and leg muscles cording tight. He lifted his face from her neck and she saw her desire, her *urgency*, mirrored in his eyes. She rose up at the same time his mouth crashed down on hers in a rough and exhilarating kiss. Sex with Harley was always fantastic, but everything felt different now. White-hot flashes of electricity coursed through her, through *them*. The raw, primal sounds they made were aphrodisiacs all on their own, each one pushing her closer to the edge. She felt *free* and safe in ways she never had. They surrendered so completely to each other, to their passion, groping and writhing as their bodies pounded together, they found a new wild tempo that bound them as one, as savage as it was luxurious.

Piper gasped for breath as wind and fire whipped through her like a hurricane and a volcano battling for dominance, filling her limbs and her core. Harley pushed his arms beneath her, cradling her head with both hands. His beard scratched her cheek and shoulder as he grunted with each hard thrust. Every pump of his hips sent pleasure shooting through her.

"Pipe—" he panted out.

She tucked her head in the crook of his neck, squeezing her legs around his thighs, tightening her arms around his back, holding on to her man—her strength, her *love*. His next thrust hit her like an earthquake, and she cried out. Her inner muscles clenched repeatedly, and he followed her over the edge, grunting out her name. Their bodies bucked and thrashed, currents of pleasure carrying them to the peak of ecstasy.

They collapsed to the mattress, clinging to each other and panting for air. Harley rolled them onto their sides and wrapped one of his legs around her, keeping their bodies flush. Their skin was damp, their heartbeats frantic, and when their eyes connected, there was no need for words. He was right there with her, just as lost in the flood tide of their love as she was.

Piper blew through the back doors of Willow's bakery later that morning, grabbed a doughnut from the counter, and met the stunned faces of all three of her sisters, her mother, Aurelia, *and* Remi. "Are you having a sugar party I wasn't invited to?"

Her mother came around the counter in one of her flowy, colorful skirts and tops and said, "From what I hear, you've been getting your sugar elsewhere for quite some time now."

The girls giggled.

Piper rolled her eyes, trying hard to stifle her own giddiness. "I'm only going to say this once, and there will be no squealing, no group hugs or any other type of girlie nonsense. Got it?"

"Are you pregnant?" Talia asked with wide eyes.

"No! I'm not frigging pregnant. Bite your tongue. You know I don't want kids anytime soon."

"Babies don't work on timelines," Aurelia said, snagging a doughnut.

"What*ever*." Piper's heart was slamming against her ribs so hard, she was sure they could see and hear it. "Do we have a deal?"

"Deal," they said in unison, crowding around her.

She'd tried to keep a straight face and lost the battle before the first word even left her lips. "I have officially joined the ranks of all you ridiculously swoony, googly-eyed girls. I'm in love with Harley, and it has *nothing* to do with lotions or potions or anything else other than *us*."

Their squeals came seconds before the arms of all six women were around her as they cheered and talked over one another. Piper soaked in every blessed second of it, though she said, "Did we *not* just talk about this?"

The women scrambled back.

"Sorry," Bridgette and Aurelia said nervously.

"We got carried away," Talia said.

"We're just so happy for you," Willow added.

Roxie put her hands on her hips, eyes narrowing as she said, "I'm your *mother*, and I will not make an excuse for hugging you and celebrating your love for Harley." Her mother's arms circled her again, and she said, "I noticed a bottle of the body wash Harley likes missing from my supply yesterday. Did you take it?"

"A little extra insurance doesn't hurt," Piper confessed. She'd ducked into her mother's workshop after meeting with her father yesterday afternoon. "Don't mention it to Harley. I put it in the store-bought bottle."

"The apple does not fall far from the tree, baby girl."

Her mother hugged her again, and the others looked on longingly, filling up Piper's heart even more. She sighed and said, "Get in here, you big pains."

More cheers and hugs ensued, and for the first time in her entire life, Piper realized she wasn't so different from them after all.

CHAPTER TWENTY-TWO

THE HARMONY POINTE Middle School gym was decorated with balloon arches over the dance floor and silver stars hanging from the ceiling. A group of high schoolers were streaming music from laptops on the stage, but nobody was dancing. Girls huddled together decked out in fancy dresses, whispering behind their hands, while fathers milled about sipping punch and trying not to look too far out of their element. Harley might be out of his element, but nothing could throw him off his game today. He was too high on love, fighting the urge to tell everyone, *Piper loves me!* She'd texted him at Dutch's earlier with the message *Get ready to strip down. Hotness is on its way.* He loved her unabashed sexual nature, and he'd gotten all revved up thinking about her coming over for some lovin' in the middle of the day. Imagine his surprise when a gift box had arrived via courier instead of his sexpot girlfriend. She'd sent him a pair of dark jeans, a crisp white dress shirt, a light purple tie, and a pair of white Converse, with a card that read *You'll be the hottest man at the dance. Love you, Trig.* He had no idea when she'd found the time to shop, much less how she knew his sizes. But when his girl had the will, she always found a way.

She'd made his day . . . again.

After work, he'd changed into the clothes Piper had sent him, which fit perfectly, and picked up a wrist corsage for Jolie from Bridgette's flower shop. Jolie, Sophie, and Delaney had gushed over it. Jolie had been a nervous wreck when they'd arrived at the dance twenty minutes ago, fidgeting with her dress and standing behind him. She was finally loosening up a little and no longer hiding behind him.

"Do you want to go talk with your friends?"

Jolie shook her head, still fidgeting with the hem of her simple light purple dress. One knee was bent, the toes of her Converse resting on the floor. She looked beautiful and innocent, just like her mother had at that age.

Harley silently vowed to do a better job of protecting her from assholes like her father than he had for Delaney. "You're the prettiest girl here. You should get out there and dance, show off that dress."

She blushed and rolled her eyes.

"You can roll your eyes, but I sure hope I have a daughter as cool as you one day. Do you think when I have kids you can teach them to play soccer?"

"Can't *you* do that?"

"Not really. I can teach them to pour drinks, play football, or pilot a boat, but I pretty much suck at soccer."

She seemed to think about that for a minute before saying, "Are you going to marry Piper?"

Surprised, he said, "Where did that come from?"

She shrugged. "She's your girlfriend."

"Couples don't always get married, Jo."

"I'm *never* getting married."

His heart hurt at that. She was too young to be making such a determination. "Aw, come on. You don't know how you'll feel when you meet that special someone and fall in love."

"I'm never falling in love," she said as casually and confidently as if she'd said her sneakers were purple.

"Well, I hope you do, because love is wonderful."

"If I don't fall in love, I won't get hurt."

He wondered if Piper had told her that and quickly dismissed the idea, knowing Piper would never thrust her views on a child. "Not everyone gets hurt when they fall in love." He held her gaze and said, "Do you remember Grandpa?"

"Yes."

"Do you remember how much he loved Grandma?"

She wrinkled her nose. "They were always kissing and holding hands."

"Exactly. Love can be wonderful. And while it's true that some people aren't meant to be in relationships, I don't think that you're one of them. You're a loving, smart girl, and one day you're going to meet someone who makes your heart flutter."

"Uncle *Harley* . . ."

"Okay, maybe your heart won't flutter. Maybe you'll go to a soccer game with him, and you'll laugh, share hot dogs, and hold hands. Before you know it, you won't be able to imagine how you ever lived your life without him in it."

She bit her bottom lip and lowered her eyes. "Do you think so?" she asked softly.

He lifted her chin and said, "I know so, because you're an amazing girl, and some lucky guy is going to see that and never let you go."

She smiled, and it reached all the way up to her eyes.

"But you're not dating until you're thirty anyway, so you don't have to worry about that for a while."

"*Thirty?* I'll be old!"

"That's okay. Old is good. It keeps Uncle Harley sane." He reached for her hand and said, "Come on. Let's dance and show these boring dads how to have fun."

She pulled her hand back. "Nobody's dancing, Uncle Harley!"

"So? Just because they don't want to have fun doesn't mean we can't."

She shook her head again.

"You're going to make me dance by myself?" He walked backward onto the dance floor.

"Don't! *Please* don't!"

Taylor Swift's "Shake It Off" came on, and Harley moved his shoulders to the beat. "I can't help it. I just keep moving." He turned in a circle and put both hands out, beckoning her to the dance floor with his wiggling fingers.

Jolie was beet red, shaking her head and covering her face, peeking out between her fingers. Her eyes darted all around her. But Harley was determined to help her have a good time, and by the way the other little girls were smiling and inching closer as he twirled and shook his hips to the beat, mouthing the words to the song—because Jolie and Sophie used to play it every time they were together—he knew they were close to a breakthrough.

"Come on, Jolie!" He danced around her as her friends closed in on them.

"Your uncle is a good dancer!" a blond girl said.

Another little girl pointed at him and said, "I wish my dad could do that!"

Harley motioned to the high schoolers to repeat the song after it was over, buying him a little more time since he had no idea how many songs he could pull this off to.

Soon a gaggle of girls were gathered around Jolie. Harley pointed to them and said, "Everyone out on the dance floor!" and a group of them ran toward him, giggling. They all started dancing. Jolie was grinning, but still standing over to the side. "Come on, Jo! Let's show them how it's done!"

"Come on, Jolie!" a dark-haired girl urged.

Two other girls ran to Jolie and took her hands, dragging her onto the dance floor. She finally relented, dancing reluctantly at first. She quickly got caught up in the excitement and danced her little heart out, laughing and wiggling to the beat. It didn't take long for fathers and more daughters to join them. They danced to Katy Perry, Pink, some boy bands, and bands Harley had never heard before.

An hour later, Harley knew most of the fathers' and little girls' names, and Jolie was no longer nervous at all.

Toward the end of the dance, while Jolie was dancing with her friends, Harley went to get some water, and two men followed him to the snack table.

"How's it going?" Harley said.

"Great. You saved our asses," a tall, lean, clean-cut dark-haired guy said. "I'm Gary Lanigan. My daughter Teri is in the red dress."

"And I'm Ike Preacher. My Kensey is in the yellow dress." Ike was burly like Harley, with a thick beard and tattoo sleeves. "We're single dads, and we don't know shit about dancing. You saved our daughters loads of embarrassment."

He shook their hands and said, "I'm Harley Dutch, Jolie's uncle. Seems like the girls are having fun."

"Yeah, it's nice to see them so happy," Ike said. "Thanks for your business, too. You hired our company, At Your Service, to bring dinners to Delaney. She's an amazing person."

"She is, thank you. It's good to meet the men behind the business. Your dinners saved her from herself. I know my sister, and she would have worn herself out trying to do everything on her own."

"No problem," Gary said. "We appreciate your business. Ike's buddies own a company called Husbands for Hire in the cities where they live. They do handyman work, mechanics, running errands, that sort of thing. We're joining forces over the next few months and expanding our services. We'd appreciate it if you'd keep us in mind."

"Absolutely. With so many single parents and families where both parents work full-time, that's a brilliant business concept."

The last song of the night was announced, and Harley said, "I'll definitely keep you guys in mind and help spread the word. I need to grab my niece for this dance, but if you're ever in Sweetwater, I run Dutch's Pub. Come by and I'll buy you a drink and introduce you around."

He found Jolie huddled with her friends from soccer. "Last song of the night, girls. Go find your fathers. I'm sure they'd love to dance with you."

The girls ran off to find their fathers as "I Hope You Dance" by Lee Ann Womack started playing. He offered his hand to Jolie, and they made their way to the dance floor.

"Did you have fun?" he asked as they danced.

"*So* much fun. Thank you for bringing me."

"It was an honor to be your date."

After the song ended, they said goodbye to Jolie's friends and their fathers. On the way out to the truck, Harley said, "Listen, Jo. I may not be your dad, but I am your uncle, and I love you and Soph. I want you to know that you can *always* count on me, no matter what. If you ever want to talk or hang out at my place. If anyone bugs you at school, or a boy asks you out and I need to give him a shakedown."

"Uncle *Harley*." She giggled.

"I'm serious. If you, Sophie, or your mom ever need *anything*, I'm here, okay? And when you grow up and go away to college, you can bet I'll visit you and send you care packages. I'll dance with you at that wedding you're not going to have, and I'll even walk you down the aisle if you're still talking to me by then."

"Why wouldn't I talk to you?"

"Because you can bet that I'll shake down the guy who you end up marrying, too."

She giggled again, the greatest sound of the night.

"Did Piper's brother shake you down?"

"He did."

"But you're still with her."

"Yes, and I hope to always be with her. A shakedown isn't to scare guys away. It's to weed through the wrong guys. Sort of like tasting ice cream to be sure the aftertaste isn't horrible."

Her brows knitted. "*Oh.* Then you *should* shake them out."

"Shake them *down.* Gotta know the lingo, kiddo." He unlocked the passenger door and said, "Just know I love you and you can always count on me, okay?"

She nodded and climbed into the truck. As she put on her seat belt, she said, "I hope when I'm twenty I meet a guy like you."

"Didn't I say *thirty?*"

"Yes, but that's old. *Twenty* is better."

He looked at her out of the corner of his eye and said, "Twenty-five."

"*Nineteen*," she countered.

Delaney was in big trouble with this one, and he told her as much when he dropped Jolie off after the dance. He was still chuckling over Delaney's response—"Guess that means you'll be sitting on my front porch with a shotgun during the girls' teenage years"—as he pulled away from the curb and called Piper.

"Is this the woman who loves Harley Dutch?" he asked when she answered the phone.

"That depends. Is this Charlie Hunnam? If so, then, baby, I'm as single as a one-dollar bill."

"That dude from *Sons of Anarchy?* He's a *squirrel*."

"A damn hot squirrel, which is a shame since I'm pretty sure my much hotter *grizzly* could shred him to pieces. How was the dance? Did Jolie have fun?"

"She was nervous at first, but I think she had a great time. She loved my outfit. Thank you for making me look good."

"You always look good."

She probably had no idea she revealed her heart in everything she did and said, and he loved it. "By the way, I'm never having daughters."

"No shit. Girls are way too emotional and hard to figure out. Maybe you can train your sperm as well as you trained Jiggs and have only boys."

He wanted to read more into her comment than she probably intended—that she might want kids with him one day and was totally up for boys, but he knew better. Besides, patience had worked so far; that's where he was putting his bet.

"I'll get right on that. I hear it takes lots of practice."

"I'm all for practice," she said seductively.

"Man, Pipe, I sure do love you, and I love that now I can say that without worrying about scaring you off. I'm heading home. Meet me at my place?"

"I've got my bag in the car. I just got back from walking Jiggs. We'll be right behind you."

He ended the call and loosened his tie as he drove by the pub, smiling to himself as Piper's earlier text came to mind. That text might have been referencing clothes, but soon he'd have his hot girlfriend in his arms and his buddy by his side. Life didn't get much better than that.

As he pulled into his driveway, his headlights illuminated an unfamiliar motorcycle with Colorado plates. He cut the engine, and as he stepped from his truck, the silhouette of a man came around the back of the house.

"Can I help you?" Harley called out.

He squinted into the darkness as the man came forward. Harley's hands fisted by his sides, years of anger and resentment storming through him as he took in the brother he hardly recognized. A thick beard and mustache disguised Marshall's face, harsh tattoos covered his flesh, but there was no mistaking his eyes, which still held the promise and arrogance of trouble in the making.

"What the hell do you want?" Harley heard the warning in his own voice. His fingers unfurled, only to recoil even tighter as Piper's truck pulled into the driveway, fueling his rage. Marshall had hurt his family—and Piper—enough. He wasn't about to let him do it again.

"Hey, Har," Marshall said in his frustratingly *typical* carefree way.

Harley didn't take his eyes off Marshall as Piper and Jiggs got out of her truck. "Don't 'hey, Har' me. What the *fuck* are you doing here?"

Jiggs bounded over, veering toward Marshall. "*Jiggs! Here,*" Harley commanded, stopping his dog in his tracks. Jiggs came to his side, and Harley touched the dog's head.

Marshall's eyes shifted in Piper's direction, his brow furrowing.

Harley's gut seized. *Don't even fucking look at her. You've hurt her enough.* He stepped into his brother's line of sight and said, "Piper, take Jiggs inside."

"Not a chance." She moved to his side and crossed her arms, glowering at Marshall.

Damn it. Why did he even try? He pinned a dark stare on Marshall. "I said, what the hell are you doing here?"

"I . . . uh . . ." Marshall's eyes moved curiously between Harley and Piper. He shoved his hands into the front pockets of his jeans and shrugged. "I wanted to come home and see everybody."

"That's just fucking great." Harley's voice escalated. "Still the same old Marshall. Where the hell were you when Delaney's husband left her with a baby and one on the way? Did you want to see everyone *then*? Did it ever cross your mind to come home and help your only *sister* find her fucking way through life without losing her mind?" He closed the distance between them, unable to temper his rage. "How about when Dad got sick and Mom needed you most? When our father was *dying*? When Delaney and the girls were so fucking scared they couldn't see straight? Where were you then? Where were you when Dad *died*?"

Jiggs growled at Marshall, standing sentinel beside Harley.

Harley grabbed Marshall by the shirt, lifting him to within an inch of his face, vaguely aware of Piper saying something, but her words were lost to the blood thundering through his ears. "I'll tell you where you were," he seethed through gritted teeth. "Off taking care of *Marshall,* just like always. I don't know who you are, but you're not a *Dutch.*"

He shoved Marshall so hard his brother stumbled, catching himself with both hands on the hood of Harley's truck.

Harley stalked over and said, "Get the *fuck* off my property." He grabbed Piper by the arm and dragged her up the porch steps with Jiggs at his heels.

Harley paced the living room like a caged panther greedy for a good slaughter, muscles corded, hands fisted, eyes as harrowing and icy as a winter storm. Jiggs kept pace beside him, looking worried. Piper didn't even know that was possible for a dog.

"What was . . . ? What the hell just happened?" She had never been on this side of that kind of anger, much less seen Harley in such a state before. She hadn't even gotten a good look at Marshall. She'd noticed Harley's hulking body language seconds before he'd tried to tell her to go inside. The source fueling his rage had become blurred by her own protective instincts.

Harley's eyes remained trained on the floor as he wore a path behind the couch. "Fucking Marshall was here when I showed up."

"What did he want?"

"Who the fuck knows?" he snapped. "He probably needs money or some shit." He pulled his phone from his pocket. "I have to warn my mother and Delaney. *Damn it.* I should have run the fucker out of town."

"Whoa, Harley." She touched his arm, trying to lower the phone. "Stop. Take a deep breath and *think* before you make that call. Did he *say* he wanted money?"

He whipped his hand away. "He didn't say *shit.* I didn't give him a chance to."

"Has he asked for money before? I thought you haven't heard from him in years."

"What the hell else could he want? He fucking shows up out of the blue and acts like he didn't abandon our family years ago? Who does that?"

"I don't know!" Her voice rose, matching his.

"I need to warn Delaney and my mother."

"Don't." She put her hand over his.

His eyes narrowed suspiciously. "Now you're on *his* side?" His eyes flashed with sudden outrage. "Did he come see you *first*? While I was at the dance? Goddamn it," he growled, breathing erratically. "I never saw *this* coming. I should have kicked his ass." He lowered his chin, and his eyes impaled her. "You're not over him, are you? Maybe you didn't even realize it until you saw him, and suddenly you can't see past your feelings. What a fucking idiot I—"

Her palm met his cheek with the sting of a thousand bees. She was shaking all over, anger exploding inside her like bombs.

He blinked several times. "Did you just *slap* me?"

"You're lucky I didn't *punch* you, the way you were spouting non-sense like it's the truth. Are you *insane*, saying all that shit after I bared my soul to you?"

The blood drained from his face, and he sank down to the edge of the couch, grinding out a curse as he scrubbed a hand over his face. "Jesus, Piper. I'm so sorry. I lost my mind."

"You *should* be. I am *always* on your side. But you don't know what he wants, and you can't make things worse between Marshall and your family just because *you're* angry with him."

"Make things *worse*? Is that what you think I want?" His voice escalated again as he pushed to his feet, agitated and pacing. "I've spent my whole damn life *protecting* them from his shit. Racing home on weekends from the city to help with the girls and make sure my sister didn't spiral into depression. Picking up all the pieces of our family, and the business, when my father was sick and after he died. Dealing with the aftermath of Marshall disrespecting our parents by showing up high as a fucking kite to my father's funeral." He grabbed his head with both hands and looked up at the ceiling as if he were trying to keep from shouting. He groaned and threw his arms down, paced again. "I'm so *angry* with him for turning his back on my sister and mother. We didn't know if he was alive or dead for all this time. You shouldn't be around me right now," he said without looking at her. "You should get out of here."

She stepped into his path and put her hands on his chest, feeling his heart hammering against her palm. "You made me fall in love with you, and I am *not* leaving just because you're so angry you can't see straight. You're *allowed* to be in a crappy mood. That's what I'm here for."

"No. It's wrong, Piper. I said awful, hurtful things to you."

"And I probably would have said worse if I were in your shoes, which means I get a free pass for when I say things I shouldn't."

His lips almost twitched into a smile, but stopped short, sorrow rising in his eyes.

"You have every right to be pissed and resentful. You might not realize this, but you said you were mad that he turned his back on your mother and Delaney. What about *you*, Harley? Where do you fit into that equation? He turned his back on *you*, too. Maybe somewhere deep inside, you miss the brother you hung out with as a kid. The brother you could relate to on some level."

He scoffed and looked away.

"Don't disregard that you matter, Harley." She put her arms around him, resting her chin on his chest, and said, "I get it. Not everyone is good with words. Sometimes you have to go to the Mad House and just get it out of your system."

He nodded. "It sucks being this angry."

"No shit. I've been there too many times to count."

"I hate that when I saw him, I wanted to beat the shit out of him, and at the same time . . ." He shifted his eyes away, swallowing hard.

"I know," she said, saving him the discomfort of saying he missed Marshall and was glad he wasn't lying dead in a ditch.

"It makes me even angrier at him that I feel that way."

"I get that, too."

His gaze softened, and he said, "I know you do. I should warn my family."

"Maybe you shouldn't *warn* them and instead just let them know he came by and you sent him away. Remember when your mom said she hoped one day Marshall would come back? She needs this, Harley, even if he digs himself a deeper hole. If he does, that's on him. But your mom's needs are different from yours, and I bet Delaney's are, too. And the girls? They're young and resilient. They'll probably be psyched to have another uncle around."

His jaw clenched, and he was silent for a minute. "And when he disappoints them and hurts them again and I'm left to pick up the pieces?"

"If that happens, then luckily, you're really good at picking up pieces and putting people you love back together. And yeah, that sucks, but he's family, and even if you don't feel it at this moment, I know you. You love him. Somewhere deep inside, past the part that wants to beat the shit out of him is the part of you that wants to see him productive and happy. But you can't if you never give him a chance to speak his mind. If he fucks up, he does. That's life. But don't make it your doing. You're not a bad guy, Harley, but if you stand between him and your family, you might be seen as one."

He exhaled a long breath and hugged her tight. "It's probably better if I don't call them tonight and just see what happens. I don't trust myself not to lose it if he's with them." He pressed a kiss to the top of her head and rested his cheek there. "When did you become the wise one about relationships?"

"I didn't. Maybe I'm wrong and he needs money, or maybe he's here to try to win me back."

He drew back, leveling her with a dark stare.

She flashed a big, cheesy grin.

"That wasn't nice, Pipe."

"No, it wasn't. I guess I was more upset over the shit you said to me than I realized." She caressed his face, hurting for him. "I'm sorry for saying that. But if you ever accuse me of being interested in another man again, I will have to kill you, and nobody would ever find your body at the Mad House."

He arched a brow. "You've put some thought into that, huh?"

"A girl's got to cover her bases."

He touched his forehead to hers and closed his eyes. "I really am sorry."

"I know, and I'm sorry for slapping you, but someone had to do it. Your words hurt, and I know mine did, too. I guess we need to work on that, but on the upside, we survived our first fight. We should take that as a win."

CHAPTER TWENTY-THREE

ON SATURDAY AFTERNOON Harley stood in his mother's kitchen filling three glasses with iced tea, wondering how he was going to break the news about Marshall without getting angry. If not for Piper, his night would have been hell. She'd suggested they take the boat out to try to clear his head. They'd taken Jiggs with them and anchored the boat far from shore, where they lay beneath the stars talking about anything *other than* Marshall. Piper was good at distracting him, making him laugh and talking him off the ledge, but even with the gentle rocking of the boat, his girl in his arms, and his dog by his side, an hour later he was still agitated. They made their way back to the house, and Piper pulled a move that was so unexpected and unlike her, there was no way he could have remained enraged. She'd suggested they take a bubble bath, and then she'd pampered the hell out of him—bathing, loving, and *soothing* his battered and bruised emotions. It had been exactly what he'd needed. *She* was exactly what he needed.

Piper's pampering had done the trick last night, calming his thoughts enough for him to fall asleep. But this morning he'd woken up with the sun, feeling discombobulated again, and with Piper fast asleep in his arms, he'd tried, and failed, to sort out his feelings about Marshall.

He'd been walking around with a gut full of lead since he'd arrived at his mother's house. Neither she nor Delaney had mentioned hearing from Marshall, which either meant they hadn't, or they were waiting to drop the bomb.

Delaney rolled her shoulders back, glancing out the patio doors at the girls sitting in the hammock together playing on their iPads.

Harley handed her a glass and said, "Are you okay?"

"Yeah. I did too much around the house yesterday. I'm just a little sore." It had been almost two months since her operation, and she was doing much better. She'd decided to work from home part-time until her breast reconstruction was complete and she healed enough to manage carrying files and working for several hours at a stretch without too much pain or fatigue.

"Damn it, Dee. Why are all the women in my life stubborn? Didn't I tell you to call me and I'd take care of whatever you needed?"

"Yes, but I don't think I need my little brother to do my laundry or run a vacuum."

He handed her a glass of iced tea and said, "I met the guys who run At Your Service at the dance. They're expanding their business to include errands, handyman duties, and even cleaning. I'll hire them for a month to help out."

"Don't you *dare*." She turned away, but not before Harley saw her blushing.

"Dee . . . ? What's going on?"

"Nothing." She tried to school her expression, but her joy broke free and she said, "*God*, I hate that I can't lie to you. Ike still brings dinner by sometimes, but I don't need him *cleaning* my house."

He took a sip of his iced tea and said, "Are you *seeing* him? I met him last night, and he seems like a nice guy, but I'm not sure that's a good idea with all you and the girls are going through right now."

"The girls and I are fine, thanks to you. As you heard when we got here, Jolie hasn't stopped raving about the dance. It sounds like you made quite an impression and left her friends wishing they had cool uncles like you. But as far as my nonexistent dating life goes, that's not your decision to make. There's no need to get all riled up anyway. I just hired him for dinners three times a week. It was easier, that's all. It's not because he's hot and smart or because his daughter and Jolie have gotten to be good friends or anything."

"You just said you can't lie to me, but you seem pretty good at it."

"I'm a lawyer, which means you have no idea if I'm lying or telling the truth, while I know one thing for sure: You look like crap. Having a hard time keeping up with your girlfriend?" she teased as they went into the living room.

"*Hardly.*" Harley handed his mother a glass of iced tea and sat down on the couch beside Delaney.

"Thank you, honey," his mother said. "I'm so glad you decided to drop by. We're taking the girls to the library later. Would you like to come?"

"No, thanks. I've got a lot to do." *Like trying not to punch a wall.*

"With Piper?" his mother asked.

"She's working right now, but later, yes."

"I don't know how she manages like she does." His mother set the glass on the coffee table and said, "She's so tiny, and she's working with big, gruff men all day long. I tried to help your father when we first moved into this house and were finishing the basement. No sooner did we start than I hit my thumb with the hammer. It was excruciating. Needless to say, from that moment on, my help consisted of feeding him while he worked."

"She's been doing it a long time, Mom. She's excellent at what she does, and the men respect her."

"If they didn't, she'd kick their butts," Delaney added.

"Yes, she's a tough cookie," his mother said.

He could talk about Piper for hours, but every second he put off what he'd come to talk about made it that much harder. "She is, and as much as I love talking about her, I have something more important to talk with you about. Have either of you seen or heard from Marshall?" Their faces filled with confusion.

"No," they said in unison.

"Have *you* heard from him?" his mother asked hopefully.

He set his glass down and pressed his hands to his thighs to keep them from clenching. "Yes. He was at my place when I got home after dropping off Jolie last night."

"How is he?" His mother shifted to the edge of the chair, eyes wide.

"What did he say?" Delaney asked, only slightly less anxiously than his mother.

"Not much. I didn't really give him a chance."

His mother sank back in the chair and said, "Oh, Harley." The disappointment in her voice was inescapable.

"What, Mom?" He was unable to keep the bite from his tone and was too agitated to sit still. He pushed to his feet and paced. "What did you want me to do after the way he abandoned you and showed up at Dad's funeral all messed up? Welcome him with open arms? Offer him a beer?"

Grief worked its way up his mother's face, forming a frown, heavy eyelids, and a furrowed brow, adding more weight to the lead in Harley's gut.

"Of course not," Delaney said. "Calm down for a second, Harley. This is a lot for Mom to take in."

"No shit, Dee. How do you think I felt last night when he showed up out of the blue?" He couldn't look away from his mother's grief. "Say something, Mom."

"Is he gone again?" she asked shakily.

"I don't know," Harley said. "I assumed he'd come here or to Delaney's."

"I haven't seen or heard from him," Delaney said. "If you went at him like you did after the funeral, he probably took off again."

"Oh," his mother said sadly, lowering her gaze to the coffee table. "He just missed Mother's Day."

"Mother's Day? Really?" He scoffed. "What the hell do you want from me? I was trying to *protect* you. I'm sure he needs something. Wait until you see him. He's covered in tattoos. We have no idea what he's gotten into, and until we find out, I don't know if I trust him around you."

His mother closed her eyes, breathing deeply. When she opened them, determination replaced the grief he'd seen. She grabbed the arms of the chair and sat up straight. "Harley, that is not your decision to make."

"Jesus, Mom. You have *always* had a soft spot for him."

"He's my *son*," she said sharply.

Years of repressed emotions rushed out. "So am *I*, and Delaney's your daughter. You had us busting our asses at the bar from the time we were kids—washing dishes, clearing tables—and *Marshall* never had a single responsibility. We've *always* been here for you."

"You loved working there. So did Delaney," his mother insisted.

"It's true," Delaney said. "But Harley has a point. Not that you chose favorites, but you have to admit, Marshall was brought up differently than we were."

"He was a different *child*. He was moody, and maybe you don't remember, but he could get very sullen and pull away from us. We didn't want to lose him altogether," his mother said, her eyes pleading for understanding. "He wasn't resilient like you two were. He was *fragile*."

Harley paced. "The only thing *fragile* about Marshall was the glass box you and Dad kept him in."

"We had a business and two other children to care for." His mother rose to her feet, speaking with her hands, which she did only when she was trying not to yell. "It was easier to let him do his own thing than to fight over what *we* wanted him to do. You and Delaney were strong

288

and even-tempered. You *wanted* to learn and to be part of the business from the time you realized there was more to our family than just what was under our roof. But not all children are the same. Maybe you won't understand that until you have your own, but Delaney should." She looked at Delaney and said, "Jolie and Sophie aren't alike in their moods or their interests. You *know* you cannot treat every child the same."

"That's true," Delaney agreed. "But that doesn't mean we didn't feel slighted because of it."

"I'm sorry, Mom, but letting him do whatever he wanted opened the door for him to blow off the few responsibilities and commitments he had, like school and family." *And Piper.*

"You're right, and it was something your father and I didn't see clearly until years later, when Marshall quit college and disappeared. I— *we*—accept responsibility for that. We did the best we could. Nowadays you can go online and find a million resources for how to handle different types of children, but it wasn't like that then." She sat down in the chair and said, "All we wanted was for our kids to be happy, and instead we lost one son, and you two are obviously resentful and angry at me and your father."

"We're not angry, Mom," Delaney said.

"No, it's true, and it's okay," their mother said. "We did the best we could. We love you all. We never meant to hurt any of you. After Marshall disappeared, I started seeing a therapist in Port Hudson, and during the three years I saw him, I learned a lot about things we did wrong as parents and things we did right. I'm not ashamed for being human."

Harley glanced at Delaney, wondering if she knew about their mother going to therapy.

"Your sister didn't know about the therapist, Harley. I felt like we'd failed Marshall, and I didn't know what to do. Your father couldn't talk about it, and he didn't want our family to be the talk of the town."

"You might have opened a door, but he's the one who walked through it," Harley insisted. "Nobody around town blames you or Dad for Marshall's mistakes."

"We don't know that, but I hope they don't. The only person who knew about my therapy was Roxie Dalton, and that's because she saw right past my pleasantries to the pain that was eating away at me. She tried to help, bless her heart. But her holistic approaches didn't work. She had a friend in Port Hudson, a psychologist, and Roxie covered for me once a week so I could go see him. I was depressed, which he said was to be expected. He helped me understand a lot of things, and it took a few years, but eventually I learned to put things in perspective and got back on track. I missed Marshall, and I'm not happy about the mistakes your father and I made, but I understand that I can't change the past."

"Wait, wait, *wait*," Delaney said. "You were *depressed* and having a hard time for *three* years? How could I miss that?"

Harley felt just as blindsided. He'd always kept in close touch with his parents. He remembered a few weeks after Marshall had first taken off when they'd been unhappy, uneasy, concerned. Hell, they all had. But he couldn't remember any *long* stretches of time when his mother had been out of sorts.

"Because, Delaney, your life was fairly messy back then. You were living in the city, you had a new baby, and you were trying to keep your head above water while attending law school and attempting to save your rocky marriage."

"I didn't do a great job of saving it." Delaney sighed and sat back against the couch cushions.

"Nobody could have fixed that douchebag," Harley snapped. "Who leaves their pregnant wife and child for some chick they met at a park?"

"Let's not go there again," Delaney suggested. "Mom, did Dad go to therapy, too?"

Their mother shook her head. "No. Your father didn't believe in it."

"I can't believe I missed the clues. I'm sorry, Mom." Harley sank down to the arm of the couch beside his mother's chair, feeling like he'd failed her.

"Oh, honey, don't do this to yourself. You were building a very important, very difficult career, and you still made time to come back and help us out at home and with the business. I never should have leaned on you for all this time." She reached over and touched his cheek, bringing his eyes to hers. "You're my boy, and I love you. But Marshall is my boy, too, and I love him, which is why you need to give him a chance to speak his mind. You need to do this for me, honey. I need to see him, even if it's just so I can apologize to him for the things your father and I did wrong."

"*Apologize?* He—"

"Harley," his mother said firmly, her unwavering gaze holding him silent. "I don't care if he hears me out and takes off again. I *need* to see him. Do you understand that?"

"Mom, we don't even know if he's still in town," Delaney reminded her as she pulled out her phone. "I can call my friend at the police station and see if he can keep his eyes open for his car."

"Motorcycle," Harley snapped, frustration stacking up inside him. "Colorado plates, but, Dee, *really?*"

"He's right. You can't call the police. If Marshall's in trouble, then we could be leading the police directly to him," his mother said.

Harley pushed to his feet again. "That is *not* what I was saying! When are you two going to stop bailing him out? How many times did Dad fix things for him in high school by leaning on his buddy, Chief Klein? If Marshall's in trouble, he should pay the price."

"Oh, sweetheart." His mother sighed, shaking her head. "The heart is a powerful thing, and it can make you very confused. You think you're angry with him. I think you're worried about him."

"I'm *way* past worrying about Marshall. I'm concerned about you and Delaney and the girls."

"You would not do well on the witness stand," Delaney said with a smirk.

He glowered at her.

"You don't believe that, Harley," his mother said. "Why do you think you're so angry at him?"

"I don't need to think about it," he fumed. "I'm angry because he screwed everyone over and doesn't care about how much he's hurt you, and yeah, Mom, I'm pissed that now you're making excuses for him to come right back into your life and hurt you again."

"And if he's sick?" their mother asked, stopping Harley in his tracks. "What if he came home because something is wrong, and you drove him away?" Her face blanched. "Oh, goodness. What if he doesn't come back?"

Guilt and frustration coiled together into a frigging noose, tightening around Harley's neck. "He didn't look *sick*. He looked *harsh*, and he acted like the same arrogant Marshall he's always been, expecting to waltz right into our lives without any remorse for what he's done." He had to get out of there before he lost it and said things he shouldn't. "I love you both, but I've got to get out of here." He headed for the door and said, "Kiss the girls for me and tell them I love them."

He climbed into his truck and called Piper as he sped away.

"How'd it go?" she asked anxiously.

He was too pissed for small talk. "Would you mind if I demolished something at the Mad House?"

Piper climbed from her truck as a visceral groan cut through the air, followed by the familiar sound of metal on stone and the dull thud of stones landing on concrete. Her heart ached for Harley. If she'd allowed herself to think about Marshall on any personal level, she might have been the one needing the outlet. But Marshall's return wasn't about *her*.

She'd forced herself to put that wall up, sealing off any thoughts about what Marshall had done to her all those years ago, so she could focus on helping Harley deal with his much bigger, more hurtful issue.

She grabbed the water bottle and towel she'd brought, wishing she could have gotten out of work earlier. It had been more than an hour since Harley had called, but they were putting the final touches on the carriage house and she'd needed to get the job done. She followed the sounds of destruction through the long grass and around one of the dilapidated buildings. Most of the knee-high stone wall that had once surrounded the patio was scattered in bits and pieces in the grass and on the patio. Harley was midswing, his skin glistening with sweat. His back and arm muscles bulged and flexed. He emitted a loud, guttural sound as he swung the sledgehammer, and it crashed into the wall, sending stones flying.

"Damn, Dutch. That was about the sexiest thing I've ever seen."

Harley turned, his surprise easing into a partial smile, which did nothing to soothe the torment in his eyes. "Hey, babe." His chest rose and fell with each inhalation.

Piper went to him, wishing she could take away his anguish. "That bad, huh? What can I do?"

Motioning to the stones, he said, "You've already done enough."

He sounded less angry and maybe a little defeated or exhausted. She wasn't sure which, but both were cause for worry. He was wrong. She hadn't done enough, but she'd continue trying as long as he'd let her. She handed him the towel. He toweled off his face and chest, then kissed her. His lips were salty and warm. It didn't matter what was going on in their lives. Every single kiss was still better than the last simply because their love was alive in them.

"I figured you probably forgot to hydrate." She handed him the water bottle.

He set the sledgehammer down and guzzled the entire bottle. "My brain's been on overdrive today."

"Your brain never thinks of *you* until everyone else is taken care of."

"You think you know me," he said, parroting her words with a playful glimmer in his eyes.

She was glad to see and hear his levity. "I know I love you. Does that count?"

"More than you could know." He kissed her again. "Thanks for bringing the drink and towel."

"I keep them in my truck just in case the urge to come here or jump in the lake hits me."

He looked doubtful. "When's the last time you jumped in the lake?"

"I can't tell you all of my secrets," she said coyly. "There'll be no mystery left between us."

"You'll never stop being a mystery to me."

"Let's hope not, but how about we take away a little of *your* mystery? Do you want to talk about what happened with your mom and Delaney? Or would you rather go back to hitting the wall? I'm cool with either."

He pulled her against his sweaty chest, and she wrinkled her nose. "You're a little *ripe*."

"And you smell like my favorite girl who worked hard all day, but you don't see me complaining."

She turned her face and sniffed her shoulder. "I smell like my mother's lavender lotion."

"Keep telling yourself that," he teased. "And I'm onto you with that love-potion lotion of your mother's adding another level of irresistibility to my girl. Just an FYI, I like you sweaty." He kissed her neck. "And I'd like to get you even sweatier."

"I'm good with that." She pressed a kiss to his chest and said, "But I'm also onto your avoidance technique."

"I learned that trick from a very beautiful, extremely wise woman."

"She must be an excellent teacher."

"Wait until you see what she taught me to do in the shower." He lowered his lips to hers, kissing her deeply.

Now she knew what Harley had felt like when she'd been closed off to him. She wanted *him* to let *her* in, but she knew she was the last person who should push anyone to talk about their feelings. At the same time, she was too worried about him not to ask. "Just tell me this. Did they see Marshall?"

"No, but they want to. I feel guilty for sending him away, but if I hadn't, I would have hit him. That would have been worse."

"Maybe, or maybe he needs to duke it out, too."

"That is not the kind of advice my mother would give me," he said.

"Mine either. My father told me that about him and his brother. They fought for years, and when they were trying to clear the air, he said they just went at each other. No words were spoken, but fists flew until they were both worn out."

"Your father? Clean-cut Dan Dalton got into a fistfight?"

"My dad's badass. How do you think I ended up this way?" She felt his tension easing and said, "What do you want to do about Marshall?"

He shrugged. "No idea, and he probably left town anyway."

"If he did, then he wasn't ready to come back. You two have a lot of bad blood and resentment between you. Maybe he just needs time."

His eyes narrowed skeptically.

"I get it. He's had *years* already, but you know what I mean. Thinking about seeing the people you've hurt and actually looking into their eyes is different. As you found out last night, suddenly all that crap you guys told yourselves that you'd do if you ever saw each other again rises to the surface."

She took his hand and said, "Why don't we put away the sledge-hammer and go home and get cleaned up?"

He put the towel over his shoulder and picked up the sledgehammer, resting it on the towel as they walked through the long grass to the barn. After they put away the tool, they headed to their trucks.

"Why was the barn unlocked when I got here?" he asked.

"The lock fairies must have come out early in the morning. They're smart like that."

He squeezed her hand, and when his loving eyes met hers, she knew her resilient man was going to be okay.

"Want to get subs or a pizza for dinner later?"

He waggled his brows and said, "Definitely. I've got a twelve-inch meat lover's for you."

"I have a tape measure, remember?"

"Come on, Trig. You *know* those things aren't accurate."

She laughed. "I don't care if you're eight or twelve inches. All I care is that you're *mine*, and to show you just how happy that makes me, I'm going to give you a Piper Special after our shower and take *all* your stress away."

"Oh, *baby*. That sounds *hot*."

"I meant a *massage*."

"As long as there's *a happy ending . . .*"

CHAPTER TWENTY-FOUR

PIPER TORE A piece of drywall off the studs and tossed it on a pile of rubbish. It was Monday afternoon, and she was strung so tight, she'd been gritting her teeth all day to keep from biting her crew's heads off. After finishing the carriage house and wrapping up the Windsor Hall project, she'd hoped to have a few days off before preparing for their next job. But she and her crew were *back* at Windsor Hall, tearing out the kitchen. She was usually patient when clients made last-minute changes or asked her to take on additional work, but she abhorred doing things ass-backward, like being asked to tear out a kitchen that her crew had just finished painting and touching up. Luckily, the guys didn't mind the extra work and had jumped right into dismantling the room.

"All I'm saying is that your bachelor party will be the last time you're going to get a free pass," Mike said to Darren Monday afternoon. "Think about it. The *last* time."

"That right there is the reason you're three times divorced," Kase said as he worked on removing the counter from the island. "Guys don't get a *free pass* before marriage any more than women do. I bet none of *your* exes got a free pass."

Mike scoffed. "Damn right."

"Has it ever occurred to you that I don't want a free pass? Man, you've got issues, Mike. I love my girl, and I don't want anyone else now, or ever." The restraint in Darren's voice heightened the tension between them. Darren was obviously hitting his limit with Mike's bullshit. He pointed to the other end of the cabinet he'd just torn out and said, "Now, get your ancient ass over here and help me carry this out."

"Kase, get that with Darren, will ya?" Piper called across the room.

Kase took off his baseball cap and dragged his forearm across his forehead. "Sure, boss."

Piper pulled another piece of Sheetrock from the wall and tossed the part that hadn't crumbled in her hands to the rubbish pile, grinding out a curse. When Darren was out of earshot, she said, "It's time to cut the shit, Mike. I'm getting tired of listening to Darren defending himself and his love for his girl."

"I'm just watching my boy's back. Last night he sounded like he had cold feet." He uncapped a bottle of water and took a swig.

"It's *marriage*!" she snapped. "It's *fucking scary*! Putting negative thoughts into his head isn't going to help whatever's going on between them."

He took another drink and said, "I was just having fun with him."

"Well, cut it out. It's grating on my nerves."

Mike set down the water bottle and said, "You and Harley are still going strong, huh?"

Kase and Darren came through the door, and Kase said, "They are, which means you lost your chance, Mike."

"As if he ever had one." Piper tossed another hunk of drywall aside.

Mike grabbed a cabinet and hefted it into his arms. "Guess he's not cockblocking you anymore."

Piper ground her teeth together, pulled off her gloves, and followed him out the door.

Today was *not* the day to fuck with her. In addition to having to do work that should have been on her original contract, she was worried about Harley. Nobody had heard from Marshall, and every day that passed brought more frustration and guilt to Harley over having sent him away. By taking off, Marshall had proven either her or Harley's theories right—he either hadn't been ready to come back, or he needed something. It didn't matter which one was right; the end result was the same. He was gone, and Harley was left trying to clean up his brother's mess. He might have been the one to send him away that night, but if their family was important to Marshall, he would have tried again. It appeared Harley was right and Marshall hadn't changed at all. Marshall's blatant disregard for Harley fueled a fire in her that she had no idea how to put out.

Mike heaved the cabinet into the dumpster, and when he turned, Piper was *right there.* He had about a foot and at least sixty or seventy pounds on her, but that didn't stop her from getting in his face as she said, "From now on, my relationship with Harley is off-limits. You want to joke around about aprons and that nonsense? *Fine.* But things have changed, and if my sex life comes up again, I'll give you bruises that you'll have a hard time explaining. *Got it?*"

Regret rose in his eyes. "Got it, boss. Sorry." His gaze shifted over her shoulder, and in a more forceful tone, he said, "Can we help you with something?"

"I'm here to see Piper."

Marshall's voice fueled her frustration, sending an icy chill down her spine.

Piper turned, feeling the scowl on her lips and the narrowing of her eyes. She knew the feel of the glacial expression she was giving off well. It was the one she'd used on Harley the night he'd found her on the dock when they were younger. She'd mastered it in the years since. It was a look that said, *Don't even try to fuck with me, because I will tear you up and spit you out.*

Marshall looked nothing like he had when they were teenagers. His hair was coarser, he was bearded, and the tattoo sleeves and the ink snaking out from beneath the collar of his black T-shirt gave him a sinister edge. His face had a tough, leatherish appearance, like he'd been roughed up so many times even his skin exuded a don't-fuck-with-me vibe. His eyes conveyed a completely different mood, hovering some-where between arrogance and uncertainty. He gave off a third, more complex wave of energy with an aggressive stance, but his arms hung loosely by his sides, strangely nonthreatening. Assembling all of those attributes was like trying to fit the pieces of several different puzzles into one. Piper's emotions tangled and fought in protection of Harley, spin-ning angrier by the second, but frustratingly tethered by some unseen leash to the past.

Mike stepped between them, facing Piper. "You okay, boss?"

"*Fine,*" she said, her eyes never leaving Marshall's.

Mike faced Marshall, and Piper knew he was sending his own silent message of protectiveness before finally walking away. She didn't need anyone's protection, but she was proud to have earned it just the same.

"Marshall." His name came out like an accusation.

"Saw your truck. Dalton Contracting? Congratulations." His eyes swept over the building. "What is this place?"

"Commercial property going on the market when I'm done with it. Stop the small talk. Why are you here?"

He took a step forward.

"That's far enough," she said sharply. She didn't know what he was thinking or what he might do. In fact, she realized she didn't know him at all. After all he'd done to his family, she wondered if she ever had.

The surprise in his eyes quickly dimmed with something akin to regret. "I thought we could talk."

"I'm not the person you should be talking with."

"Yeah, well, I was hoping you could help me with that."

She folded her arms and said, "Then you can take that hope with you when you walk off this job site."

"Come on, Piper. Obviously you and Harley have something going on. Can't you talk to him for me?"

"What Harley and I *have* is none of your business, especially after the way you've treated him. Harley has been here to help your family through more than any family should ever have to endure, and he's done it *alone*. I have absolutely nothing to say to you, and if you think I'll try to sway Harley one way or the other, you're wrong." A thread of guilt wound through her. This might be her only chance to help Harley and his family by helping Marshall see the error of his ways. But that would be digging him out of his hole, doing *exactly* what Harley *didn't* want and what Marshall *didn't* need. So she squared her shoulders and said, "This is your mess, Marshall. A good man would do whatever it takes to clean it up. Harley's not just a good man. He's the best man I know. Unfortunately, right now I can't say the same about you."

She turned around and found eight good, strong men standing shoulder to shoulder, arms crossed, all eyes on Marshall. Her crew, her *family*, had her back, causing a freaking lump to lodge in her throat.

"You're *wrong* about me, Piper," Marshall called after her.

She gritted her teeth, hands flexing, heart thundering, and glanced over her shoulder. "Prove it."

She strode around the corner of the building and walked inside, unwanted tears vying for release—for the support of her crew *and* for the hope that Marshall might try to prove her wrong.

The men followed her inside, talking loudly on their way to the kitchen. Piper kept her back to them, willing her tears to remain at bay. She heard Kase guiding them away from her and breaking up a couple of guys who must have been horsing around, giving her time to pull herself together.

"A'right, let's get back to work," Kase said loudly in the other room.

A few minutes later, the sounds of men working brought relief, and Piper felt a comforting hand on her back.

"You okay, boss?"

She inhaled deeply and faced Kase. "Yeah. Thanks for rallying the troops."

"I didn't do it. Mike did. We've always got your back."

Mike, even after I reamed him. "I appreciate that."

"Who was that guy?"

"Harley's brother. He hasn't been around for a while . . . and I might have gone out with him in high school."

Kase's lips tipped up at the corners, and he said, "Guess that explains it. You handled him well. Harley should be proud."

"Thanks. I need to make a call."

"Take all the time you need. I've got this."

She headed outside and walked away from the building to call Harley.

He answered on the first ring. "Hey, Trig. What's up?"

"Marshall was just here."

"Son of a bitch," Harley growled. "What'd he say?"

"He wanted me to talk to you for him, but I told him I wouldn't and that he had to clean up his own mess. He may be heading your way."

He ground out a curse. "Did he get into anything with you? If he said or did anything nasty, I'm going to kill him."

"First, that's inappropriately *hot*. Second, I didn't give him the chance, and all my guys were behind me."

"Good. Sorry you had to deal with that, babe."

"It's fine. At least you know he's still around."

Harley exhaled loudly. "Right. I need to call my mom and Dee, let them know he's still in town."

"Okay. Hey, Harley?"

"Yeah?"

"Whatever does or doesn't happen between you two, I'm here. You're not alone in this anymore."

He was quiet for a beat, and she knew him so well, even in the silence she heard his gratitude.

"I love you, babe," he finally said. "Meet me at my place after work?"

"Sure, but you'll see me for dinner. After the day I've had, I need a double order of Dutch's wings, a cold beer, and about a hundred kisses from the hottest bar owner in Sweetwater."

"My lips are waiting."

"Hey, man, I think that glass is clean," Jasper said, breaking through Harley's thoughts.

Harley looked down at the glass in his hands. He hadn't even realized he was still holding it. The bar was closed, and they were getting ready to leave for the night when Harley had decided to have one drink to calm his nerves. He'd spent the evening in fluctuating states of anxious contempt and hostility. Marshall hadn't shown up, and he hadn't gone to see their mother or sister, either, which Harley was glad about. The only bright light of his evening had been when Piper had come by for dinner. She'd told him what had happened with Marshall, though neither one of them knew how he'd found her on the job site.

"You've been drying that thing for eight minutes," Jasper pointed out. "Does that mean you're relieved or angry that your brother didn't show up?"

Harley put the glass away and said, "I don't really give a shit either way." He had no idea if that was true or not. That was how jumbled his thoughts were. All he knew for sure was that he didn't want Marshall anywhere near Piper.

"I'm going to call that *relieved*," Jasper said as he walked around the bar. "Want me to lock up on the way out?"

"No. I'll be right behind you."

"All right, man. Try to relax tonight."

After Jasper left, Harley let out a long breath. *What a fucked-up day.* He'd held his breath, readying for a fight every time the damn door opened. He'd spoken to his mother around nine o'clock, and she'd sounded upset that Marshall hadn't come by to see any of them. When he'd called Delaney, she'd sounded disappointed, too. Their conversations had tweaked his guilt, but their willingness to look past everything Marshall had done had just pushed his need to protect them into hyperdrive. He went into his office to shut down his computer, and his gaze fell to the picture of his parents on the corner of the desk. He picked it up and sat down, wondering what his father would have done the other night when Marshall had shown up.

A few months after Marshall had quit college and lost touch, Harley had asked his father if he should go after him. His father had said, *Marshall doesn't need us to find him. He's on a solo journey to find himself.* At the time, Harley had thought leaving them in the dark was the most selfish thing his brother could do. But he'd been wrong. The most selfish thing wasn't his leaving. It was that he'd stayed away for so many years.

Harley ran his fingers over the glass covering the picture, remembering what his father had said the only other time Harley had brought up Marshall. It was when his father had gotten sick, and Harley had come home to take over Dutch's. Harley had spent weeks trying to find Marshall, calling the last place he'd worked, tracking down people he'd worked with, following bread crumbs until he'd finally heard back from Marshall. He'd sounded drugged out, and it had disgusted Harley, but he'd told him that their father was on death's door, and he should get his ass home. When their father's health had taken a dismal turn, Harley had apologized to his father for not being able to bring Marshall back to say goodbye. He'd never forget the regret in his father's eyes as he'd said, *He's too lost to be found.*

Now anger flared inside Harley, burning in his chest. *You've got to be a fucking mess for your own father to give up on you.* "Fuck it."

He put the frame on the desk and shut down his computer, in a worse mood than he'd been in all night. *Fucking Marshall.* He pulled out his keys on the way out of his office, nearly barreling into his brother.

"*What the f—*"

"We need to talk," Marshall said, holding Harley's stare.

He held a leather jacket over his right shoulder, and Harley had the odd thought that the damn thing had to be easier to carry than the chip he'd been lugging around forever because of his brother. That thought fueled his rage. "Like hell we do. Stay the fuck away from Piper."

"Harley—"

Harley dropped his keys on a table as he closed the gap between them, getting angrier by the second at the thought of him with Piper. He shoved Marshall back with one hand to the chest, seething. "I don't live life on *your* terms, little brother. I spent *weeks* trying to track you down to let you know our *only* sister had cancer. Do you have any idea how *lucky* you are that the surgery cleared her? That we didn't *lose* her?" Harley was hollering, out of control. There was no stopping the rage exploding inside him. "She could have *died* without ever seeing you again. Do you know how hard that would have been for *her*? Do you have any concept of the pain you've caused everyone in this family?"

Marshall gritted his teeth and threw his jacket on the floor, locking a cold stare on Harley. Harley shoved him again. Marshall stumbled back, knocking over a chair. He found his footing and came at Harley swinging. Harley dodged a punch, catching Marshall in the jaw. Marshall flew back and Harley grabbed him by the shirt, hauling him upright.

"I don't know why I ever expected anything from you." Harley's tone was venomous, his fight unyielding as he let another punch fly.

Marshall blocked his punch and threw one to Harley's gut. Harley doubled over, and Marshall's fist connected with his cheek, sending him stumbling sideways. Adrenaline surged inside him. He ran toward Marshall at full speed, taking them both down to the floor, sending chairs scattering as they competed for dominance. They wrestled, knocking into chairs and tables, fists flying, getting out *years* of anger.

Marshall wrenched out of Harley's grip and punched him in the ribs. "Same old fucking holier-than-thou Harley!"

"You should've been there for *Delaney*," Harley seethed.

They were both on their knees, breathing hard, their bodies swaying. Harley threw another punch, connecting with Marshall's eye. Marshall keeled sideways, and Harley made his move, putting him in a headlock. Harley's muscles strained against his brother's efforts as he wrestled him down to the floor, Marshall's back to his chest.

Harley tightened the headlock and growled, "You should've been there for Mom and Dad."

"Fuck you." Marshall clawed at Harley's arms.

Harley wrapped one leg around Marshall's from behind, trapping them as his brother fought futilely, trying to wrench free.

"Your nieces don't even *know* you," Harley ground out through gritted teeth. "You'll never change, and I'm not letting you hurt them *ever* again."

"Always the fucking *hero*," Marshall accused.

"I never wanted to be a hero, you *asshole*. I've spent my life cleaning up your messes, trying to minimize the damage you left behind. How many times did I cover for your lame ass? Drive a fucking hour and a half from the city to pick up your drunk ass? I finished the boat for Piper because you were too busy screwing up to do it yourself. I should have ratted you out." A painful realization slammed into him. He'd enabled Marshall's behavior as much as his parents had. *Holy shit.*

Marshall pushed back against Harley's chest. "You *loved* being the hero."

"Wrong. I loved *you*, and that was a big mistake."

Marshall scoffed, thrashing from side to side, trying to break free. "You loved making that fucking boat for *her*."

"Don't you *ever* talk about Piper." He tightened his arm around Marshall's neck. "You were never good enough for her."

Marshall clawed at Harley's forearm, throwing himself forward and back, making strangled noises, but Harley was blinded with fury, his brother's sounds drowned out by the blood thundering in his ears. Marshall's arm stretched shakily out to his side, and his index finger straightened. His second finger followed, creating a trembling peace sign, kicking Harley's brain into firing again as memories rolled in and he recognized the signal for surrender they'd used as kids. Marshall's third finger rose, his hand shaking so hard, his fingers blurred together. Harley released him, backing away in a state of panic. Marshall bent forward, coughing and gasping for air.

Harley ground out, "*Fuck.*"

"I coulda had you." Marshall was bent over, his back to Harley, both palms flat on the floor. His head hung between his shoulders, his body heaving as he noisily dragged air into his lungs.

"*Asshole.*" Harley coughed out a laugh. "You and what army?"

"I didn't come here for this shit."

Harley used his heels to push back against the wall and tipped his face up. "Why are you here, Marshall?"

Marshall turned haunted eyes in Harley's direction. His face was a mask of pain. He held up his left hand, showing Harley a gold wedding band. "To make sure my wife's death wasn't for nothing."

CHAPTER TWENTY-FIVE

MARSHALL HAD GOTTEN married and had never told them? His wife had *died*? Harley couldn't process the information. He didn't even know where to begin. The ghosts in his brother's eyes rose to the surface. Harley knew about the hope-sucking anguish of grief from losing their father, but he couldn't imagine the magnitude of despair if something ever happened to Piper. The thought of his brother actually loving a woman enough to marry her, and then losing her, brought Harley's walls crashing down. "You're *married*?"

"Widowed."

Marshall's eye was already turning purple from their fight, but Harley knew that pain was nothing compared to what his brother had already endured. "Why didn't you tell us?"

Marshall dragged himself over to the wall beside Harley. "After what I just told you, *that's* the part you zeroed in on? You're losing your hero touch, bro."

He swallowed hard, trying to assemble his fractured thoughts. "I'm beyond sorry for your loss. I'm just trying to process everything. It's a lot to take in."

"Tell me about it." Marshall sighed. "Losing Annie fucked me up. Not that I wasn't already messed up, but we were good for a while. Better than good."

Despite everything that had gone down between them, Harley was glad to hear that his brother had been good for a while. "Where have you been all this time? When did you meet her? *Annie?* What happened?"

"Life, man. Life happened. After I left school, I headed out to California with a buddy of mine and worked as a firefighter. With training and the right connections, we made it to a hotshot crew." Hotshots were elite teams of wildland firefighters. They were fearless, highly skilled hand crews trained to battle all phases of the most serious wildland fires in the nation.

"That's impressive. *Dangerous*, but you always wanted to be a smoke jumper."

"Yeah, I blew that when I didn't finish school. But I loved my job. It was good for me, you know? No chance to get bored, worked with a great group of guys. That's when I met Annie. I was coming out of a bar with my buddies and she was just standing there looking up at the stars, like an angel who had been dropped in my path. She was beautiful to me, maybe not so much to the other guys. She had bright red, almost orange hair, cut super short, and she had acne scars and *other* scars. The kind of scars most people turn away from, brought on by a rough life and mean hands. Not mine, though. Never mine." Marshall looked down at his hands, tears glistening in his eyes. "From the moment she looked at me, I felt sparks, man. I'm talking where-have-you-been-all-my-life sparks. I'll never forget the way she looked me up and down, like she'd seen far better men, and I'm sure she had, but it just made me want to be better than them. The first thing she ever said to me was, 'If you were a bird and could go anywhere in the world, where would you go?' My buddies walked away at that point. But I couldn't have walked away if I'd wanted to. I had only one answer. I said, 'I'd follow you,' and she said, 'Cool. Let's go.'" Marshall wiped a tear from his cheek. "She was reckless and crazy and so fucking smart I could barely keep up with her thought processes."

"She sounds incredible," Harley said, clearing his choked-up throat. "I'm sorry I didn't get to meet her."

"We'd planned to come here. She was twenty when we met. I was twenty-four. We were wild. *Too* wild, and reckless, drinking, smoking, living what we thought was the good life. When things got too heavy, we partied harder."

Harley silently prayed his brother hadn't been the cause of her death, because that was a torment he didn't think anyone could get past.

"After a while she realized she'd missed a few periods, and when we found out she was four months pregnant we stopped all that shit." Marshall made a fist and covered it with his other hand. "We were going to do everything *right*, be responsible parents. We both got life insurance, got clean, and figured when the baby was born we'd come back here and try to start over. We thought the baby would be a way to break the ice, you know? Who can turn away an adorable baby girl? We had big plans. Annie had run away when she was fourteen. We were going to head to Colorado with the baby and find her family after we were settled back here and things were good with you guys." He pressed his lips together, his eyes glassy again. "Life was good, you know? I mean, Annie's moods were up and down, but we figured that was hormones. But then our little girl . . ." He held his hands out, palms up, and tears spilled from his eyes, pulling tears from Harley's. "She was . . ." He gritted his teeth, cleared his throat. "*Destiny*, that was her name. She was stillborn."

Harley opened his mouth to speak, tears wetting his cheeks, but there were no words to soothe his brother's pain. He opened his arms and Marshall moved into them, struggling to regain control.

"She was so small, so *perfect*, Har," Marshall choked out. He pushed back from Harley's embrace and pulled his wallet from his back pocket. "Annie insisted we take a picture. I didn't want to, but I'm glad we did. It's all I have left."

He pulled out the picture and handed it to Harley. His sweet wife lay in a hospital bed holding their tiny baby in her arms. The baby was swaddled in a pink-and-white blanket. She had wisps of red hair, and she looked peaceful, like she was sleeping. But the anguish in Annie's eyes told their sorrowful story, drawing more tears for his brother's losses. The picture was creased and faded, the corners curled and frayed. Harley could only imagine the hours Marshall had spent looking at it.

"They're both beautiful," Harley said. "I'm sorry, Marshall."

"I know. It was a long time ago. Six years since we lost her." He wiped his eyes with the base of his hand and said, "After that, we both went to shit. We moved from one town to the next, trying to start over, but we'd fallen too far. We were both devastated, but Annie couldn't break out of it even when she was drunk, you know? She couldn't let go enough to find herself. I tried to get her help, took her to doctors." He wiped the remaining tears from his cheeks and said, "They gave her meds, but she wouldn't take them. I felt like the pill police, and it fucking sucked. I became the bad guy, and I lived up to it, Harley. I never physically hurt her. I'd never do that. But we argued, and I'm not proud of that. But it was hell losing the baby, and the truth is, when we lost Destiny, I also lost Annie. And then . . ." He ground out a curse. "Annie tried to commit suicide. That was when Dad got sick. I was in the hospital with her when you called, and I couldn't leave her, man. I couldn't do it."

Harley's breath rushed out. He felt gutted. "Why didn't you tell me? I would have come there to help."

"The last thing I needed was my brother the *hero* swooping in to save the day."

"That's not fair, Marshall. I was thrust into that role, and you know it."

Marshall's jaw clenched so tight the veins in his temples bulged. "I thought I could help her. I got clean again, and I tried, man. Damn it, I tried so fucking hard." He shook his head, fresh tears wetting his cheeks.

"She did it when I was at work, had it all planned, like a damn grocery list. I found her in the bathtub, her wrists cut, and a note."

"Jesus, Marsh." Harley couldn't hold back his own tears. "I'm sorry." He didn't ask what the note said. Marshall had shared enough of his pain.

"Me too. After that, I left all my shit and took off on a bender. Ended up at this biker bar in Colorado a few months later, the Roadhouse. I found the biggest, meanest-looking biker and tried to start a fight. I wanted to *hurt*, Harley. I wanted to *die*."

Harley tried to swallow past the thickening of his throat, but it was too painful to think his brother had suffered so much and had been all alone.

"I called him names, threw his beer bottle against the wall," Marshall said. "I shoved him, but the guy was like a fucking mountain, muscles upon muscles, with a lethal stare. The coldest, deadest eyes I'd ever seen. I egged him on, throwing punches, which had the impact of a flea. All these big-ass guys surrounded us, wearing leather and biker patches, but it was like they deferred to him, looked to him for direction, you know? The alpha of the pack. I was sweating bullets, fighting a guy who refused to fight back, knocking bottles off the bar, shoving chairs and tables out the way, and saying God knows what. The guy, Diesel, told me later that I was shouting and rambling, apologizing to Annie and Destiny."

Harley put his hand on Marshall's fist and held it. "Grief is a powerful thing, and you're lucky—*we're* lucky—that guy didn't kill you."

"He *saved* me." Marshall met Harley's gaze, trying to blink away tears. "Those guys surrounded me and waited until I wore myself out and collapsed to the floor like a fucking pussy, crying and so damn lost. The bikers who I *wanted* to kill me sat on the floor of the bar talking with me, *to* me, for hours. They told me their own horror stories of loss and battles. And then they told me about the Dark Knights motorcycle club."

Marshall must have seen the worried look in Harley's eyes, because he said, "It's not a gang. They do good. Just look at me. They took me in, brought me to the Redemption Ranch, run by Tommy Whiskey. He goes by the biker name Tiny." A wry smile curved his lips. "They must have fortified water out there, because *Tiny* was probably three hundred pounds, a big, bearded, and tattooed guy who looked soft. Not muscular, just heavy. But *man*, he is tough as nails. They rescue horses, and as in my case, they rescue people. They hire ex-cons, recovering drug addicts, people with social and emotional issues. And they *help*, Harley. You don't just work on the ranch, although that's a must. They give people a *purpose*, a reason to push past their pain and get moving again. Tiny's wife, Wynona—*Wynnie*—is a licensed psychologist. She and a host of other medical professionals, mostly comprised of Dark Knights and their family members, hold daily therapy sessions, group and individual. There was always someone there to pick me up and remind me that I'm not alone."

"We've been here, Marshall. Your *family*. If we'd known, we would have been there to do the same."

"Sure, once we got past our shit. But I couldn't come home like that. I couldn't have done that to Mom, to Delaney and the girls. To *you*."

"I wish you had," he said, tears burning his eyes again.

"Thank you for that, but I did what I thought was right. With their help, I grieved until I couldn't grieve any more, for my baby girl and my beautiful wife. I learned just how fucked up I was, how Annie's issues were chemical, which was why she spiraled so far out of control. I knew she was depressed, but I *stopped* fighting with her to take those pills because it just pulled us apart. But then I learned what I could have— *should* have—done for her. She wasn't just depressed. She was bipolar. I was told that when we were mired down with grief, but I couldn't process it until I was seeing clearly again. And I've got my own issues, Har. I wasn't just a troublemaker when we were younger. I was trying to outrun my own demons and anxiety. You wouldn't think a teenager could have demons, but I did. Once I could see things more clearly, I grieved all over again for all the things I never did and all the people I hurt. Those men and their families, the Dark Knights, they helped me finish school, helped me find peace of mind. They showed me what I could *be*, and it was who I *wanted* to be for Annie, for Destiny, for you and Mom and Dee. For *Dad*."

"*Fuck*, Marshall. I gave you hell when you came home for Dad's funeral . . ." Harley's voice was lost to a wave of guilt and regret.

"I was grieving three people I loved in the only way I knew how."

"I'm sorry for all the shit I gave you. I'd give anything to take it back."

Marshall shook his head. "You did the right thing. I would have torn our family apart. I wasn't ready. I needed to find that bar in order to find my way. I think Annie led me there."

"Did you find her family?"

"No, but I will."

"I'm here if you want help. Marshall, I'm glad you had those guys, but we could have found a way to help you. You have to know that."

"Don't you get it?" Marshall said angrily, sitting up straighter, hands fisted. "I had nothing to offer but heartache. I was a broken brother and son. A waste of life."

"Who gives a fuck? We're *family*." Harley banged his chest with his fist. "*I* should have been there for you. *I* should have gotten you help."

"*No!* Stop it! You are *not* making this about you. This is *my* heartache! *My* pain, and damn it, Harley, this is *my* redemption. You cannot take that away from me."

"Take it away? I don't want to take it away," he said angrily. "I feel like shit for not being there for you, for sending you off without hearing you out. I'm your older brother, the guy who should have had your back."

Marshall scoffed. "Yeah. I know a thing or two about hindsight and just how fucking painful it is. Don't go down that dark, angry, painful path. You don't deserve it, not for a second. I wanted to explain all of this the other night, but you didn't give me the chance, which was fair given my history. I should have been strong enough to break through and tell you my side of the story, but man, your reaction sent me right back into defensive mode. And when I saw *Piper* standing with you like she was on your side, all I could think was that you *finally* got your girl."

"What do you mean *finally?*"

Marshall closed his eyes and rested his head back against the wall. "You've been in love with her forever."

"No I haven't. A few *years*, but not forever."

Marshall opened his eyes and looked at Harley like he'd lost his mind. "Do you know why I didn't come back after I quit school?" He didn't give Harley a chance to answer. "Because from the moment you found out I cheated on Piper, you were always up my ass. You might have been working in the city, but you kept tabs on me, you called and harassed me, you came home on weekends—"

"To help Dad at the pub or to bail you out of trouble!"

Marshall sat up straight, anger rising in his eyes. "Keep telling yourself that, but I saw the truth. That fucking black eye you gave me for cheating? That told me how much you cared about her."

"You *hurt* her. I would have done that no matter who you cheated on," Harley insisted.

"Is that what you tell yourself?" he asked calmly. "Because I remember things a little differently. When I went out with Evie Collier, you knew I cheated on her. You gave me hell, but you *never* touched me. When Piper got that horrible flu and I promised her I'd finish the boat so she'd have it for the summer boat race the next weekend and then I blew it off, you tracked me down. You pulled me out of a party and beat the living hell out of me for leaving her hanging. Then you finished building and painting her boat. You loved her then, man. It's a *good* thing. *Own* it, because the way she stood up to me today told me that you two are right as rain together. You should be damn proud of that

315

woman. She's only gotten better with age. And you were right: I didn't deserve her. But you sure do."

Harley's mind reeled back in time, spinning with memories of racing home on the weekends to work at the pub, bailing Marshall out of trouble, and a dozen other reasons he'd come home. But he felt the pulse of the truth getting louder, breaking free from its burial ground deep inside him. He'd shoved the truth down so deep, he'd never seen it. Because he felt like he was betraying his brother? He couldn't be sure. But memories rushed in, of standing outside the pub, hoping he'd see Piper on the dock. Looking for her everywhere, wondering if she was home for the weekend, too, once she'd gone away to college.

"You remember, don't you?" Marshall asked.

"I didn't . . . I wasn't trying to take your girl," Harley said, dumbfounded by the truth.

"I know that. You were driven by your emotions. I can see that now. I understand it, and I'm not pissed at you anymore. I was angry for a long time, feeling like you chose her over me. But then I met Annie, and I finally *got* it. I felt *love* like you must have, and I knew I'd do anything for her. That's why I'm here. I became a Dark Knight, and through them I've had a chance to help others the way the Dark Knights helped me. For the first time in my life, I have a clear direction, a clear head, and I know what I was meant to do. With their assistance and guidance, I came up with a business plan to open an emotional wellness center, Annie's Hope."

"Marshall—"

"Just hear me out. I know it's a big endeavor. I have Annie's life insurance money, and I want to put it to good use. I've been clean and sober for two years, and I'm never going back to that life again. Not when I realize how much I could have done to save my girls. I'm not talking about a huge medical clinic. I want to create a more welcoming, less threatening environment. A coffee-shop atmosphere for meetings, offices that are like living rooms, with medical professionals, volunteers, mentoring programs, work programs. My plan is a solid one. I've had it reviewed by several mental health professionals in Colorado. It would be similar to AA or NA. I don't have a medical degree, but I don't need one to be the person who pulls it together. My experience—the experiences I've learned about with others—are what guided me to the concept. I need to do this, Harley, and I can do it with or without your support. I know that I can stand on my own two feet, and the Dark Knights, the brotherhood, have my back. There are chapters everywhere."

Harley looked across the room, where his brother's leather jacket lay in a heap, the Dark Knights patches facing them, as if they were in the room with them, giving Marshall the support he needed. Despite Marshall's forgiveness, Harley would always regret turning him away. He wanted to give him the support he was asking for, but he also wanted to protect him.

He met Marshall's gaze and said, "I support you, brother, but I think it's only fair to you, and to the rest of us, if you give it some time. We have a lot of anger and hurt to work through as a family, and I don't want you to stress yourself out and end up in a bad place again."

Marshall laughed under his breath, shaking his head. "Still the hero."

"I didn't mean it like that," Harley said sharply.

Marshall's lips quirked up, familiar and *arrogant*. "Just giving you hell. You're right. That would be smart. I need to find NA meetings around here anyway, get my stuff sent from the ranch, and touch base with the psychologist they referred me to out here. But my first order of business is seeing Mom and Dee. Think you can go with me to talk to them tomorrow? I have to figure out how to explain to Delaney's girls who I am and who I was."

"Absolutely."

Marshall carefully put the picture of his wife and baby in his wallet and shoved the wallet in his back pocket. His expression turned serious again, and he said, "If Annie and Destiny, Dad, and the stories of my Dark Knights brothers taught me one thing about life, it's that we don't know how long we'll be on this earth. We have no guarantees of tomorrow, and neither do the people we love. I did the best I could at the time, but I'll never get back the years I missed out on with Dad. I don't know what your plans are with Piper, but I know love when I see it, and you two give it off in droves. Don't waste a second of the life you have with her. Don't put everyone else first, and yourself last, which is what you've always done. I'm not surprised you didn't realize you loved her when we were younger. You were in *hero* mode, and that's not a bad thing, Harley. Dad raised you to be a good man, to take care of the rest of us. You were saving Piper from me, and you did a good thing. But don't stay in the background. Give her *all* you have *now*. And don't just be *her* hero. Be your *own* hero. Because while you're busy putting off your dreams, thinking in terms of *one day*, that dream can be stolen away in a heartbeat."

The door to the pub opened, and Jiggs bounded over, covering Harley's face with sloppy kisses. "Guess you should meet my buddy Jiggs." Jiggs climbed on Marshall, covering his face with kisses.

Marshall loved up Jiggs and said, "He's as touchy-feely as you are."

Harley's heart beat impossibly faster as Piper stepped inside, looking sweet and worried in a sweatshirt and cutoffs. After everything Marshall had said, he wanted to run to her, sweep her into his arms, and never let her go.

"Do I need a body bag, a medic, or a bottle of tequila?" Piper asked as she stepped into the bar, closing the door behind her.

Marshall looked at Harley and said, "Don't waste a second."

He didn't plan to. Not with Piper and not with him.

"I saw Marshall's bike and figured Jiggs and I would wait out on the stoop," Piper said, righting chairs as she approached. "But it went silent for too long, and I thought you'd killed each other."

"No dead bodies," Harley said as he pushed to his feet, wincing.

Jiggs sniffed Marshall as Harley offered his brother a hand, helping him to his feet.

"Just a couple of bruised egos," Marshall added.

"It looks like a little more than that. Ouch, Marshall, that black eye looks like it hurts. At least you got the burly one back on his cheek." She put her arms around Harley, and he winced. She lifted his shirt, revealing hints of what he was sure would be bruises on his ribs by morning. She pressed a kiss there, and then her lips curled into a sassy smirk and she said, "Where else did you hit him?"

Marshall and Harley chuckled.

"In the heart mostly," Marshall said. He started to pick up fallen chairs. "I'm going to head out after we get the place fixed up and give you guys some privacy. Unless you want me to stick around to go over things with Piper?"

"I think I can handle it." Harley touched Marshall's hand, stopping him from fixing the chairs, and said, "I've got this."

"Sorry, brother, but I clean up my own messes these days," Marshall said, and he went back to helping put the room back in order.

When they finished, Harley asked Marshall where he was staying.

Marshall picked up his leather jacket and said, "With Ike Preacher, a Dark Knight over in Harmony Pointe."

"Really? I hired his company to bring Delaney meals after her surgery," Harley said as Jiggs came to his side. He scratched Jiggs's head. "I think she's got the hots for him."

"He's a good guy," Marshall said.

Harley grabbed his keys from the table where he'd left them and offered them to him. "Stay at my place."

"Let's not push our luck," Marshall said.

"We can stay at Piper's, give you privacy," Harley suggested.

"No, really. I'm good. As you said, we have a lot to work through, and one of my issues is standing up for myself, not needing a savior. I appreciate you being there for me, but it's healthiest if I find my own way, overcome my own obstacles." Marshall glanced at Piper and said, "Thanks for giving me a shove in the right direction, Piper. I needed it."

"You know how much I like bossing people around. You should put some ice on that shiner."

"Nah. Battle wounds are to be worn proudly." Marshall winked at Harley.

Harley called Jiggs from where he'd wandered behind the bar. He slung an arm around Piper, and they all headed out to the parking lot. It was a brisk, starless night, and as Harley locked the door, he said, "Why don't we meet at Dee's tomorrow morning around nine? The girls will be at school. That'll give you and Delaney a chance to figure out how to talk to them about everything."

"Can we make it eight? I'd like to try to do it as soon as possible, if you don't mind. It's hell trying to sleep these days with all of this on my mind," Marshall said.

"Sure. The girls will be on the bus by then. I'll text Dee and Mom."

"I've learned to always try to say goodbye when given the chance." Marshall looked tentatively at Harley and said, "Mind if I give your girl a hug?"

"Of course not."

Marshall embraced Piper and said, "You've got the better man. Treat him well."

Harley's heart swelled, but now that he knew what Marshall had been through, he wasn't so sure his brother was right. "I'd say we're neck and neck."

"That's generous of you. Thanks for hearing me out. I won't let you down." Marshall opened his arms and waited for Harley to take him up on the embrace. When he did, Marshall whispered, "Don't forget what I said. For once in your life, be your own hero. You deserve it."

They exchanged phone numbers, and Harley tugged Marshall into another hug. "I'm glad you're back. I love you, man."

"I love you, too." Marshall gave Jiggs a pat on the head and climbed on his motorcycle.

As he drove away, Harley filled Piper in on what had transpired, from the first punch to the deaths of Marshall's wife and child, the Dark Knights, Marshall's recovery, and every heart-wrenching detail in between. He got choked up again, and Piper's eyes teared up as he answered her questions, and then he wrapped her in his arms and counted his blessings. His brother was back in town trying to rebuild a life he'd never known, his sister was healthy, and his mother was getting her son back. Harley had his pup by his side and his girl in his arms. He was on top of the world.

"I can't get over all that he's been through." Piper rested her chin on his chest and said, "He's lost so much."

He thought of how much he'd already lost—his father, time with Marshall, time with Piper before—and he thought about how much the people he loved had lost, and the people Piper loved. In the space of a few fast heartbeats, Marshall's warning magnified. Harley knew what he wanted, what he'd *always* wanted, and there beneath the starless sky, in the parking lot of his family's pub, he went after it with everything he had.

He took Piper's hands in his, gazing deeply into her eyes, and said, "We have all lost too much. I don't want to risk losing anything else, Piper. I don't want to wait another minute to tell you how I feel."

He got down on one knee, and Piper's face blanched.

"What are you doing?"

"Seizing the moment," he said as Jiggs came to his side.

"*Nonononono. Harley*, you can't do this." Her warning was clear, but so was that smile tugging at her lips.

"Oh, I'm doing this," he said playfully, trying to snap her out of her shock. "Piper, my sweet girl with a hair trigger, these last several weeks have been the best of my life. I was wrong when I said I'd be okay just dating you. You're my best friend, my lover, and my beer-drinking, sports-watching, sass-talking, wing-eating goddess. I love you so damn much. I want forever with you—a ring on your finger, babies, burnt cookies. I want it *all*. And I know you thought you didn't want to get married, but I'm hoping you feel the same way I do."

Tears streamed down her cheeks.

"Say you'll marry me, Pipe, and I promise you we'll have a *great* life together."

As he rose to his feet, she covered her mouth with a trembling hand.

"How *could* you?" she accused through a rush of tears, stumbling backward. "Everything was so good. We were *happy*! You promised not to try to change me. I *trusted* you! I can't . . ." She ran toward her truck.

He was momentarily frozen. But then his brain kicked in and he took off after her, snagging her by the wrist. Her tears sliced through him like a knife. "I thought things had changed for you, too."

"They did, but *that* didn't!" she hollered, hurt welling in her eyes. She pulled her arm away, stumbling around Jiggs. "I won't change my mind about marriage, Harley. I *know* that about myself."

She was so *mad*, shaking and crying, but if she could just see them more clearly, he was sure she'd calm down.

"But you've *already* changed. We sleep together every night. We stay at *your* house, which according to you is huge. You told me that I wasn't alone in this thing with Marshall anymore, and I *know* you meant it. I heard it in your voice. Don't you see, Pipe? We're already building a life together as a couple." He paused to let his words sink in, but her tears kept falling. "What do you think has been happening between us? You can try to deny it, but you love me, and you love Jiggs, and damn it, Piper, you *know* I love you."

"I *knew* you wanted marriage!" she said angrily. "I never should have believed you when you said you were okay with the fact that I wasn't looking for that. If that's what you need, then maybe . . ." She squeezed her eyes shut, as if the words trying to escape were too painful to even think about.

His gut seized, and the truth rushed out. "What I need is *you*, Piper, *any* way I can have you. I just got carried away. I started thinking about the time I lost with Marshall, about Bridgette losing her husband right after Louie was born and Marshall losing his wife and baby, and how we lost my father." He couldn't rein in his emotions. "I don't want to look back and regret not telling you how I feel. I want every second I can have with you. Is that such a crime?"

She shook her head. "No, *but* . . . I can't think right now." She dug her keys out of her pocket and said, "I need space. I need *time* . . . I need . . ."

"You love me, Trig," he said softer. "You're just scared, babe. *Yes*, I want to marry you, but that's not because I want to change *who* you are."

She rolled her eyes and said, "That's *exactly* what marriage does." Her voice changed as she said, "Mrs. Harley Dutch! *Fuck* Piper Dalton. She'll fail to exist the second we say 'I do'!"

"You know that's not true, and you know I don't want *that*. Look at your sisters and Aurelia. Look at your parents, Piper. I know you've had shitty boyfriends in the past, my brother included, but I'm *not* them."

She shook her head, and he had no idea if she knew how wrong she was, or if she felt too sucker punched by his impromptu proposal to think straight. Either way, he had to fix this.

"Then don't change your name, baby. I'm not asking you to give up your job and be a stay-at-home mom. I'm only asking you to commit to loving me—loving *us*—forever."

She pulled open the door of her truck and took a few steps toward him, then veered away, like she was confused. He stepped forward, but she held up her hand and said, "Please *don't*, Harley. I need to go to my house and figure things out. I need you to give me space."

Space was the opposite of what they needed. He took another step toward her. "Pipe—"

"*Stop!* I *can't*, Harley!" She looked down at her keys and said, "Don't come after me. I'm not saying that so you'll swoop in like a knight in shining armor. I'm saying it because I can't look at you right now without falling apart."

His chest constricted. He couldn't let her go, not like this. "Baby, that's the last thing I wanted. Just give me a chance to explain."

She shook her head, tears spilling from her eyes. "You just did. If you love me, you'll give me time to think."

She climbed into her truck and sped out of the parking lot, leaving Harley to wonder if he'd just made the biggest mistake of his life.

CHAPTER TWENTY-SIX

PIPER SPED THROUGH town, trying to see through the blur of tears. She kept her eyes locked on the road, gripping the steering wheel so hard her fingers hurt. Her thoughts were drowned out by the stupid whimpering sounds she had no control over. She flew into her driveway and threw the truck into park. As she lowered her face to her hands, she caught movement in her peripheral vision and jumped as a growling-whimpering sound rang out. Her gaze darted to the right, and there on the floor was Jiggs, looking at her with the saddest eyes she'd ever seen.

"*Damn it.*" Sobs bubbled out. "It's like you two know just how to get to me!" She narrowed her eyes and said, "You did this on purpose so I'd go back. Well, I have news for you, buddy. You're stuck with me tonight."

She threw open her door, and Jiggs bounded across her lap onto the grass. She followed him out. "If you have to go to the bathroom, you'd better do it now, because I'm *not* walking around this block and letting my neighbors see me like this."

Jiggs whimpered and lowered his chest to the ground, wiggling his butt.

"*No.*" She walked past him and sat down on the porch steps. "Go do your business. I'll wait here."

Jiggs sat in front of her, put his chin on her knees, and whimpered.

"What are you? Part *Harley*? Go pee already." She pointed to the yard, feeling numb, which was better than feeling like her heart was being crushed. "If there is a higher power, then he'll give me a break and you'll march out there and do your thing."

Jiggs barked as a motorcycle roared past her house. *Marshall.* Her heart lurched. Could tonight get any worse? The bike stopped a few houses down, turned around, and pulled up to the curb across the street. Marshall took off his helmet and climbed from the bike, heading her way.

She was going to *kill* Harley. "You can tell your brother that *needing space* means *not* sending his brother."

"What are you talking about?"

"Why are you here?" she seethed.

"Because you sped past the church like a bat out of hell." He petted Jiggs and sat down beside her on the porch. "You're crying."

She swiped at her eyes. "*So?*"

"Piper, what happened? You guys seemed so happy."

"What happened? You came back and ruined my life. *Again.*"

He huffed out a sort of chuckle. "I knew it. Harley doesn't trust me, does he?"

"Yes. I don't know. I think he does. What are you *talking* about?" Her brain was overloaded.

"I'm just trying to figure out how you went from hugging my brother to looking like he just broke up with you and stealing his dog."

She groaned and closed her eyes. "He didn't break up with me. He *proposed.* And I didn't steal his dog. Jiggs was a stowaway, and I'm sure Harley made him do it just so I had a reason to go back."

As if on cue, Jiggs climbed onto the step and pushed his chin onto her lap.

Marshall looked confused. *Join the club.*

"Aren't women usually *happy* about proposals?"

"Probably! But I don't want to get married, and he *knows* it. Everyone in this town knows it, for Pete's sake."

"Wait, the girl who planned out our entire life when we were teenagers doesn't want to get married?"

"What are you talking about?" She sighed. "I'm not in the mood for games. You should go be with your brother, and take Jiggs to him."

His gaze moved slowly over her face. "You really don't remember, do you?"

"I remember seeing you and Victoria Mathers half-naked behind the boathouse, which is something I'd really like to forget."

"I'm sorry for that," he said kindly. "Do you know why I cheated on you?"

"Because you were a selfish asshole." A breeze swept up the yard, and she crossed her arms, rubbing them against the chill.

Marshall took off his leather jacket and draped it over her shoulders. "I *was* a selfish asshole, but do you know why else?"

"Because I wouldn't put out for you."

"I was definitely a horny kid, but that's not the real reason." He leaned his forearms on his knees, worrying with his hands, and said, "You planned out our life. You said we'd both go to college, then move back to Sweetwater, where you'd make your *handygirl* service into a full-time job. I'd become a fireman, we'd have two kids, a boy and a girl. Is any of this ringing a bell?"

She shook her head. "Definitely not."

"Damn," he said with a sigh. "I must have really screwed you up. Those life plans of yours were the biggest reason I cheated. I tried to break up with you by saying I was sick of you not putting out, but you were so stubborn. You argued with me, telling me that real relationships weren't based on sex. Do you remember that?"

It was starting to come back to her now, the pain, the challenge of getting him to love her, the hurt when he'd cheated. But apparently Marshall didn't need an answer, because he continued telling her about who she'd been.

"You scared the hell out of me, Piper. I was a stupid kid with anxieties that I didn't understand, and you were so organized and ready to take on the world. But no matter what I did to show you we weren't right for each other, you held on tight."

"Well, I never held on tight again, that's for sure."

"Until my brother," he said.

She clenched her teeth, fresh tears stinging her eyes.

"I'm sorry, Piper. I'm sorry for cheating on you and for hurting you. I didn't realize I ruined your love of romance and your dreams of marriage. I take full responsibility for ruining your past, and I'd give anything to take it all back. Every hurt I ever caused anyone. But don't blame Harley for my mistakes. He's a good man, and he's loved you for as long as I can remember."

"Nice try, but we both know he barely saw me when I was younger."

Marshall shook his head. "What is it about you two? You're both too damn blind to see what's right in front of your eyes. Do you remember my Jet Ski accident?"

"Right after we broke up. You got hurt pretty bad."

"There was no Jet Ski accident. Harley beat me up for cheating on you."

Piper's jaw dropped.

"Yeah, the guy who *didn't* have feelings for you. Remember when I dared you to streak?"

She nodded.

"I was stupidly bragging to him when he came home that weekend, and he roughed me up pretty good. How about the boat? Did he tell you he was the one who finished it?"

She shook her head, floored at what she was hearing.

"I blew it off and went out with my friends instead of working on it. He tracked me down, beat me up again, and told me to straighten my ass out and do right by you."

"That doesn't make sense," she said. "When you left it in my yard, the note said you finished it for me."

"Harley wrote it. He didn't want you to be hurt because I'd dropped the ball, and he knew if he told you the truth, you'd be sad. He was saving you from me." He raked a hand through his hair and pushed to his feet.

Jiggs lifted his head, watching him.

"I take full responsibility for hurting you, Piper, and for ruining your past. I can't fix that," he said regretfully. "But I can do my best to learn from it and try not to hurt anyone else, including you and my brother. He's got a hero complex, Piper."

"Watch it, Marshall," she warned.

He held his hands up in surrender. "That can be a horrible thing, but in Harley's case, it's a good thing. He's got a big fucking heart, and I sure as hell wish I could have inherited one-tenth of it. You'll do what you want, but I'm sure somewhere inside you that teenage girl who looked at me with hope in her eyes is trying to climb out because she realizes my brother is the best man she'll ever know. I hope you let that girl shine, Piper, because while your hurtful past is on me, if you let Harley go, your unhappy future is on *you*."

He turned to leave, and she slipped off his jacket. "Marshall." She held it out to him and said, "Can you take Jiggs to him? He should be with Harley. I'm not the most tactful person."

"Sorry, Piper, but one thing I've learned is that we all need to take responsibility for our own actions and clean up our own messes."

She looked down at Jiggs as Marshall drove away. "Guess you're spending the night with me." She tipped her head back and looked up at the dark sky. "Thanks a lot. All I wanted was for Jiggs to pee, not a trip back in time *or* a look in the mirror."

329

Harley felt like he'd opened his mouth beneath a spigot and swallowed a gallon of heartache. He was an idiot. He wished he could take back what he'd said to Piper, even though he'd meant every word of it. He hadn't meant to hurt her, but she was right. He'd made her a promise, and he'd gotten carried away and broken his word to the person who mattered most. Now he might have lost her for good, and that thought made him sick and lonely and so fucking sad he couldn't see straight.

Harley wanted to go to her, to apologize and do whatever it took to make things right, but he knew better than to defy his girl's request for space after what he'd done—and he refused *not* to think of Piper as *his girl*. She *was*, and if he had it his way, even if it took years to win her trust back, she'd be by his side forever.

At least she wasn't alone tonight. She had Jiggs, and while his boy might not be a great wingman, he was a superb companion. He'd seen his pooch slink into Piper's truck when they were arguing, and he'd thought about calling him back. But then he'd figured Jiggs had sensed that Piper needed him tonight more than Harley did. Jiggs was smart like that. His heart was always in the right place. Harley had expected Piper to turn around and drop Jiggs off right away, which would have given him a chance to apologize, but three hours later, he was still sitting alone on the stoop at Dutch's, typing messages to Piper, then deleting them.

He pushed to his feet and headed for his truck, but the thought of going home without her to sleep in a bed that would smell like her and feel too empty, or on the couch where she tucked her feet beneath her and rested her head on his shoulder was too much to bear. He turned around and headed back into the pub. The couch in his office would have to do.

CHAPTER TWENTY-SEVEN

WHERE THE HELL are you, Willow, and why the frick don't I have a key for emergencies? Piper tried for the third time to pick the lock on the back door of the bakery. Jiggs went paws-up beside her, sticking his nose between her and the door.

"Stop, Jiggsy." She wiggled the piece of metal she was using to pick the lock, and it broke off. *"Fucker."*

She was in no mood for this shit. It was almost four in the morning, and she hadn't slept a wink. Jiggs had only made it worse. He kept crawling over to Harley's side of the bed and whining. As if Piper didn't already miss Harley enough? Every time she'd closed her eyes she'd seen the joy in Harley's eyes when he'd gotten down on his stupid knee, and the confusion when she'd gotten mad. *Confusion!* As if he'd lost his freaking mind and forgotten who she was and what she *didn't* want.

Damn him.

She stalked to her truck, ignoring the sharp pebbles cutting into her bare feet, and rummaged through her tools, cursing herself for forgetting shoes . . . and *pants.* She'd gone to bed wearing one of Harley's T-shirts because she'd wanted to feel closer to him, but she'd gotten frustrated at herself for lying there sad and angry, listening to Jiggs whimper. She'd pulled on one of Harley's sweatshirts and rolled the sleeves up because it was made for giants. She'd grabbed her keys and her trusty stowaway sidekick, and then she'd bolted, desperately needing to drown her sorrows in sugar.

She snagged a crowbar and stalked back to the door.

Putting one foot against the doorframe, she wedged the crowbar between the lock and the frame and jimmied it with all her might. The sucker was stubborn.

Where was her sledgehammer when she needed it?

Images of Willow's delicious doughnuts, Loverboys, and cake flew into her mind. *Oh yes, cake!* With renewed motivation, she forced more pressure, feeling the wood give. She was going to eat every frigging thing Willow had in the display cases and the refrigerator. And anywhere else she might have sugar, because Piper needed enough sweets to put her out of her misery. She pushed with all her might again. She could see the hardware. She squeezed her eyes shut, jimmying as she threw her body against the door. It *flew* open, sending her sprawling into a counter. Her hip slammed against the edge, and she dropped the crowbar right on her bare foot. She cried out. Tears burned her eyes as she hopped on one foot, holding the other.

Jiggs ran around her, barking and whining.

"*Shitshitshit!*" She glowered at the offending crowbar, sucking in gasps of air to keep from sobbing.

She let go of her foot, but when she put weight on it, pain radiated all the way up to her ankle. She cried out again, sending Jiggs into another flurry of whining and barking. Piper dropped to her knees, gritting her teeth against the pain in her foot as she crawled to—and through—the doors that led from the kitchen into the bakery.

Jiggs licked her face.

"Bet you somehow planned that injury, too, right? Just to get me down to your level."

He licked her face again.

"That wasn't fair. I know. Sorry. I'll give you some goodies, but no chocolate. *But* if you knock into my foot, I'll have to kill you." Using the counter, she pulled herself up on one foot and hopped a few feet to the basket by the register, which was filled with bags of yesterday's goodies. She sank down on the floor with the basket in her lap and tore open the bags, shoving doughnuts, croissants, and muffins into her mouth as quickly as she could fill her cheeks. She closed her eyes, reveling in the deliciousness as sugary goodness exploded in her mouth. She tore off a piece of a glazed doughnut and handed it to Jiggs.

"Don't tell your daddy." The words made her chest ache. She shoved a chocolate doughnut in her mouth, and ate it in three bites, crumbs falling like rain on her clothes and legs.

Jiggs scarfed down the entire glazed doughnut and shoved his nose into a bag.

"Hey, now." She took his face between her hands, remembering how Jiggs had jumped on Harley the first afternoon when she'd brought him home from the hospital and how Harley had loved him up despite his pain. Tears filled her eyes, and she touched her forehead to Jiggs's. "What have I done, Jiggs? What is wrong with me?"

Jiggs licked her mouth, which brought more tears. She didn't think it was possible to feel this bad or for a heart to actually hurt. She gave Jiggs a croissant and shoved another doughnut into her mouth. But no matter how much she ate, the pain in her chest persisted. She put a Loverboy in each hand, eating them ravenously. But she still felt empty inside. She knee-walked to the display cabinet and took out the cake box she'd spied on her way to grab the basket. She sat down with the box in her lap and lifted the top, hoping the green-frosted cake would do the trick.

She pulled off a hunk with her fingers to see if there was any chocolate in it. Jiggs pushed his nose toward the cake, blocking her view.

"Give me a second, Mr. Big Head." She peered around his noggin and saw that the cake was vanilla. "Okay, you're good, but you're probably going to shit like a monkey after eating this, so don't do it in here."

She tore off the top of the box, used her fingers to cut the cake in half, and put Jiggs's half in the box top beside her.

"Go for it, Jiggsy."

Jiggs shoved his face in the cake, smacking his lips as he ate. Piper ate with her hands, enjoying every second of her sugar rush, when she heard a siren. She froze, eyes wide, fingers full of frosting, mouth full of cake. Jiggs lifted his head, ears perked up, frosting and cake all over his snout.

"Piper!" Willow hollered, panic evident in her shrill tone. "Are you okay? Who broke in?" She flew through the kitchen door in her pajamas and slippers, her hair askew, and skidded to a stop at the edge of the counter. Her eyes bugged out. "*Holy . . .* Are you okay? What's going on?"

Zane peered around her and chuckled. "I think Piper had a rough night."

Two policemen appeared behind them.

Great.

Piper had gone to school with Teddy Mercer, the brown-haired policeman trying not to laugh, and Ben had gone to school with the blond guy, Phil Sanders, who looked awfully confused.

"Piper?" Phil said quizzically. "Was there trouble here tonight?"

"Yeah. I didn't have a key and needed sugar." She shoved a handful of cake in her mouth and said, "It's okay, Jiggs. You can eat. Unless my sister is going to have us arrested?"

"What? Nobody's getting arrested, but what happened?" Willow crouched beside Piper, her gaze sailing over her. "And *what* are you wearing?"

Piper glanced down at her clothing, which was covered in crumbs and smeared with icing, as were the floor and Jiggs. She shoved a hunk of cake into her mouth, speaking accusingly around the food. "When did you get an alarm system?"

"When *Mason* told me to," Willow said. "I mentioned it to you. You said it was a good idea."

"Well, it *wasn't*. You shouldn't listen to me." She dug into the cake with her fingers and put more in her mouth. "This is good. What is it, anyway?"

Willow looked at the demolished cake and sighed. "It *was* Mrs. Larson's daughter's birthday cake."

Piper mumbled, "Sorry." She looked at Jiggs and mouthed, *Oops.* "I'll pay for the damages to the door and all the food, and I'll hire cleaners."

"You know the convenience mart is open twenty-four-seven and has doughnuts, right?" Teddy asked, earning a laugh from Zane.

Willow glared at him.

Zane mumbled an apology and ushered the police toward the back door, reassuring them everything was cool.

"Sorry about your door," Piper said. "And your food. But . . ." Tears sprang from her eyes and she cried, "Harley *proposed*." Her words came out strangled, and cake fell from her lips as she threw her arms around her sister and cried on her shoulder.

"Piper! That's wonderful! I've never seen you cry happy tears! I know you're excited, but couldn't you have waited to celebrate with me instead of breaking down my door?"

"*Happy?*" She cried louder. "You *know* I don't want to get married!"

"Oh no, no, no. Piper, breathe, honey." Willow sat right down on the mess and held her, rubbing her hand down her back. "Harley loves you."

"And I love *him*," she whined. She pulled back and used the bottom of her sweatshirt to wipe her tears.

"Then why are you doing this?" Willow petted Jiggs and said, "And why did you steal his dog?"

Piper choked out a laugh. "I didn't *steal* him. He hid in my truck when Harley and I were fighting. And I'm doing this because I didn't know what else to do. You should have given me a key!"

"I did, when you renovated. Remember?"

"Shoot." She exhaled loudly and picked up a piece of a muffin. "Sorry. I'll fix everything."

Jiggs ate the muffin out of her fingers.

"Glutton," Piper said.

Jiggs cocked his head to the side.

"I think Jiggs shares your eating habits," Willow said.

"What am I going to do, Willow? He got down on one knee and I couldn't breathe."

"Then maybe you do want to get married."

"You wish. I *panic* at the thought of marriage. My hands sweat and my throat swells. It's not pretty. But he wants the ring, *forever*, the whole deal."

Willow moved Piper's hair away from her face and said, "And what do you want?"

"*Him! Forever.* But no contract. I know that's my own hang-up, and you and the rest of the world think I'm crazy. But it is what it is, and it's not going to change."

"It's a little weird, Pipe," she said softly.

"That's okay. So am I. Willow, he *wants* to get married. I can't hold him back from what he wants, but I love him too much to walk away." She leaned back against the cabinets and said, "What should I do? And don't say walk away, because I couldn't bear to see him with another woman. I'd have to move away from Sweetwater and become a cat lady, because I'd have no friends, no job, no family, and I'd never be able to have a dog without thinking of Jiggs and Harley. And you know how much I hate cats. I don't want to move away from him, but he probably hates me because I was a freak and bitchy. I don't want him to hate me!" She threw her arms around Willow again, sobbing. "I want him to *love* me!"

Willow gasped. "I've got it!"

Piper sat back, her heart racing.

"Negotiate the terms, just like you do for work," Willow said excitedly. "A client brings you a contract, and you go back with a counterproposal. Give Harley a counteroffer, on *your* terms. The worst that can happen is he'll say no, and then you'll eat more sugar and we'll figure out how to survive losing the man you love."

"Oh *God*!" Piper's chin fell to her chest.

Jiggs licked her cheek.

"You could hold Jiggs hostage until he agrees," Willow said. "But Harley loves you, and you love him. You guys will find a way to make it work."

"He wants a *ring* and the whole nine yards." An idea formed in Piper's mind. "Oh my God. I know what I have to do!" She jumped to her feet, sending pain searing through her foot, and collapsed to the floor with a wail.

"What?" Willow asked frantically.

"You need to help me. I hurt my foot." She put her arm around Willow's neck and hopped toward the kitchen. "Come on, Jiggsy!"

Jiggs trotted behind them as they walked into the kitchen.

Zane came through the back door, took one look at them, and said, "You're on the move. Is that good or bad? What's happening?"

"I think we're closing the bakery for the day," Willow said. "Can you handle this?"

"I'm borrowing your wife!" Piper snapped. "Do *not* tell anyone you saw me here or I won't bring her back. Walk *faster*, Willow!" As they hobbled out the door, she said, "I'll call Kase to fix the door!"

Tuesday morning Harley was exhausted, worried, and stressed out beyond belief. He'd finally given in and texted Piper at six thirty, but she'd never responded. He'd driven by her house, but her truck was gone. He'd gone inside to get Jiggs, but Jiggs was gone, too. He'd driven by her siblings' houses, thinking maybe she'd stayed with one of them, but her truck wasn't there, either. He'd gone to the Mad House, and when there was no sign of her there, he'd headed to her job site, but Kase said nobody had heard from her, either. He'd run out of time and had finally gone to meet Marshall at Delaney's.

Marshall was waiting on his bike in front of Delaney's house when he arrived. As Harley climbed from the truck, Marshall closed in on him with a concerned look in his eyes.

"Oh man, Har. You look like hell."

"Rough night, but I'm here." *When I really want to be trying to figure out where the hell Piper is.*

"I need to tell you something, and I hope you're not going to get pissed."

"No promises. I'm in a shit mood. Piper and I got into a fight last night."

"I know. I saw her speed past the church last night and followed her home. She was a mess."

"You saw her? I've been looking for her all morning. Do you know where she is?"

He shook his head. "No. I was only there a few minutes, and when I left she was sitting on the porch with Jiggs. She told me you proposed."

"I was an *idiot*. She told me she'd never get married, and I got carried away. If I lose her, I don't know what I'll do."

"She loves you, Harley. I know she does. This is all my fault, and I'm sorry. I knew I hurt her in high school, but I had no idea how badly. I thought she'd just written me off as an asshole and moved on. She never wallowed around giving me nasty looks in the halls like most chicks did when they got burned. But I don't think she ever wrote *me* off. I think she just changed who she was, got tougher, and threw away the notion of marriage and forever. That's on me, man, and I've been up all night wishing I could fix it."

"It's not on you," Harley said with a heavy heart. "You might have been the start, but a lot of the guys she's gone out with have wanted her to change in some way. Now I'm on that damn list, too. Let's get this over with so I can find Piper."

"You can go, Harley. I can do this."

"No way. I always honor my wo—*Damn it*. I always *try* to honor my word."

"Okay, thank you. What did Delaney and Mom say when you talked to them?"

"They both wanted to know everything, but I felt like that's your story to tell. I told them you were back, hopefully for good, and that you wanted to see them. I apologized to them for not trying harder with you and not giving you the benefit of the doubt, and I warned them about your black eye and my bruised cheek to spare them the shock of it."

"Probably a good plan. Thanks. I appreciate you doing this with me."

"No problem. Delaney didn't mention that you were staying with Ike."

"She'd have no way of knowing. A Dark Knight's business never leaves the group unless it's requested by the member," Marshall explained. "You should think about prospecting to become a member."

"No thanks, brother. I'm glad you're doing it. But I'm a lover, not a biker."

Marshall clapped a hand on Harley's shoulder with a tease in his eyes and said, "Yeah, you're probably not cool enough anyway."

The front door opened, and Delaney and their mother stepped onto the porch.

Harley lowered his voice and said, "Don't say anything to them about Piper. They have enough to deal with."

Their mother's eyes filled with tears as she descended the steps. "Marshall," she said as she embraced him. She put one hand on the back of his head, like she used to do when they were little. "I've missed you."

Delaney sidled up to Harley and said, "You okay? You don't look so good."

"Yeah, just tired."

"Did you hear about Willow's bakery? Mom went by this morning to get Marshall's favorite muffins and it was closed, but Zane was there. He said someone broke in last night and told her he was sending everyone to the bakery here in town. Luckily no one was at Willow's when it happened. Did you hear anything about it?"

"No, but I'm glad Willow wasn't there when it happened."

Marshall glanced over, and Delaney said, "My turn! But don't hug me too tight. I'm still a little sore."

She hurried over to Marshall, and their mother joined Harley. She touched his bruised cheek and *tsk*ed. "A little bird told me it's going to be a good day for all of us."

Harley wasn't so sure.

Marshall touched Delaney's wrist. "I see you got my gift."

"It's from you? There was no card. How did you know about my surgery?"

Marshall glanced at Harley and said, "My buddy lives here, and he's part of a club I'm in. I'll explain when we go inside."

"I love the bracelet. Thank you. Let's go in," Delaney said. "Nice shiner, and I like your wheels." She touched Marshall's arm as they went inside and said, "One of those tats had better be in my honor."

Marshall laughed. "I've missed you, Dee."

"Me too," Delaney said. "I'm glad you're back."

Their mother fussed over them in the kitchen, giving Marshall an orange-cranberry muffin, his favorite, and Harley a blueberry scone. She looked ten years younger than she had on Saturday, all because of Marshall's return, driving Harley's guilt even deeper for running Marshall off after their father's funeral. He had a feeling he'd better get used to that guilt. It clung to his bones, like an unwanted yet *deserved* hitchhiker.

They settled in around the kitchen table, where the remnants of Delaney's favorite chocolate croissant littered her plate.

"You boys need to learn to speak with words, not fists," their mother said. "Can you do that for me? Please?"

"Yes," they answered in unison, sharing a knowing grin.

Delaney said, "You shouldn't lie to your mother. I can't get over your beard, Marsh, and all that ink. You look so different."

"I am different," Marshall said, and then he told them about where he'd been and all he'd gone through. He showed them the picture of Annie and Destiny, and their mother and Delaney cried. Marshall put on a brave face, shifting a tight expression to Harley.

Harley knew he was seeking support and nodded accordingly. He tried to focus as his mother told Marshall about how depressed she'd been when he'd disappeared, but Harley couldn't stop thinking about Piper, wondering if she was okay and where she was. He touched his phone in his pocket, wishing she'd text or call.

"I'm sorry, Mom. I had no idea I'd hurt you so badly. You and Dad must have hated me," Marshall said, bringing Harley's mind back to their conversation.

"No, honey," their mother said emphatically. "We could never hate you. We missed you, and it was easier for your father to let you go than to think about all the things he felt he'd done wrong that made you leave. He wasn't happy that you gave up on college when your dream was to become a smoke jumper, but he put that blame on himself for not doing more to help you."

"Nobody made me leave, Mom," Marshall said, glancing at Harley again. "I blamed everyone else for a long time: Harley for being hard on me, Dad for giving up on me and treating me like I would never amount to anything, while he helped Harley and Delaney learn all kinds of shi—*stuff*. But I left of my own accord, and I know that blame was misplaced."

"Honey, your father didn't think you'd never amount to anything," their mother said. "He—*we*—were trying to give you what you needed, not force you to be someone you didn't want to be and fight with you about it."

Marshall put his hand over their mother's and said, "I've gone through enough therapy to understand that now, but as a kid I didn't see anything very clearly. I don't want to rehash all of that. I'm in a good place now, and I'm on medication for depression, which I should have probably been on even as a teenager, when I felt like my world was spinning out of control. It wasn't, but that's what anxiety does to a person."

Marshall went on to tell them about his idea for Annie's Hope, and Harley's thoughts turned to Ralph. He said, "When I lived in the city I had a friend who fell apart under the pressure of the job and became suicidal. A place like Annie's Hope could have offered help and hope. I think what you're planning will be beneficial for many people." *Myself included if Piper ends things with me.*

"I would have loved to be able to walk into a café setting for a support meeting when I was first diagnosed with cancer," Delaney said. "We met at the YMCA in a meeting room, and it always felt cold and weird. Are you thinking of helping kids, too? Teenage years are so hard, and if there are peer groups and therapists who can sit down and talk in a comfortable setting, maybe more kids could get help instead of bottling everything up."

"That's the hope. We'll serve all ages. Wynnie, the therapist I told you about, will help me connect with medical professionals in the area, from pediatrics to geriatrics," Marshall explained. "Mental health issues don't discriminate by age. I'd like to create an environment where dealing with emotional issues isn't seen as something that sets people apart, but a place where it brings them together for support. Imagine if there was a meeting for stressed-out single fathers, like the buddy I'm staying with? I bet they'd love to have a place where they didn't need to pretend everything was cool all the time."

Their mother fidgeted with her napkin and said, "Your father could have used a place like that, too, even though he never would have gone."

"Dad wasn't depressed," Harley said. "The man worked like a dog. He had a right to be moody."

"I never said *depressed*," his mother clarified. "But he had his own issues."

"Wouldn't we *know* if Dad had emotional issues?" Delaney asked.

"Not necessarily," she said. "He was a proud man, and you kids were busy living your lives when you were still at home. Then you were off at college, and then you were off *building* your futures, getting started with your careers."

"I would have noticed. I was home every weekend," Harley said.

"He was proud of the way you stepped up to help Delaney when she moved back home, honey," their mother said. "But there was no reason for your father to be on your list of people to watch over."

Harley sat back, feeling like he'd somehow failed his father.

"Harley, don't beat yourself up. Why do you think Dad worked so many hours?" Marshall asked. "It's a trick people use to keep themselves distracted from the things they can't control."

"He's right, sweetheart," their mother said. "The mind is a powerful thing. Your father would have worked himself to death before he'd let you kids see him as something less than the man you needed him to be."

Harley shook his head. "So he suffered *alone*."

"You can't go back and be his hero, Har," Marshall said. "Don't take on that burden. You've got enough on your plate. Besides, Dad's generation was built on tough love. He wouldn't have known what to do with you hovering over him."

Delaney looked at Harley over the rim of her coffee cup as she took a sip. Her joy was apparent in her eyes. She set her cup down and said, "Looks like our baby brother has become all kinds of smart."

"He's always been smart," their mother said. "And he's right about our tough-love generation, which was probably why Harley was so tough on Marshall when you boys lived at home."

Harley and Marshall exchanged a glance. Even with their fights, they'd never ratted on each other.

Their mother looked at them coyly. "Come on, boys. Give your mama a little credit. Do you think I really bought all those tales you two told when you were kids? How many accidents can two kids have? Bicycle, skateboard, Jet Ski, or—your father's favorite—the one you told all the time when you were just little boys and you'd both come home with bruises and scratches."

Marshall chuckled. "The one where we said we fell down a hill chasing Mrs. Treadway's lost dog and then climbed under the boathouse at the marina when it hid there?" Mrs. Treadway was a teacher at the elementary school.

"I thought that one was our best," Harley said.

"It might have worked if Mrs. Treadway had a dog," Delaney said.

A dog barked outside. "Jiggs!" Harley jumped to his feet and looked out the window. Jiggs was standing by the passenger door of Piper's truck barking, and Willow was walking around the front of the truck, wearing pink pajamas and slippers. *What the . . . ?*

"*Jiggs?*" Delaney asked, popping to her feet next to Harley.

"Why is Willow wearing pajamas?" Marshall asked from behind Harley.

"No idea." Harley ran to the front door with his family close behind and flew out the door. He ran down the steps, and Piper hobble-hopped toward him with one arm around Willow's neck, her right knee bent. His chest constricted. She was barefoot, and her right foot was swollen and black-and-blue. Her hair was tangled and streaked with green, as were her cheeks. She didn't appear to have any pants on, only one of his sweatshirts, which hung halfway down her thighs.

Jiggs was running between the truck and Harley, barking.

Piper looked up, locking eyes with Harley as he closed the distance between them. She put her hand out and said, "Stop."

He stopped cold a few feet away. The fissures the long night had left in his heart split wide open. "What happened?"

"Don't ask," Willow said.

He was going to fucking ask—*after* he apologized. "Piper, I'm sorry about—"

"Stop talking or I'll cry!" Piper snapped. "Please don't say a word. *Darn it!*" She motioned impatiently with her hand, beckoning Harley closer.

He took a few steps. Jiggs ran over and sat beside him. Harley absently scratched his head. Now that he was closer, he saw pieces of food in Piper's hair and on her sweatshirt. He couldn't miss her red-rimmed eyes or the dark circles beneath them, sending his heart into another frenzy of distress.

She took his hand, and he felt hers trembling, breaking his heart even more.

"I'm sorry for freaking out," she said softly.

"It's okay. I shouldn't have proposed."

"You *proposed?*" his mother said from behind him.

He'd forgotten his family was there.

"She's not wearing a ring," Delaney said. "Oh my God! Did you say *no?*"

Harley said, "Delaney!" at the same second Piper said, "Yes!"

"Yes, you said *no?*" Delaney asked. "Or *yes*, as in you *accepted?* Did you know this, Marshall?"

Harley looked over his shoulder, scowling at Delaney. "The first one. Now, can you *please* give her a chance to speak? I'm dying here." He turned his attention back to Piper and said, "Sorry."

"I have to start over," Piper said anxiously.

She inhaled a few deep breaths, exhaling so damn slowly Harley thought he'd lose his mind.

"I'm sorry I freaked out," she said shakily. "I know I'm messed up because I don't want to get married, but—"

"*Ever?*" Delaney asked.

"*Shh*, honey," their mother chided her.

Piper's eyes remained trained on Harley as she said, "I don't want to get married, but that doesn't mean I don't want forever with you. I want the same things you do, Harley. I want to have our babies one day—not right away." She glanced apologetically at his mother. "But one day. And I want to be with you and know we've committed ourselves wholly and completely to each other—"

Her words were drowned out by a line of cars and trucks honking their horns as they pulled up to the curb. Piper glared at Willow.

"I didn't do it! It must have been Heaven," Willow said frantically.

Heaven? Harley was officially *lost*.

"Wait!" Bridgette yelled as she, Bodhi, Zane, and Louie climbed out of her minivan. Louie sprinted across the lawn toward them.

The rest of their family members piled out of their cars and trucks, followed by Remi, Mason, Kase, and a few of the other guys who worked for Piper. Louie skidded to a stop beside Jiggs. Jiggs leapt up to lick his face, and Louie tumbled down in a fit of giggles as Jiggs smothered him with sloppy kisses. Bea wiggled from Ben's arms and held his hand as she toddled across the yard.

"Marshall?" Ben extended his hand. "Good to see you, man. Derek, Mason, get over here and meet Harley's brother."

"Are you freaking kidding me?" Piper said, exasperated. "I'm kind of in the middle of something here!" She looked like she was chewing on nails as everyone gathered around them, murmuring behind their hands.

Roxie linked arms with Harley's mother and said, "We did good, Mama."

Harley arched a brow in his mother's direction. She and Roxie mimed zipping their lips and throwing away the key.

"I don't know who spilled the beans about this, but somebody's head is going to roll," Piper said with a scowl. She looked around, and pain rose in her eyes. Her shoulders slumped. "Jolie and Sophie should be here. It's practically their fault I'm doing this, and Sophie knew about the nachos . . ."

"Nachos?" Harley asked, earning an adorable eye roll from a very flustered and injured beauty.

"I've got this," Delaney exclaimed, and she whipped out her phone. "Thank goodness for videos."

Piper sighed with relief. "Thank you. Willow, can you help me down, please."

"*Down?*" Harley watched as Willow helped Piper down to her knees, her injured foot dangling a few inches off the ground. Harley followed suit and started to get down on his knees.

Piper gave him a deadpan look and said, "You're supposed to *stand.*"

He straightened up. He'd stand on his head spitting wooden nickels if she asked him to.

She took his hand in hers and said, "Harley, I love you with every ounce of my stubborn soul. I know that when you proposed, you were speaking from the heart, and now I'm speaking from mine."

His heart filled to near bursting as the pieces fell into place, and he got all choked up.

"Harley, I want to spend the rest of my life with you, every free minute. I want to hang out at the pub while you work, watching sports and watching my man. I want to go on moonlight boat rides and take Jiggsy for walks."

He heard sniffles behind him and noticed Bridgette wiping her eyes. Would they think he was lame if the tears he was holding back fell?

Piper squeezed his hand and said, "The truth is, I don't care what we're doing as long as at the end of the day, it's you that I get to come home to. I love you, Harley, and I know you want marriage, but I'm hoping you're willing to meet me in the middle and accept me as I am, quirks and all." She inhaled a loud breath and blew it out fast. "Will you do me the honor of being my partner in life, forever and always, without a contract saying we have to?"

Harley dropped to his knees as "Hell yes" fell from his lips. He swept his arms around Piper and kissed her.

Cheers and applause rang out, causing Jiggs to bark and run around them.

Harley lifted Piper onto his lap. He gazed into her teary eyes and said, "I love you so damn much. You've always been my forever, but it took Marshall to get me out of my own way and show me that. I promise to never ask you to change or to marry me again."

Piper laughed and wound her arms around his neck. "Never is a long time."

"So is forever and always, and I'm *in*, baby. I'm *so* in." He pressed his lips to hers, earning more cheers and whoops.

Willow yelled, "Wait!" The cheers quieted to murmurs as she crouched beside them. Ignoring Piper's death stare, she said, "This girl is one hot mess, Harley. She broke into my bakery and ate *everything* without caring about the damage she caused. She forced me to help her wake up Heaven Love at an ungodly hour, and—"

Piper gasped and thrust out her hand. "Give them to me! I almost forgot!"

Willow reached into the pocket of her pajamas and set something in Piper's hand. Piper turned to him, clearly elated. Her eyes were brighter than the sun. "I know you wanted rings, so I had them made for us." She handed him a thick silver band and said, "Read the inscription."

He needed someone to pinch him to be sure he hadn't keeled over and gone to heaven. He read the engraving aloud: "*Back off, bitches. I'm taken.*" A deep laugh rumbled out, and he hauled her in for a kiss.

Laughter, cheers, and barks ensued.

"That's my girl," Piper's father called out.

As Piper slid the silver band on his left ring finger, he said, "Taken by the best woman in the world. I couldn't love our commitment, my ring, or *you* more than I do right now."

"I bet you will in a second," Piper said, handing him the other ring. "Since I ripped you off of having a *Mrs. Dutch*, mine's engraved on the *outside*."

Tears stung his eyes as he read the inscription. *"Harley's."* He slid the ring on her finger, and the love in her eyes nearly did him in. He said, "I love you, baby," and pressed his lips to hers.

"Congratulations, boss!" Kase hollered, causing another uproar of cheers.

"Are they married?" Louie asked.

"*No*," Harley and Piper said at once, making everyone laugh.

Piper gazed into Harley's eyes and said, "But in our hearts we are."

"Always and forever," he said, and then he sealed their promises with a kiss, silently thanking the powers that be for the water on the floor that had caused him to fall and land in the hospital all those weeks ago.

CHAPTER TWENTY-EIGHT

"HOW ABOUT 'OLD lady'?" Harley asked later that evening. He'd spent the last ten minutes trying to come up with a word to use instead of *wife*.

"Sure. Unless you like your *balls*." Piper snuggled closer to him on the couch.

After her proposal, Delaney had picked up the girls early from school, and they'd celebrated with their family and friends, messy cake-hair, pajamas, and all. When she and Harley had finally come home, Harley had taken his sweet and ever-so-delicious time helping her bathe. They'd made *excellent* use of the bench she'd installed in the shower. He helped her ice her foot and rearranged his schedule to chauffer her to and from the job site for the next few days until her foot was better. He'd always been good to her, but she hadn't expected him to be good *for* her. He made her see him for who he really was, forcing her to open her eyes and *feel* his love—and to see that she was not only lovable for-ever, but that she had loads of love to *give*, too. She looked forward to giving him every ounce of it for the rest of their lives.

"Well, I can't use *spouse*, and *partner* is too generic." He held up his left hand, admiring his ring for the millionth time that evening. "How about my sexy *thang*?"

"Too hookerish."

He chuckled. "Sex slave?"

"Let's see how that'll go over in public. 'Hi, God-loving friend. Meet my sex slave, Piper.'"

"You're probably right. It's not politically correct. How about *forever fuck buddy?*"

She elbowed him in the ribs.

He *oomph*ed, and his arm shot across his body.

"Oh shoot! I'm sorry! I forgot Marshall hit you there." She lowered her voice and said, "But you deserved it. I am *way* more than your fuck buddy."

Jiggs's head shot up from where he slept on the floor, he yawned, and put his head back down.

"I know you are, Trig, but I love riling you up. Just keep your elbows to yourself." He pulled her onto his lap, wincing with the effort, but still, his smiling eyes caught hers. "What I want to call you is *mine*, but that's going to sound funny to other people, so I think I'll stick with *my girl, my better half,* and *my forever love.*"

"And I'll call you my *everyday man candy.*" Piper wound her arms around his neck and pressed her lips to his. She'd never felt happier and her world had never felt more right than the moment she'd told Harley she wanted *forever* with him and he agreed to her unconventional proposal.

"Do you think you can fit twelve-inch in there somewhere?"

She put her face beside his and whispered in his ear, "This twelve-inch friend must be very important to you, but sorry, Dutch, I'm not into threesomes."

He grabbed her sides, and she squealed, trying to wiggle out of his lap as he lifted her and gently tossed her onto her back on the couch.

"I thought your ribs hurt!" she said through a laugh as he came down over her with a devilish grin, carefully avoiding her injured foot.

"I will never be too hurt to do this." He pressed his lips to hers. "And I'll never share you with a soul."

"Then stop with the hugeness references. What would I do with *twelve* inches?" She was unable to keep from giggling, and she didn't care that she sounded like a goofy, swoony girl. "It's too much. It won't *fit*. You don't see me upsizing my boobs."

"I love your boobs." He dipped his head and kissed them. "I love all of your perfect little parts."

"I know you do, and I love your blissmaker." She slid her arms down his back to his butt and patted it. "And your butt." She trailed her fingers from his wrists to his shoulders. "Your arms and *all* of you. But do you want to know what I love most about you?"

"My heart?"

"You do have an amazing heart, and you prove it with the way you love me and everyone else in your life, especially Marshall."

Marshall and his family would surely go through difficult times when their pasts rose to meet their present, which they all knew would happen from time to time. And they were prepared to deal with the hurt that had been overshadowed by the joy of their reunion. But they were all determined to rebuild their family, and the relief that brought Harley showed in the new light in his eyes. Harley had even mentioned possibly investing in Annie's Hope. But for now Marshall was going to focus on reconnecting with his family. With the help of their friends and family, Piper was moving into Harley's house this weekend—*their* house—and Marshall was moving into Piper's house once the renovations were complete.

Piper reached up with both hands, running her fingers along Harley's handsome face, and said, "I love your heart, but your *mind* is my favorite part, because it allows you to love me for who I am. You could have turned me down today, and I'd have to move away and become a cat lady."

As if on cue, Jiggs pushed his snout between them and licked their faces. Then he lay down beside the couch with a heavy sigh.

Harley chuckled. "Our jealous dog didn't like the sound of that."

"Neither did I, but I love the sound of *our* dog."

"We've always been yours." He kissed her softly and said, "I'd have to be a fool to turn you down. I can't help but think that our moms' behind-the-scenes magic had something to do with it."

While Sophie swore Piper and Harley's relationship developed because of the nachos Harley had made for her, their mothers thought otherwise. They were taking full credit for Harley and Piper's relationship because of a matchmaking scheme they'd hatched long ago, which apparently included more than potions and a ride home from the hospital. They'd gushed about watching Harley and Piper's love blossom in the minutest of ways over the years. With nudges from their mothers, the rest of Piper's family members had also unknowingly been involved. So many things made sense now: Roxie's random requests for Piper to drop things off at the pub, their friends making sure they were always on the same basketball team, spur-of-the-moment get-togethers for drinks at Dutch's, Piper's sisters backing out of evening plans at the last minute, leaving her free to spend time at the pub when Harley just *happened* to be working. They'd learned that even Harley's taking care of the girls had started as part of their mothers' matchmaking scheme. Their mothers had been *certain* he'd ask Piper to help with his nieces, and when Harley had outshone their expectations, proving himself to be the greatest uncle in the world and messing up their plans, their devious and determined mothers had connived a backup plan. But they'd never put it into action, because fate had stepped in and sent Harley to the hospital. Their mothers refused to reveal what their plan had been, claiming they might need it for future love matches.

"I've been thinking," Harley said. "Do you know how I found out that Marshall had cheated on you when I was away at school? My mother called in the middle of the week and said she thought a storm might be brewing and would I please come home for the weekend to help with the fallout, *just in case*. I didn't think anything of it back then, but I do remember that the weather was clear. The other thing is,

I used your mom's body wash for years before you threw them out. I'm pretty sure she put some kind of hypnotizing potion in it that made it impossible *not* to love you."

Piper loved how he believed some magical powers had brought them together, and though she was taking extra precautions just in case, she said, "Or maybe your mom really thought there would be a storm and my mom's body wash did nothing."

"Is that why you've been sneaking it into the bottles you buy at the grocery store?"

Her jaw dropped. "You *knew*?"

"They smell completely different." He kissed her again and said, "I love that you believe in it, too."

"I do *not*. Not *really*," she said. "It was just a little extra insurance because I'm not exactly the easiest person to love."

His brows slanted. "You *are* easy to love. You're the only woman I have *ever* been in love with. I know you think people change for the worse, but I promise you that twenty, forty, *sixty* years from now the only thing that will change is that I will love my nacho-eating, hammer-yielding, loud-swearing, beautiful better half more with every passing second. You are easy for *me* to love, and I'm the only one that matters in the loving-you equation. Don't ever doubt that, Pipe."

For the millionth time, her insides fluttered, and she whispered, "I never will."

"I don't know if I believe in matchmaking, fate, or the power of nachos," he said as he cradled her beneath him and rolled them onto their sides, nose to nose. "All I know is that I love hearing my nieces call you Auntie Piper and knowing that every morning I'll wake up next to the woman of my dreams. We're in this together, babe, *ringed* forever."

He kissed her slow and deep. She finally knew what to do with warm and wonderful—*embrace it*. She gave herself over to their kisses, melting against him, their hearts beating as one.

He moved his leg over hers, bringing their bodies even closer, and said, "This not-married stuff is pretty fucking great, and I think we should celebrate."

"With expensive wine and caviar?" she teased.

Heat sparked in his eyes. "I believe my girl prefers beer, nachos, and no less than three orgasms."

She whispered, "*Each*," as his warm, loving mouth claimed hers, carrying them to their breathtaking, *ringed-forever* ecstasy.

EPILOGUE

PIPER LOOKED OUT the second-floor window of Windsor Hall, which Marshall had purchased over the summer. Piper and her crew were handling a few final renovations before the upcoming grand opening of Annie's Hope. She could hardly believe it had been fifteen months since she and Harley had moved in together and way too many months since they'd found out she was pregnant. She was due any day, and she was truly, *blissfully* happy. They each had their pet peeves, like the toilet seat being left up and Piper leaving her clothes on the floor, but they were small prices to pay for a life with Harley that was even more amazing than she'd hoped. After she'd moved out of her house, she and her crew had finished the renovations, and Marshall had moved in. He was in the process of buying it from her. He and Harley had gone through a few hairy moments, but thankfully, none of them had ended with fisticuffs. Debra and Delaney had enjoyed a smoother transition with Marshall's return, and Jolie and Sophie were thrilled to have their uncle in their lives—almost as thrilled as Roxie and Debra were to have another future matchmaking victim on the hook. Harley and Ben and Ben's business partner, Aiden, were all investing in Annie's Hope, and the community had rallied in support of Marshall's efforts. Piper couldn't be happier about the way Marshall and his family had come back together, or all the ways her life with Harley was blossoming.

She took one last look around the room that would become Marshall's office and said, "Looks good, Kase. I want to check out the progress on the café." They had taken down most of the walls on the first floor to create an inviting café. They'd kept all of the original moldings, and they were building meeting *nooks* throughout the café, separated by half walls that would double as bookshelves and would offer self-help books and uplifting fiction.

As they descended the stairs, a dull ache crept across Piper's back. She gripped the handrail, stopping halfway down the stairs. She breathed deeply, rubbing her lower back, which had been killing her from carrying around twenty-five pounds of burgeoning baby and bulbous boobs, both of which Harley was madly in love with.

"Are you okay, boss?" Kase asked, bringing rise to the familiar, and *frustrating*, worry she'd seen in his eyes nearly every week since she'd announced her pregnancy.

"I'm fine. This is totally normal." Talia and Aurelia had reassured her of that several times over the last two weeks. They'd both experienced the same thing. Talia called it her body's way of practicing for the big day. She had given birth to her adorable little boy, Evan, named for Derek's mother, Eva, just after Christmas, and Aurelia had delivered her and Ben's impossibly cute son, Christopher, right after the New Year.

"You should go home and put your feet up," Kase said for the tenth time in as many minutes.

She glowered at him. "If you and Harley and everyone else in my life does not stop helicopter parenting/sistering/brothering/friending me, I'm going to kill all of you." She continued descending the steps and said, "Remember, I've had nine long months to figure out where to hide the bodies, and I've put every puking, amazing moment of it to good use."

"I still can't believe Harley let you come to work when you're almost ready to pop."

Piper rolled her eyes. "When have I ever allowed a man to *let* me do anything?"

Kase mumbled, "Whoever said motherhood softened a woman was dead wrong."

"Nobody has *ever* said that. If anything, motherhood makes you stronger. I'd like to see a man carry a human inside them for months without losing their minds. See how guys feel when the baby jumps on their bladders the second they finally fall asleep or makes them puke every time they try to eat a frigging doughnut." Puking had been her first clue that something was off with her body. She'd been at Willow's bakery with her sisters before work one morning when she'd eaten her normal goodies and puked them up five minutes later. Her sisters had felt her head, asked her all sorts of annoying and personal questions, and within minutes they'd decided she was pregnant.

They'd decided.

Piper, on the other hand, had taken more convincing.

She'd taken *three* home pregnancy tests, all of which were positive. For the life of her she hadn't been able to remember ever missing a birth control pill. Her doctor had gone through a list of medications that could hinder the effectiveness of pills, but she hadn't taken any. He'd then gone through other sources of potential conflicts, like *flaxseed*, which was the most ridiculous thing she'd ever heard. Her doctor had doubted that the amount of flaxseed Willow had used in the health-nut muffins she'd started making over the holidays was enough to cause issues, even though Piper had been eating them nearly every day. He'd said Piper was simply among the few who could get pregnant while taking birth control pills. Her mother swore it was the extra *F* she'd been putting in Piper's lotions, and Harley claimed it was his *supersperm*.

She didn't know *why* her birth control had failed, but she had a feeling that life just had a way of tripping people up now and then, and if her life with Harley was any indication of how good *tripping* could be, she couldn't wait to be tripped up time and time again. One thing she did know for sure was that love as powerful as theirs was meant to be shared, and she was looking forward to the day they'd meet their little bundle of joy. They'd decided not to find out the sex of the baby, and they'd gone with a neutral theme in the nursery: white walls with randomly placed quarter-sized black polka dots. It was clean and simple, with a white crib and dresser and a picture above the dresser that read YOU ARE OUR GREATEST ADVENTURE. They decorated with stuffed giraffes, rabbits, and elephants and pictures of the same. Piper built a white ladder-style bookshelf, and her father had made a gorgeous rocking bassinette. Piper had spent far too many hours in the rocking chair John Love had made for them, dreaming about what it would be like to have their baby sleeping in that room and what it would feel like to see Harley holding their little one.

She followed Kase into the bright, cheery café. Marshall had hired Everly Love to paint colorful murals on the walls, and they never failed to fill Piper with happiness. Sunlight spilled through the large windows, gleaming off the refinished hardwood floors. The ordering area of the café was to the right of the main entrance. There was going to be open seating at the front of the café, and the meeting nooks would be in the rear. It was wonderful to see Marshall's vision coming to fruition.

"The rest of the bookshelves will be installed today. It's really coming together nicely." Kase motioned to the marks on the floor outlining the locations of the remaining partitions. "Creating meeting nooks with sofas and armchairs was genius."

"Yeah," she said, reaching for the wall as a cramp shot across her lower back.

"You okay? Want to sit down?"

If he *mothered* her one more time, she was going to smack him. She reminded herself she had only about two more weeks of coddling and said, "I'm fine."

Mike poked his head in the door and said, "Lunch is here."

They went outside, where the guys were digging into boxes of Dutch's wings.

"Yes," she said under her breath. Her man was so good to her, even if he made her check in every two hours while she was at work. He was such a worrier, but at least he'd stopped showing up on the job sites unannounced to make sure she wasn't doing too much. Though she'd never admit it because he'd only hover more often, she loved that he cared so much.

She reached for a plate, and a sharp pain shot through her lower belly. *"Holy . . ."* She grabbed the table, bending over as the pain worsened.

"Oh *shit*," Mike said.

She glared at him, gritting her teeth against the pain as the men closed in on her, panic gleaming in their eyes. When the pain eased, she let out a long breath. "Well, that *sucked*. You can back off now."

"You sure, boss?" Darren asked.

"Yes, I'm fi—" She doubled over again as pain clutched her. *"Fuuck,"* she said, just as a gush of wetness soaked her maternity jeans. *"Fuck. Me . . ."*

The men began running around her like chickens with their heads cut off, shouting nonsense. "Call an ambulance!" one of them hollered.

"What should we do?" Darren looked at Kase. "Does anyone know how to deliver a baby?"

"Put her in the back of the truck!" Mike said.

"The *front*!" Kase shouted. "This wasn't in Harley's emergency plan!"

Piper pulled out her phone to call Harley and started to climb into her truck.

Kase grabbed her arm. "You're *not* driving."

"Yes I am." She yanked her hand away, navigated to Harley's number on her phone, and put the phone to her ear.

"The hell you are. Harley would kick my ass." Kase moved between her and the truck and held out his hand. "Give me the keys."

She handed him the keys as Harley's voice came through the phone. "How's my baby mama?"

She used the truck for balance as she walked around to the passenger door. "I need you to meet me at the hospital." Another pain clutched her. She grabbed the passenger door with one hand and her belly with the other, cursing as the worst pain of her life tore through her.

"What's going on? Piper, talk to me!"

The panic in Harley's voice rattled her, but the pain made it impossible to speak.

"I knew you should have stopped working—"

"Harley!" she gritted out. "It's *time*." She panted as the pain eased. "Our baby's coming. Drive fast."

"I'm coming! I love you!" Harley shouted, and then there was a crash.

As Kase helped her into the truck, she heard heavy footsteps racing across the floor through the phone, and then she heard Harley shout, "We're going to meet our baby!" in the distance and realized he'd dropped his phone and run out of the pub.

Kase sped toward the hospital rambling about hanging in there and how she was going to be fine. Fine was not even close to how she felt when the next contraction hit. She mentally scrambled for something to focus on besides the pain. Her mind raced to the last time she'd been to the hospital, when she'd picked up the wonderful man with whom she'd fallen so deeply in love.

She closed her eyes, breathing deeply and preparing to meet the next special person in her life, who had already stolen her heart.

Harley had no idea how the doctor could be so calm when his beautiful girl was in so much pain, cursing like a sailor and threatening Harley's life with every contraction. Piper had been too far along to get an epidural when she'd arrived at the hospital, and she seemed to think that was Harley's fault.

"I'm never letting your fucking blissmaker near me again!" Piper fumed through gritted teeth, sweat beading her forehead. "How could you do this to me?"

She was right; it was all his fault. He couldn't keep his hands off her.

"You're doing great, Pipe." He brushed her hair from her forehead.

She smacked his hand away as another contraction hit. They were coming so fast, she barely got a break. He wished he could endure the pain for her.

"I'm going to make you pay for this, Dutch!" she cried.

"You're amazing, baby." He'd never loved her more than he did right then as she dug her nails into his hand, bearing down to birth their baby.

"*Never* again!" she panted out.

"You're doing great," the doctor said. "Coming down to the homestretch."

"Fuck the homestretch," Piper growled as she was engulfed in another contraction. "Get this thing out of me before it splits me in tw*ooooo—oh shiiit!*"

"You've got this, baby." Tears sprang to his eyes as their baby's head appeared. "Piper, it's coming! I see our baby's head!"

"Okay, Mama, one more big, hard push," the doctor said.

She curled up as she bore down, crying out, clinging tightly to Harley's hand as he cheered her on and watched their baby enter the world.

Tears spilled unabashedly down his cheeks as he and the doctor said, "It's a girl," in unison, and Piper collapsed against the pillows.

"A girl, Pipe!" Harley kissed Piper, their tears mingling on her cheeks. "You did it, baby. You did it! *We* did it. I love you. We have a daughter!"

"Is she okay?" Piper asked, laughing and crying at once.

"She's perfect," the doctor said.

"We have a girl," Piper said dreamily as Harley leaned in for another kiss. "That was *awful*. I hope you're happy with one child, because I'll *never* do that again."

"One is perfect. You're perfect. I love you so much." He kissed her again. "I love you *both* so much."

"Would you like to hold your daughter?" the doctor asked.

"Yes!" Piper's arms shot out faster than Harley could blink. The doctor placed their tightly swaddled daughter in her arms. Piper mouthed, *Oh my God*. She lowered her face toward the baby's and said, "Hello, baby girl. I'm your mama." She peered up at Harley and said, "And that big handsome grizzly of a man is your daddy, and he's going to spoil you rotten."

They were both crying as he kissed the baby's forehead. She had a dusting of light hair, the tiniest, most adorable nose, and sweet bowed lips. "I love you, little one," Harley said, and kissed her again.

"She's perfect," Piper said, tears flooding her cheeks. "Oh my gosh, I love her so much already. I can't believe she's here. Harley, look at her. She's so tiny, and so beautiful. She's going to keep us up all night, and she's going to pull Jiggs's ears and throw tantrums. She's going to be a big pain in the ass when she's a teenager, and she'll probably try to sneak out, and I don't even care. I want her to do it *all*, to experience everything good in life. Can you believe we made such a beautiful little creature?" She wiped her tears, and in a choked voice she said, "Excuse me, Dr. Baldwin?"

"Yes?"

Piper looked up at Harley and said, "When can we have another?"

Harley was sure he'd heard her wrong. "You want *more*?"

She nodded, crying and smiling and making his heart hurt with joy. "Don't you? Look at her! She needs a brother or a sister, someone to talk to, to look after and to have her back, a friend to commiserate with about their crazy parents. Between you spoiling her and me being *me*, she's definitely going to need an outlet."

"I want as many as you want." With a heart so full he felt gluttonous, he brushed a kiss over their daughter's forehead and said, "Welcome to our family, little one. I hope you grow up to be just like your mama."

Time blurred, and before Harley knew it, they were in a hospital room surrounded by their family. Everyone was admiring the baby, taking pictures, and talking in a hundred different directions. But Harley couldn't stop looking at his incredible girls. Piper had just finished nursing their precious little girl, and she was gazing lovingly down at her. Her eyes flicked up to Harley's and she mouthed, *I love you.*

I love you both, he mouthed back.

Marshall sidled up to Harley and said, "It's hard to believe you made something so small."

"Small packages pack a lot of sass," Aurelia said.

Harley was counting on their little girl being just as feisty as her mother.

"Six pounds, eight ounces of pure adorableness." Dan patted Harley on the back and said, "Remember that when she's up all night with colic."

Derek looked down at baby Evan, fast asleep in his arms, and said, "Your lives are never going to be the same."

"They're going to be better," Ben reassured them.

Harley looked at his mother, who was standing beside Piper's chair, gazing down at the baby, and said, "I wish Dad were alive to meet her."

"He's here, honey," his mother said. "Can't you feel his presence?"

Tears stung Harley's eyes again. He swore that *he'd* gotten an extra dose of hormones with Piper's pregnancy.

"Have you thought of a name yet?" Willow asked.

They'd tossed around a number of names over the months. Harper, Delilah, and Lara were their three favorite names for a girl, but they'd wanted to wait until they met their baby to decide.

Harley looked at his brave, beautiful better half and said, "Pipe? What do you think?"

She caressed their baby's cheek and said, "What do you think about Frankie, after your father?"

"Frankie," he said, choked up again. "That's perfect."

"Frankie Dalton Dutch?" Piper asked, and in the next breath, tears sprang from her eyes, and she frowned.

Harley crouched beside her. "What's wrong?"

"I made a really big mistake. A *huge* one," she said in a strangled voice, tears streaking her cheeks.

"What do you mean?" His gut seized. "I don't understand."

"She's just overwhelmed," his mother said anxiously.

Roxie hurried over with Willow, Talia, and Bridgette, crowding in on them.

"Having a baby makes your hormones go crazy. That's all this is, honey," Roxie reassured her.

"You're going to be a *great* mother," Willow reassured her.

"And we'll all help you," Talia added, glancing at Evan, fast asleep in Derek's arms. "I know lots of tricks of the trade."

"We'll make sure to babysit often, so you can catch up on your sleep, pumpkin," Dan said. "You'll be fine."

"Have you all *lost* your minds?" Piper cried. "I'm not worried about being a good *mother*! I don't want to be a *Dalton* while my baby and husband are *Dutches*! I want to be a *Dutch*. I'm proud to be Harley's permanent other half, and I know he's not going to try to change me! He doesn't have to. Frankie already *has*."

Harley couldn't breathe, couldn't believe his ears.

"Do you think I want our daughter having to explain why her parents don't have the same last name?" Piper gazed down at their daughter.

Then she looked at her family and said, "That would suck, and sure, it would make her tougher, but what if she's a girlie girl like Bridgette? Kids will just pick on her, and then Louie, Evan, and Christopher are going to have to kick some little kids' asses, which will only make Bridgette and Bodhi, Talia and Derek, and Ben and Aurelia hate me. I can't do that to our baby." She looked at Harley with red-rimmed eyes and said, "Will you marry me, Harley?"

He couldn't stop an elated, relieved laugh from bubbling out. "Do you think we should wait until your pregnancy hormones level out, so you don't change your mind in a month and blame me for trying to change you?"

Piper's brows knitted, and she pressed her mouth into a tight line.

"Oh shit," Ben muttered.

"Bad move, bro," Marshall added.

Roxie nudged Harley and said, "Take it back, *quick*."

"Maybe you're right," Piper said before he could get a word out. "Maybe we shouldn't do it. Oh *wait*," she said sarcastically. "*That* would be the *dumbest* idea *ever*." She touched his face, her eyes turning warm and loving again as she said, "But hearing you say that proves how much you love me, so I'll ask you again and again until you say yes."

"How about if you let me do it this time?" He took a velvet bag from his pocket and withdrew the white-gold diamond eternity band he'd had made for her.

There was a collective gasp as he squared his shoulders, already down on one knee, and said, "This is an eternity band and was *not* supposed to be an engagement ring. I want to make it very clear that I had *not* planned to ask you to marry me."

Chuckles sounded around them.

"I had it made as a thank-you gift for you, for selflessly enduring nine long months, many of which were without doughnuts, to bring us our beautiful daughter. But it'll work as an engagement ring. Piper, my love, my best friend, and my forever girl, will you marry me?"

"Yes! Yes today, yes tomorrow, and yes forever."

Everyone cheered and clapped as he slid the ring onto her finger.

He gazed deeply into her eyes and said, "I love you, and I promise I will make you and Frankie the happiest people on earth."

"You already have." Tears slipped down Piper's cheeks. Their daughter yawned, and Piper glowed as she gazed down at her. Then she turned loving eyes on Harley and said, "Thank you."

"For what?"

"For opening my eyes to everything love is supposed to be and more."

A NOTE FROM MELISSA

I hope you enjoyed Piper and Harley's love story as much as I enjoyed writing it. They are two of my favorite characters, and I couldn't get enough of Jiggs! I'm looking forward to spending more time with the Daltons and all of their wonderful friends who are still awaiting their own love stories. Each of Piper's siblings has their own book and have found their happily ever afters in the Sugar Lake and Harmony Pointe series, which are now available for your binge-reading pleasure. You might want to start with Willow and Zane's story, *The Real Thing*, the first book in the Sugar Lake series.

If you've already read the Sugar Lake and Harmony Pointe books and would like to read more about the Daltons, they were first introduced in *Wild Boys After Dark: Logan* and seen again in *Bad Boys After Dark: Mick*. I hope you'll also check out the rest of my Love in Bloom big-family romance collection, starting with *Lovers at Heart, Reimagined*, the first book in my beloved Braden series. Characters from each series make appearances in future books, so you never miss an engagement, wedding, or birth. A complete list of all series titles is included at the start of this book, and downloadable checklists, free series starters, and family trees are available on the Reader Goodies page of my website (www.MelissaFoster.com/RG).

Be sure to sign up for my newsletter to keep up to date with my new releases and to receive an exclusive short story (www.MelissaFoster.com/News).

Happy reading!

Melissa Foster

ACKNOWLEDGMENTS

I am so thankful for the inspiration I receive on a daily basis from fans and friends and to all of the kind people who patiently answer my never-ending research questions. Thank you from the bottom of my heart.

If you'd like sneak peeks into my writing process and to chat with me daily, please join my fan club on Facebook. We talk about our lovable heroes and sassy heroines, and I always try to keep fans abreast of what's going on in our fictional boyfriends' worlds. You never know when you'll end up in one of my books, as several members of my fan club have already discovered (www.Facebook.com/groups/MelissaFosterFans).

Follow my Facebook fan page to keep up with sales and events (www.Facebook.com/MelissaFosterAuthor).

I'm forever grateful for my assistants and friends Sharon Martin, Lisa Filipe, Lisa Bardonski, Missy Dehaven, and Shelby Dehaven, who kick my butt when I need it, talk me off the ledge, and cheer me on. Thank you for always having my back.

A special thank-you to my wonderful and patient editor Maria Gomez and the incredible Montlake team. As always, heaps of gratitude to editors Kristen Weber and Penina Lopez and to my team of proofreaders. And, of course, to my very own hunky hero, Les, and my family, thank you for your ongoing support. I couldn't create the worlds I love without your encouragement.

ABOUT THE AUTHOR

Photo © 2013 Melanie Anderson

Melissa Foster is the award-winning, *New York Times* and *USA Today* bestselling author of nearly one hundred books, including *The Real Thing* and *Only for You* in the Sugar Lake series, and the Harmony Pointe novels, *Call Her Mine* and *This Is Love*. Melissa's work has been recommended by *USA Today*'s book blog, *Hagerstown* magazine, the *Patriot*, and others. She has also painted and donated several murals to the Hospital for Sick Children in Washington, DC.

She enjoys discussing her books with book clubs and reader groups, and she welcomes an invitation to your event. Visit Melissa on her website, www.MelissaFoster.com.